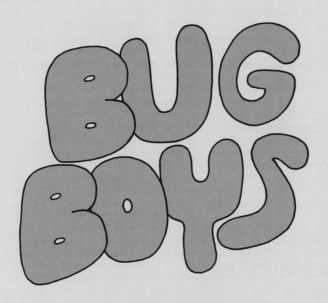

BUG BOYS

By Laura Knetzger
Colors by Lyle Lynde

RH GRAPHIC

Bug Boys was made with pen and ink on Bristol board and Photoshop.

—

All rights reserved. Published in the United States by RH Graphic, an imprint of Random House Children's Books, a division of Penguin Random House LLC, New York. Originally published in the United States in black and white and in different form by Czap Books, Providence, Rhode Island, in 2015.

RH Graphic with the book design is a trademark of Penguin Random House LLC.

Visit us on the Web! RHKidsGraphic.com • @RHKidsGraphic
LauraKnetzger.com

Educators and librarians, for a variety of teaching tools, visit us at RHTeachersLibrarians.com

Library of Congress Cataloging-in-Publication Data
Names: Knetzger, Laura, author, illustrator. | Lynde, Lyle, colorist.
Title: Bug boys / by Laura Knetzger ; colored by Lyle Lynde.
Description: First RH Graphic edition. | New York : RH Graphic, [2020] |
"Originally published in the United States in black and white and in
different form by Czap Books, Providence, Rhode Island, in 2015." |
Summary: Follows two bug friends, Stag-B and Rhino-B, as they explore
their world and share adventures.
Identifiers: LCCN 2019018102 | ISBN 978-0-593-12522-9 (library binding) |
ISBN 978-1-9848-9676-6 (hardcover) | ISBN 978-1-9848-9677-3 (ebook)
Subjects: LCSH: Graphic novels. | CYAC: Graphic novels. | Insects—Fiction. |
Adventure and adventurers—Fiction. | Best friends—Fiction. |
Friendship—Fiction.
Classification: LCC PZ7.7.K655 Bug 2020 | DDC 741.5/973—dc23

Designed by Patrick Crotty
Colored by Lyle Lynde

MANUFACTURED IN CHINA
10 9 8 7 6 5 4 3
First American Edition

A comic on every bookshelf.

To Bob and Deb

Special thanks to:
Kevin Czap
Mark Friedman
Stuart Solomon
Christopher Wessel

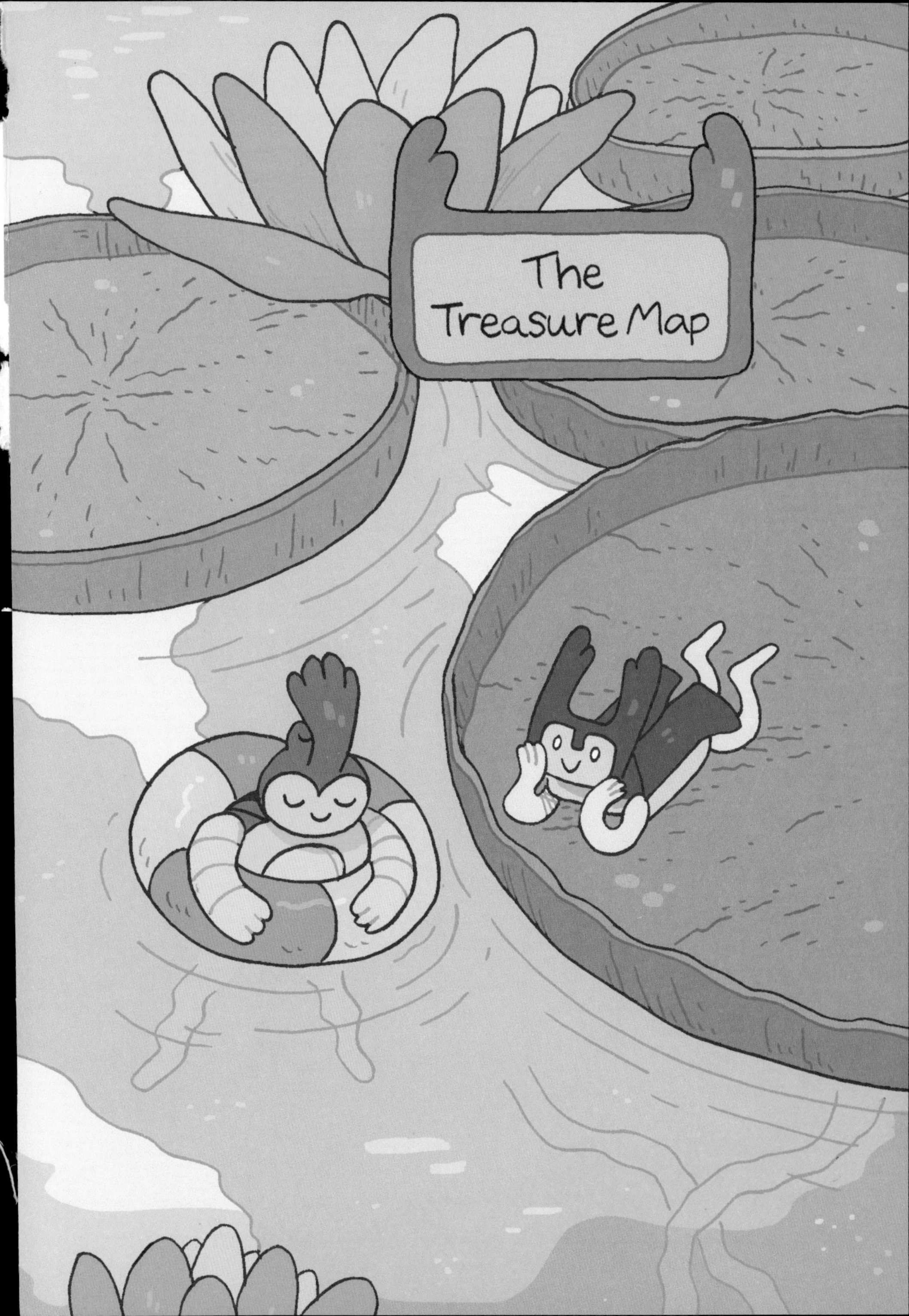
The
Treasure Map

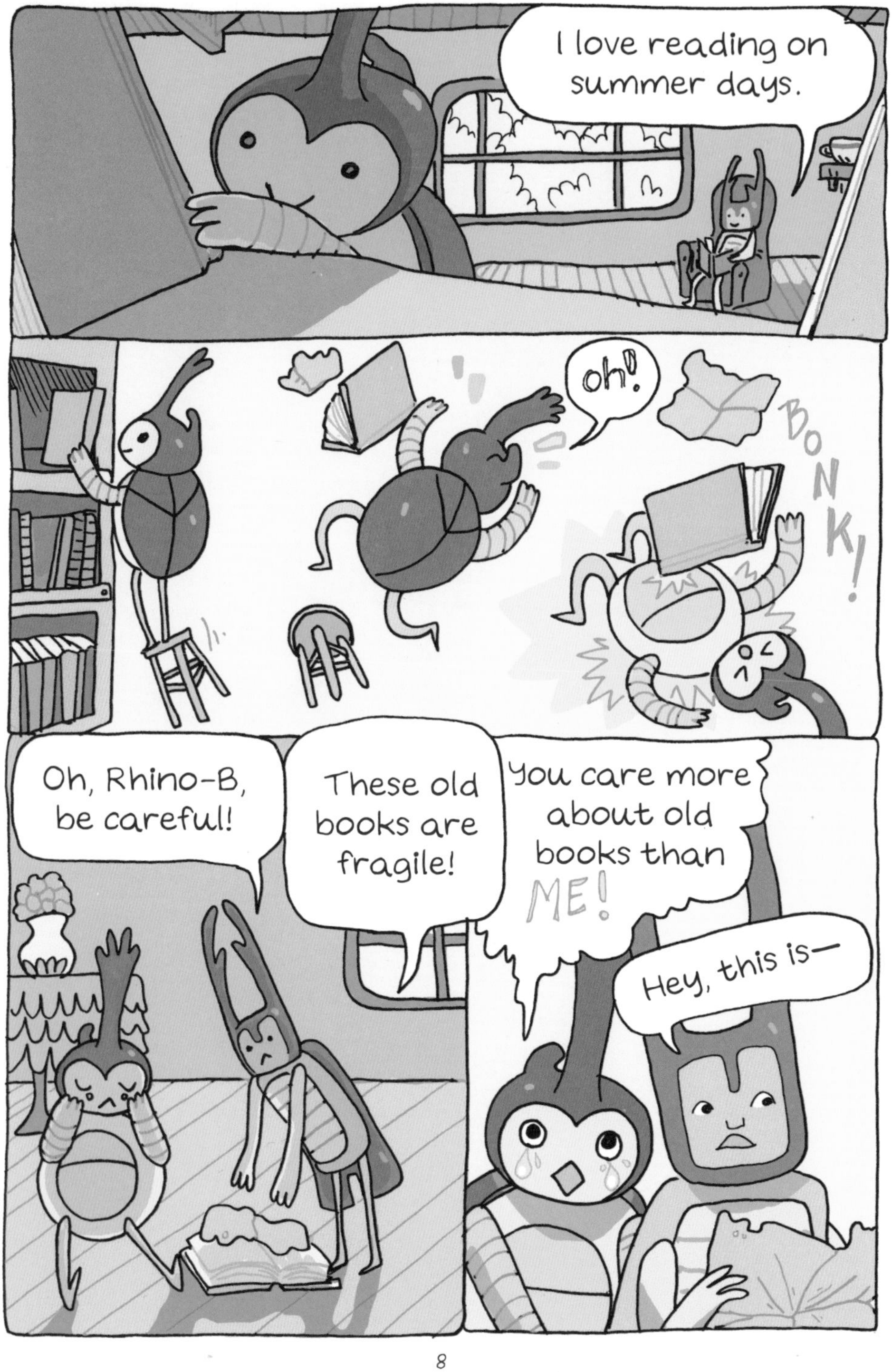
I love reading on summer days.
oh!
BONK!
Oh, Rhino-B, be careful!
These old books are fragile!
You care more about old books than ME!
Hey, this is—

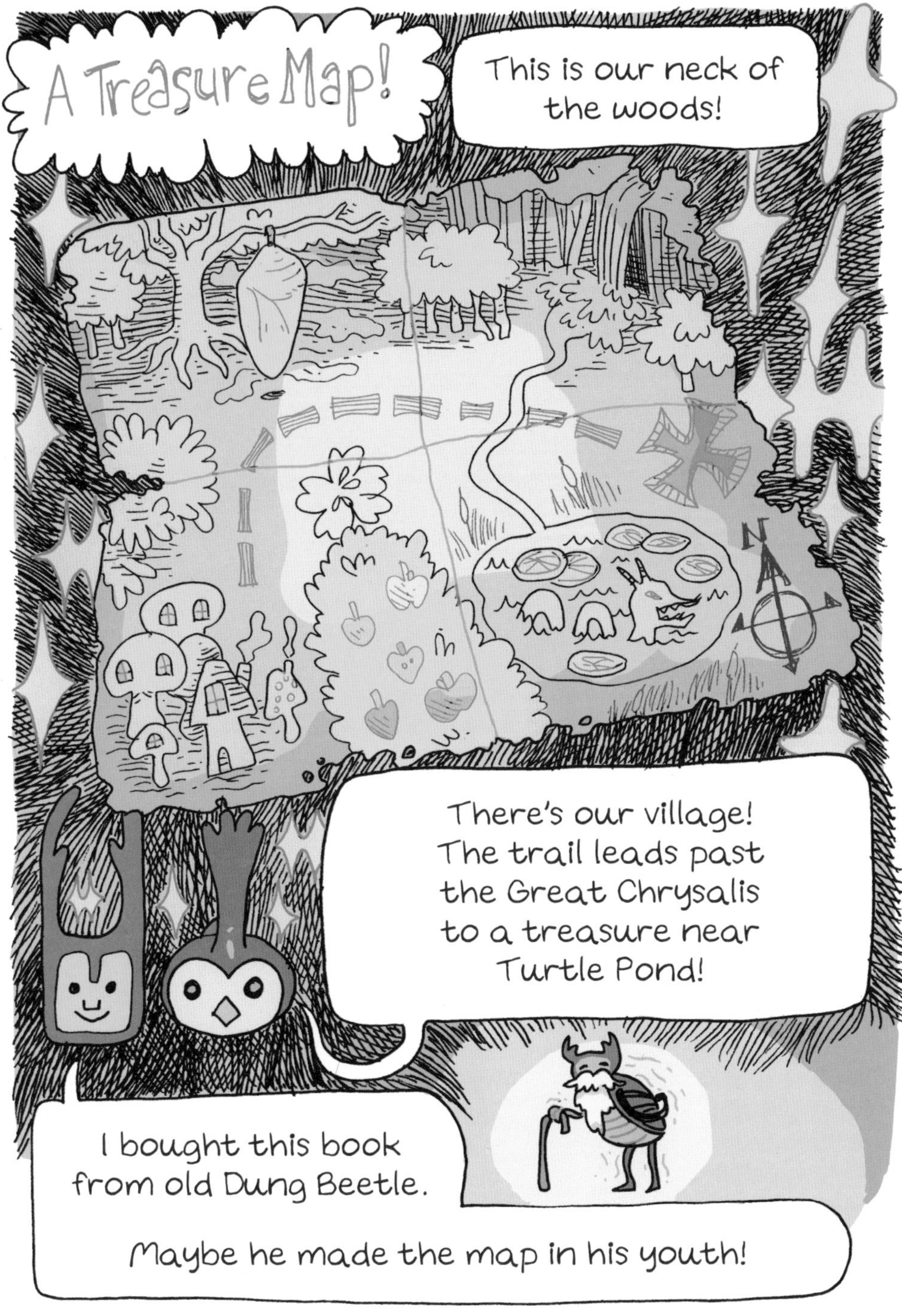
A Treasure Map!
This is our neck of the woods!
There's our village! The trail leads past the Great Chrysalis to a treasure near Turtle Pond!
I bought this book from old Dung Beetle.
Maybe he made the map in his youth!

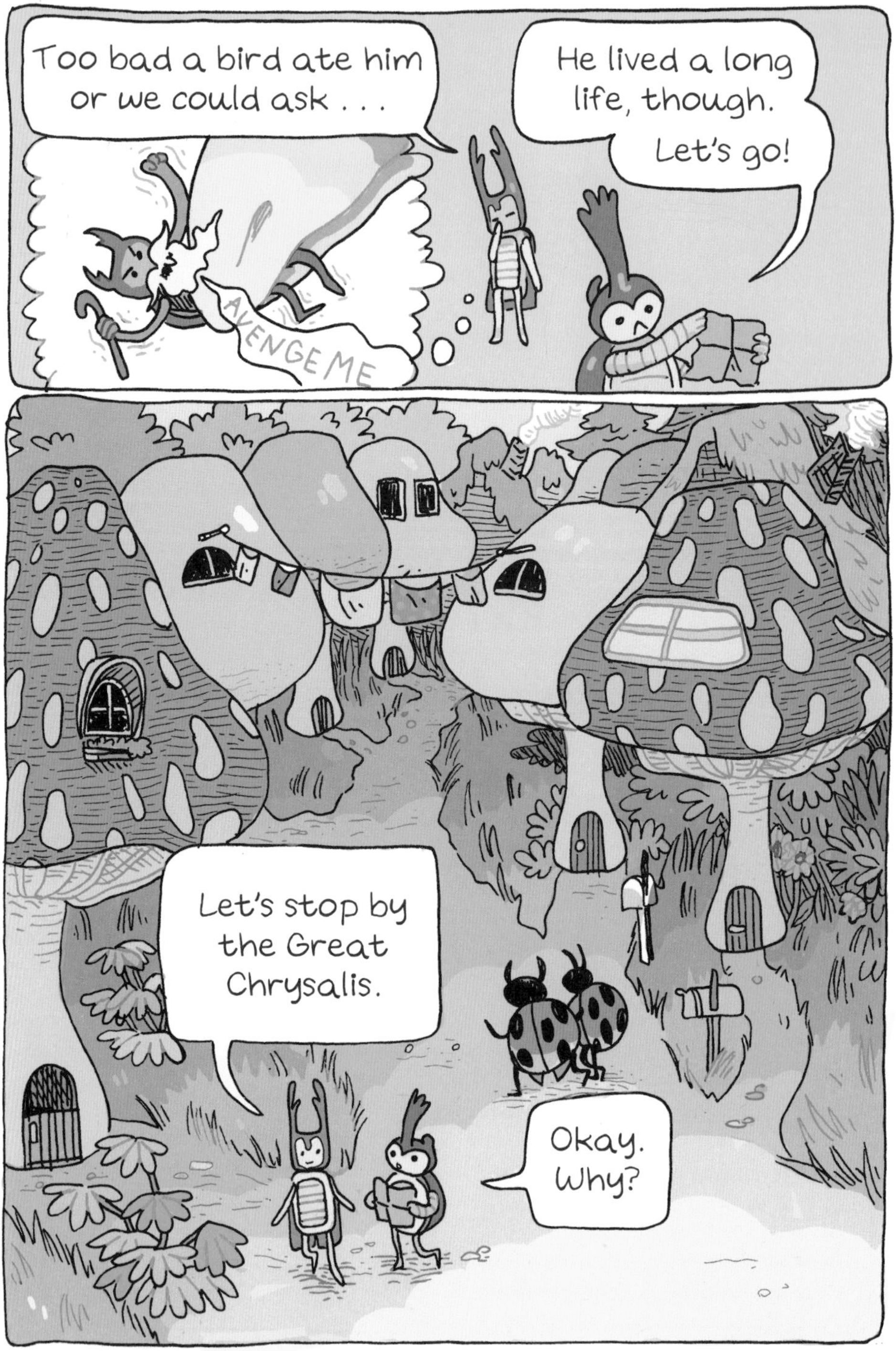
Too bad a bird ate him or we could ask . . .
AVENGE ME
He lived a long life, though.
Let's go!
Let's stop by the Great Chrysalis.
Okay. Why?

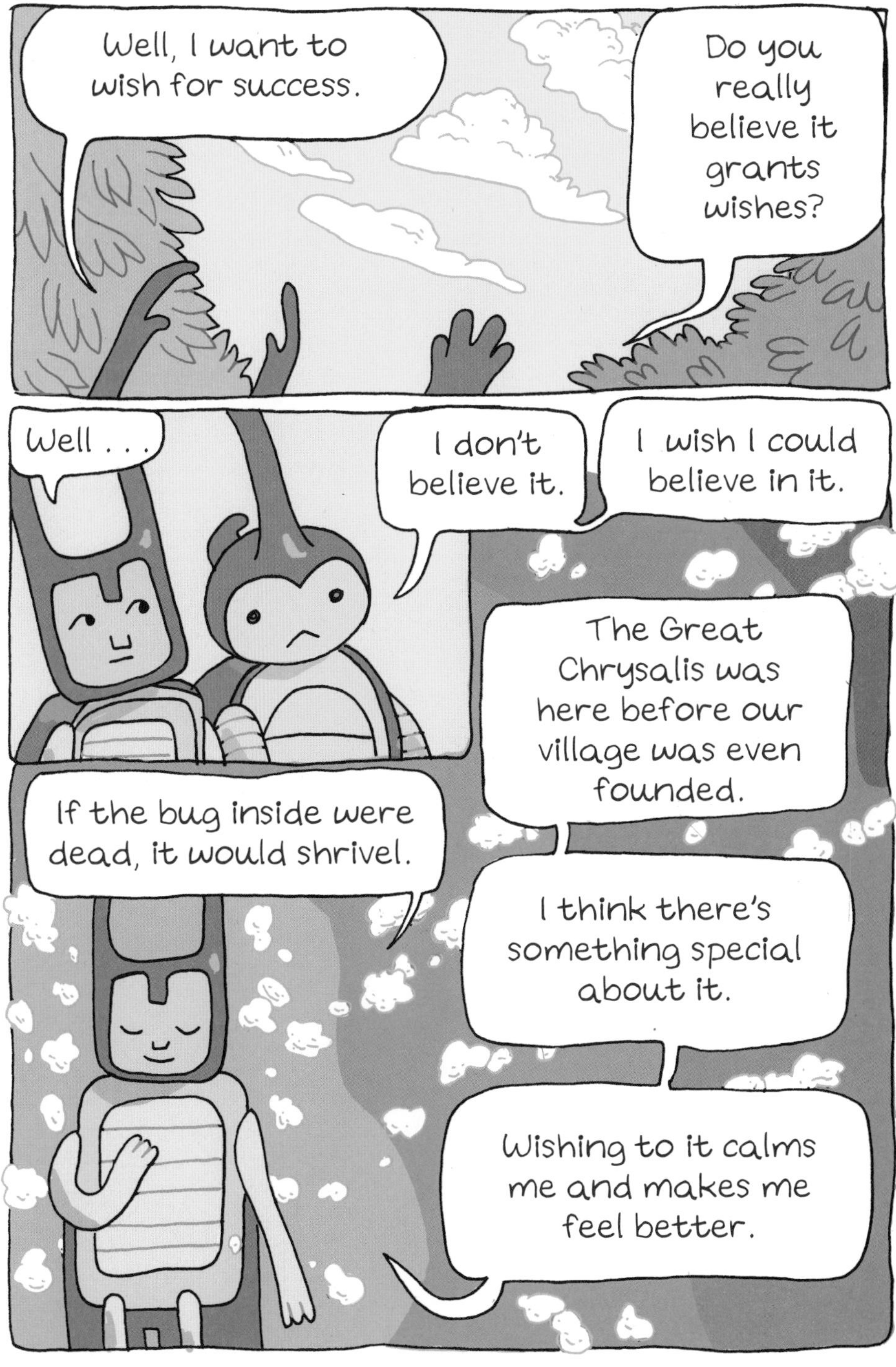
Well, I want to wish for success.
Do you really believe it grants wishes?
Well . . .
I don't believe it.
I wish I could believe in it.
The Great Chrysalis was here before our village was even founded.
If the bug inside were dead, it would shrivel.
I think there's something special about it.
Wishing to it calms me and makes me feel better.

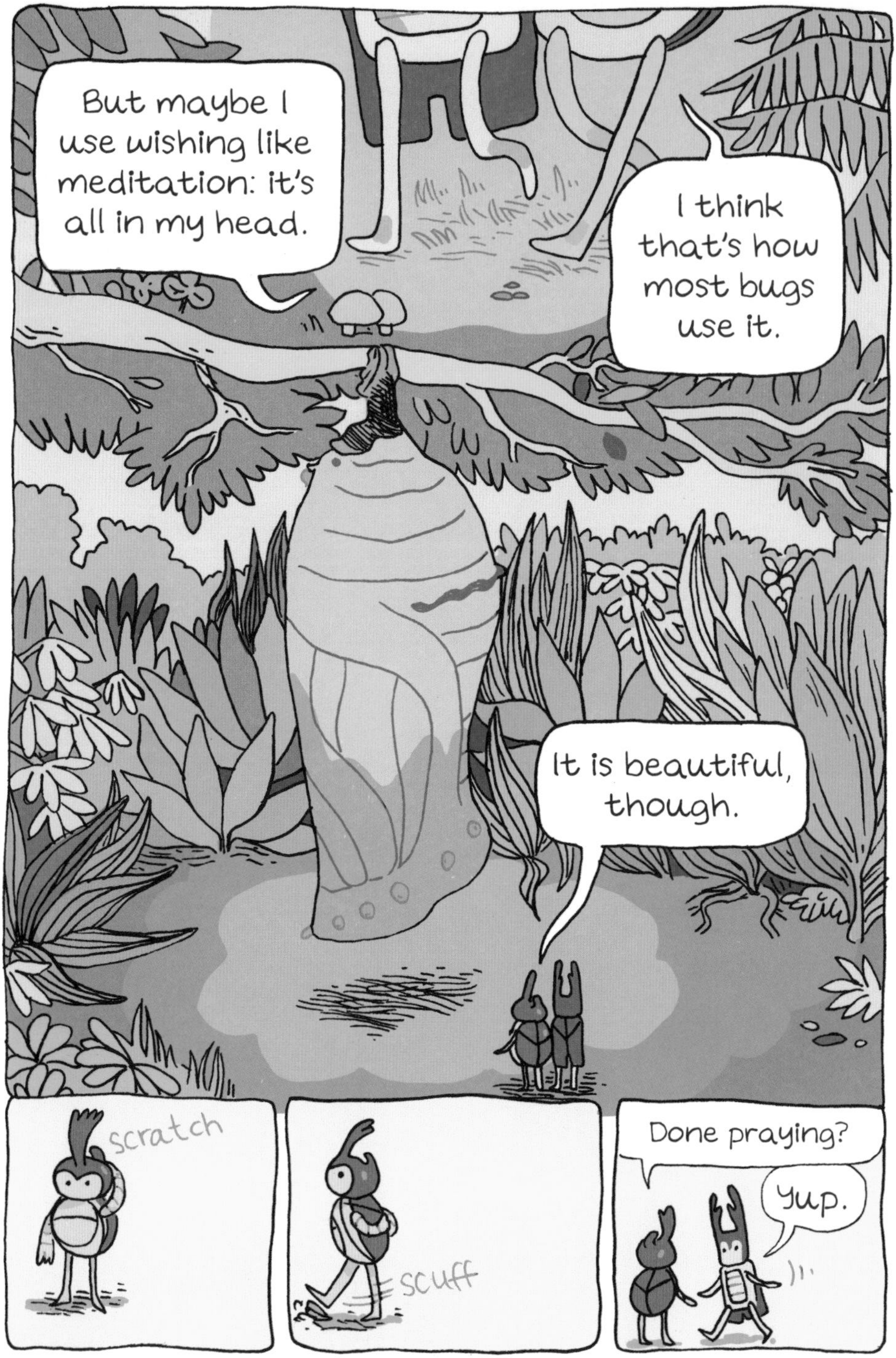
But maybe I use wishing like meditation: it's all in my head.
I think that's how most bugs use it.
It is beautiful, though.
scratch
scuff
Done praying?
Yup.

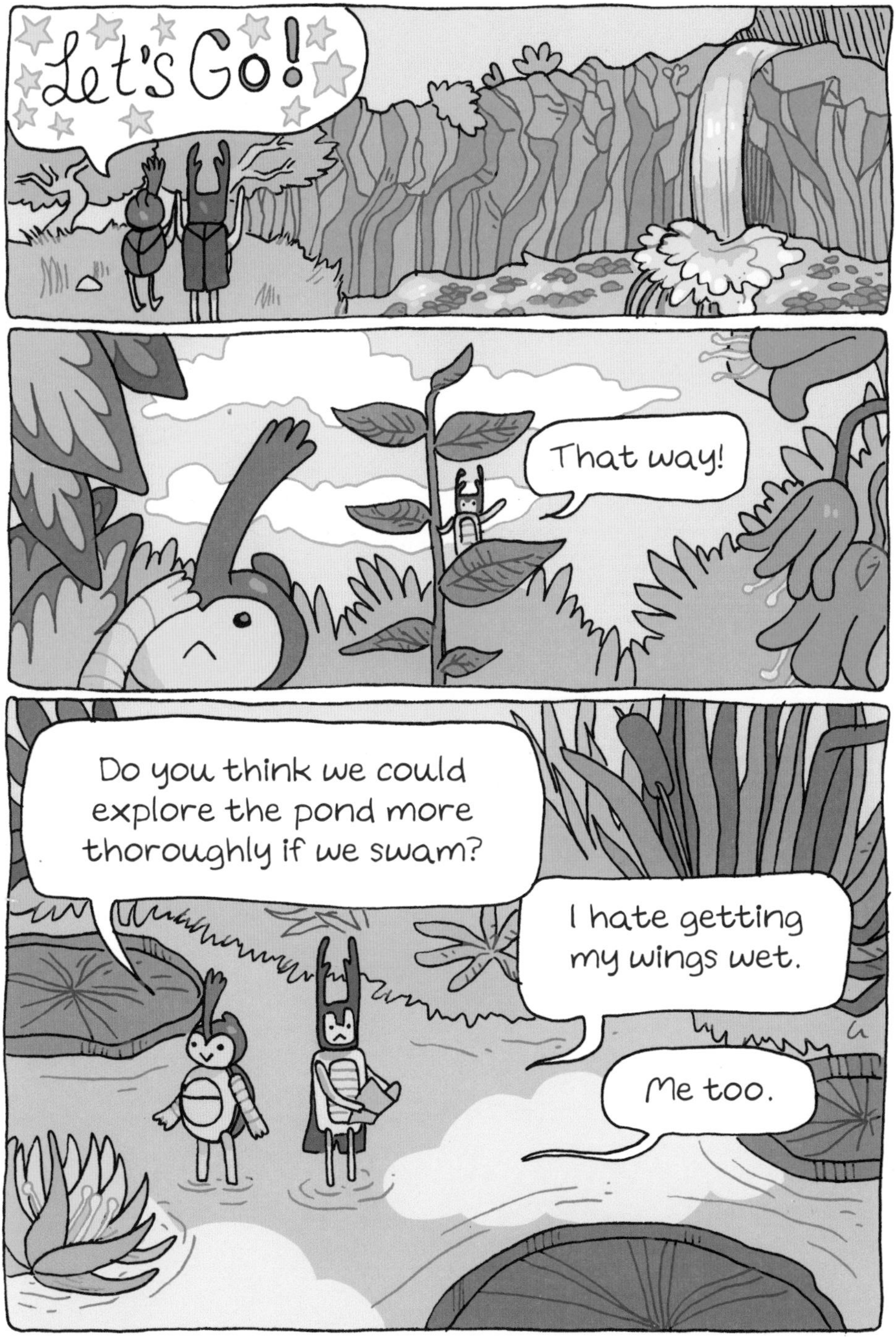
Let's Go!
That way!
Do you think we could explore the pond more thoroughly if we swam?
I hate getting my wings wet.
Me too.

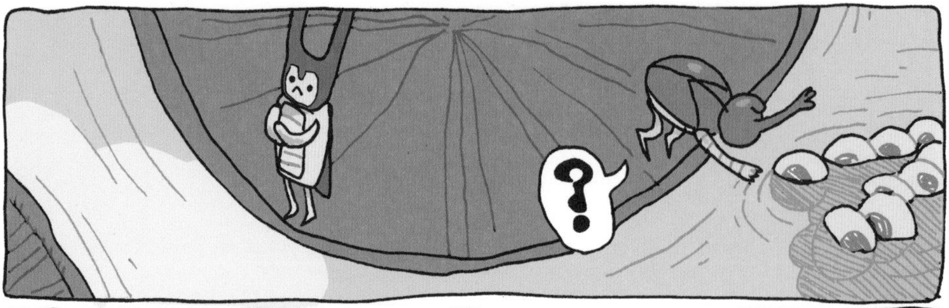
?

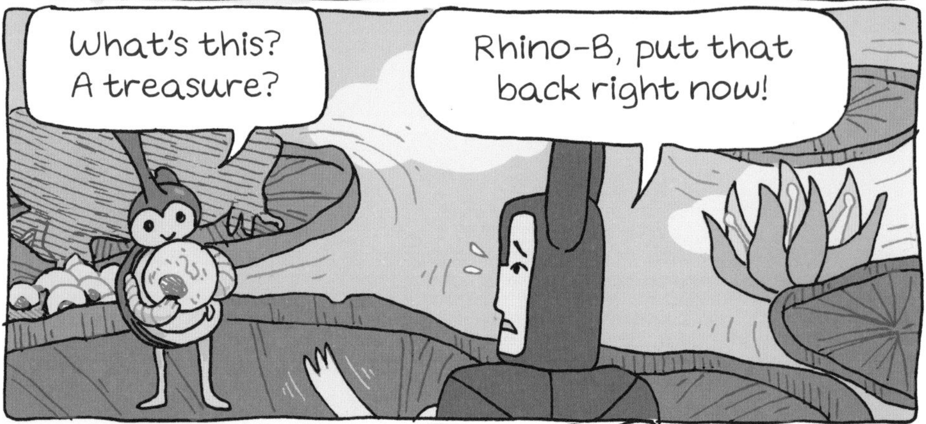
What's this? A treasure?
Rhino-B, put that back right now!

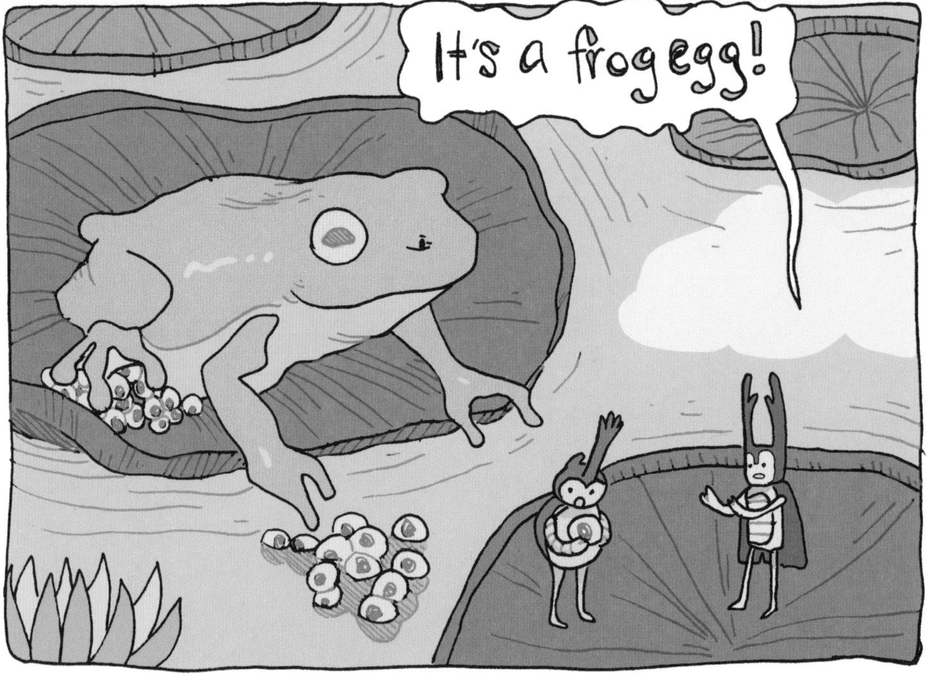
It's a frogegg!

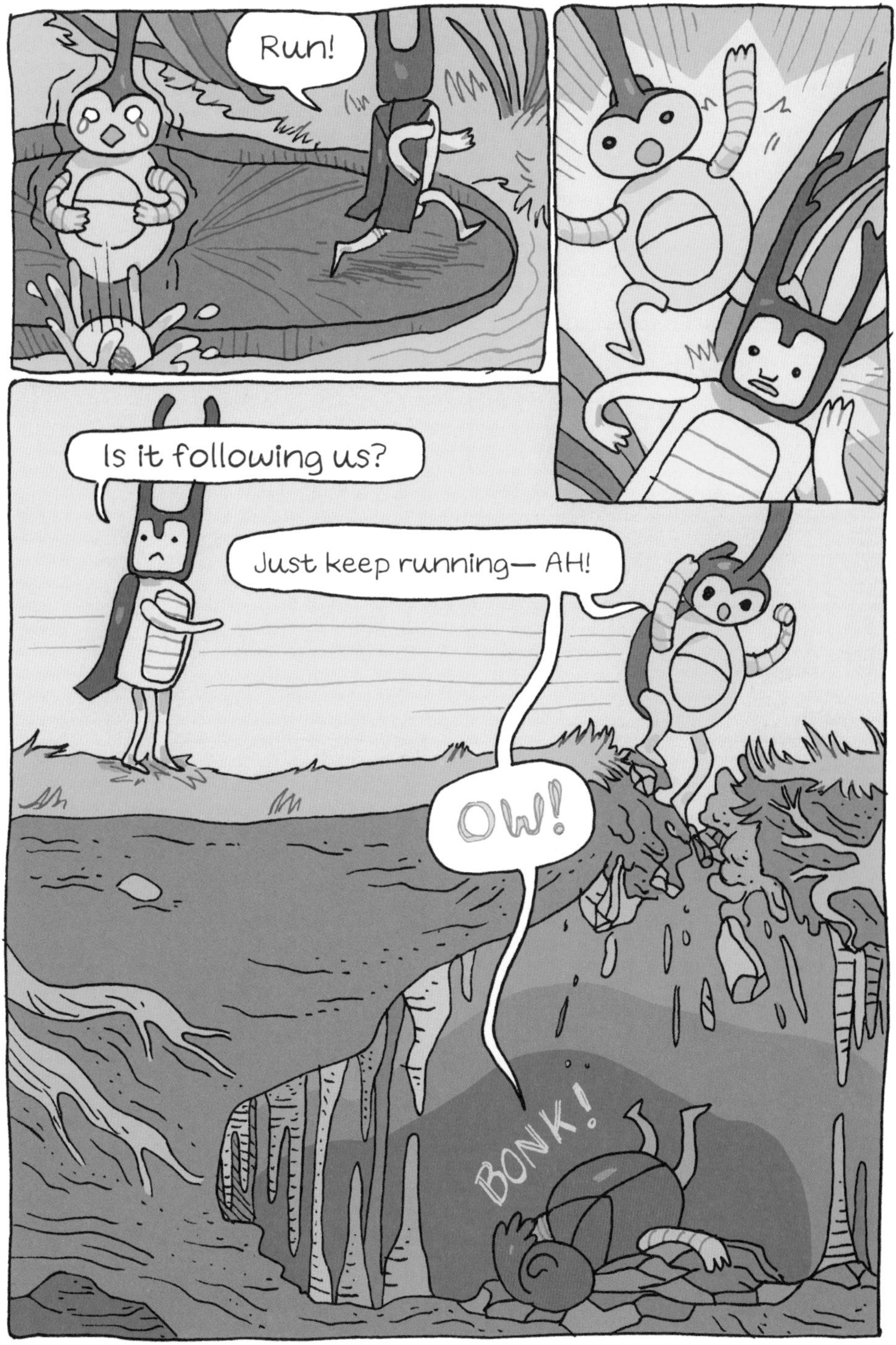
Run!
Is it following us?
Just keep running— AH!
OW!
BONK!

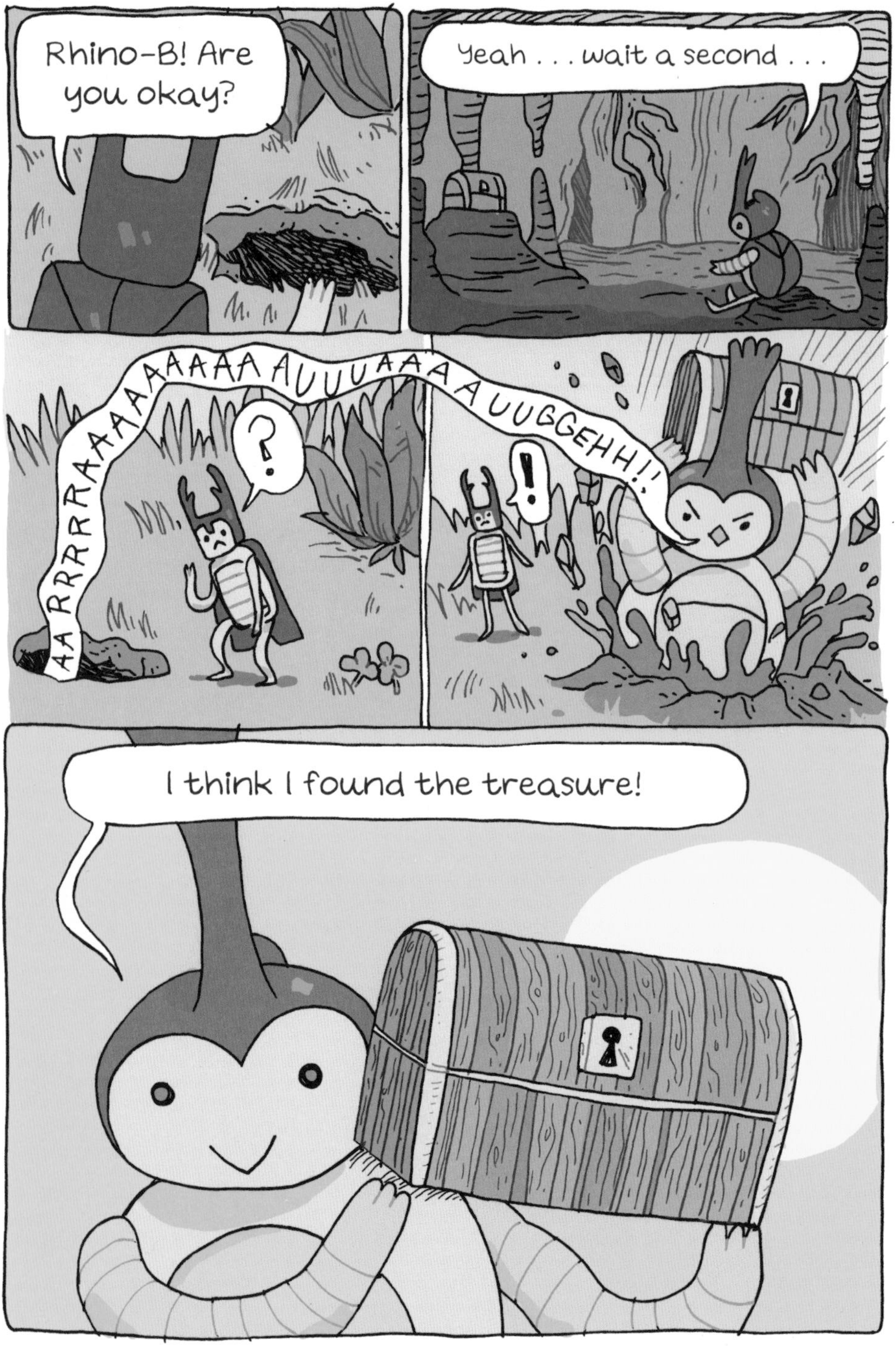
Rhino-B! Are you okay?
Yeah . . . wait a second . . .
AARRRRAAAAAAAAAA AUUUAAAAAUUGGEHH!!
?
!
I think I found the treasure!

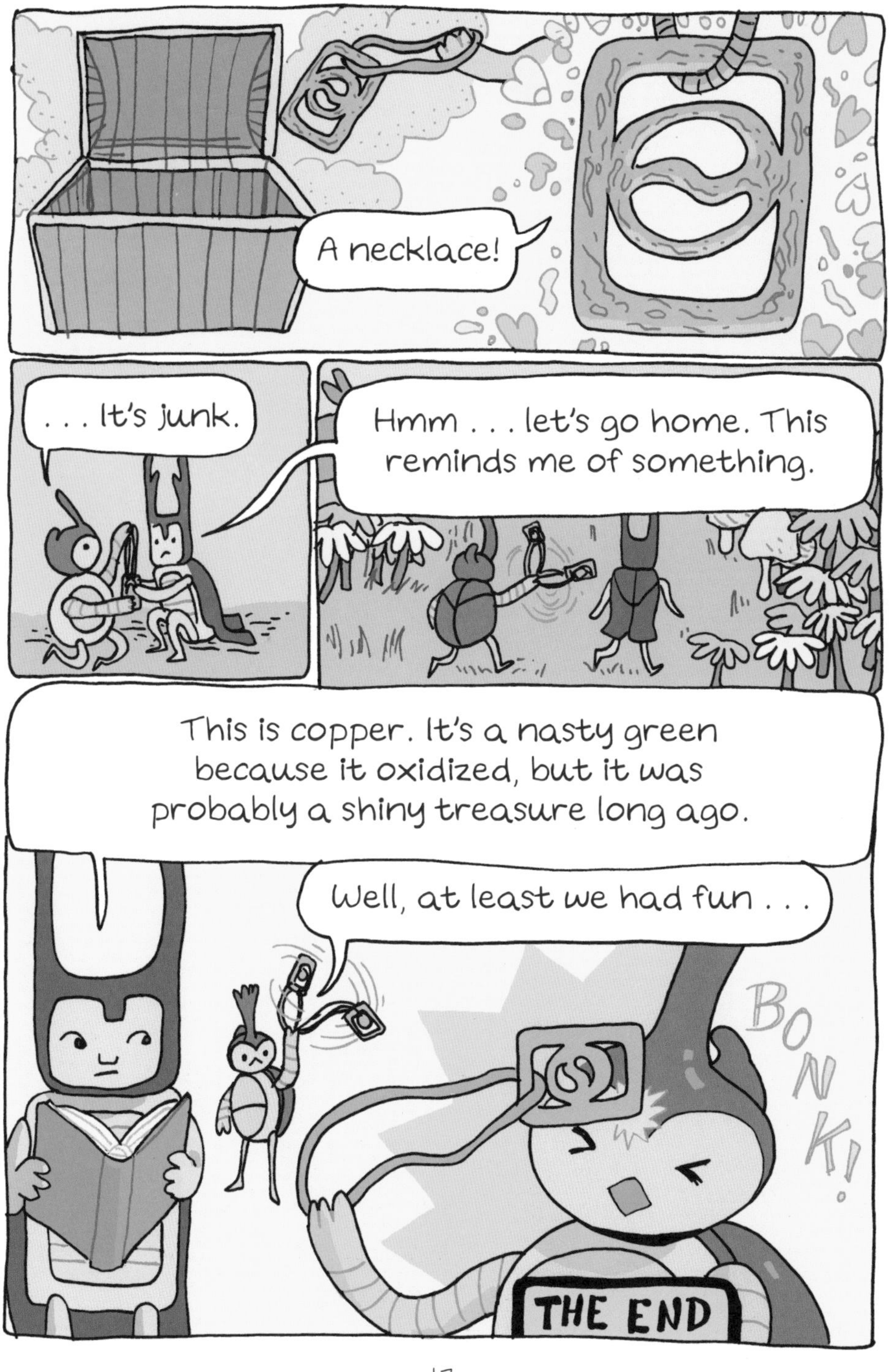
A necklace!
. . . It's junk.
Hmm . . . let's go home. This reminds me of something.
This is copper. It's a nasty green because it oxidized, but it was probably a shiny treasure long ago.
Well, at least we had fun . . .
BONK!
THE END

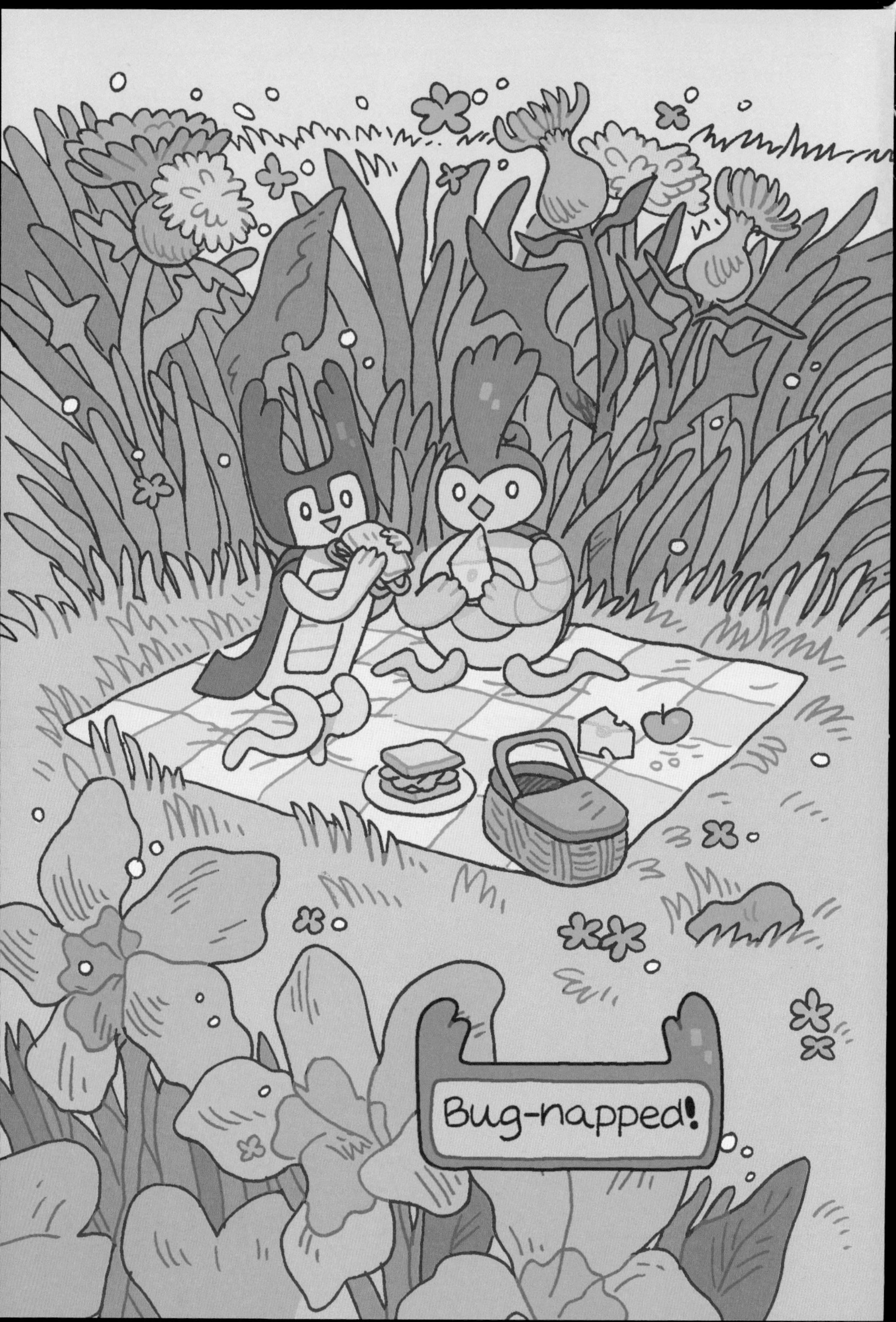
Bug-napped!

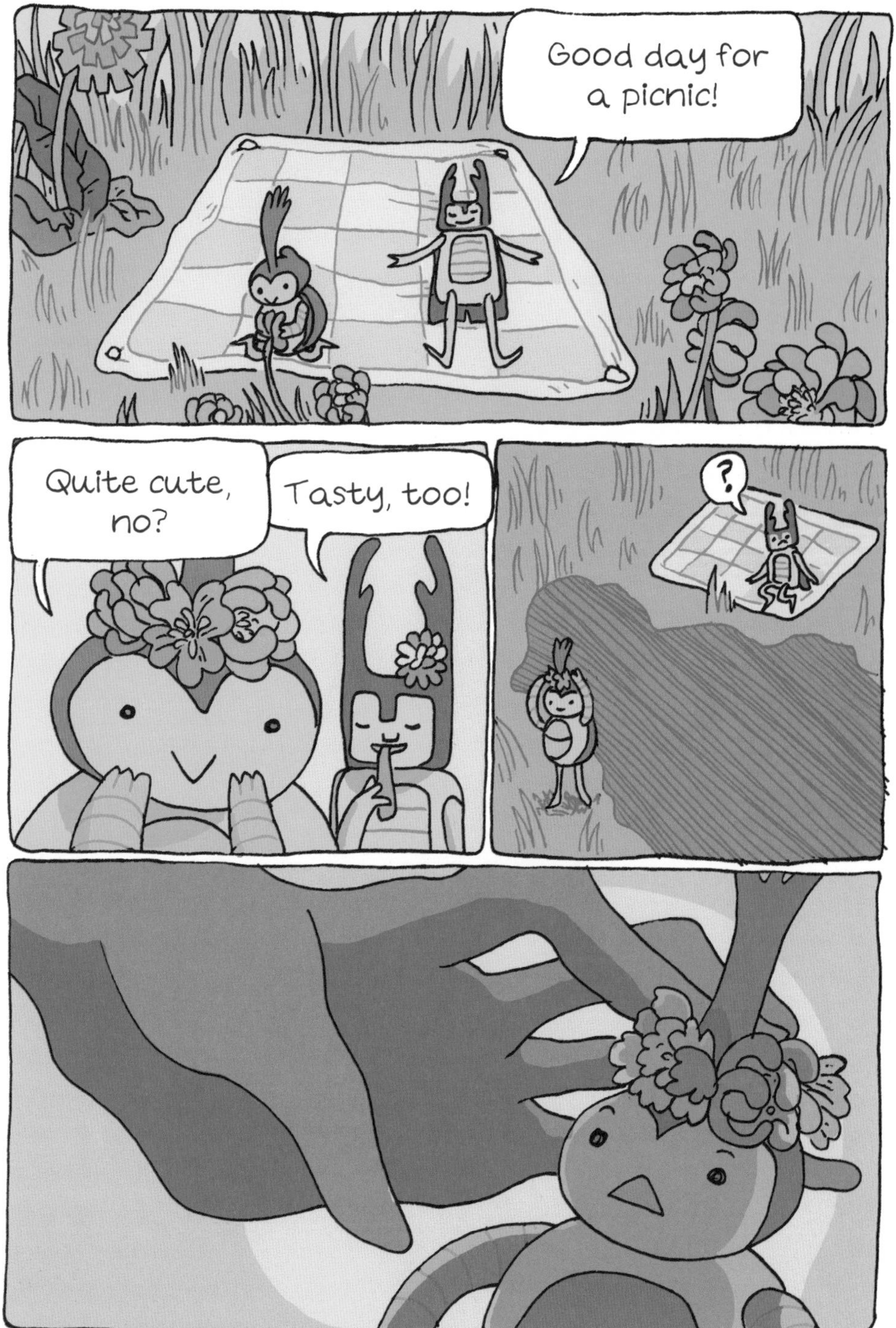
Good day for a picnic!
Quite cute, no?
Tasty, too!
?

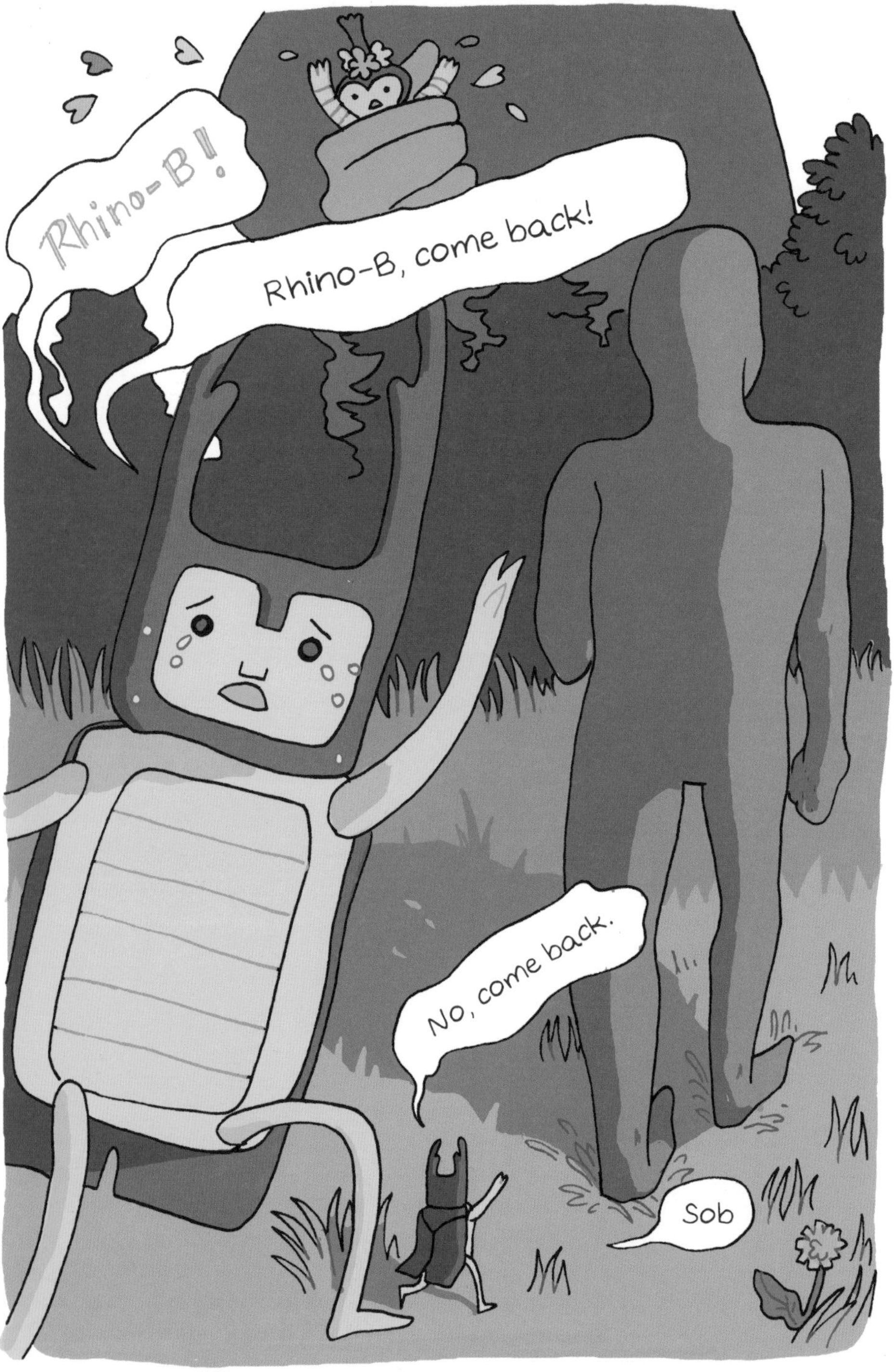
Rhino-B!
Rhino-B, come back!
No, come back.
Sob

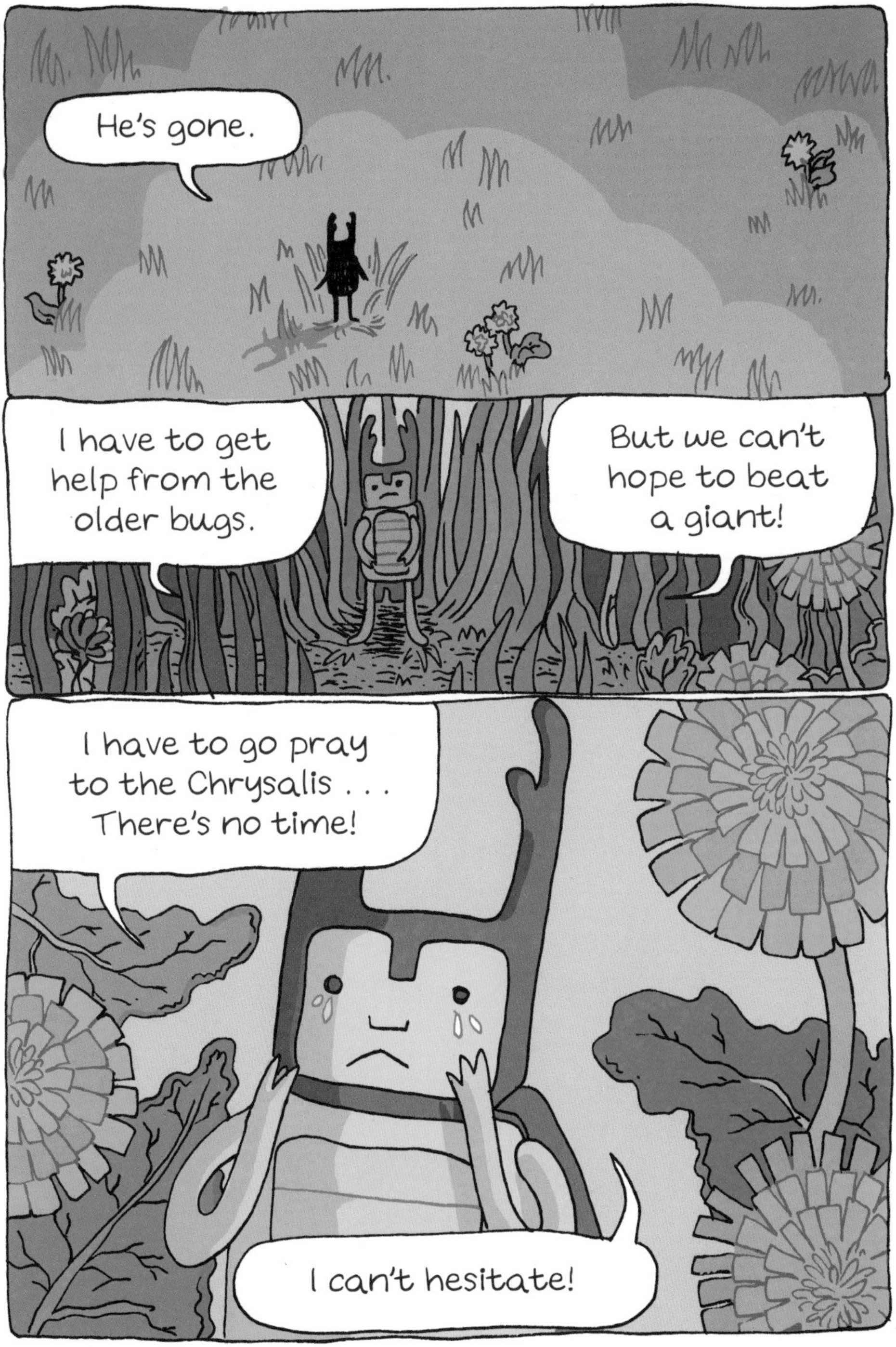
He's gone.
I have to get help from the older bugs.
But we can't hope to beat a giant!
I have to go pray to the Chrysalis . . . There's no time!
I can't hesitate!

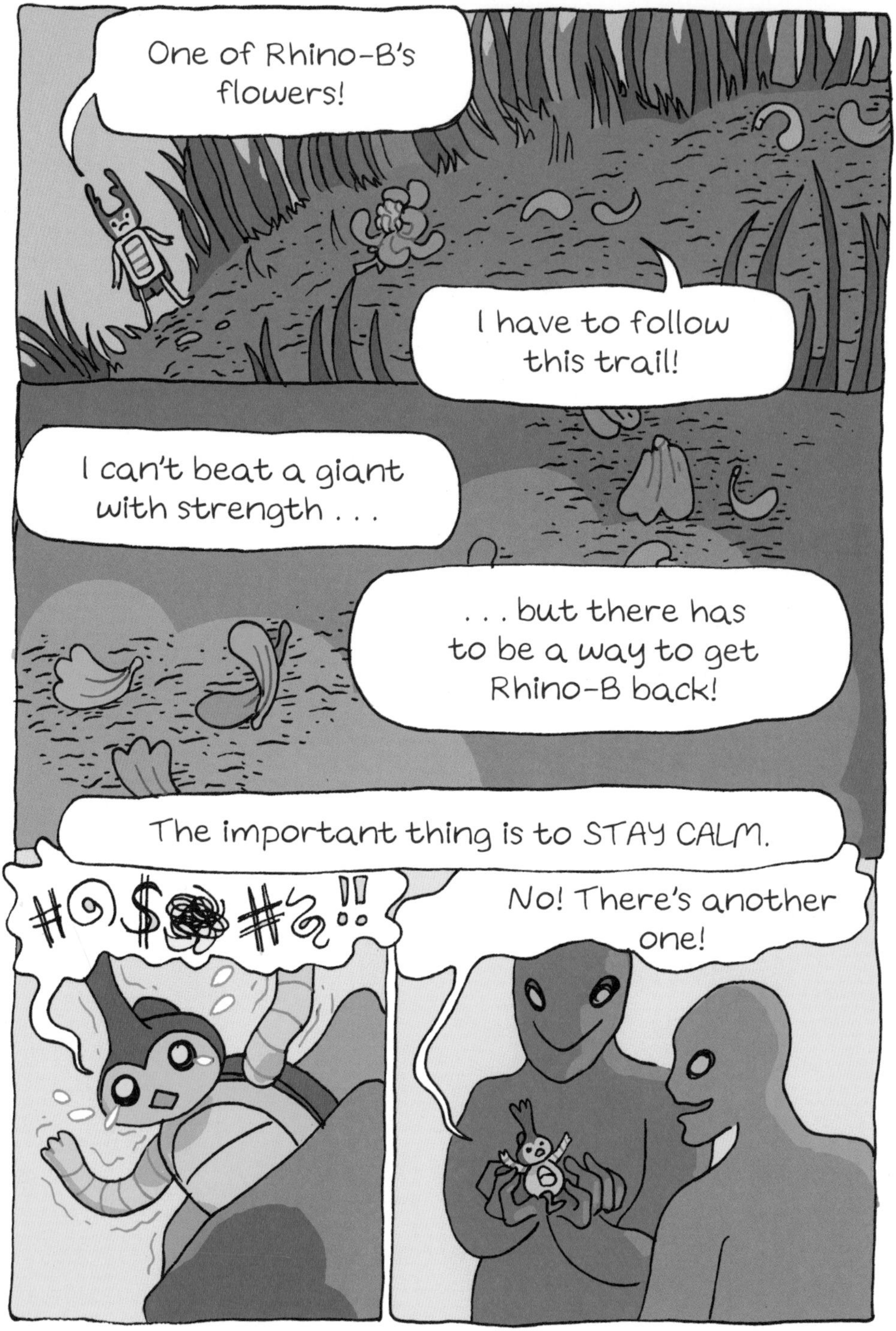
One of Rhino-B's flowers!
I have to follow this trail!
I can't beat a giant with strength . . .
. . . but there has to be a way to get Rhino-B back!
The important thing is to STAY CALM.
#@$@#&!!
No! There's another one!

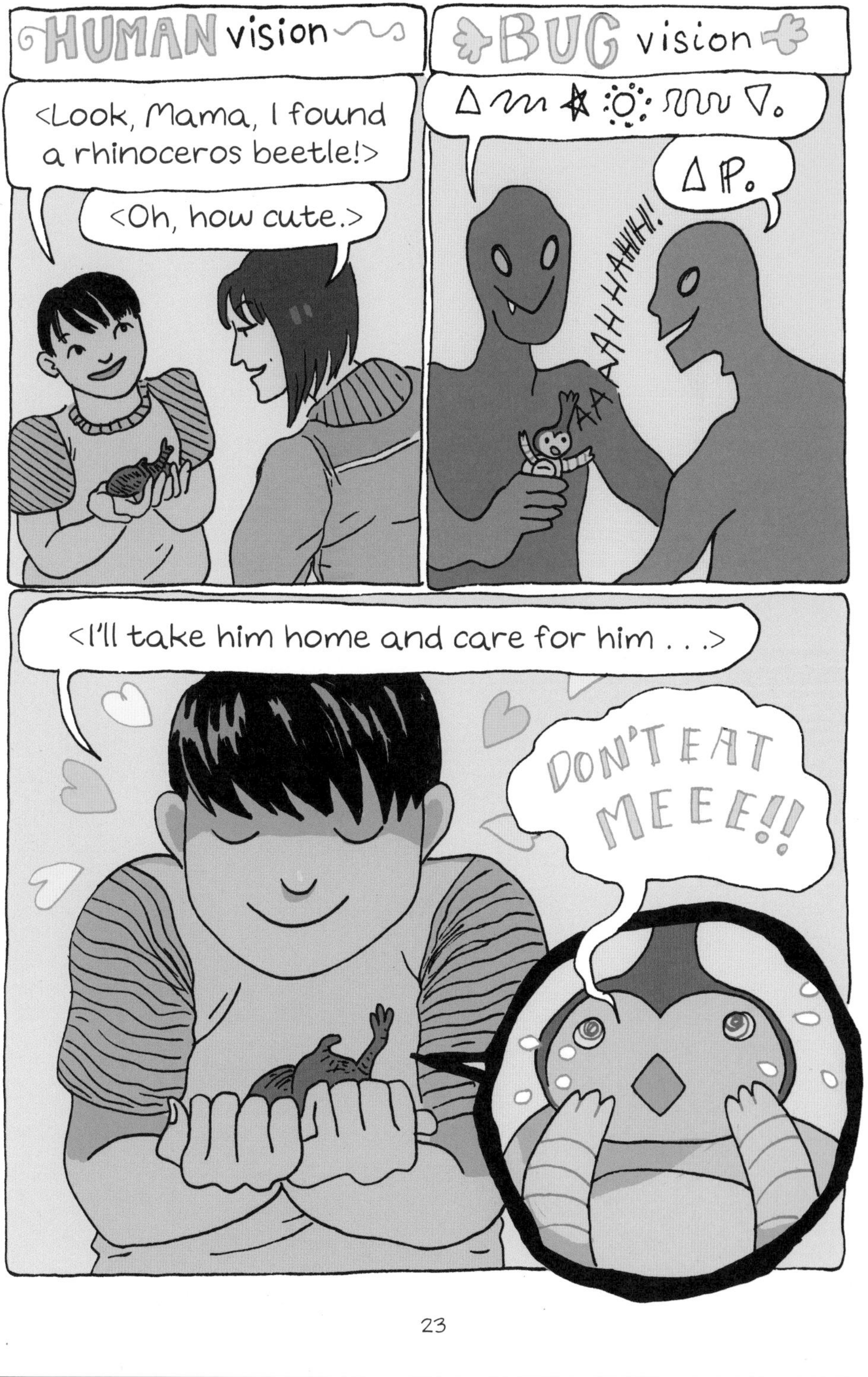
HUMAN vision
BUG vision
<Look, Mama, I found a rhinoceros beetle!>
<Oh, how cute.>
AAAAHHAHHH!
<I'll take him home and care for him . . .>
DON'T EAT MEEE!!

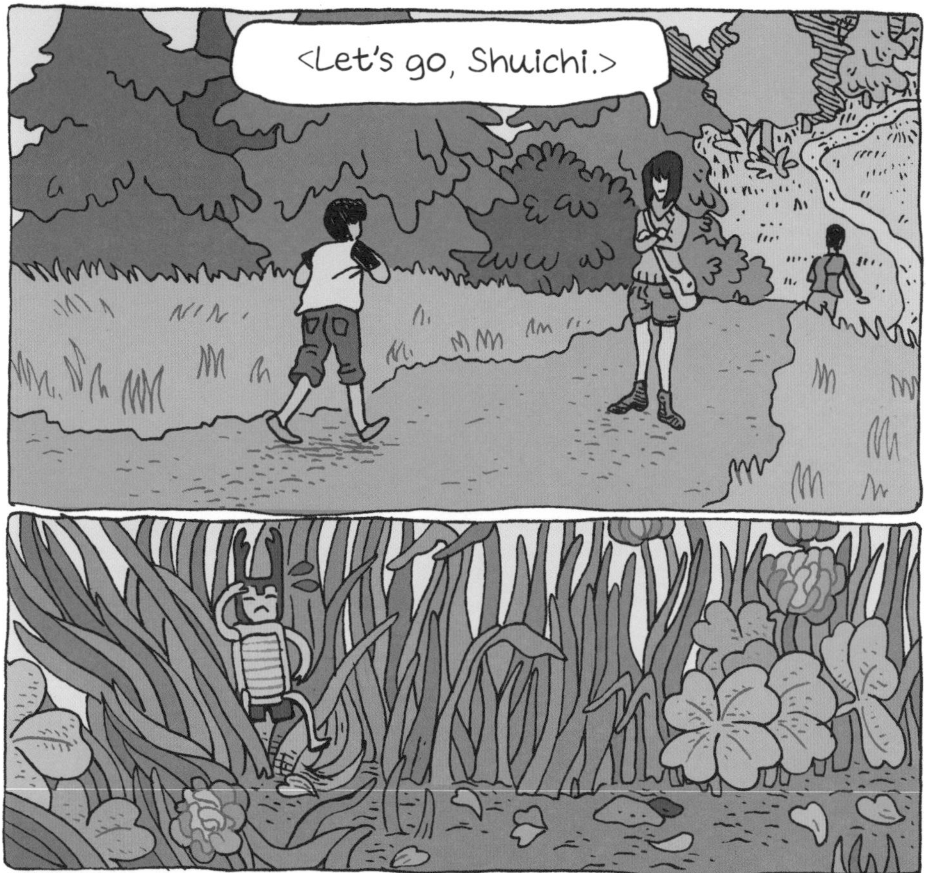
<Let's go, Shuichi.>
They went in there . . .

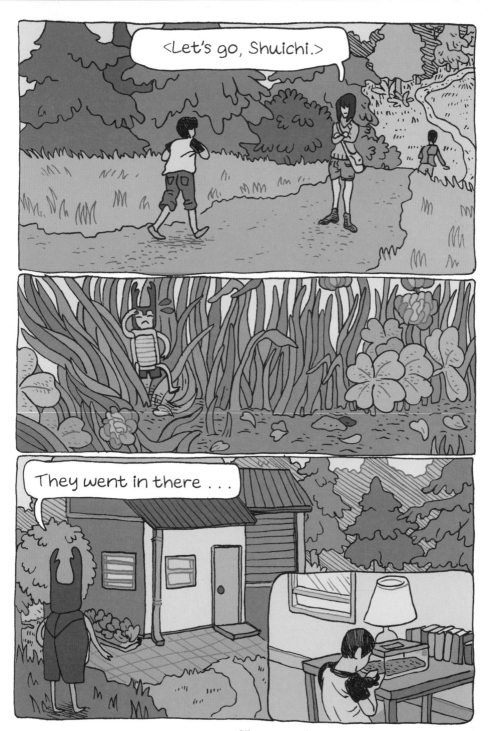

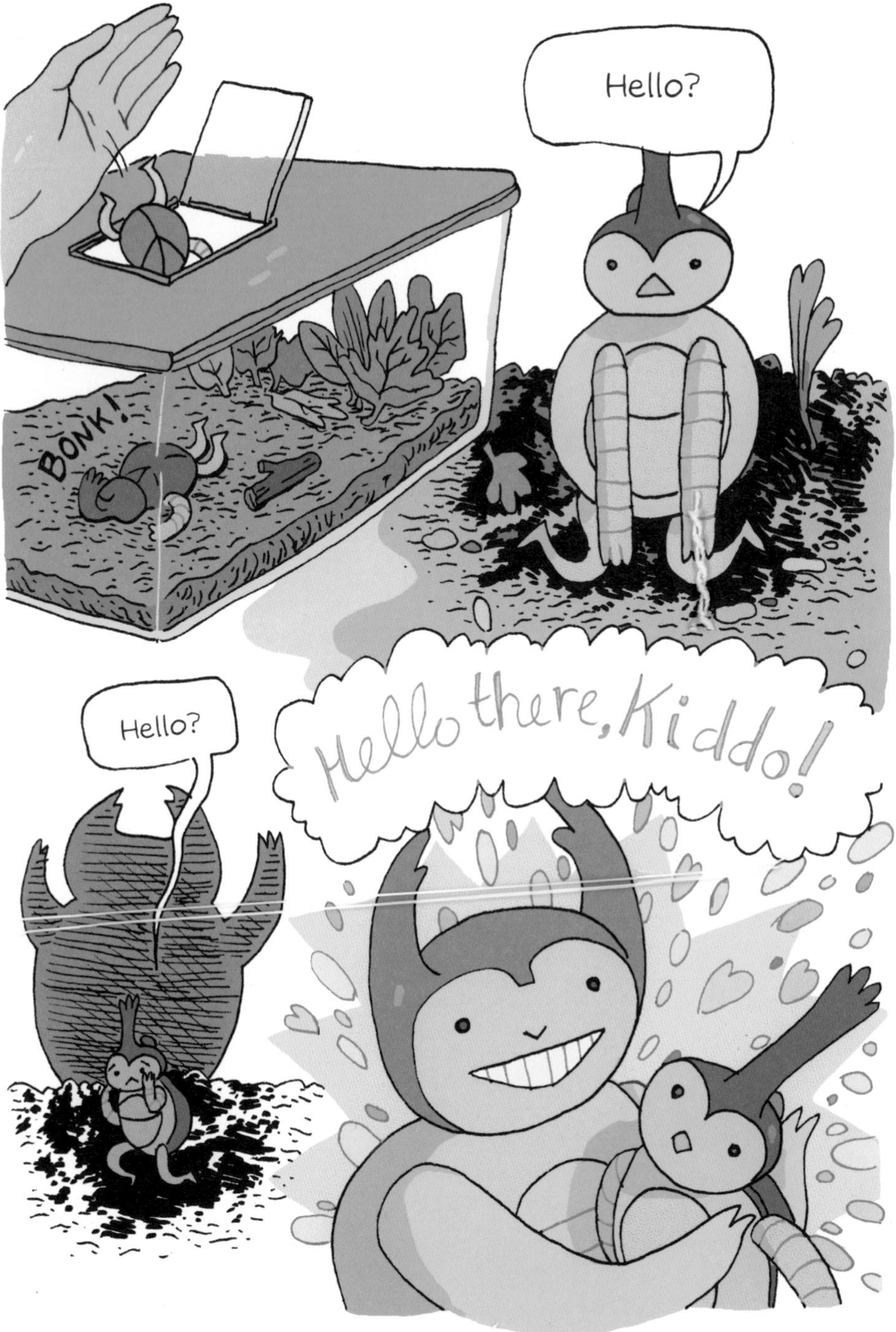
BONK!
Hello?
Hello?
Hello there, Kiddo!

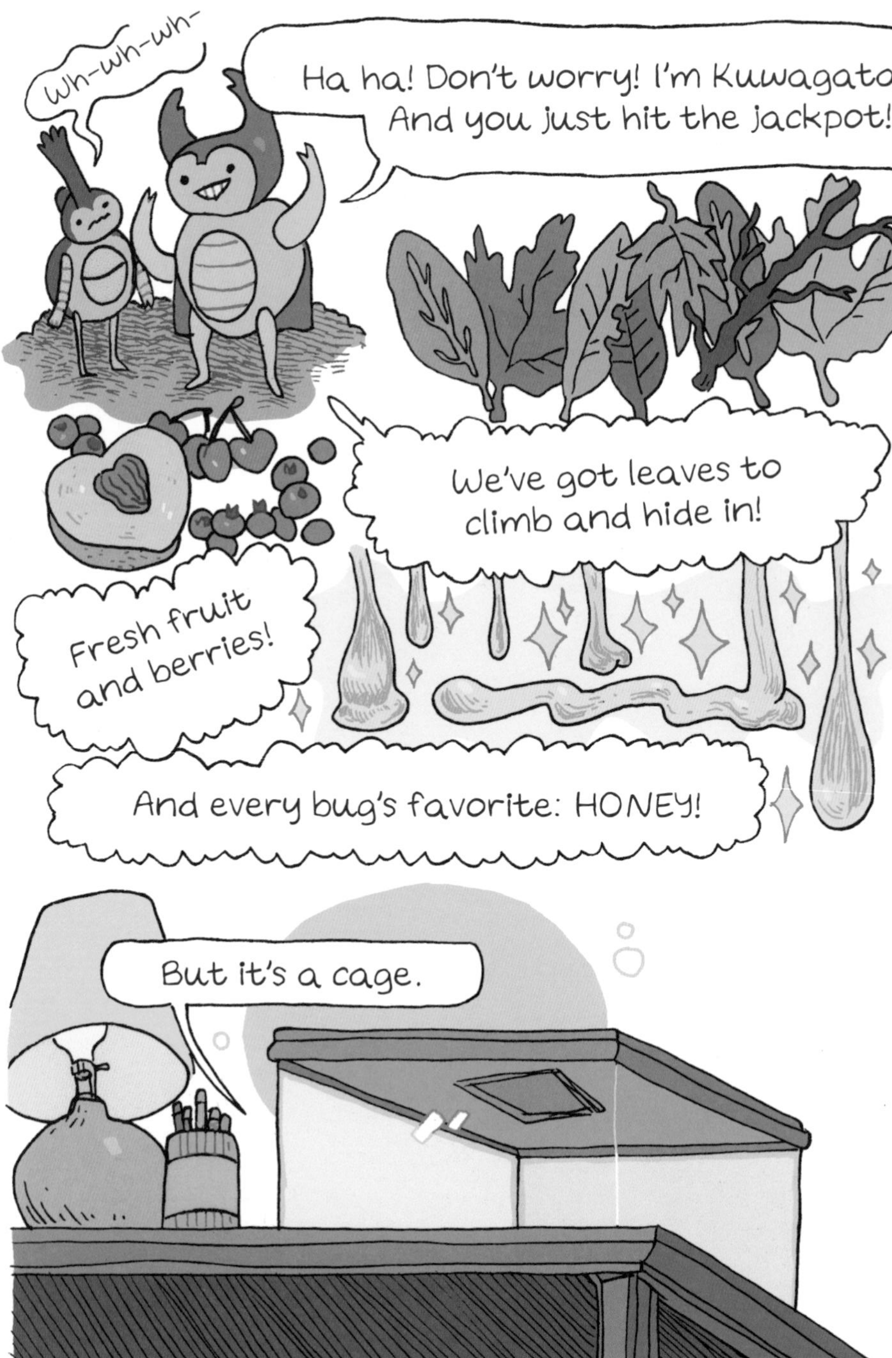
Wh-wh-wh-
Ha ha! Don't worry! I'm Kuwagata. And you just hit the jackpot!
We've got leaves to climb and hide in!
Fresh fruit and berries!
And every bug's favorite: HONEY!
But it's a cage.

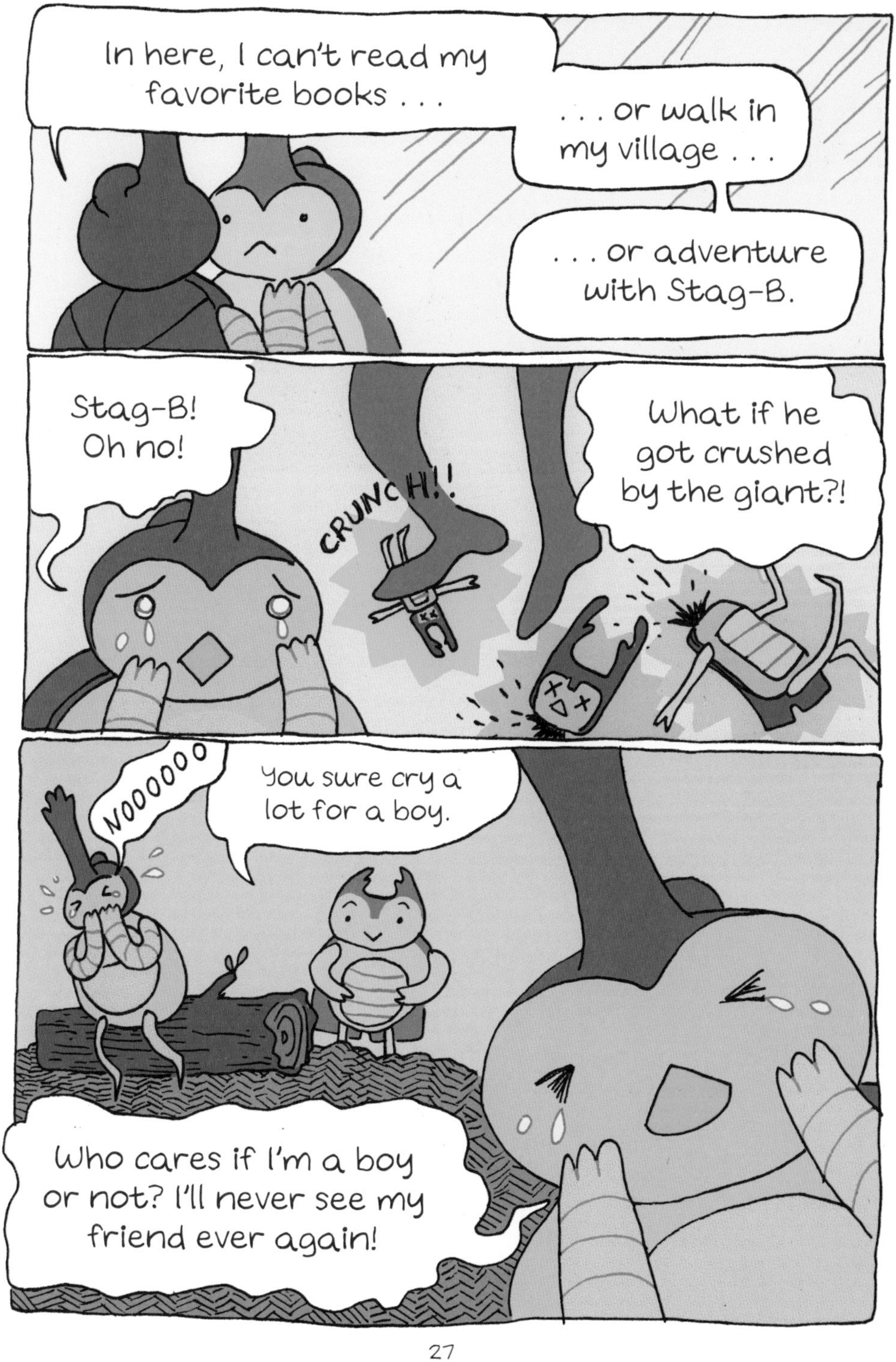
In here, I can't read my favorite books . . .
. . . or walk in my village . . .
. . . or adventure with Stag-B.
Stag-B! Oh no!
CRUNCH!!
What if he got crushed by the giant?!
NOOOOOO
You sure cry a lot for a boy.
Who cares if I'm a boy or not? I'll never see my friend ever again!

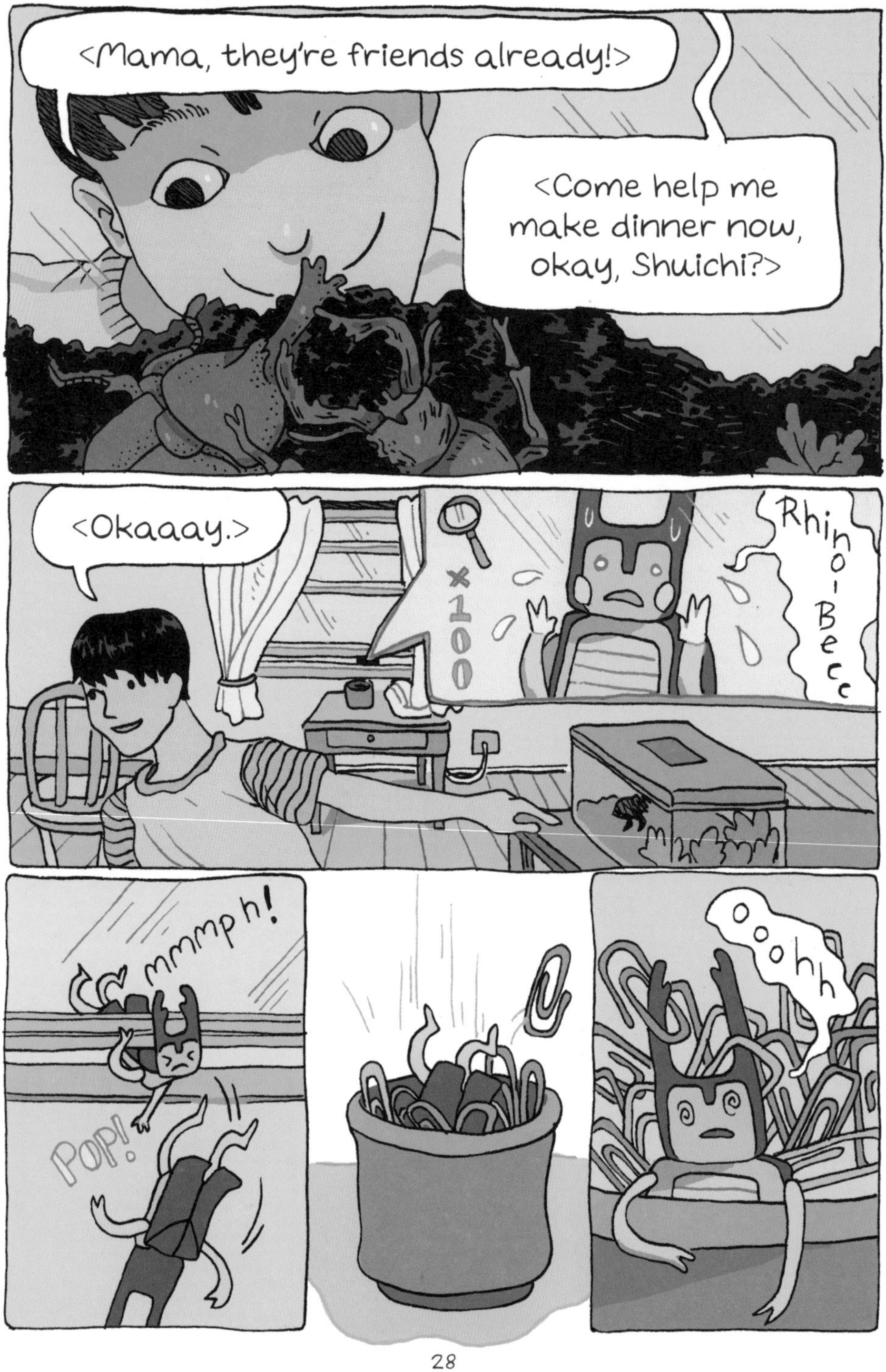
<Mama, they're friends already!>
<Come help me make dinner now, okay, Shuichi?>
<Okaaay.>
×100
Rhino-Becc
mmmph!
POP!
Ooohh

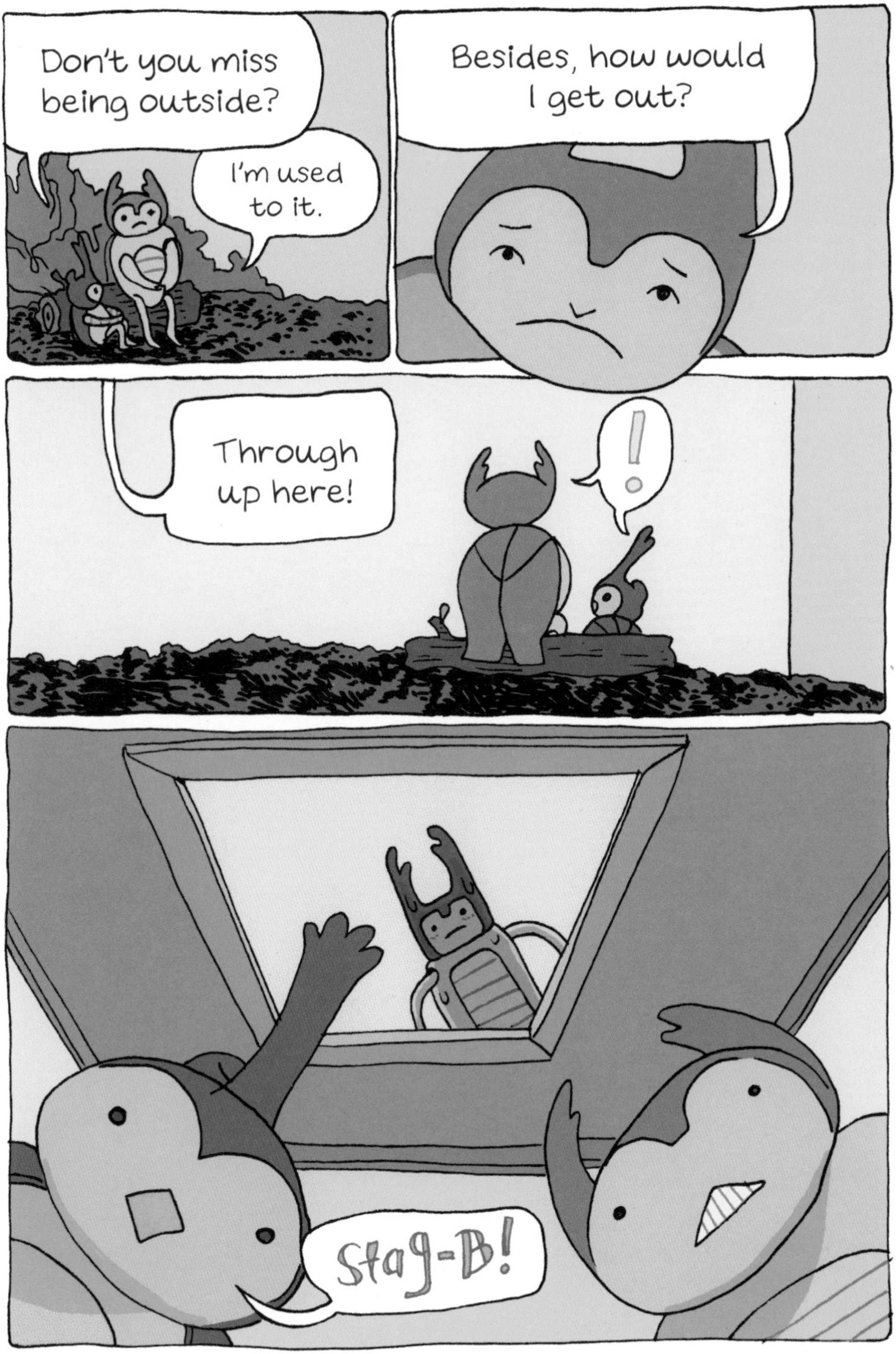
Don't you miss being outside?
I'm used to it.
Besides, how would I get out?
Through up here!
!
Stag-B!

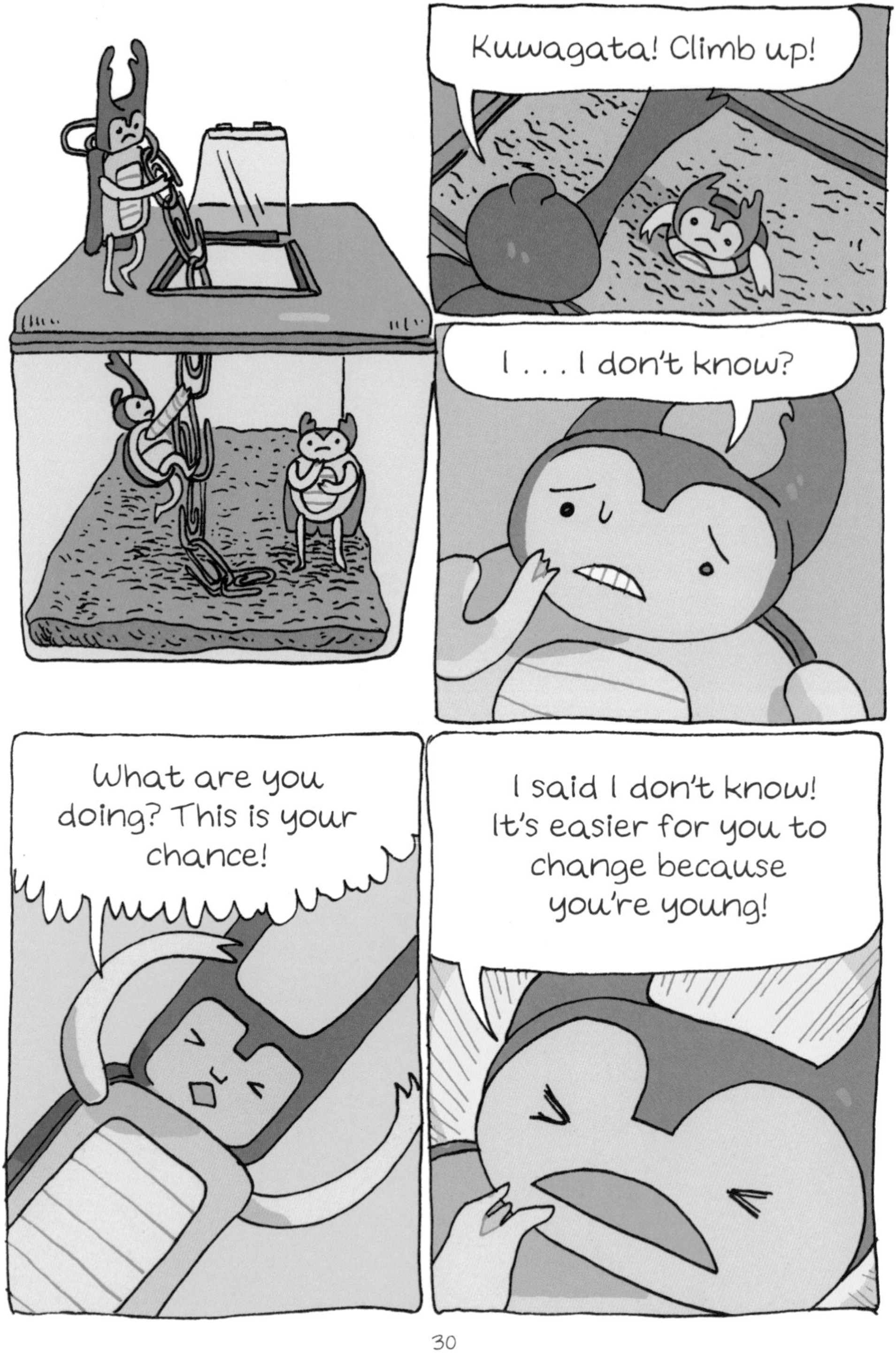
Kuwagata! Climb up!
I . . . I don't know?
What are you doing? This is your chance!
I said I don't know! It's easier for you to change because you're young!

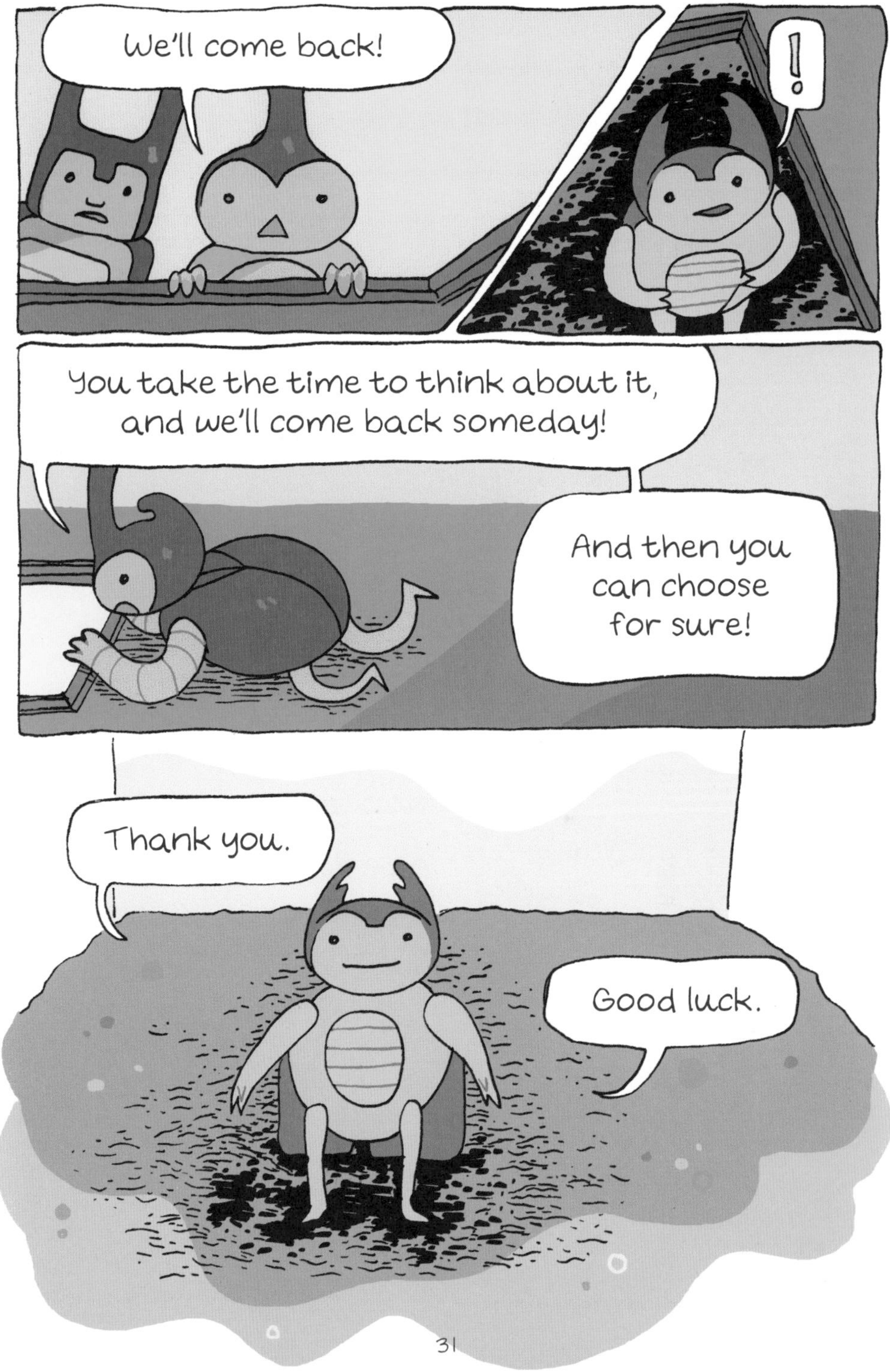
We'll come back!
!
You take the time to think about it, and we'll come back someday!
And then you can choose for sure!
Thank you.
Good luck.

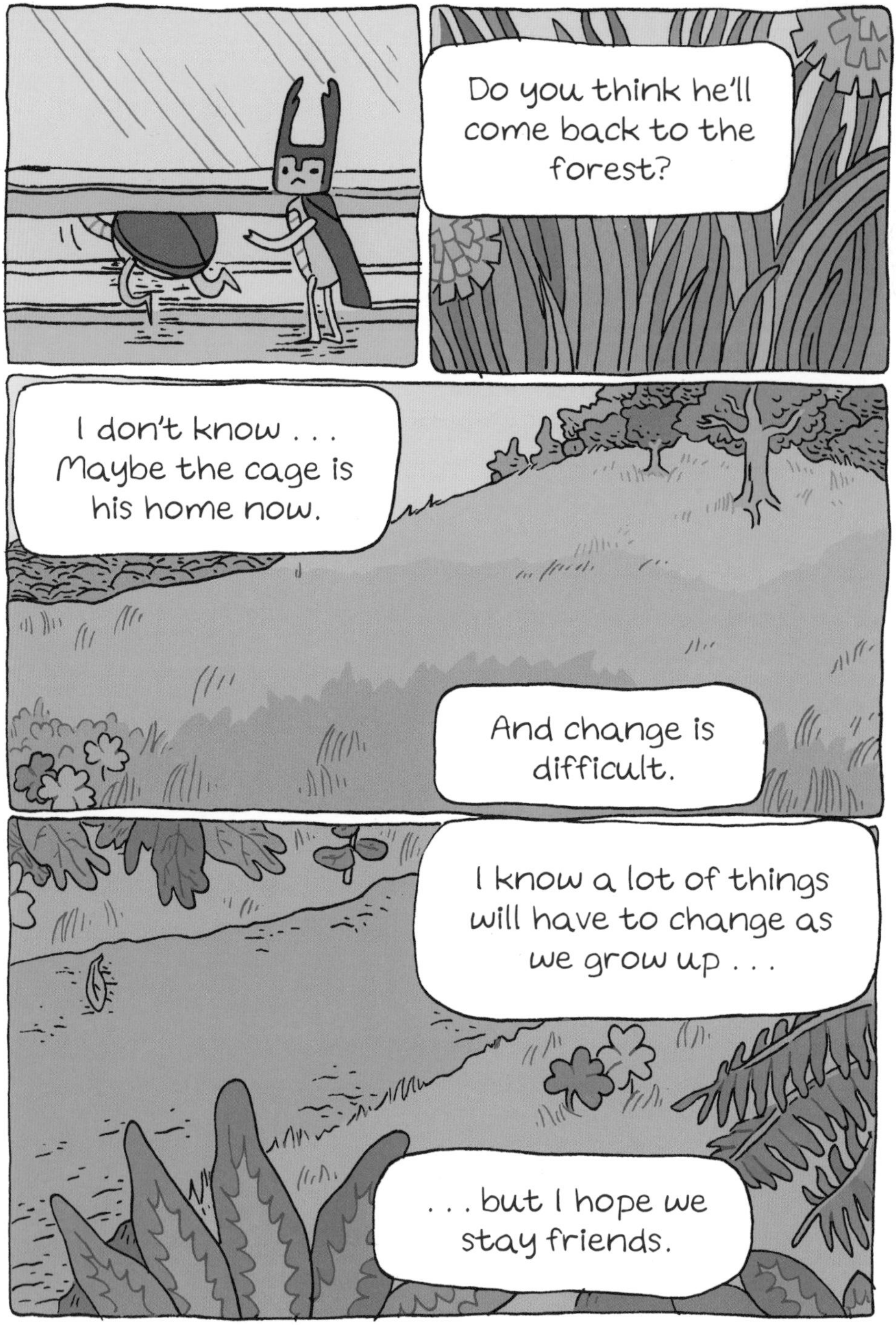
Do you think he'll come back to the forest?
I don't know . . . Maybe the cage is his home now.
And change is difficult.
I know a lot of things will have to change as we grow up . . .
. . . but I hope we stay friends.

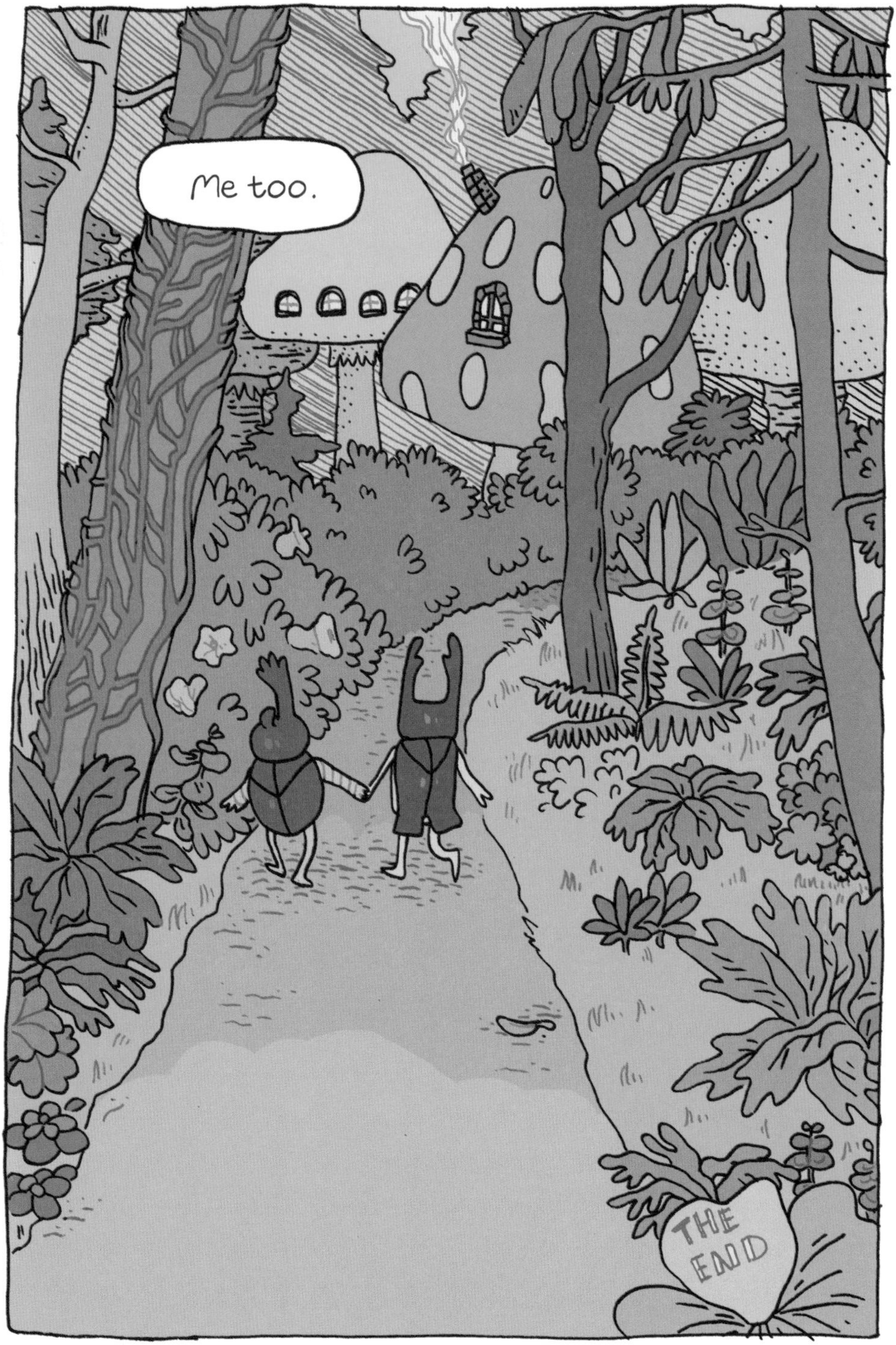
Me too.
THE END

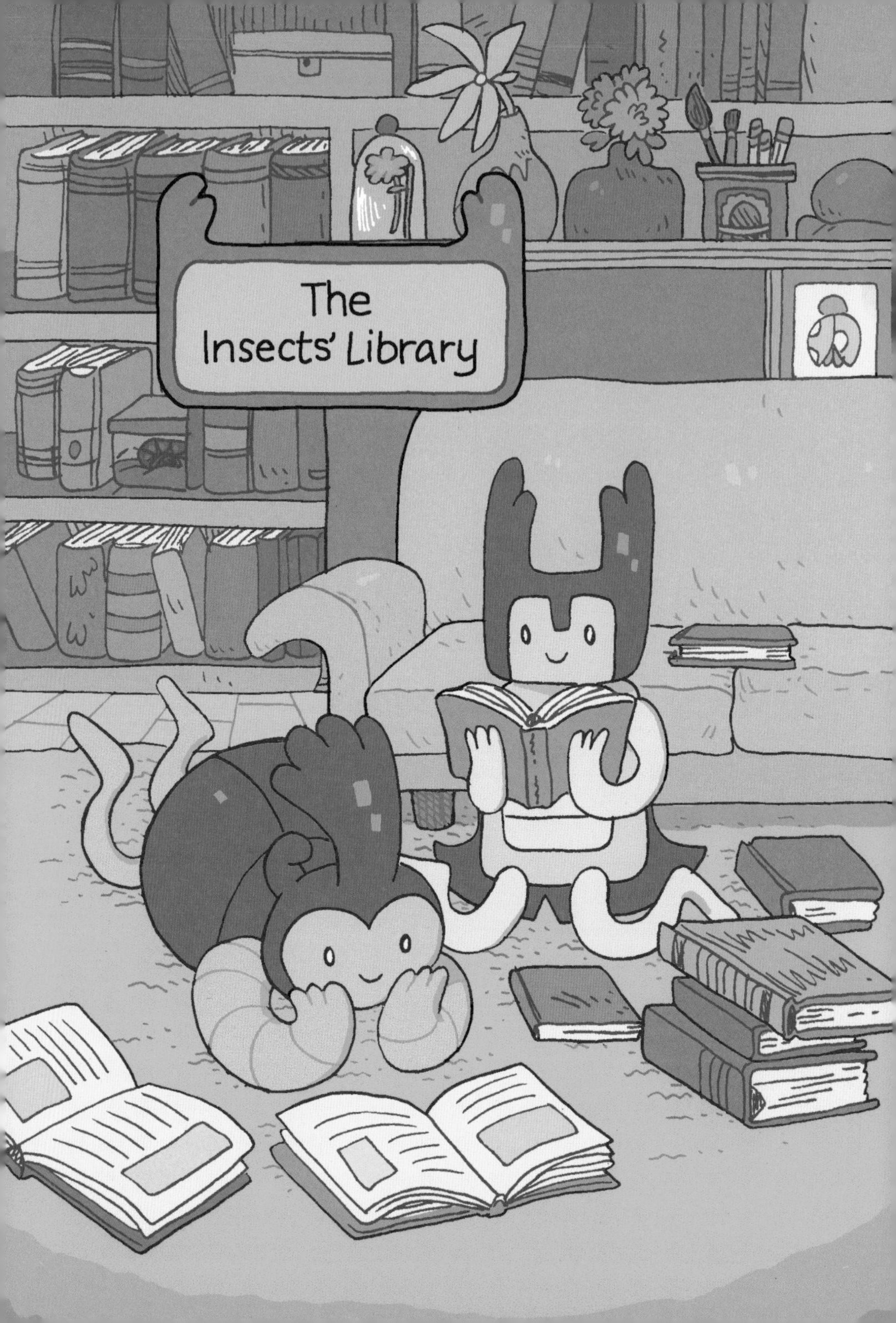
The
Insects' Library

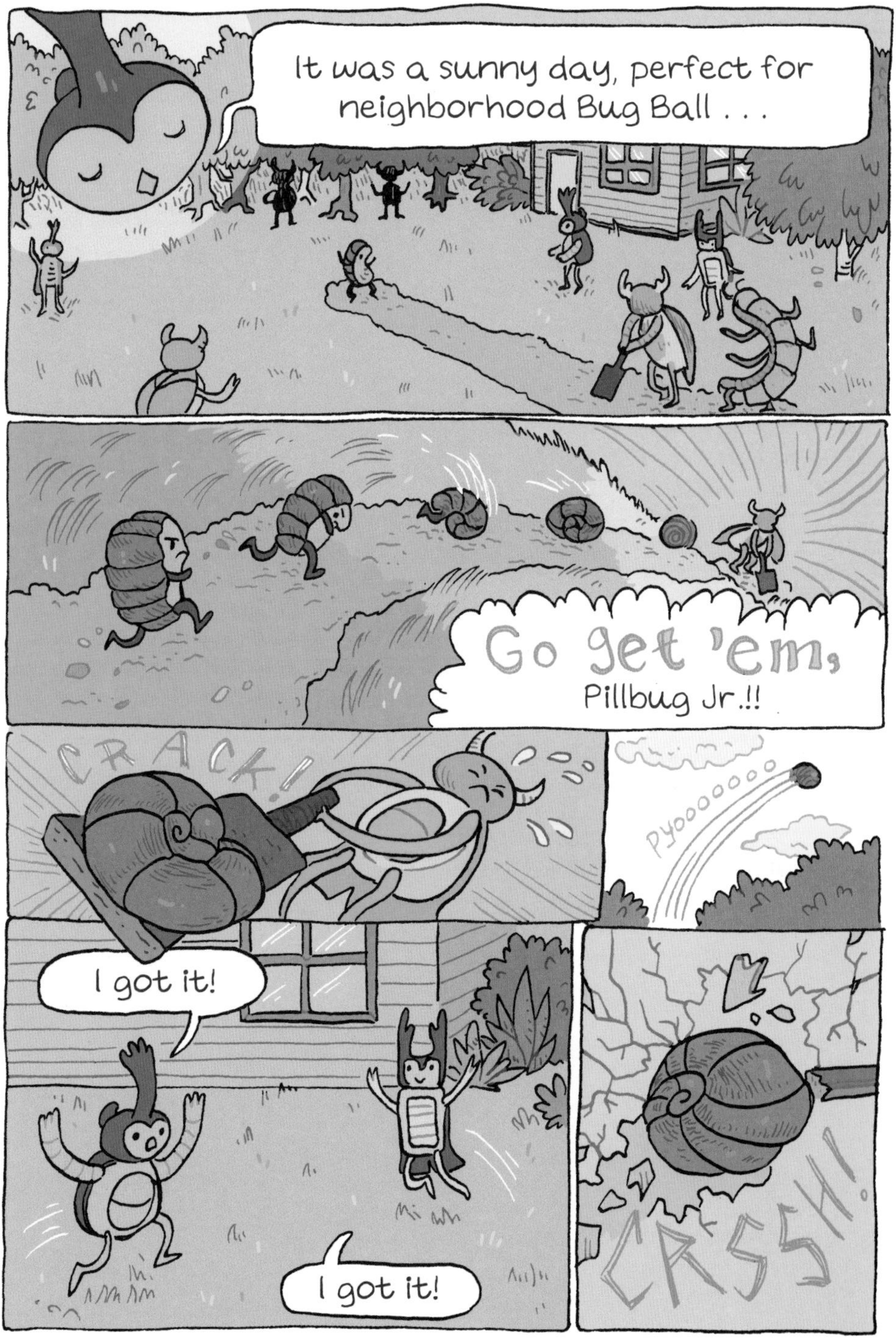
It was a sunny day, perfect for neighborhood Bug Ball . . .
Go get 'em, Pillbug Jr.!!
CRACK!
Pyoooooooo
I got it!
I got it!
CRSSH!

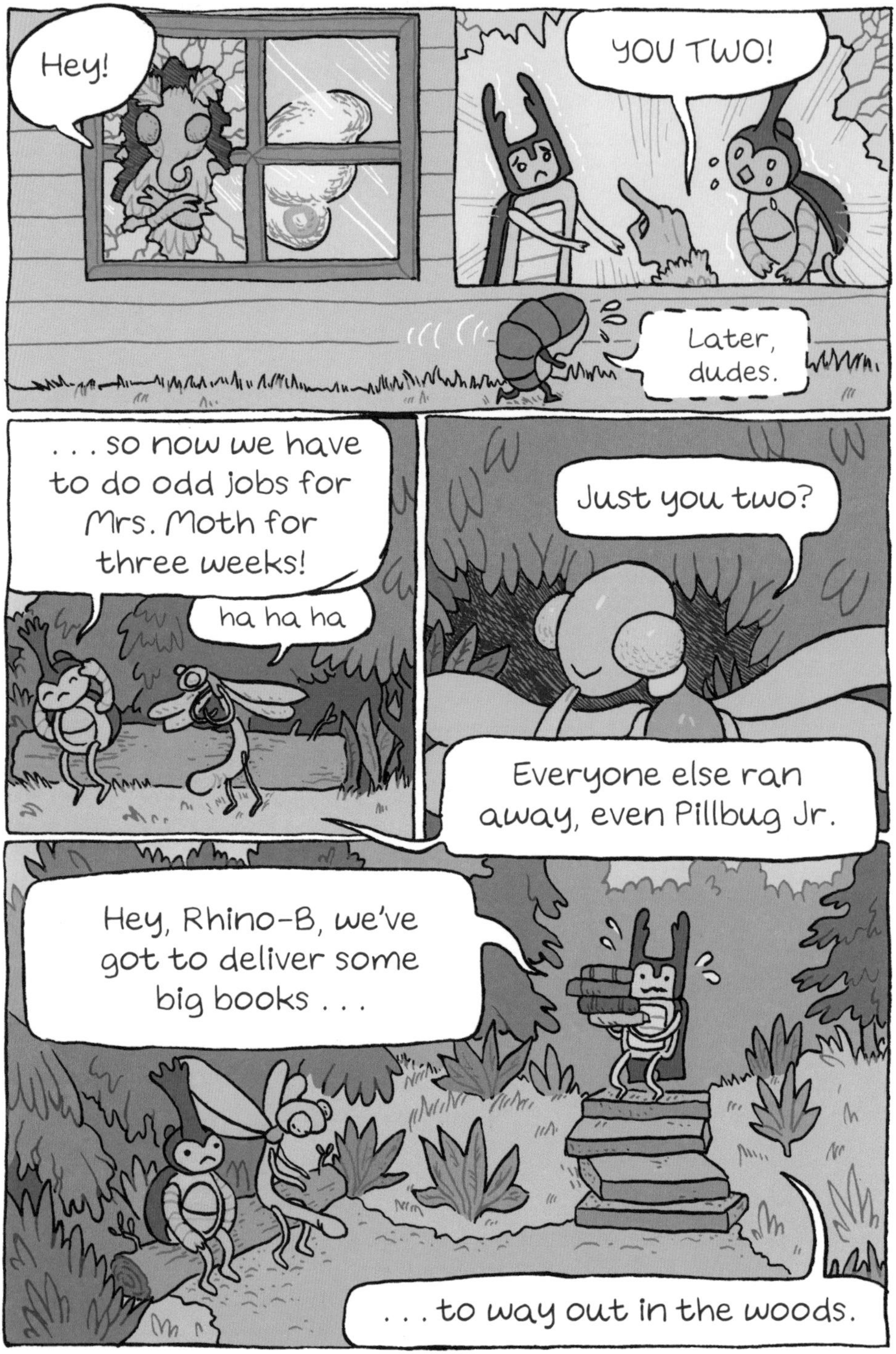
Hey!
YOU TWO!
Later, dudes.
. . . so now we have to do odd jobs for Mrs. Moth for three weeks!
ha ha ha
Just you two?
Everyone else ran away, even Pillbug Jr.
Hey, Rhino-B, we've got to deliver some big books . . .
. . . to way out in the woods.

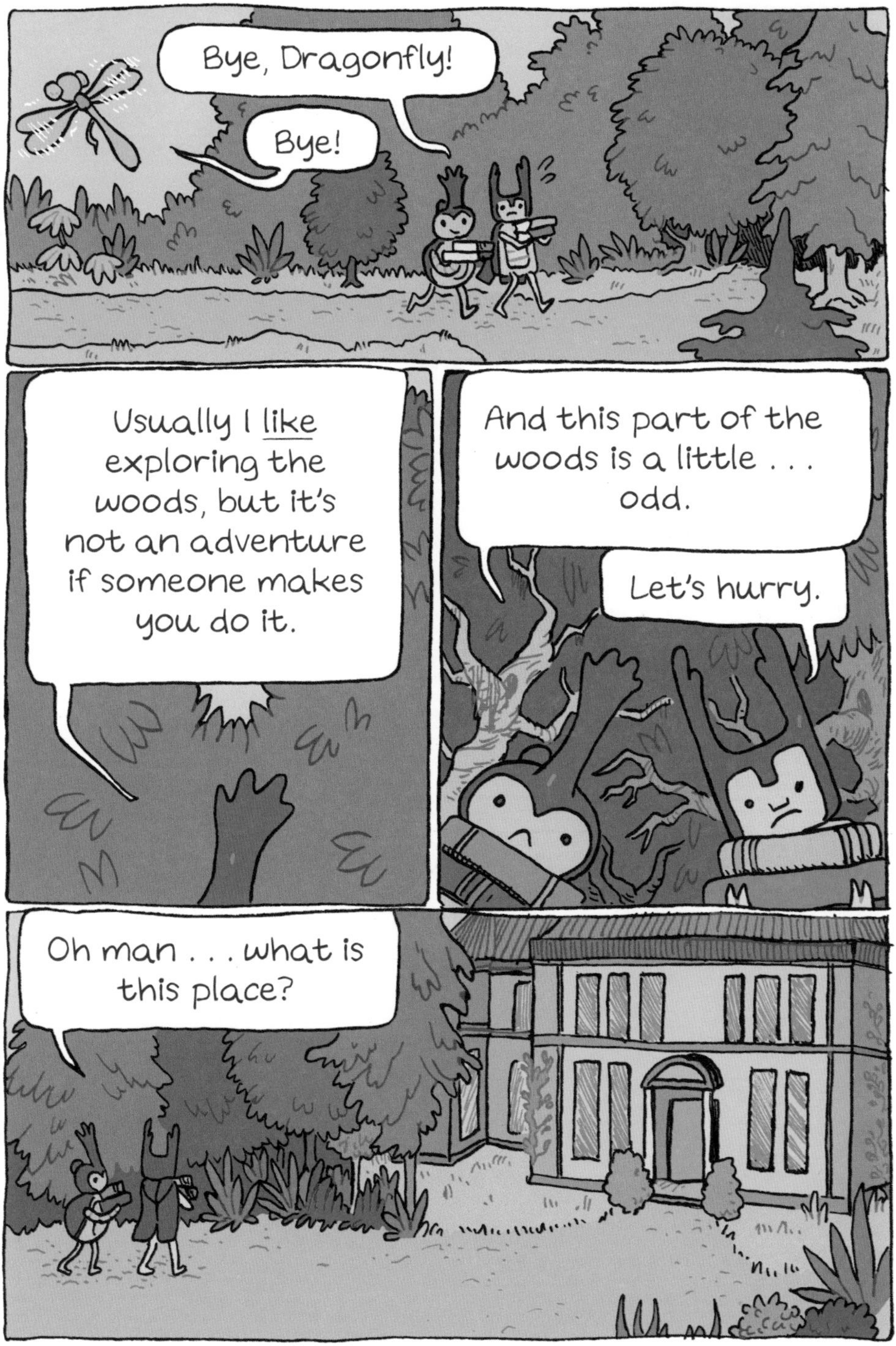
Bye, Dragonfly!
Bye!
Usually I like exploring the woods, but it's not an adventure if someone makes you do it.
And this part of the woods is a little . . . odd.
Let's hurry.
Oh man . . . what is this place?

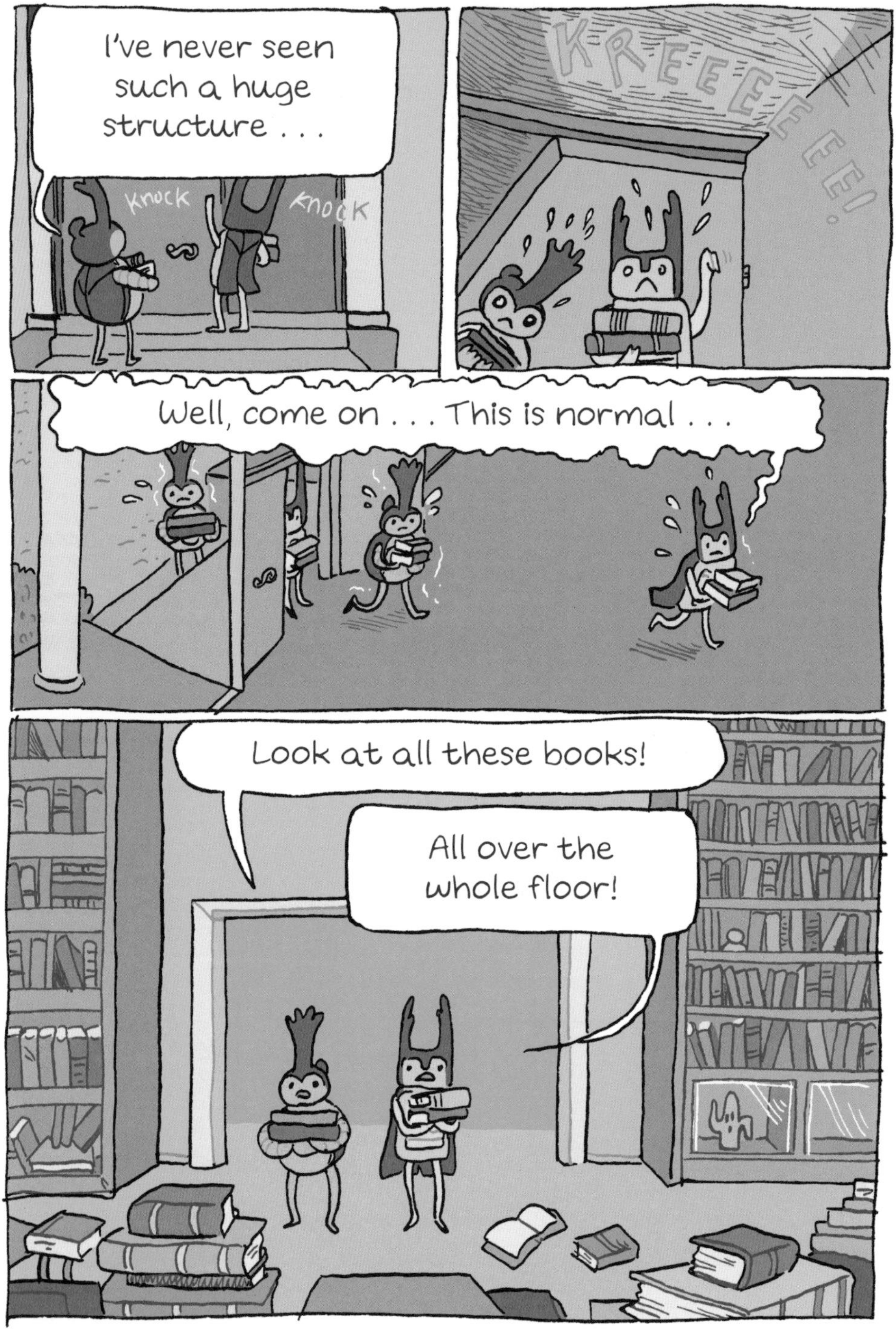
I've never seen such a huge structure . . .
Knock
Knock
KREEEEEEE!
Well, come on . . . This is normal . . .
Look at all these books!
All over the whole floor!

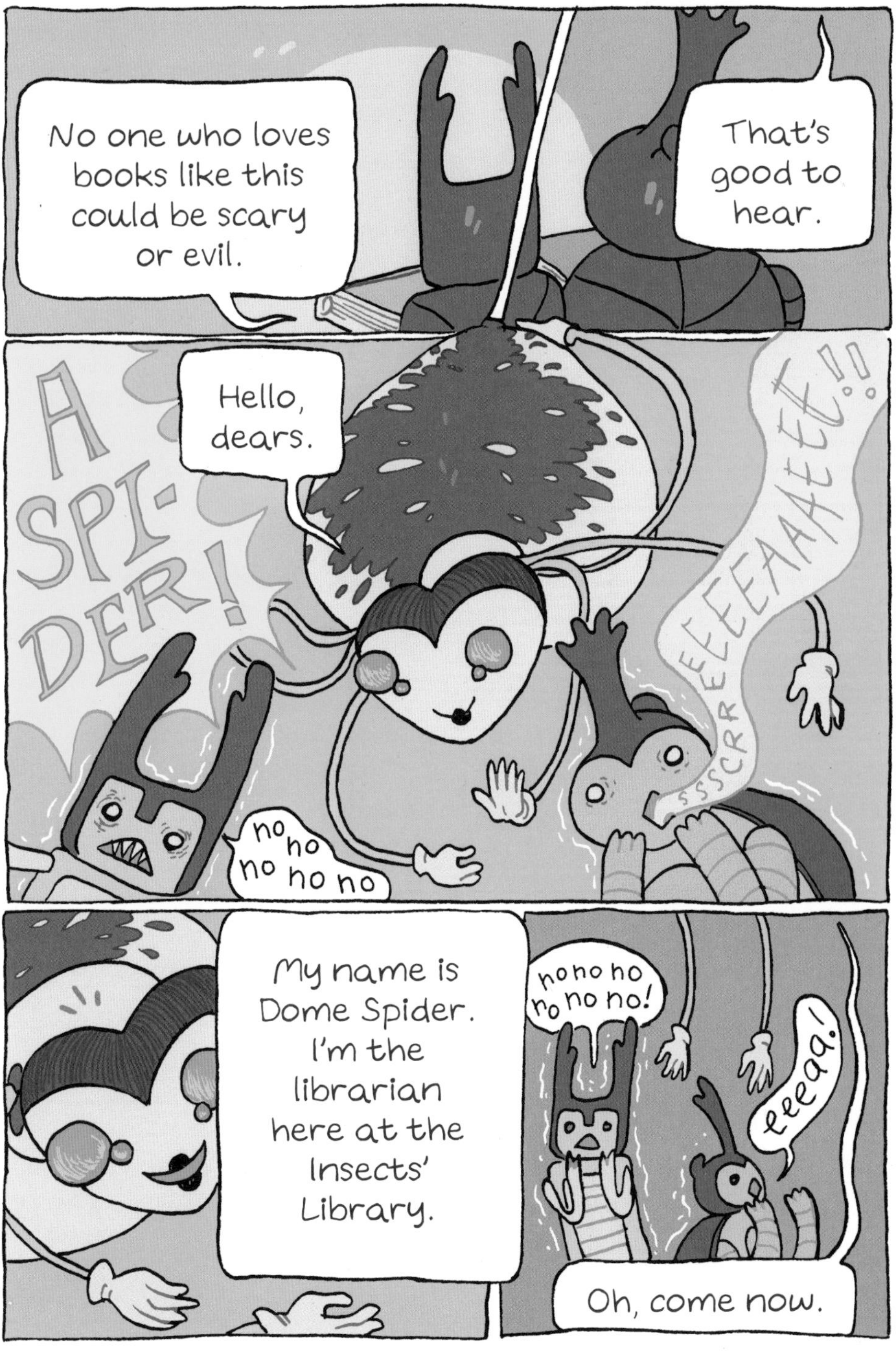

No one who loves books like this could be scary or evil.
That's good to hear.
A SPI-DER!
Hello, dears.
SSSCRREEEEEEAAAEEE!!
no no no no no
My name is Dome Spider. I'm the librarian here at the Insects' Library.
no no no no no no!
eeeaa!
Oh, come now.

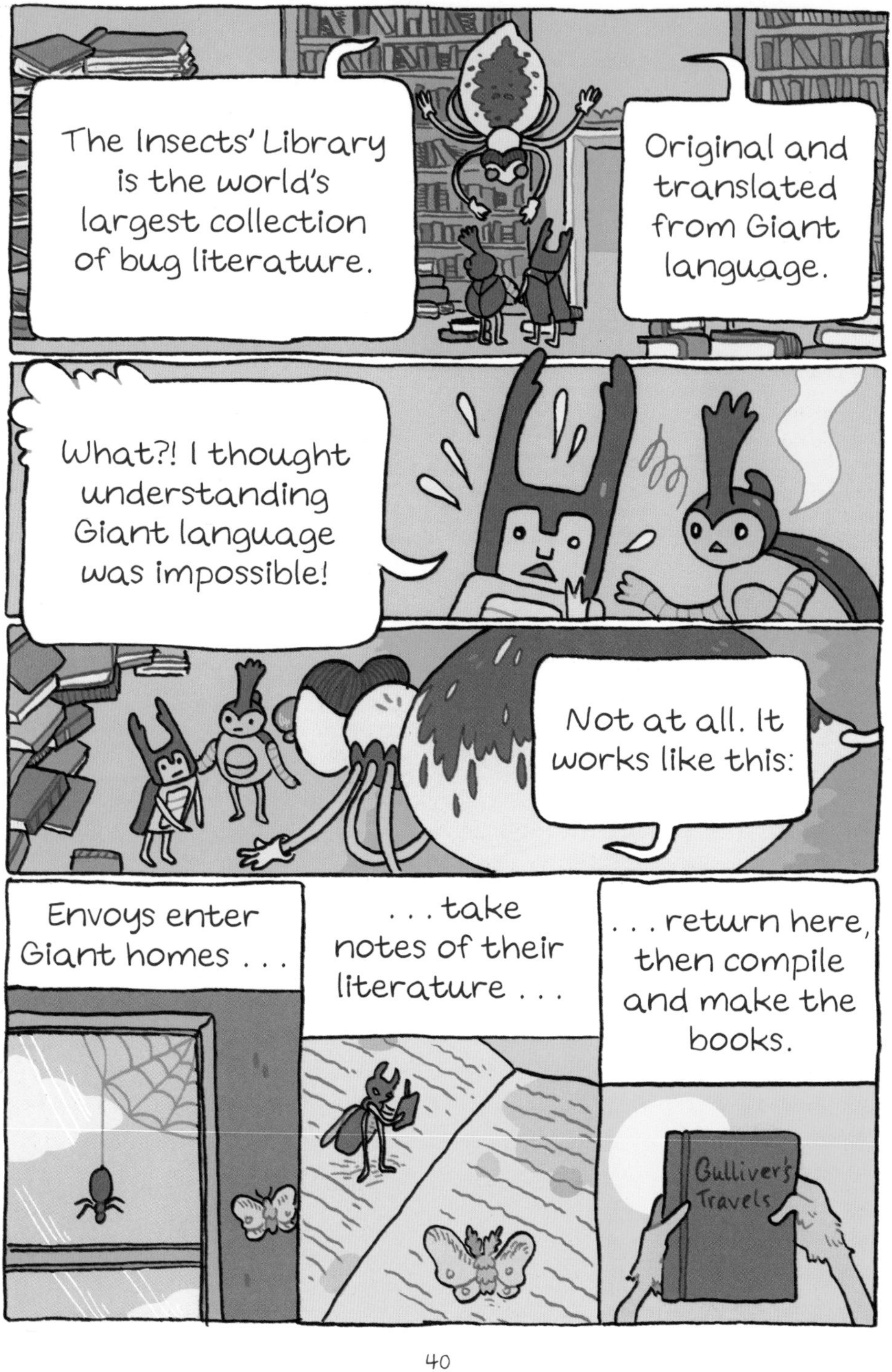
The Insects' Library is the world's largest collection of bug literature.
Original and translated from Giant language.
What?! I thought understanding Giant language was impossible!
Not at all. It works like this:
Envoys enter Giant homes . . .
. . . take notes of their literature . . .
. . . return here, then compile and make the books.
Gulliver's Travels

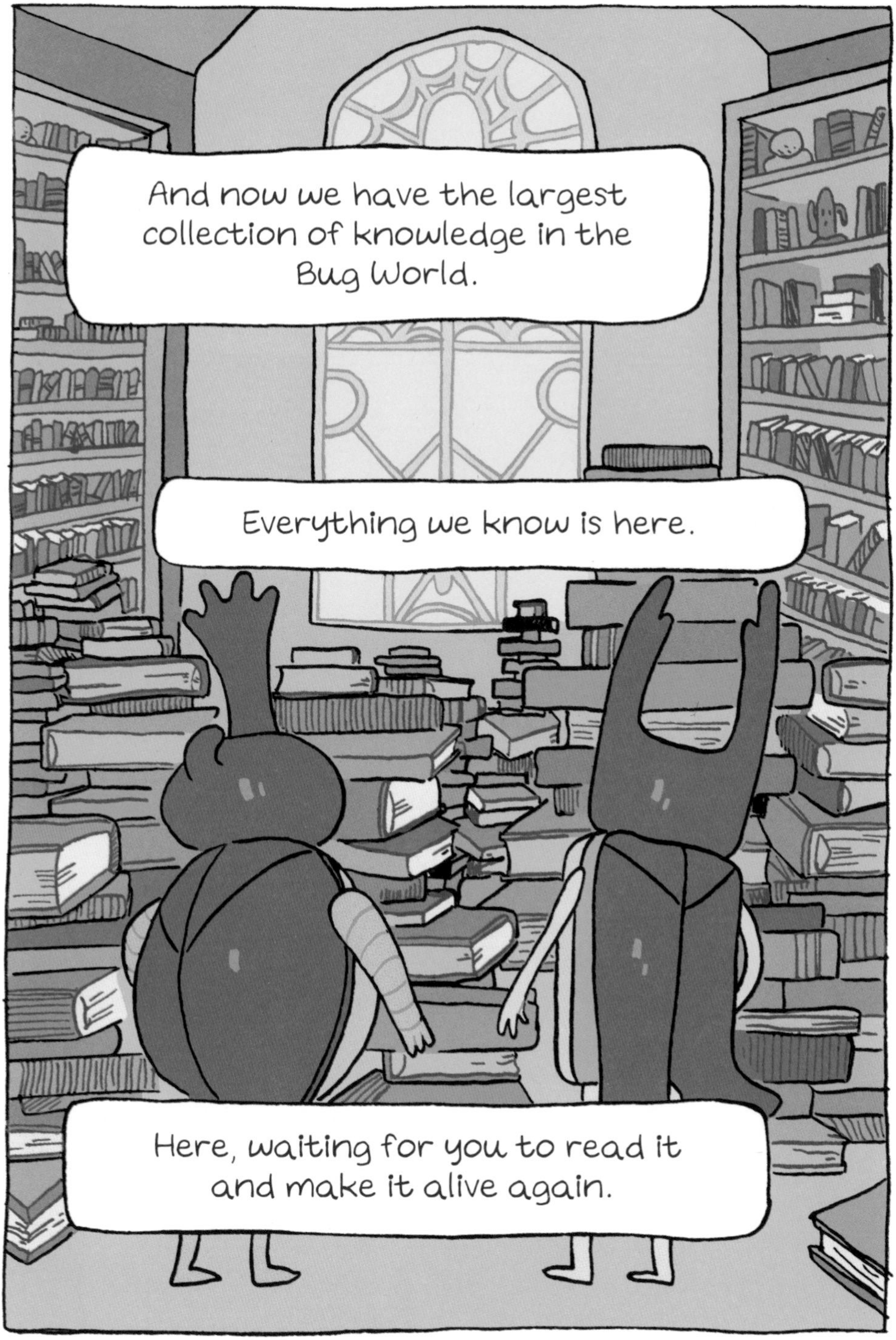
And now we have the largest collection of knowledge in the Bug World.
Everything we know is here.
Here, waiting for you to read it and make it alive again.

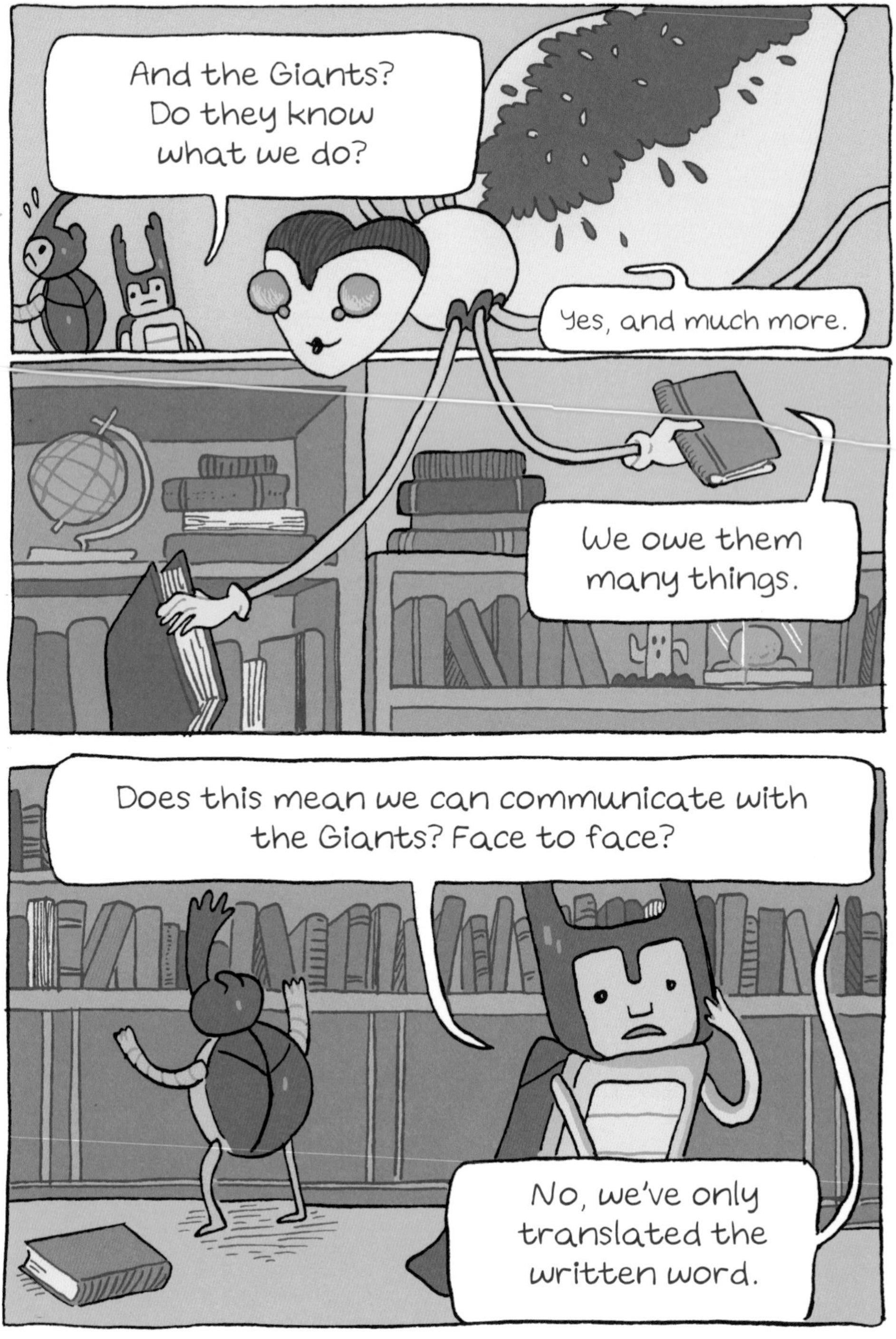
And the Giants? Do they know what we do?
Yes, and much more.
We owe them many things.
Does this mean we can communicate with the Giants? Face to face?
No, we've only translated the written word.

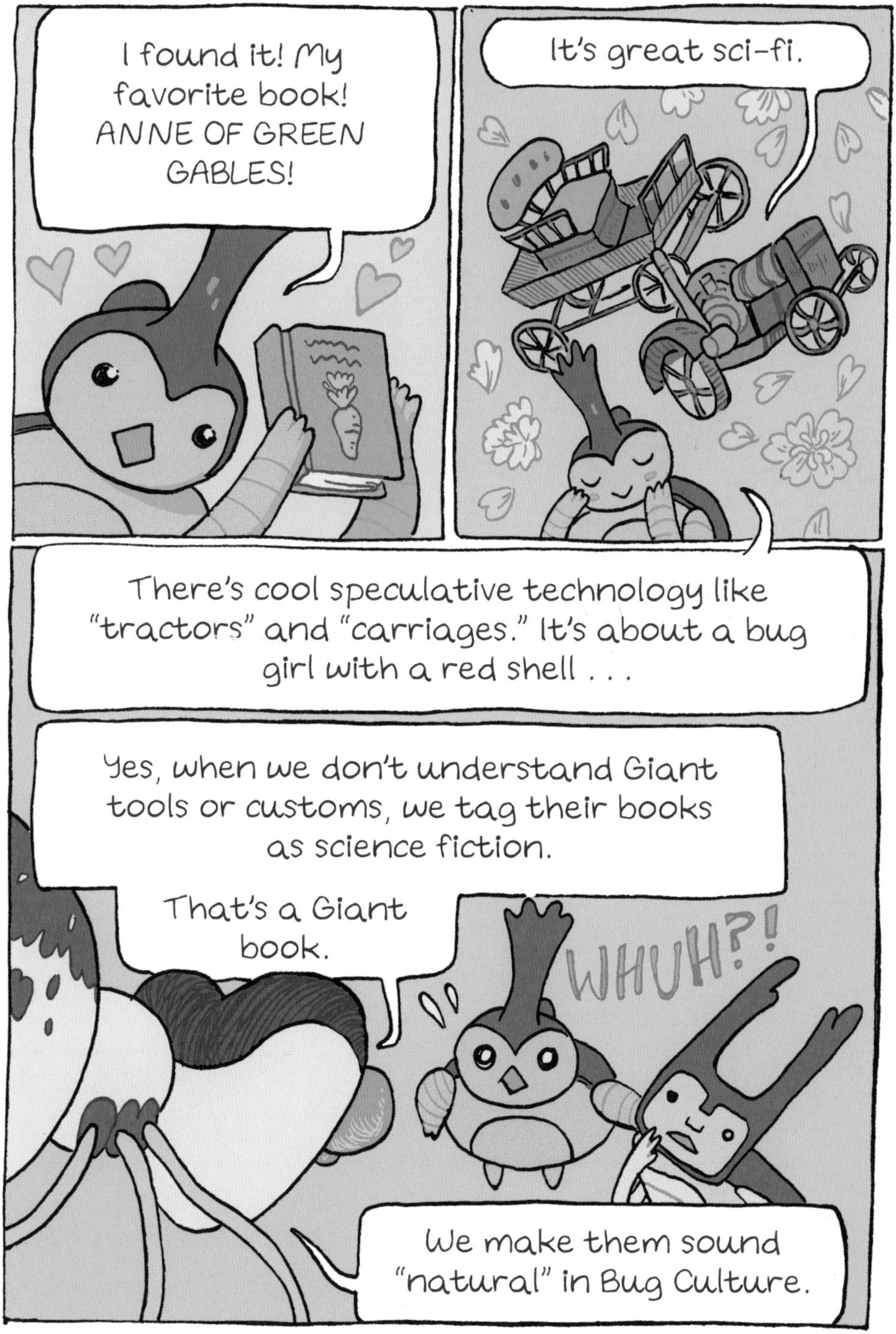
I found it! My favorite book! ANNE OF GREEN GABLES!
It's great sci-fi.
There's cool speculative technology like "tractors" and "carriages." It's about a bug girl with a red shell . . .
Yes, when we don't understand Giant tools or customs, we tag their books as science fiction.
That's a Giant book.
WHUH?!
We make them sound "natural" in Bug Culture.

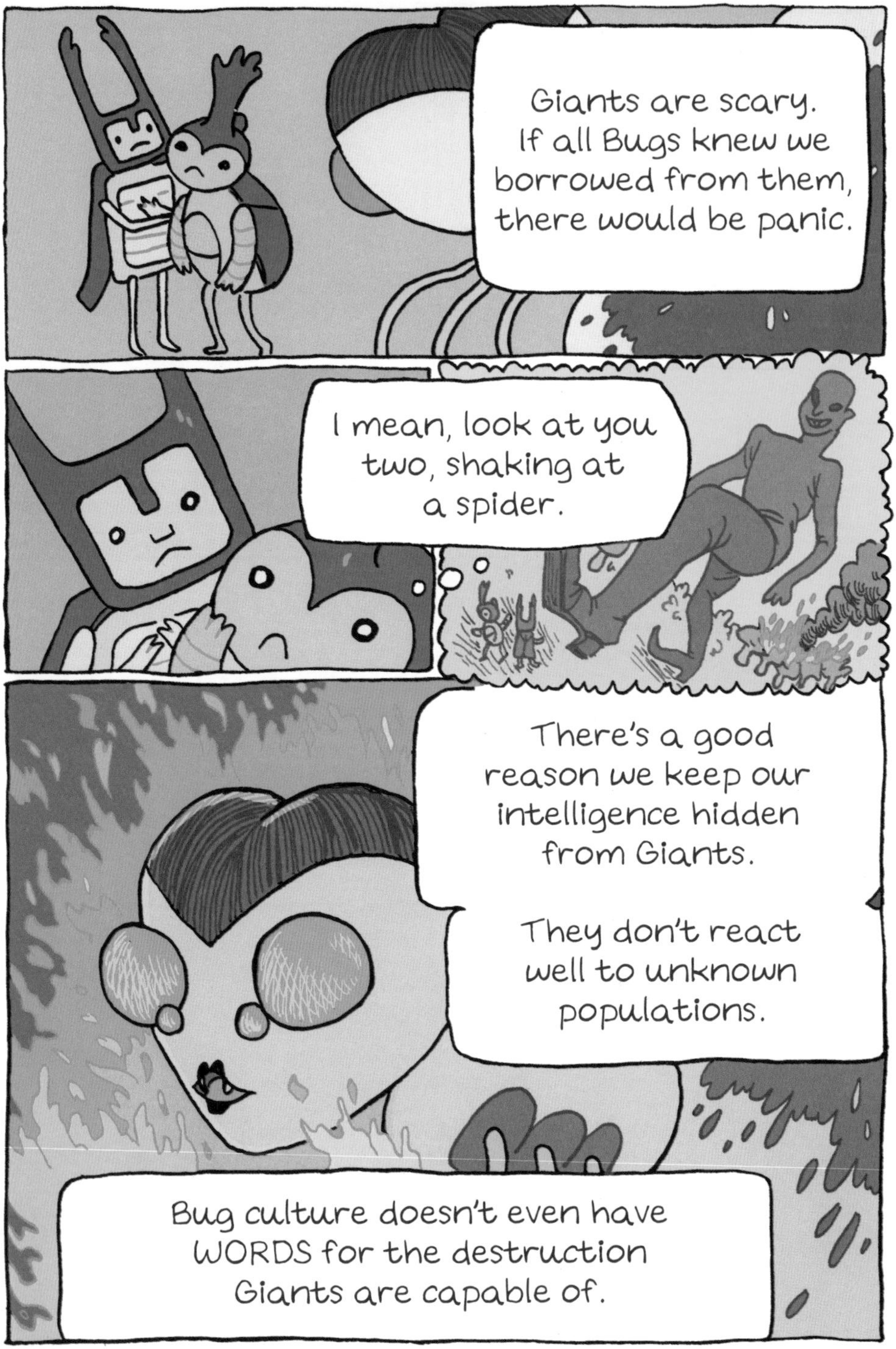
Giants are scary. If all Bugs knew we borrowed from them, there would be panic.
I mean, look at you two, shaking at a spider.
There's a good reason we keep our intelligence hidden from Giants.
They don't react well to unknown populations.
Bug culture doesn't even have WORDS for the destruction Giants are capable of.

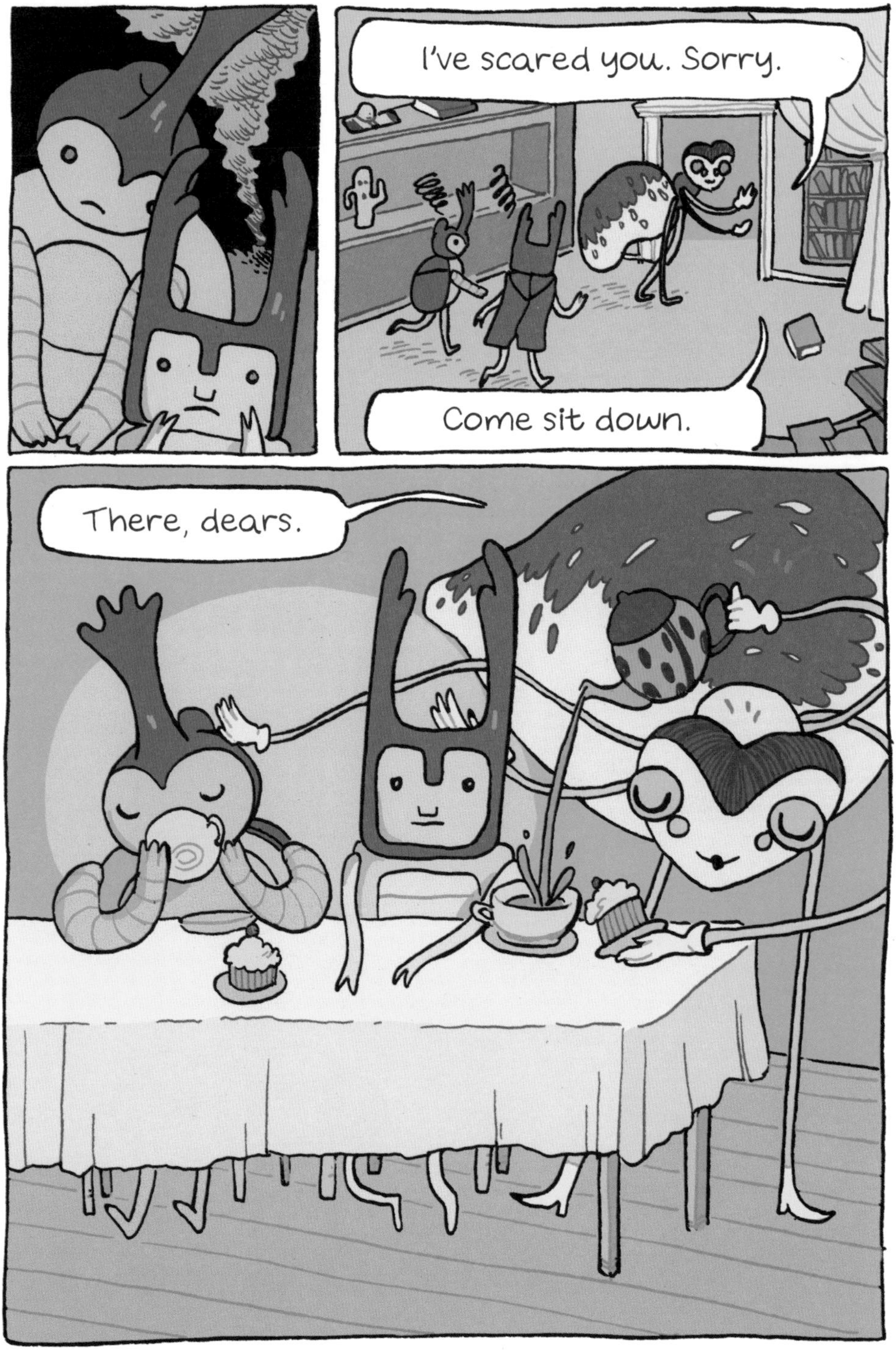
I've scared you. Sorry.
Come sit down.
There, dears.

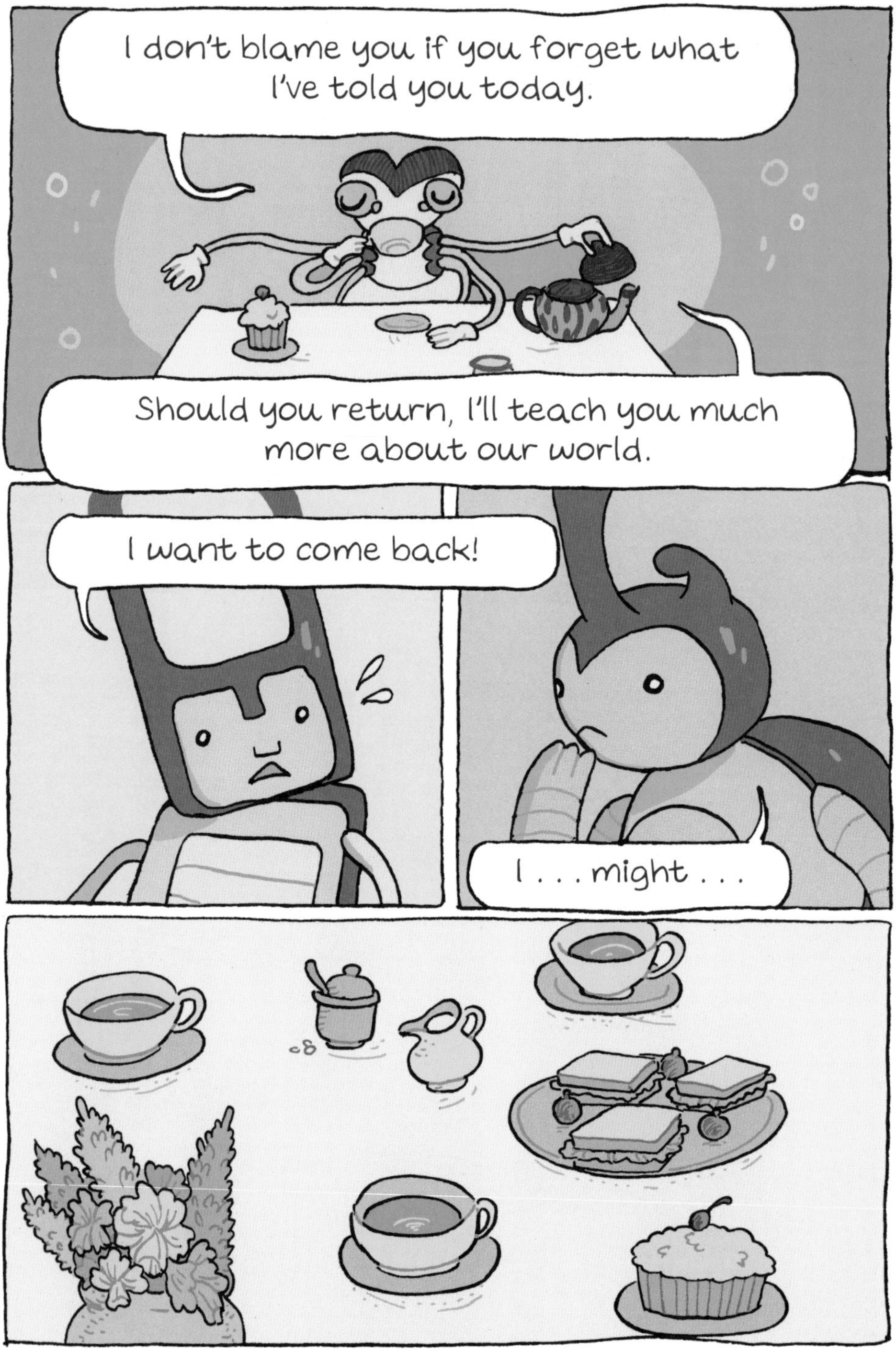
I don't blame you if you forget what I've told you today.
Should you return, I'll teach you much more about our world.
I want to come back!
I . . . might . . .

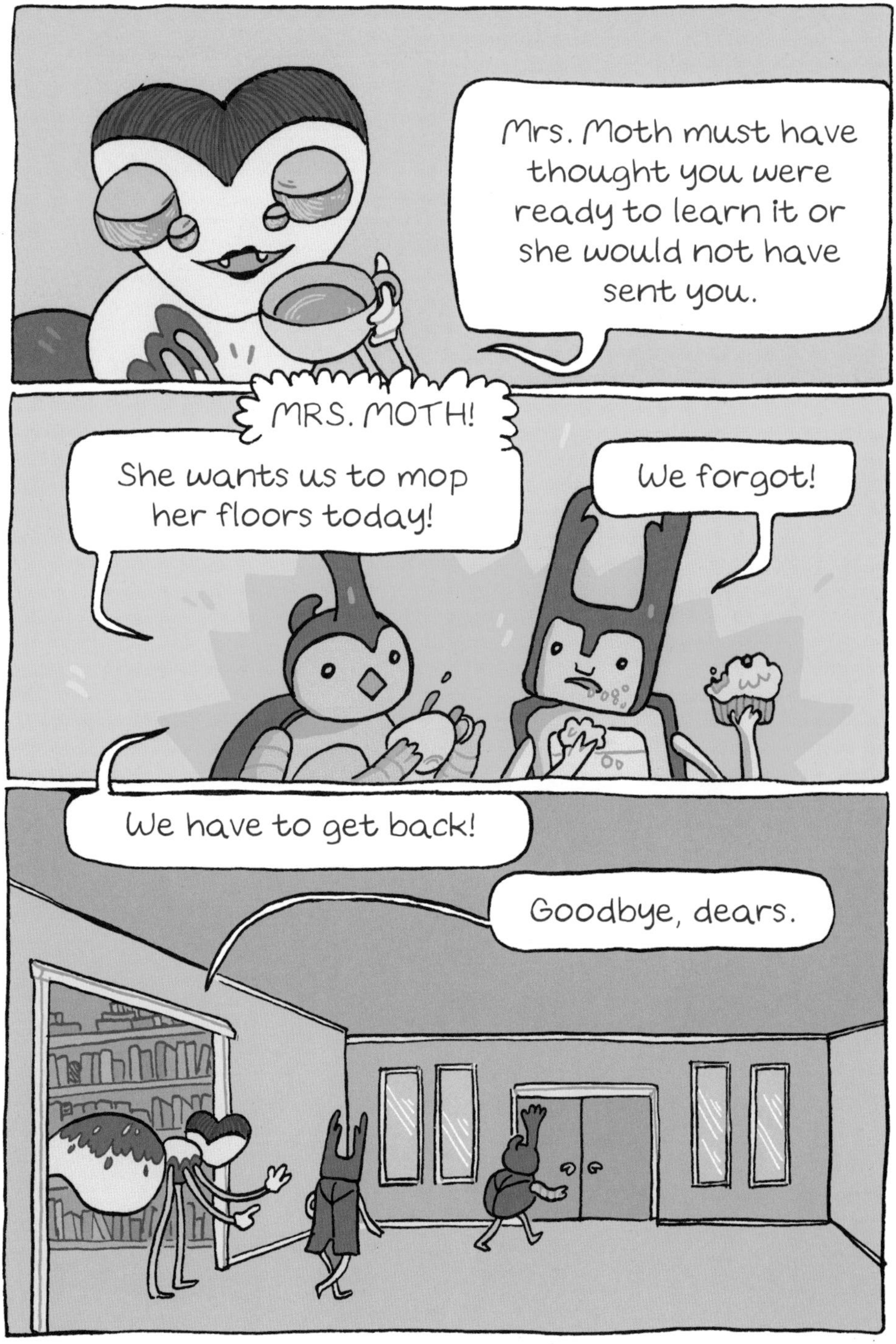
Mrs. Moth must have thought you were ready to learn it or she would not have sent you.
MRS. MOTH!
She wants us to mop her floors today!
We forgot!
We have to get back!
Goodbye, dears.

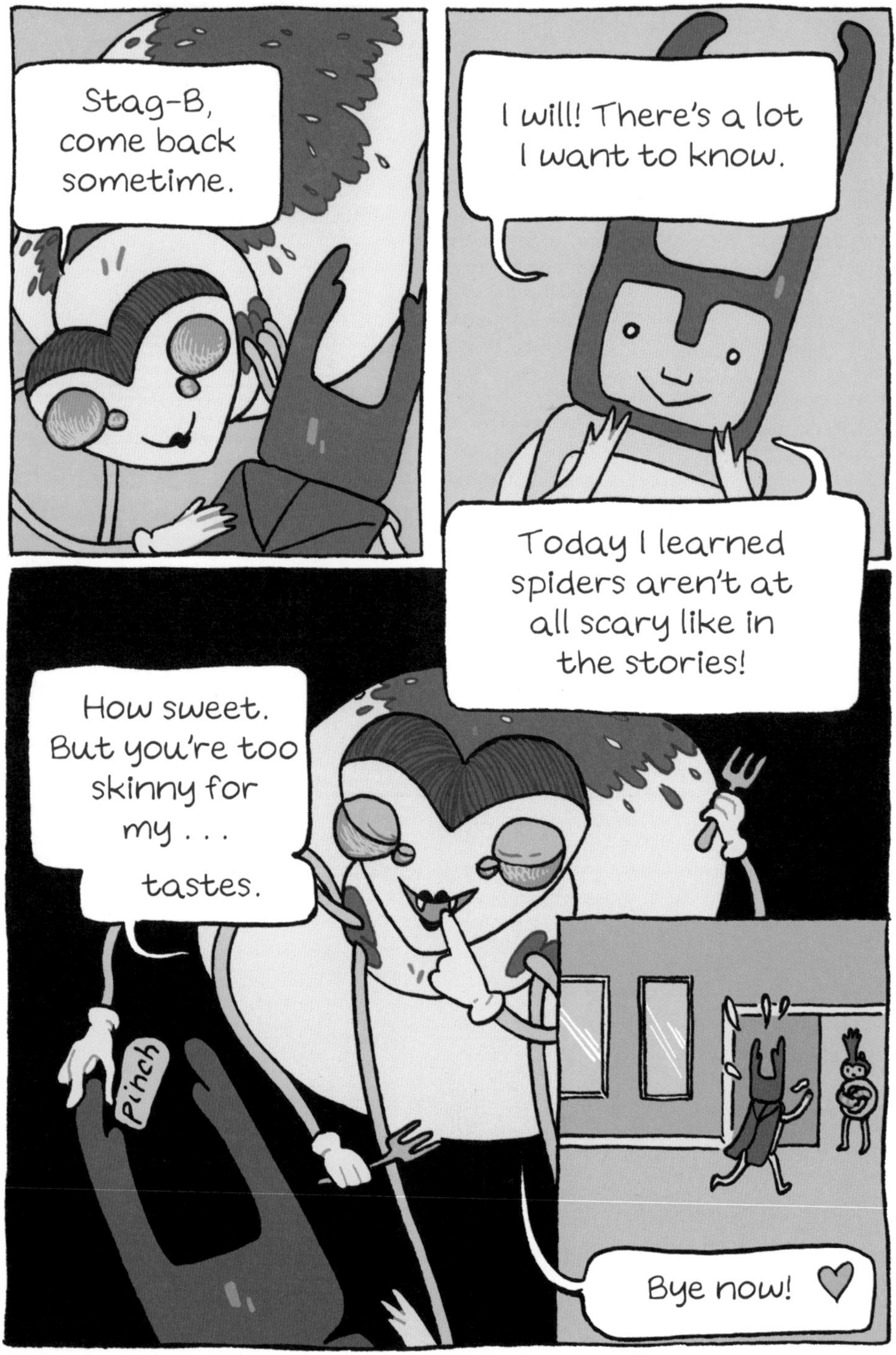
Stag-B, come back sometime.
I will! There's a lot I want to know.
Today I learned spiders aren't at all scary like in the stories!
How sweet. But you're too skinny for my . . .
tastes.
Pinch
Bye now!

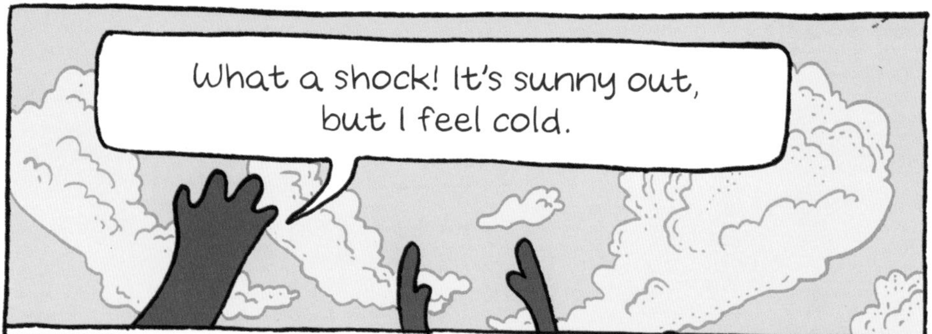
What a shock! It's sunny out, but I feel cold.

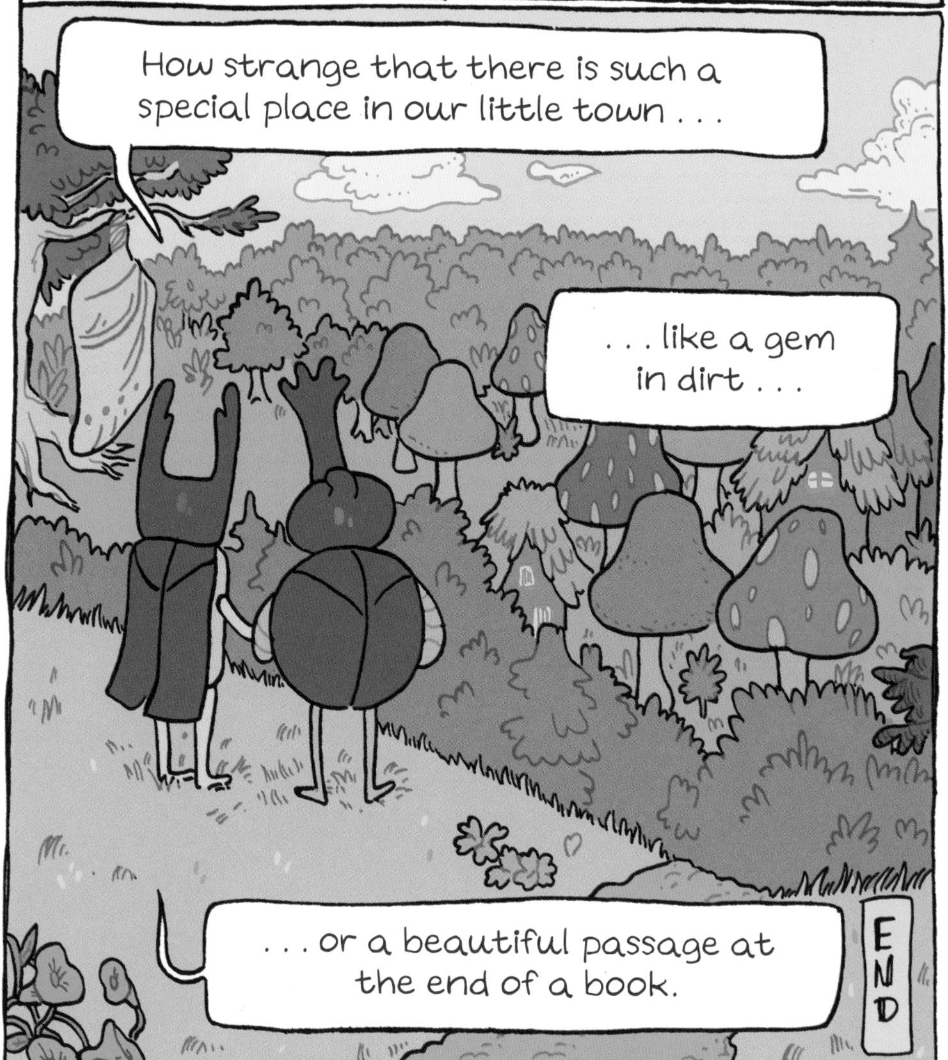
How strange that there is such a special place in our little town . . .
. . . like a gem in dirt . . .
. . . or a beautiful passage at the end of a book.
END

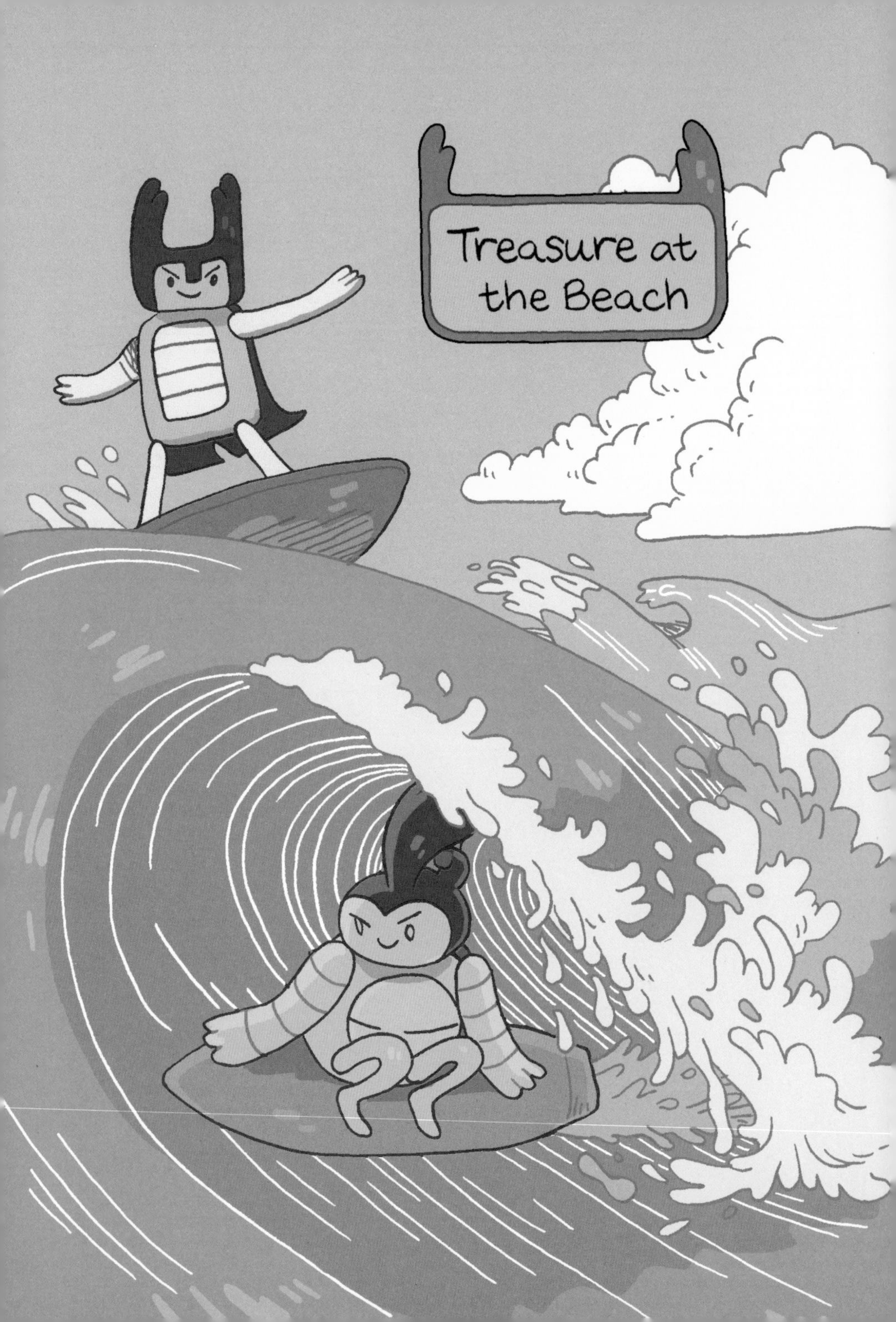
Treasure at the Beach

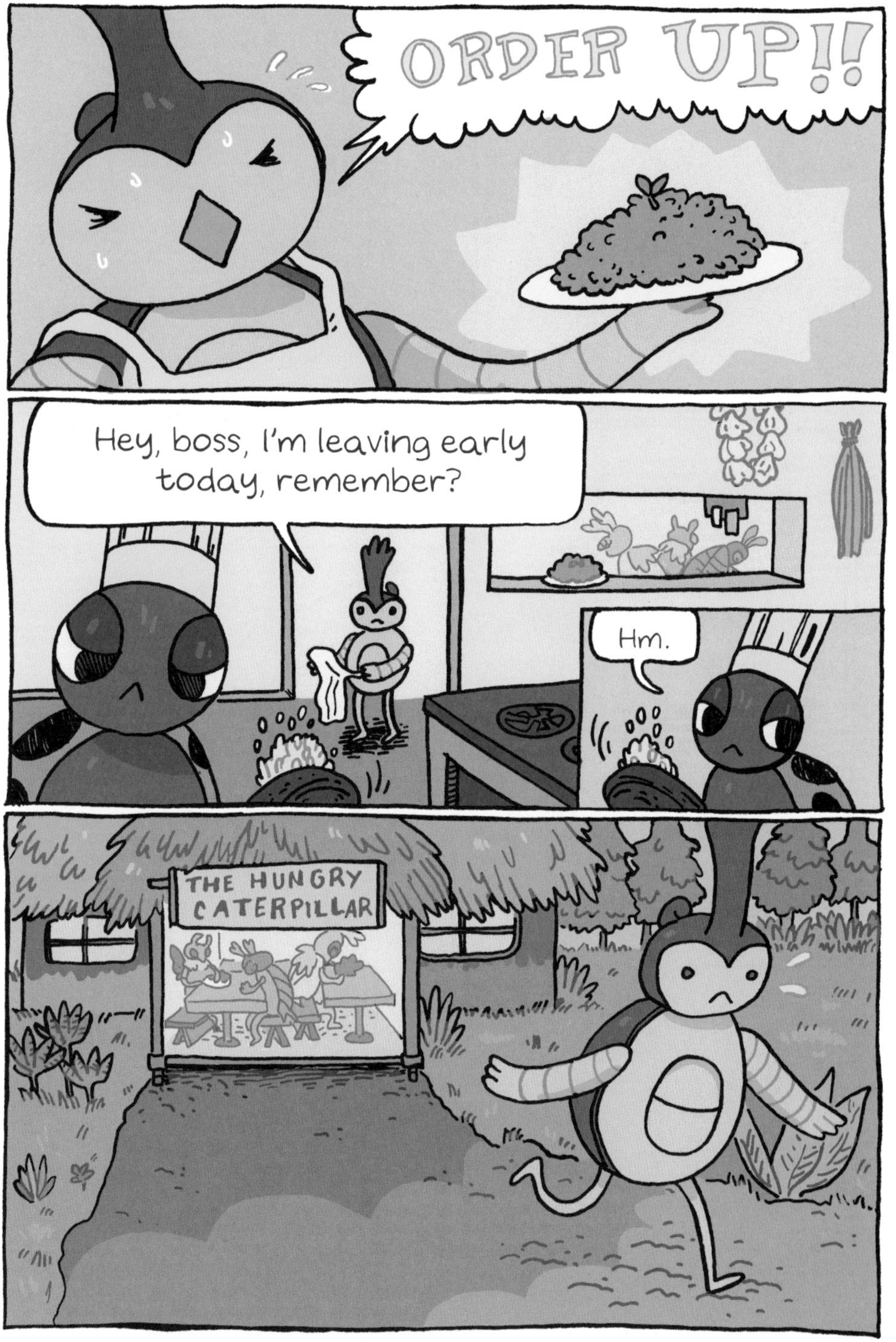
ORDER UP!!
Hey, boss, I'm leaving early today, remember?
Hm.
THE HUNGRY CATERPILLAR

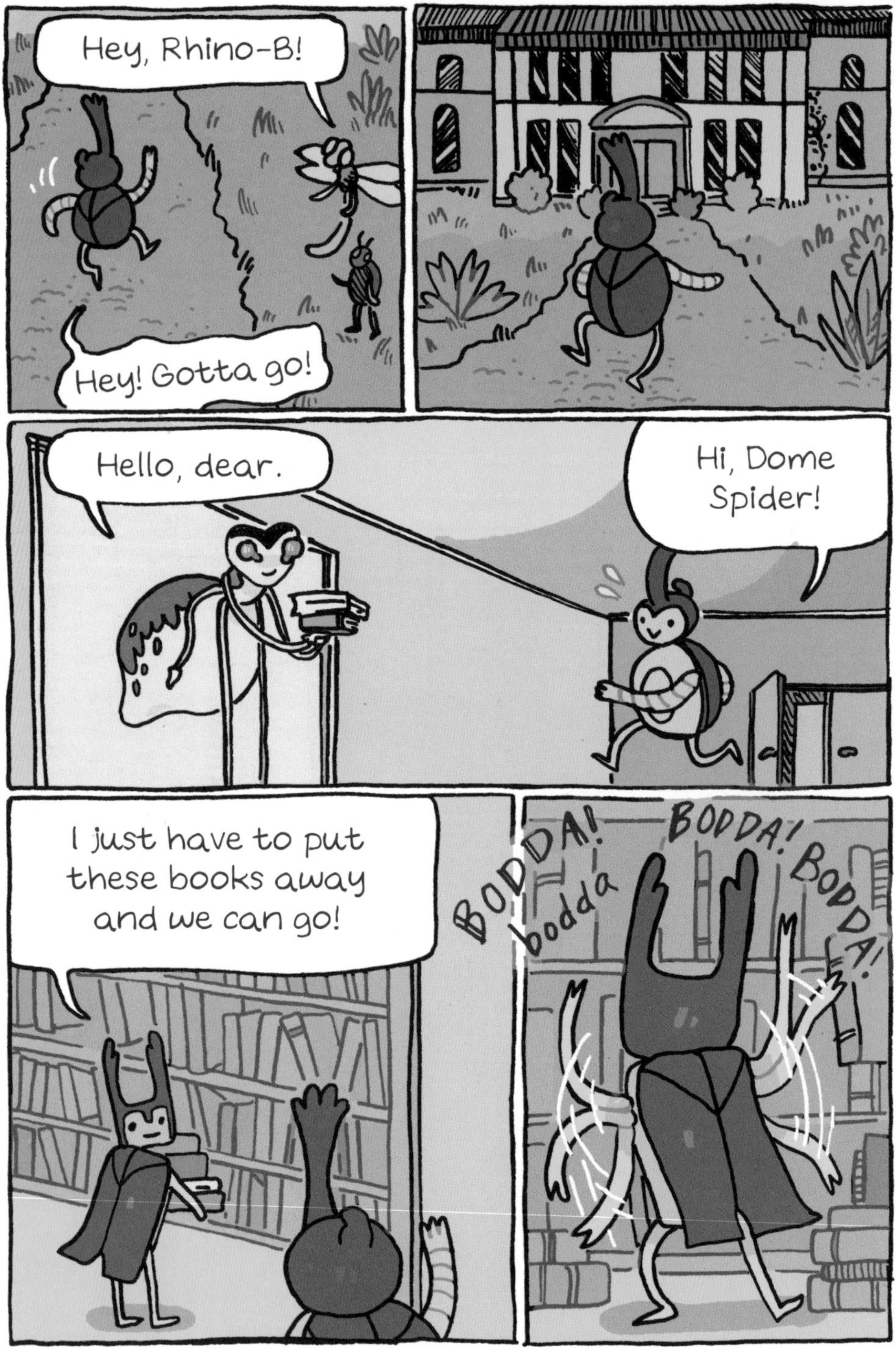
Hey, Rhino-B!
Hey! Gotta go!
Hello, dear.
Hi, Dome Spider!
I just have to put these books away and we can go!
BODDA!
bodda
BODDA!
BODDA!

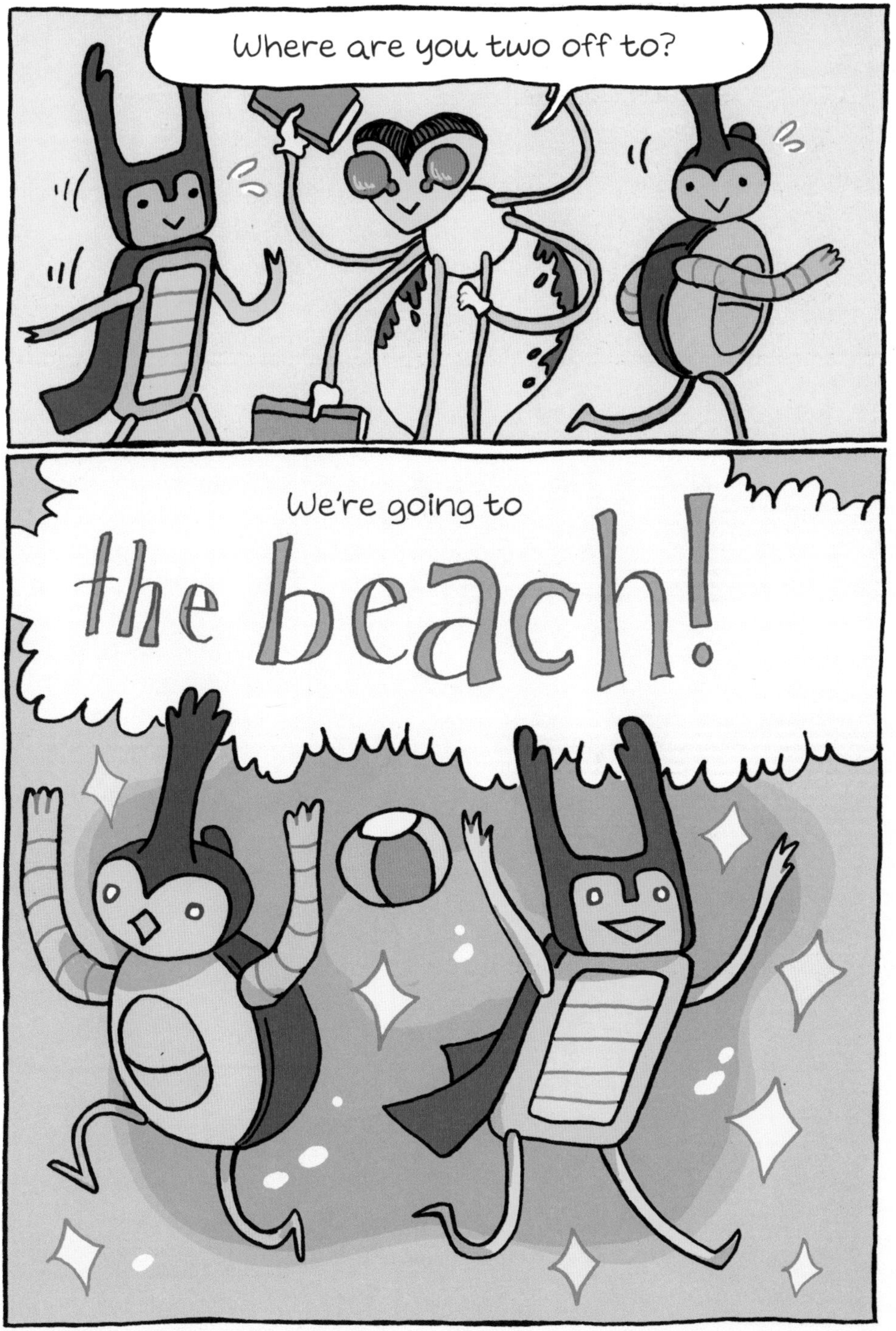
Where are you two off to?
We're going to
the beach!

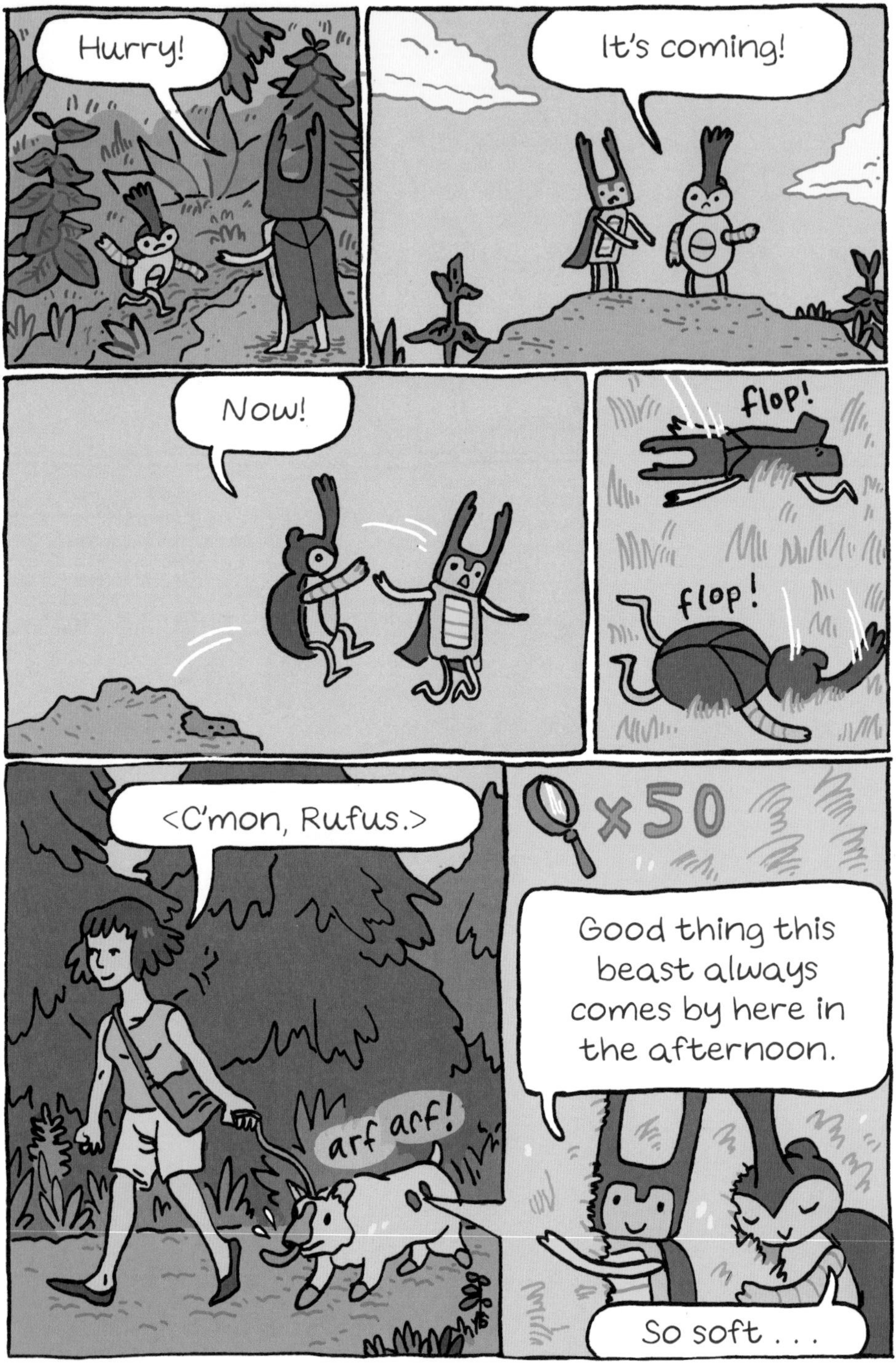

Hurry!
It's coming!
Now!
flop!
flop!
<C'mon, Rufus.>
arf arf!
×50
Good thing this beast always comes by here in the afternoon.
So soft . . .

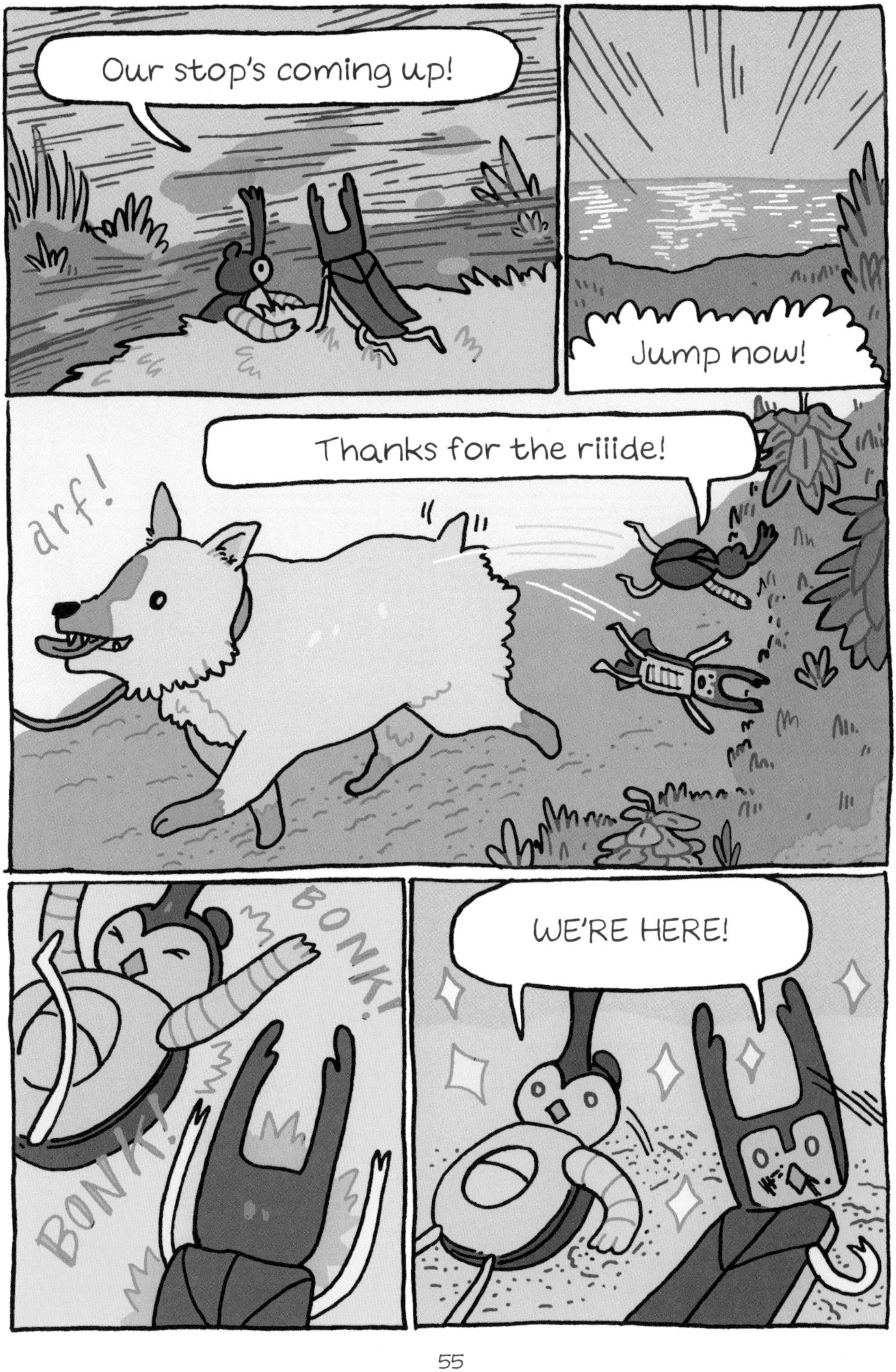

Our stop's coming up!
Jump now!
Thanks for the riiide!
arf!
BONK!
BONK!
WE'RE HERE!

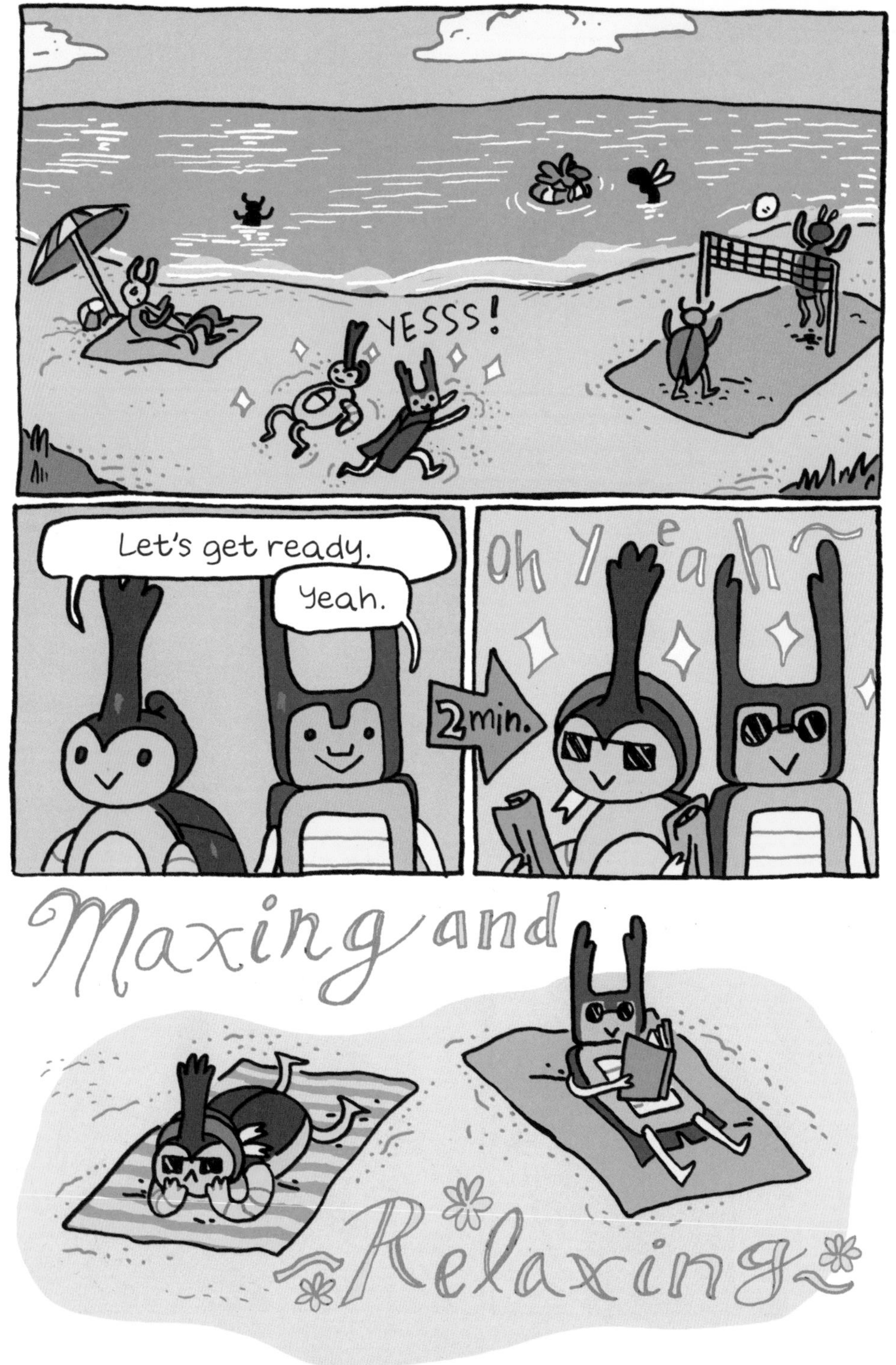
YESSS!
Let's get ready.
Yeah.
2 min.
Oh Yeah
Maxing and Relaxing

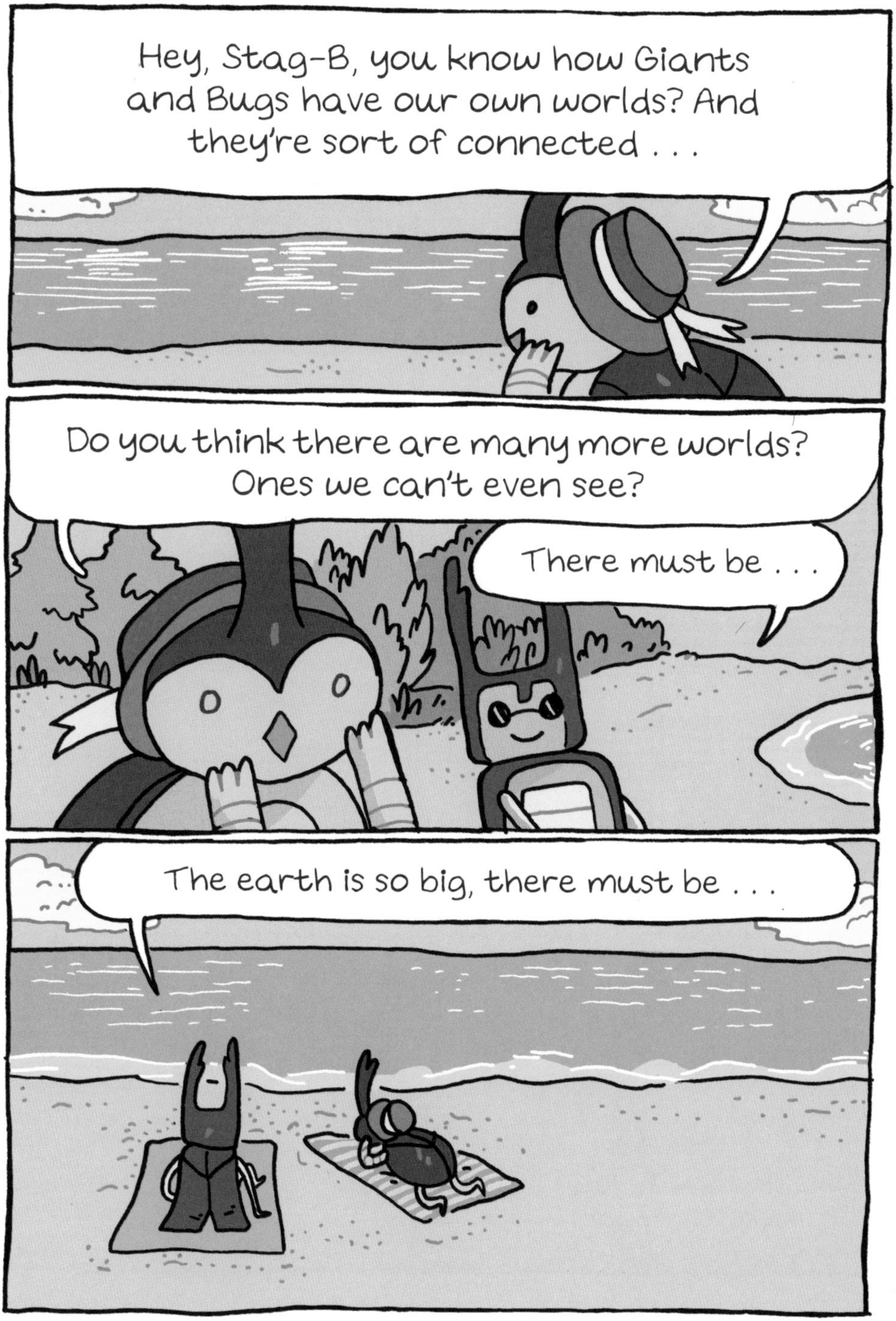
Hey, Stag-B, you know how Giants and Bugs have our own worlds? And they're sort of connected . . .
Do you think there are many more worlds? Ones we can't even see?
There must be . . .
The earth is so big, there must be . . .

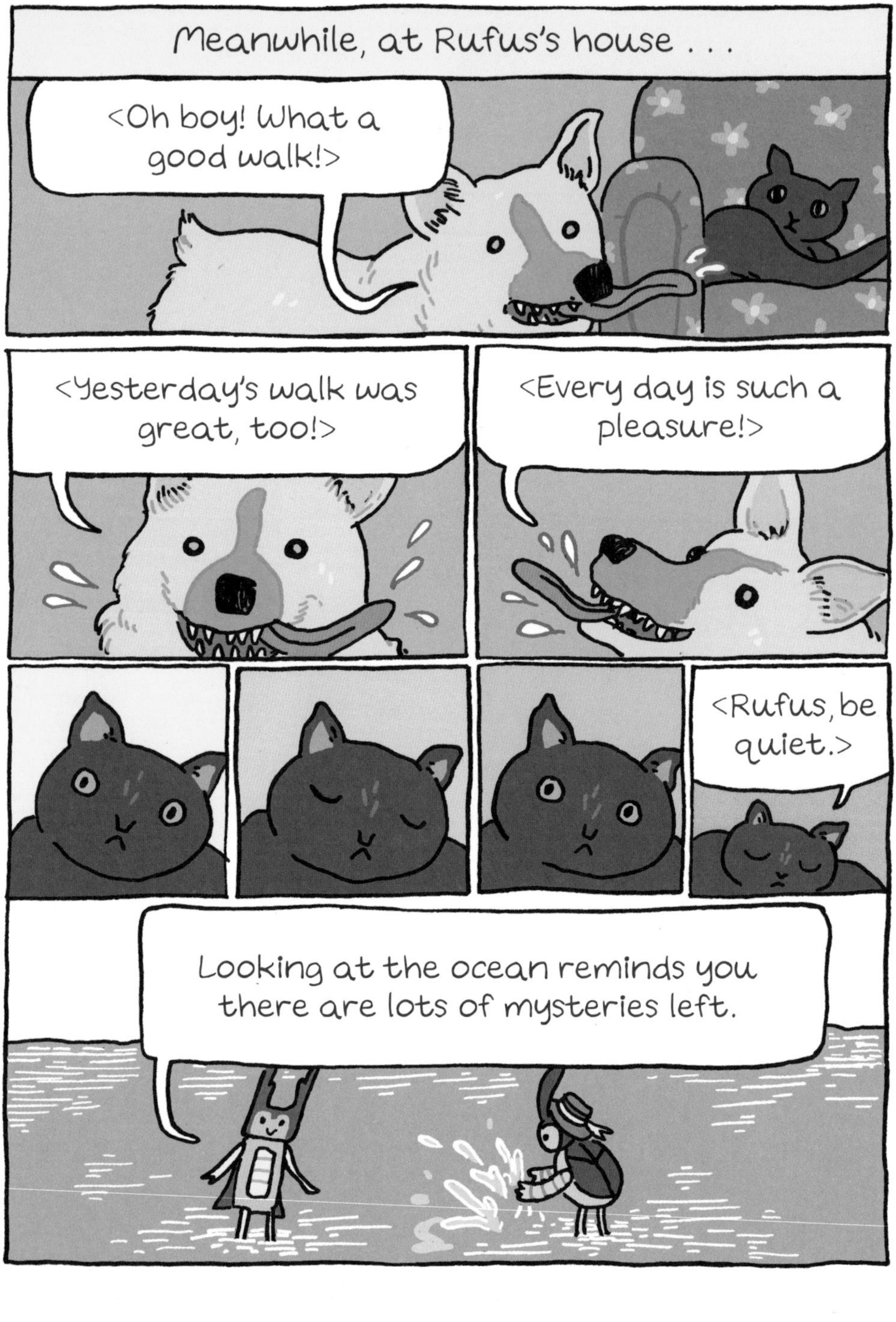
Meanwhile, at Rufus's house . . .
<Oh boy! What a good walk!>
<Yesterday's walk was great, too!>
<Every day is such a pleasure!>
<Rufus, be quiet.>
Looking at the ocean reminds you there are lots of mysteries left.

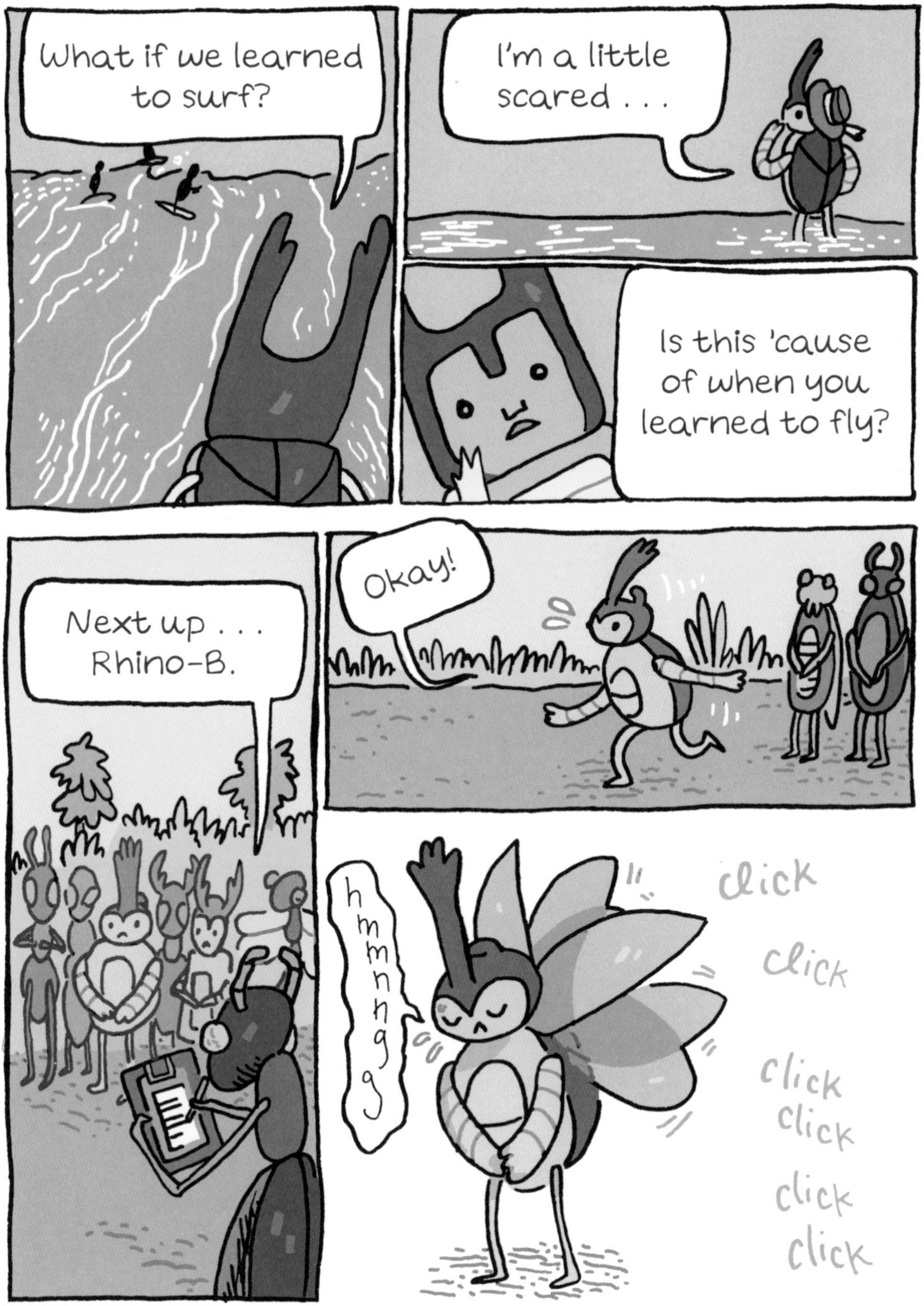

What if we learned to surf?
I'm a little scared . . .
Is this 'cause of when you learned to fly?
Next up . . . Rhino-B.
Okay!
hmmnngg
click
click
click
click
click
click

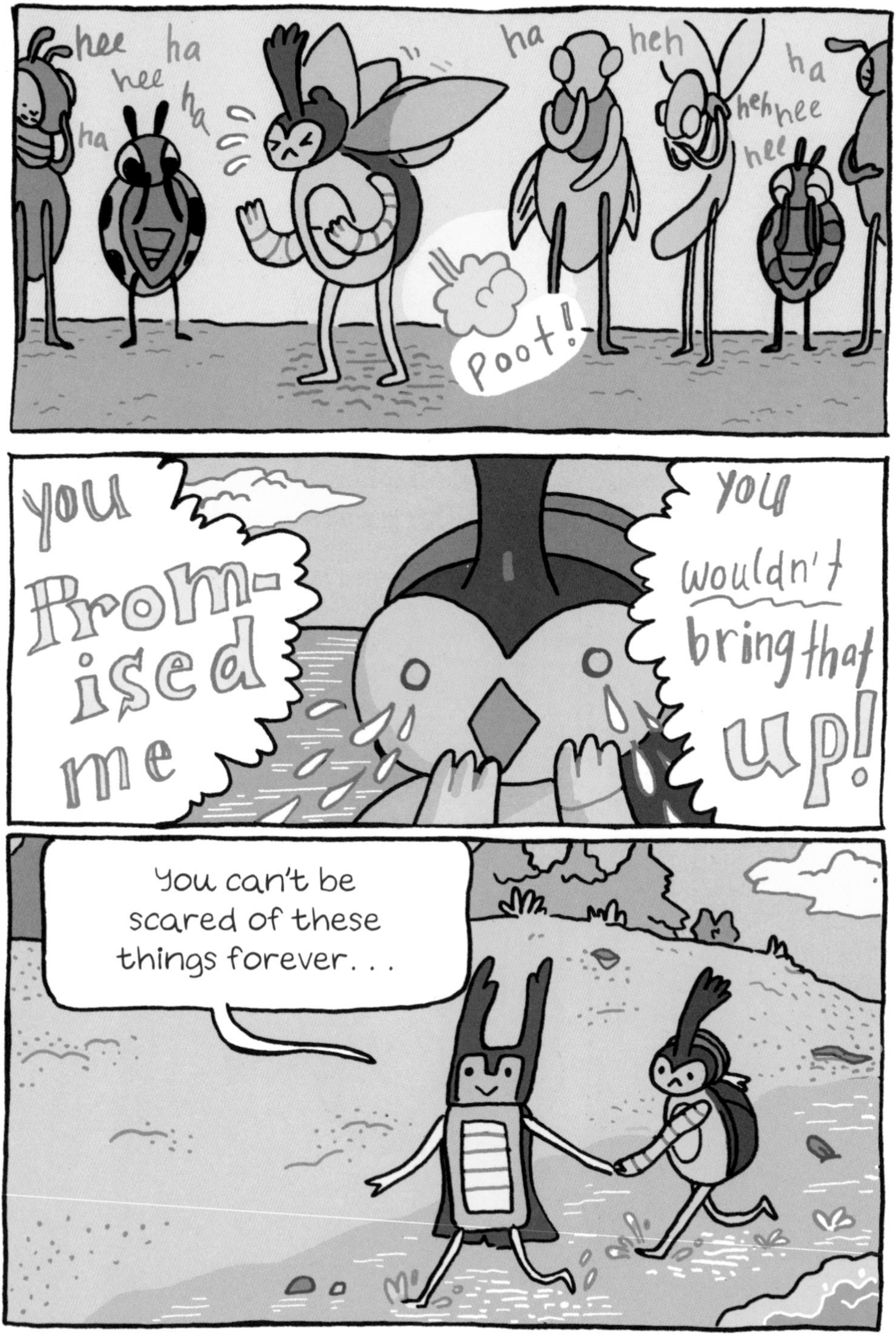
hee ha
hee
ha
ha
ha
heh
ha
heh hee
hee
poot!
you Prom-ised me
you wouldn't bring that up!
You can't be scared of these things forever. . .

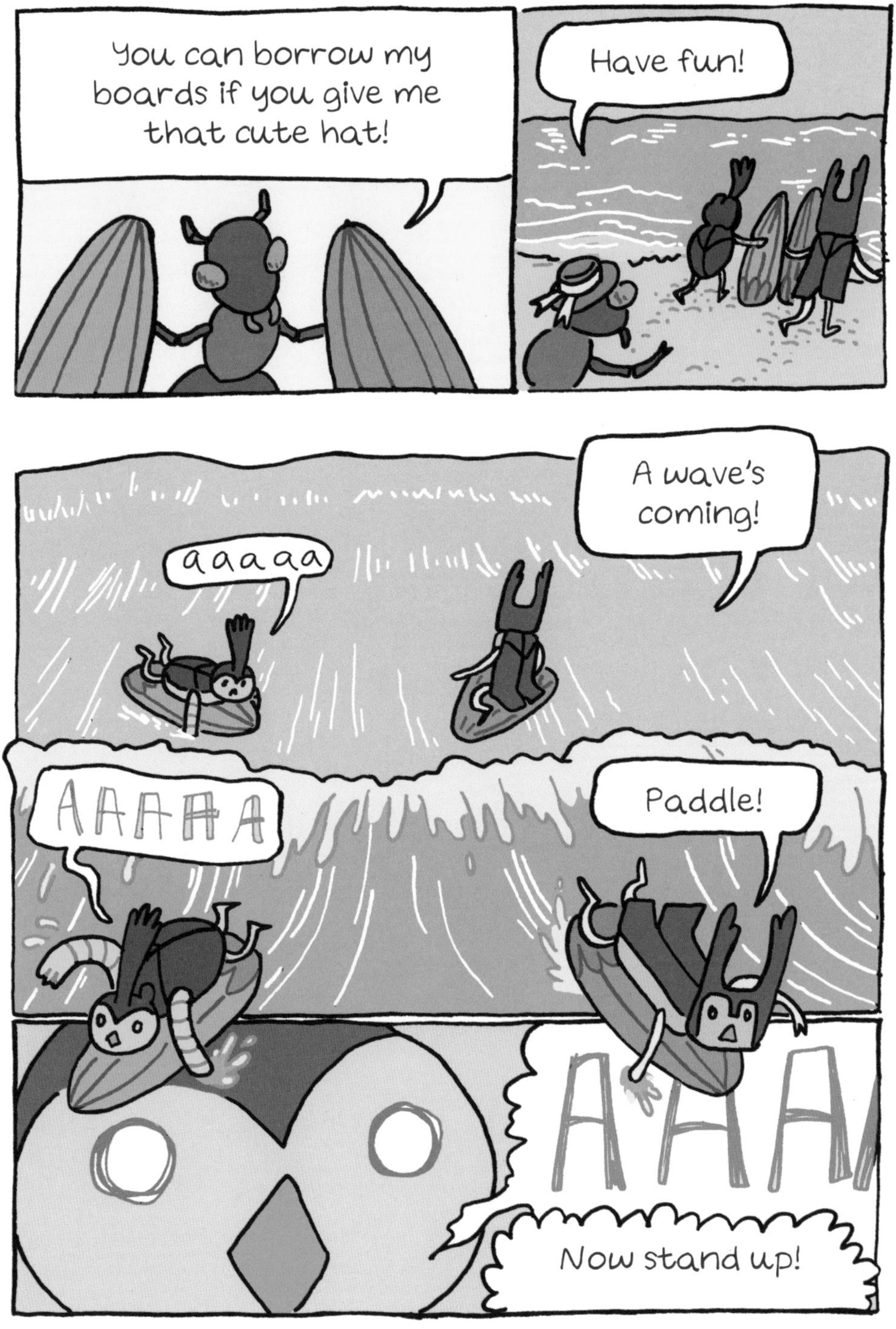
You can borrow my boards if you give me that cute hat!
Have fun!
A wave's coming!
aaaaa
AAAAA
Paddle!
AAAA
Now stand up!

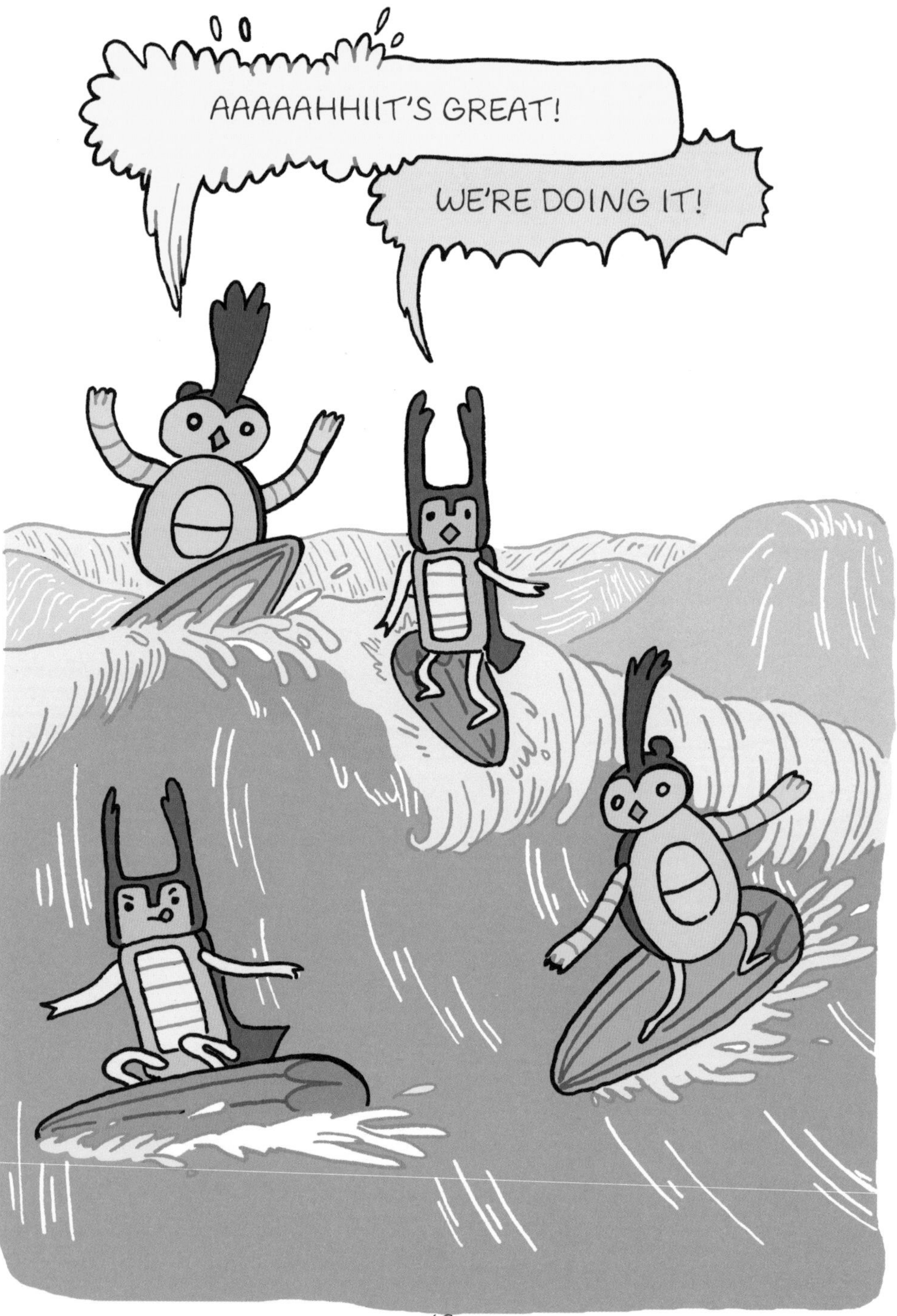
AAAAAHHIIIT'S GREAT!
WE'RE DOING IT!

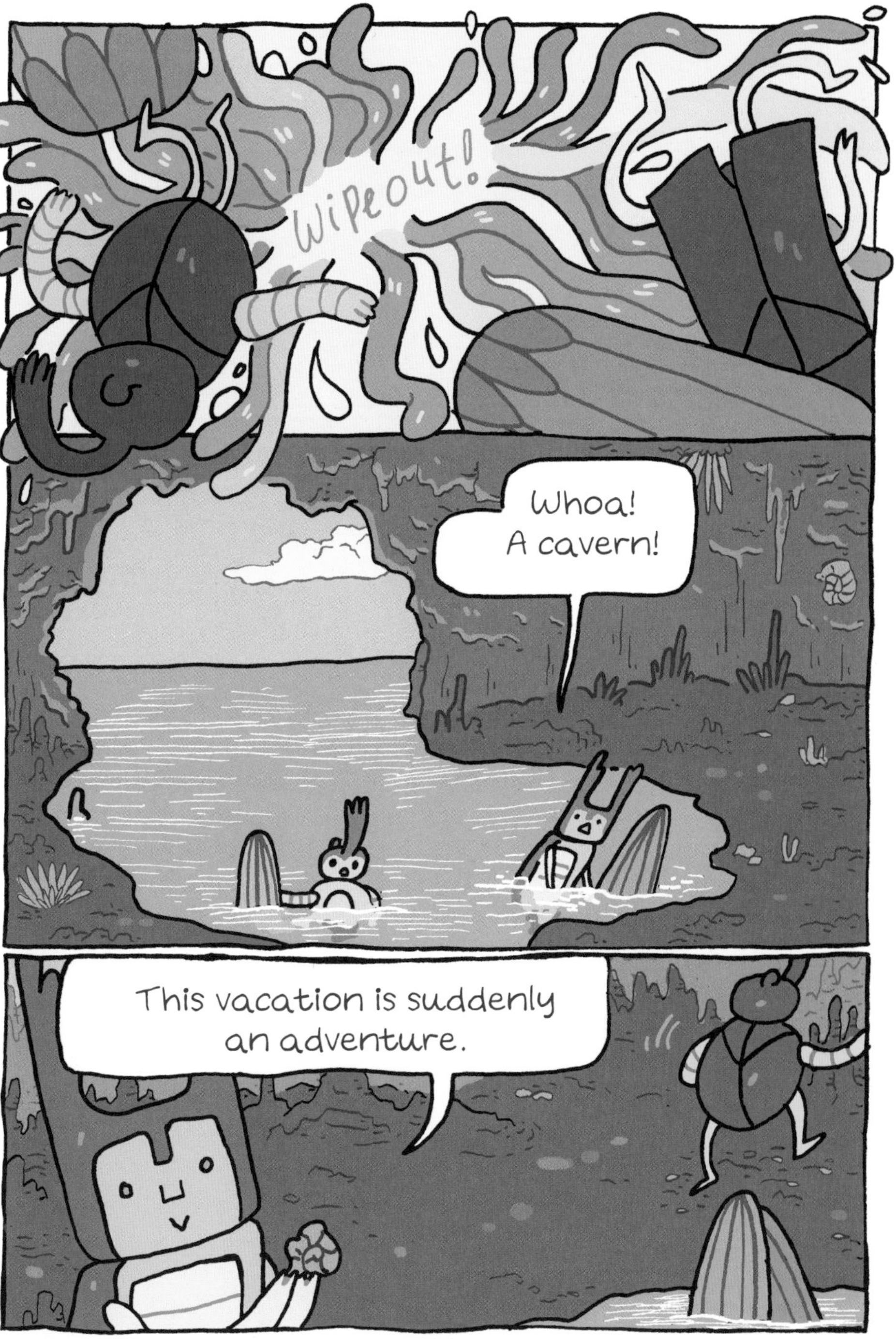
Wipeout!
Whoa! A cavern!
This vacation is suddenly an adventure.

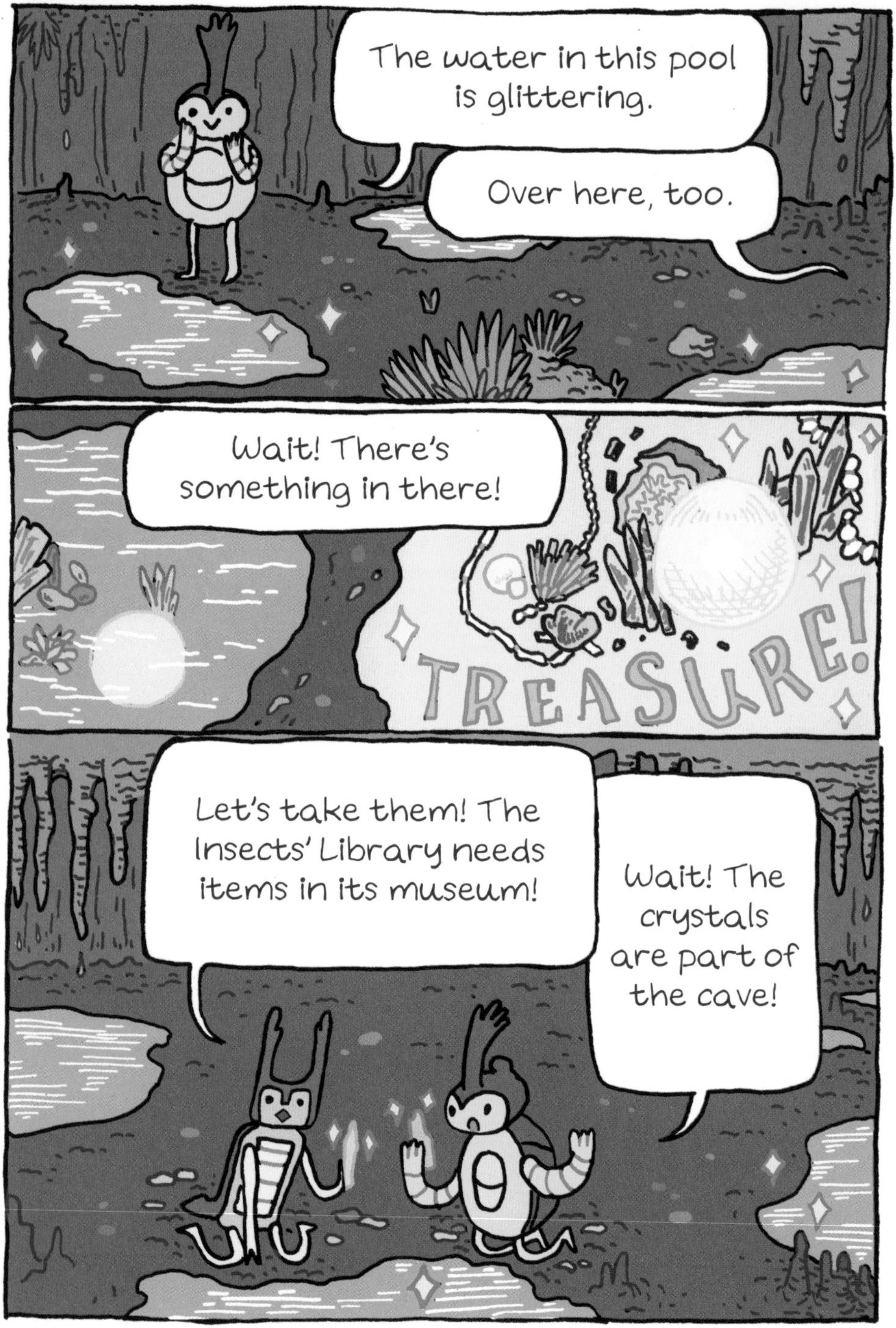
The water in this pool is glittering.
Over here, too.
Wait! There's something in there!
TREASURE!
Let's take them! The Insects' Library needs items in its museum!
Wait! The crystals are part of the cave!

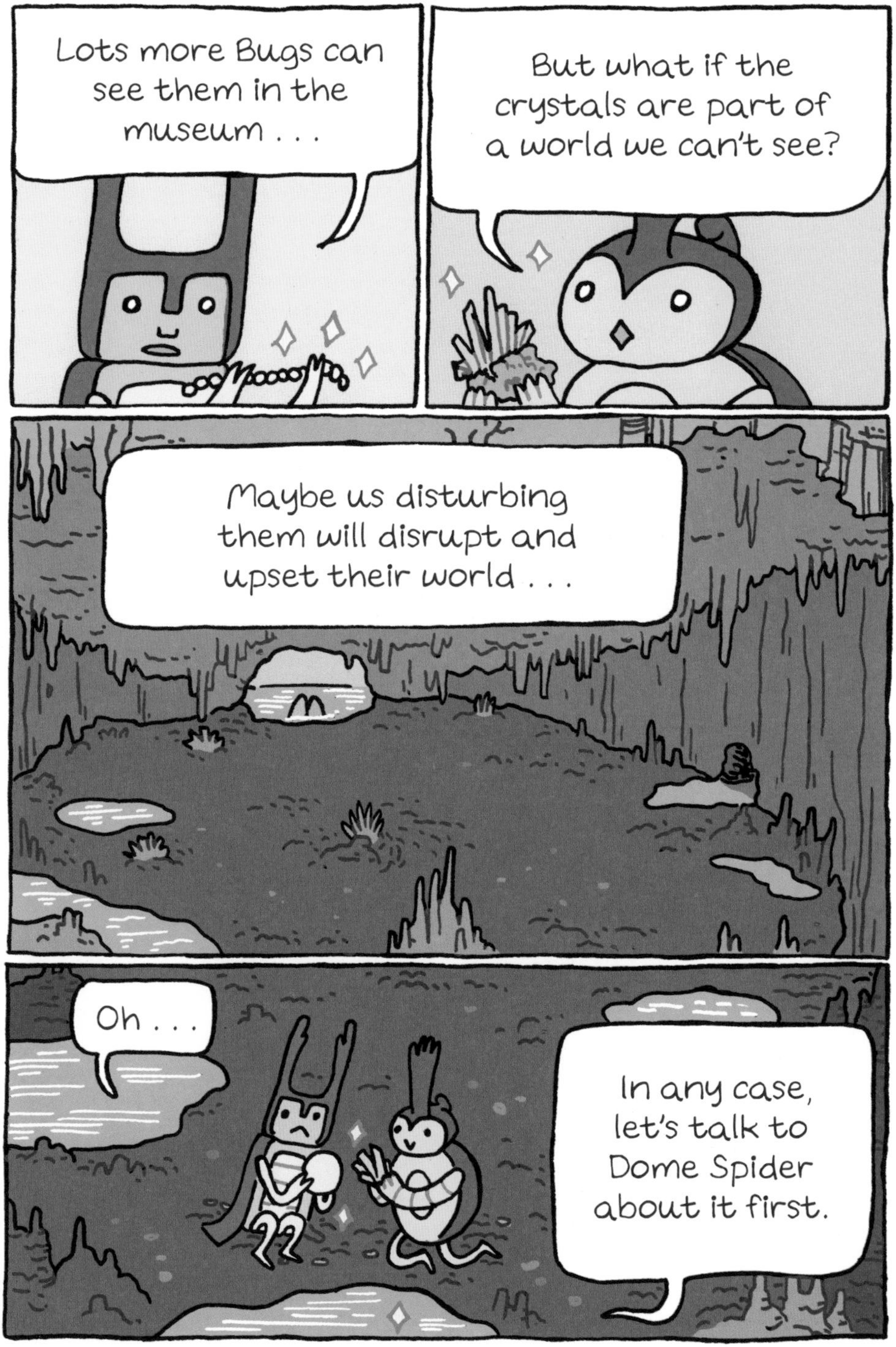
Lots more Bugs can see them in the museum . . .
But what if the crystals are part of a world we can't see?
Maybe us disturbing them will disrupt and upset their world . . .
Oh . . .
In any case, let's talk to Dome Spider about it first.

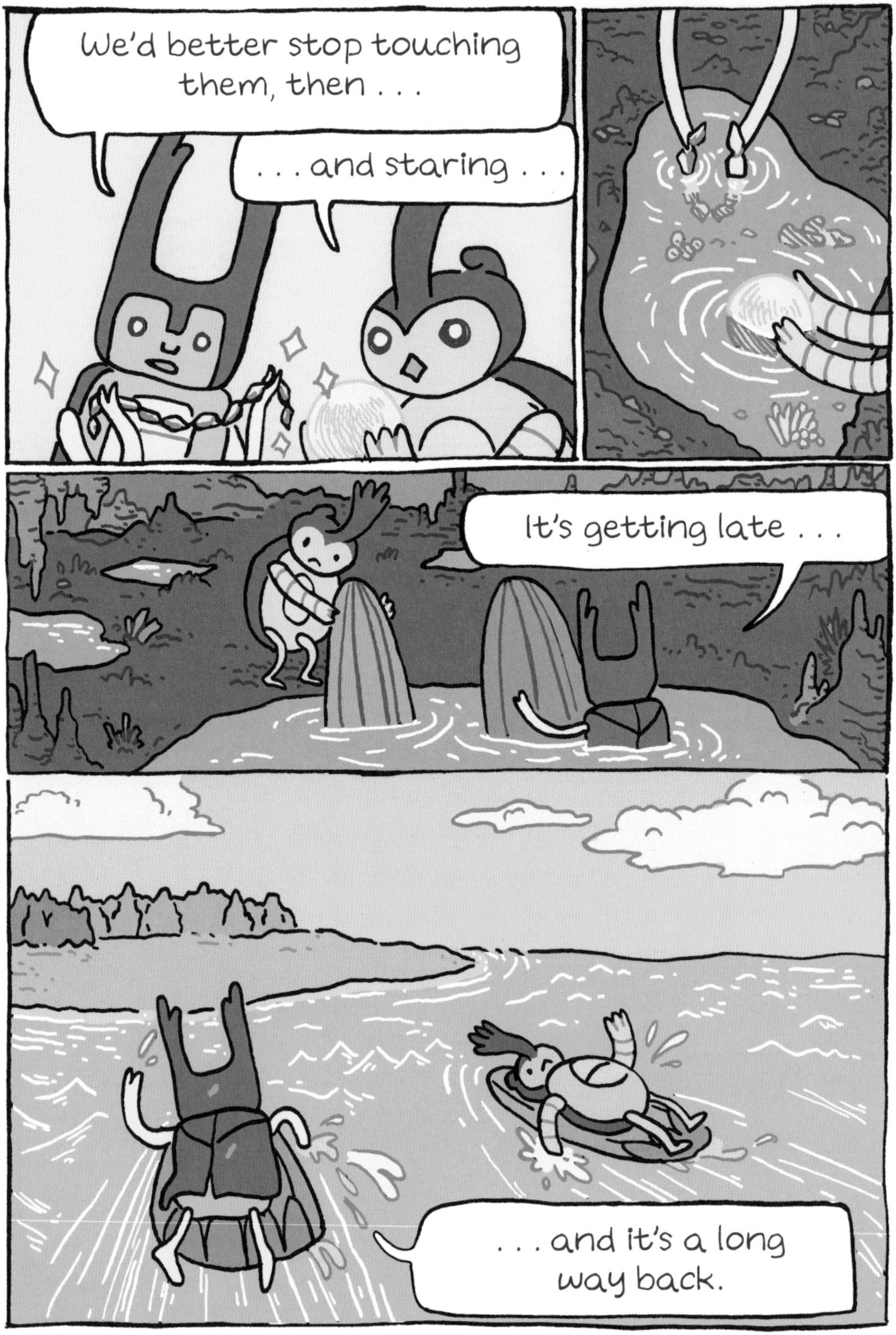
We'd better stop touching them, then . . .
. . . and staring . . .
It's getting late . . .
. . . and it's a long way back.

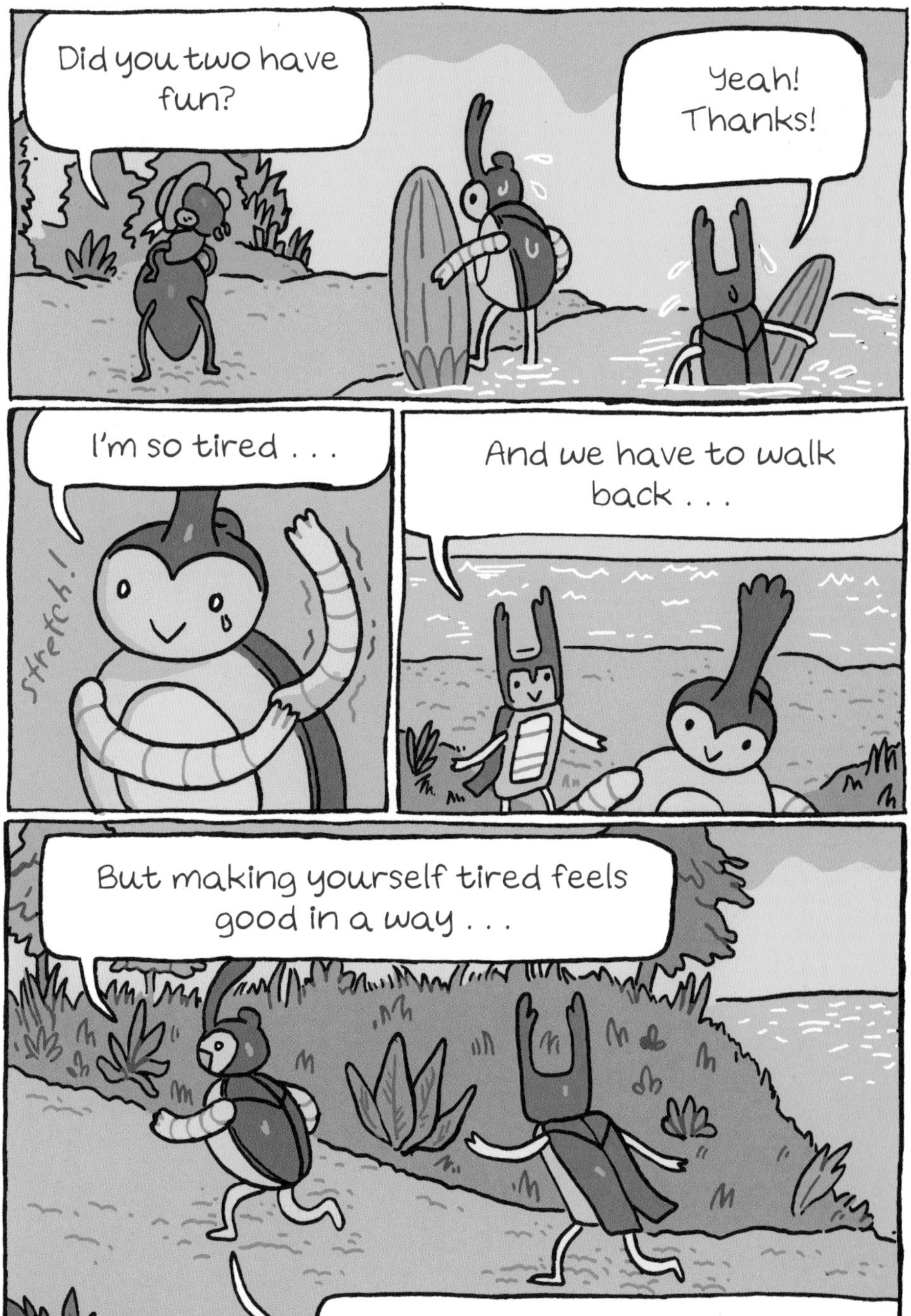
Did you two have fun?
Yeah! Thanks!
I'm so tired . . .
stretch!
And we have to walk back . . .
But making yourself tired feels good in a way . . .
. . . and you'll sleep well.

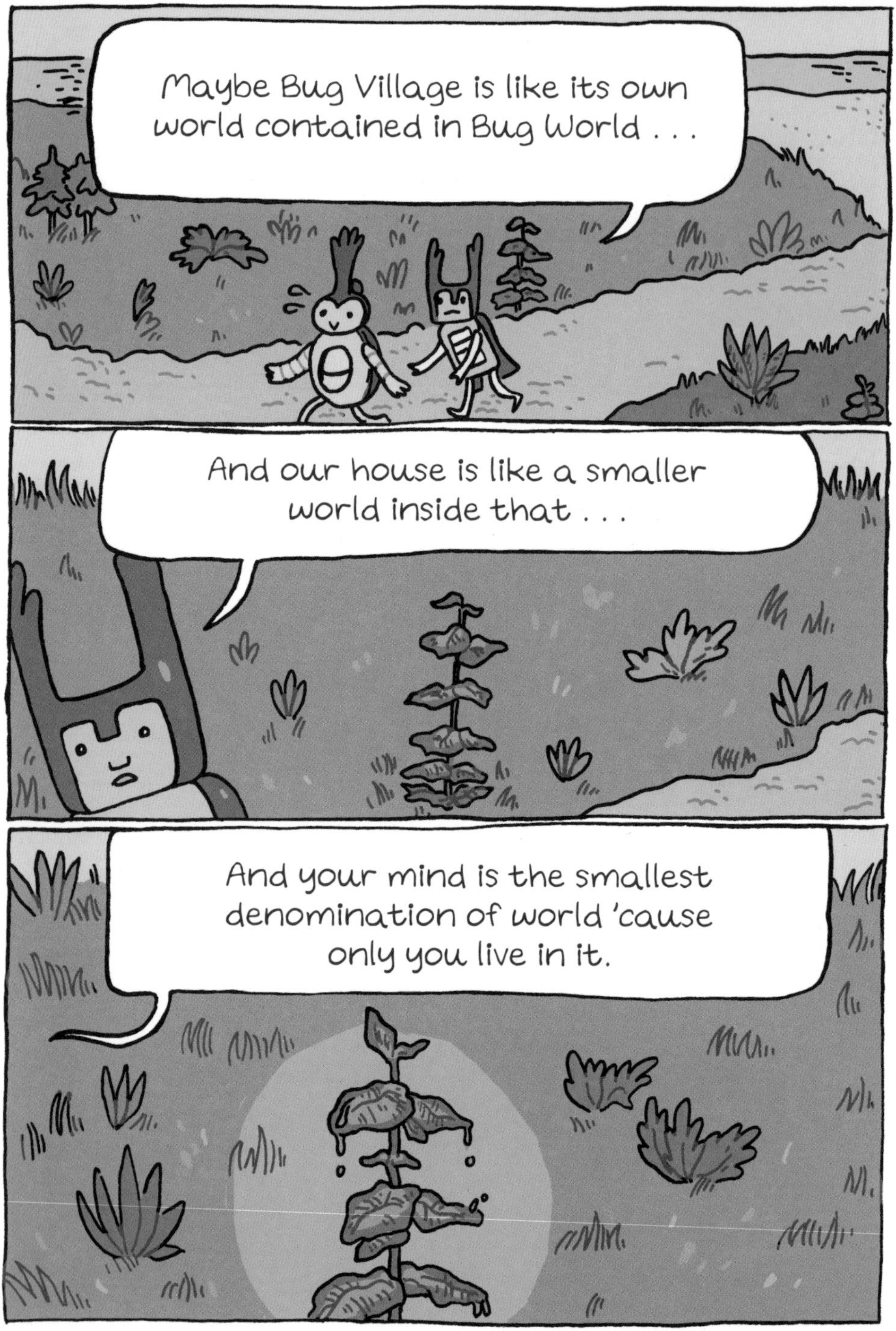
Maybe Bug Village is like its own world contained in Bug World . . .
And our house is like a smaller world inside that . . .
And your mind is the smallest denomination of world 'cause only you live in it.

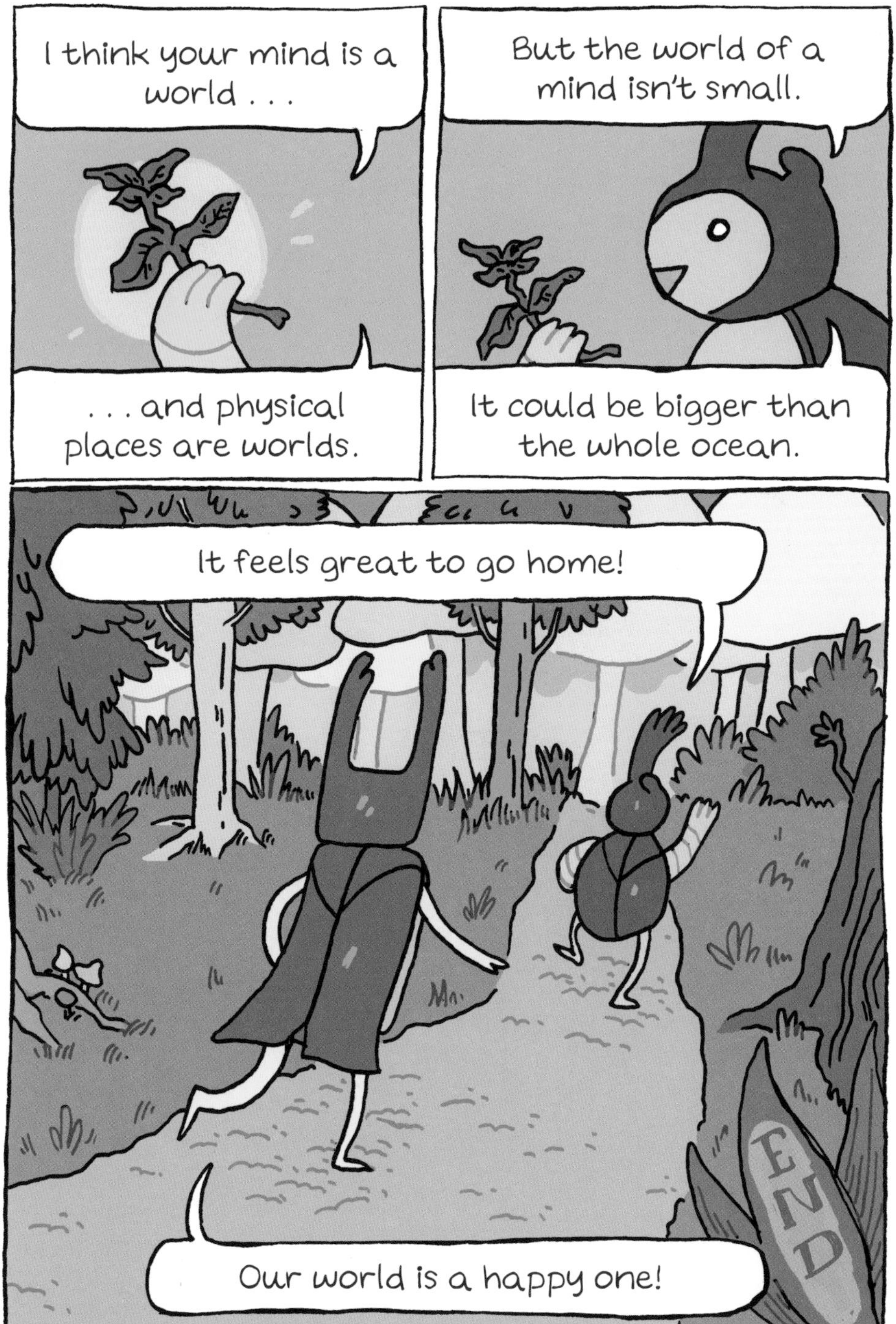
I think your mind is a world . . .
. . . and physical places are worlds.
But the world of a mind isn't small.
It could be bigger than the whole ocean.
It feels great to go home!
Our world is a happy one!
END

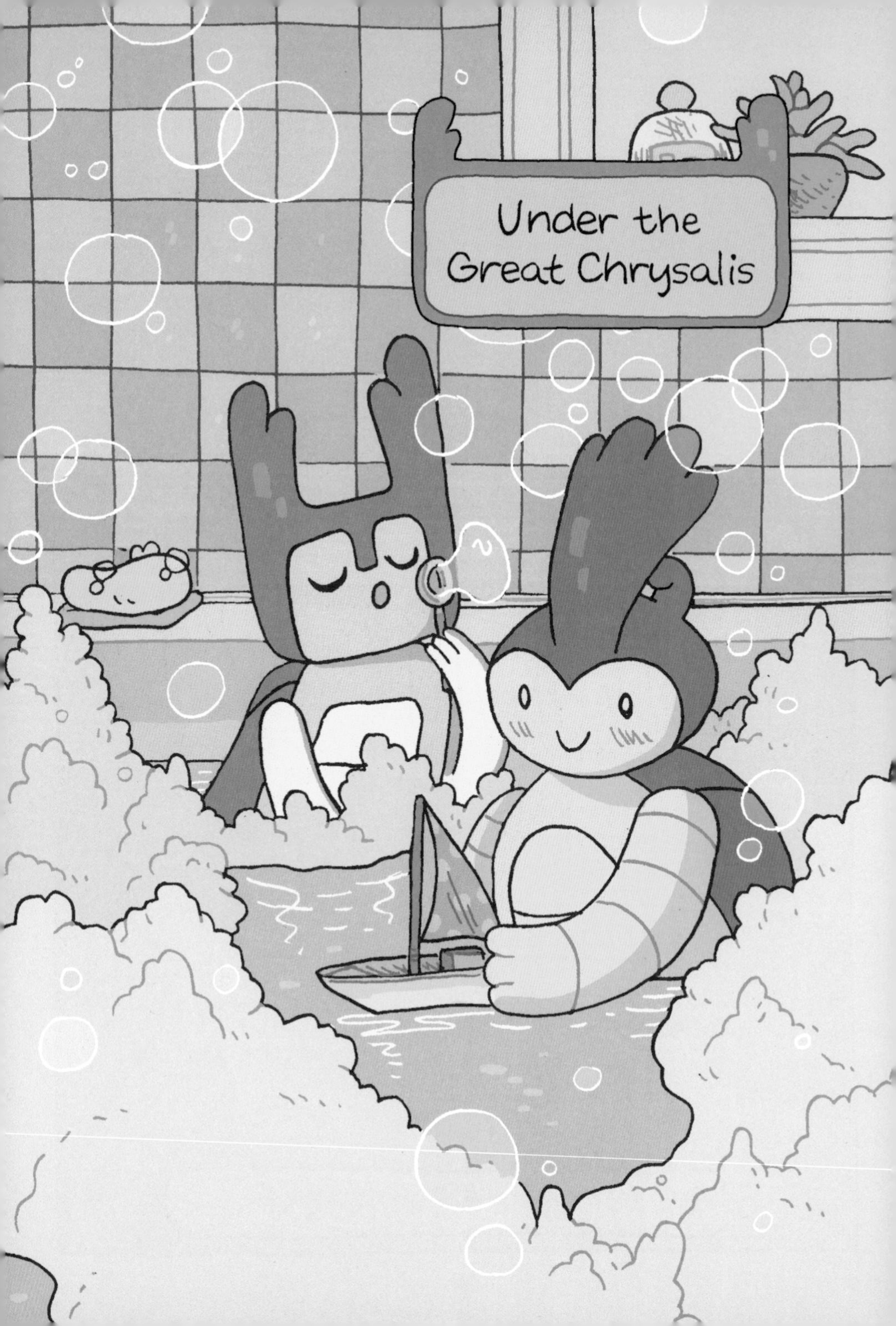
Under the
Great Chrysalis

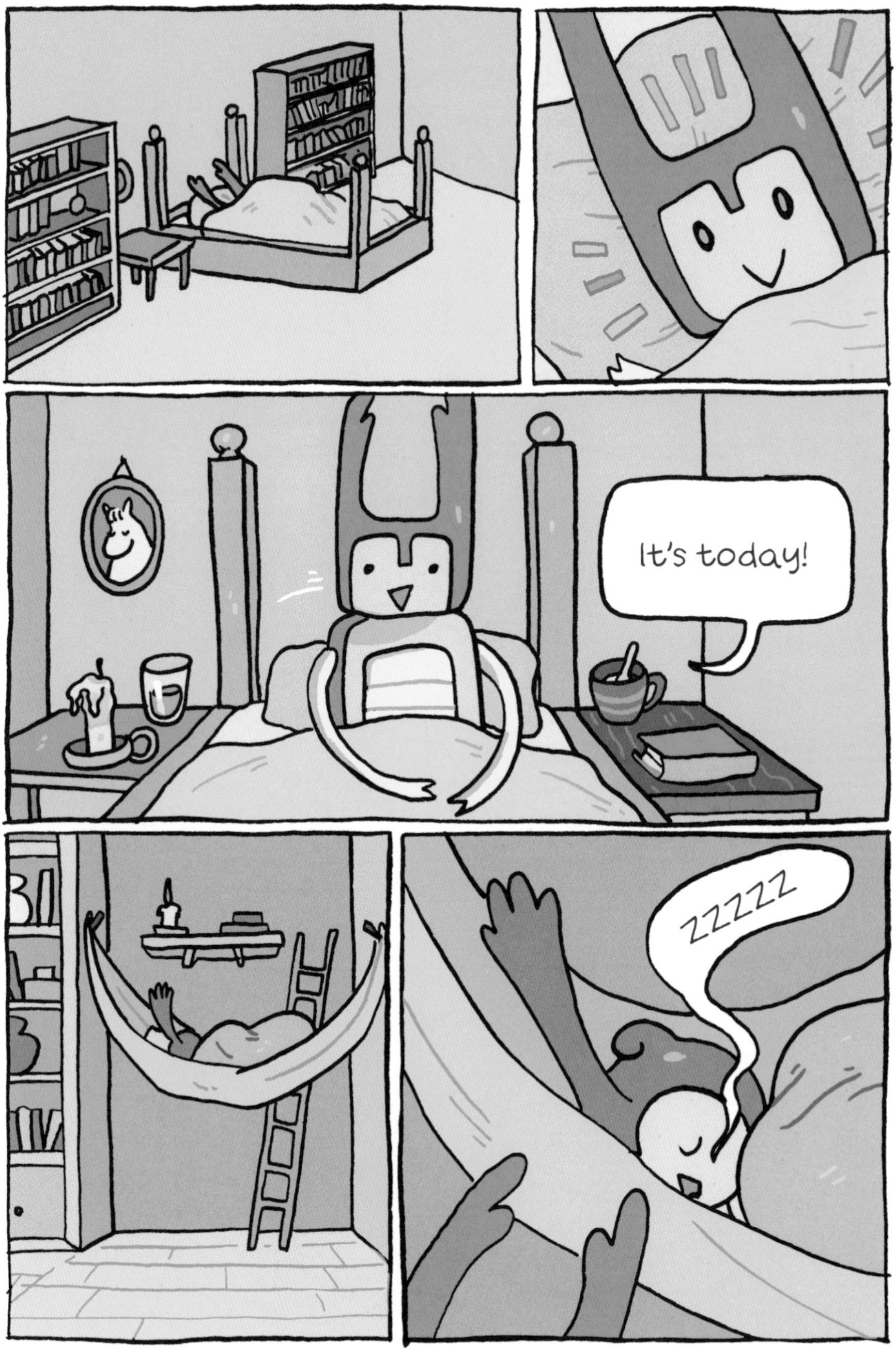
It's today!
ZZZZZ

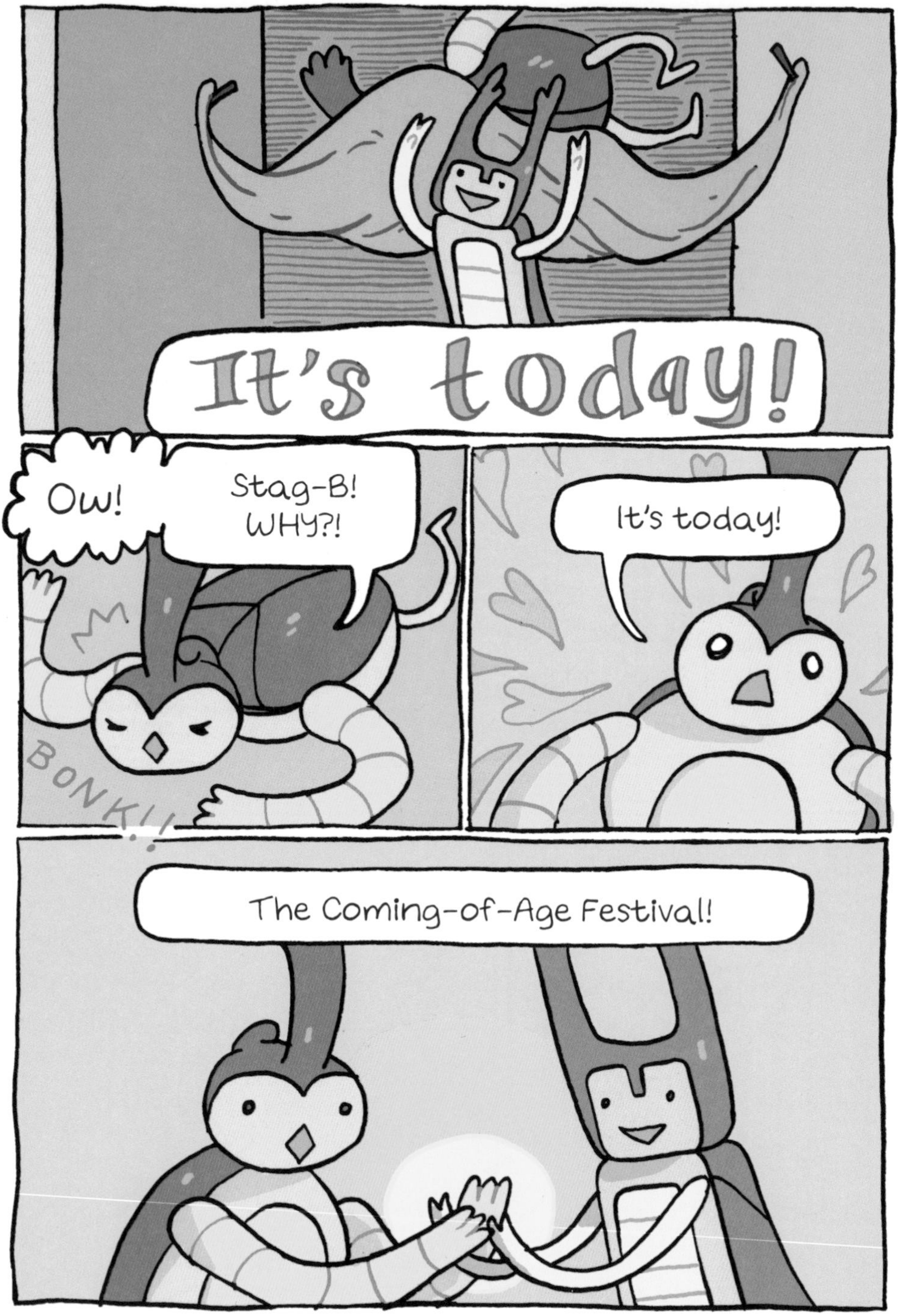

It's today!
Ow!
Stag-B! WHY?!
BONK!!
It's today!
The Coming-of-Age Festival!

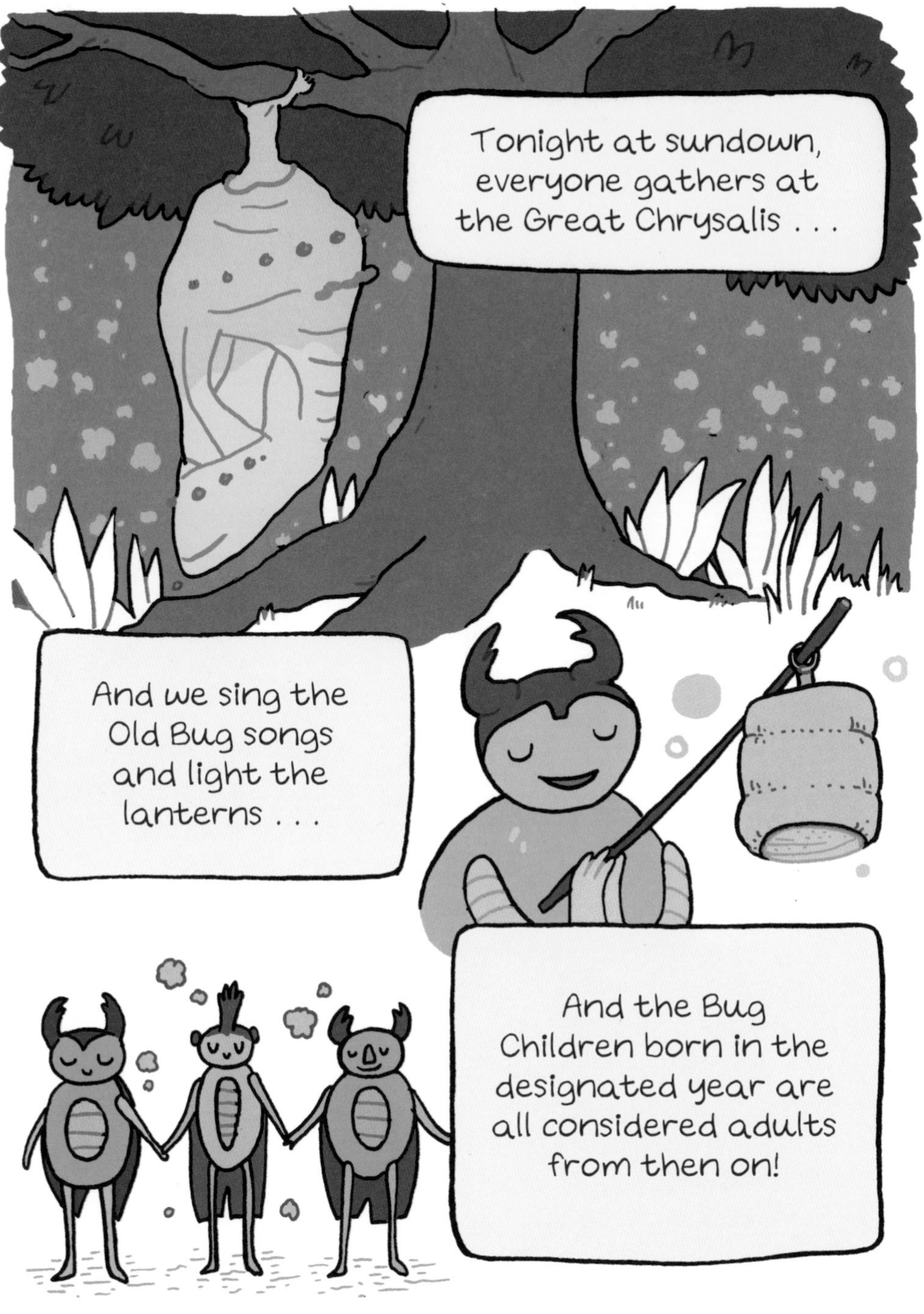

Tonight at sundown, everyone gathers at the Great Chrysalis . . .
And we sing the Old Bug songs and light the lanterns . . .
And the Bug Children born in the designated year are all considered adults from then on!

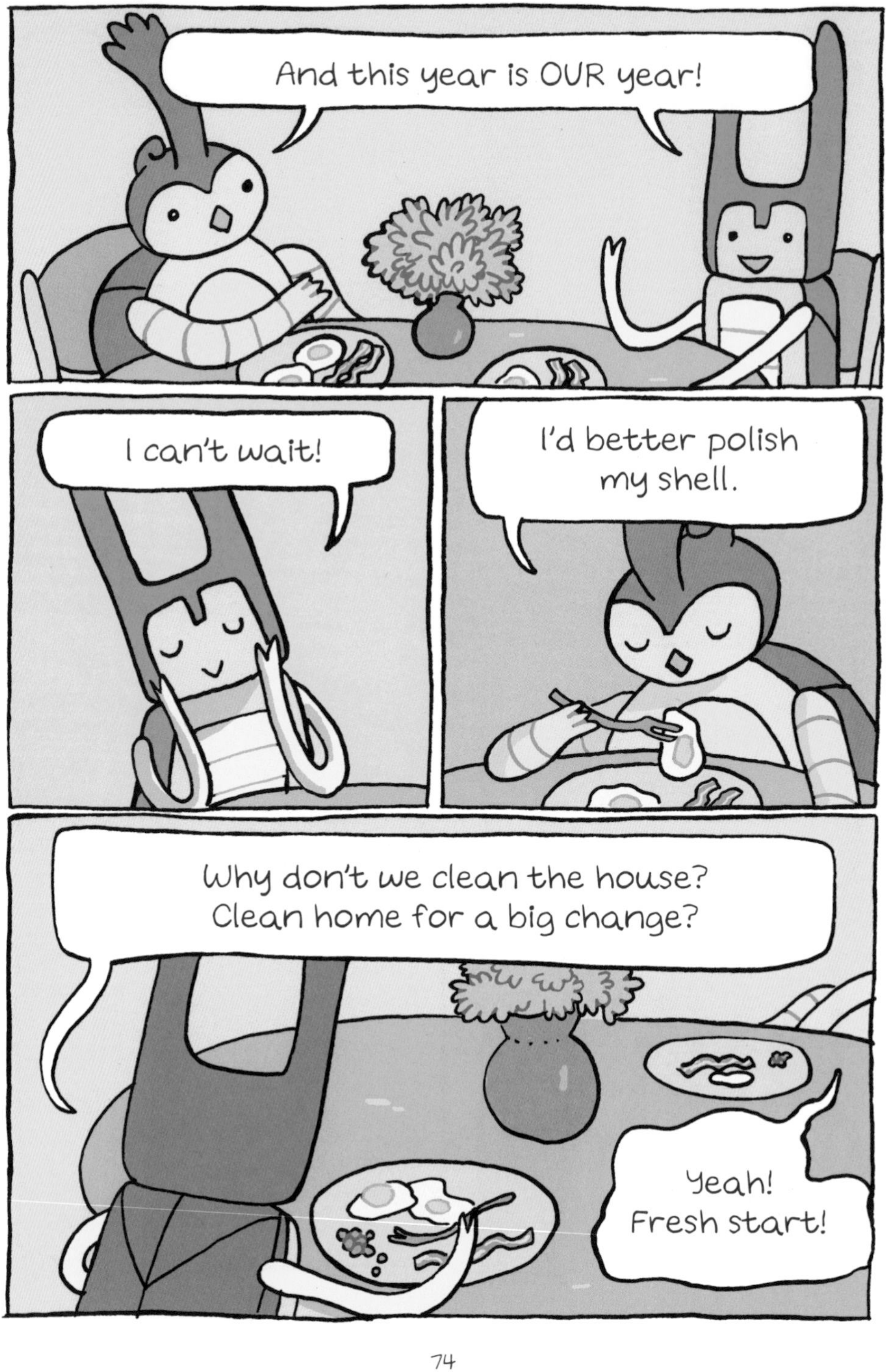
And this year is OUR year!
I can't wait!
I'd better polish my shell.
Why don't we clean the house? Clean home for a big change?
Yeah! Fresh start!

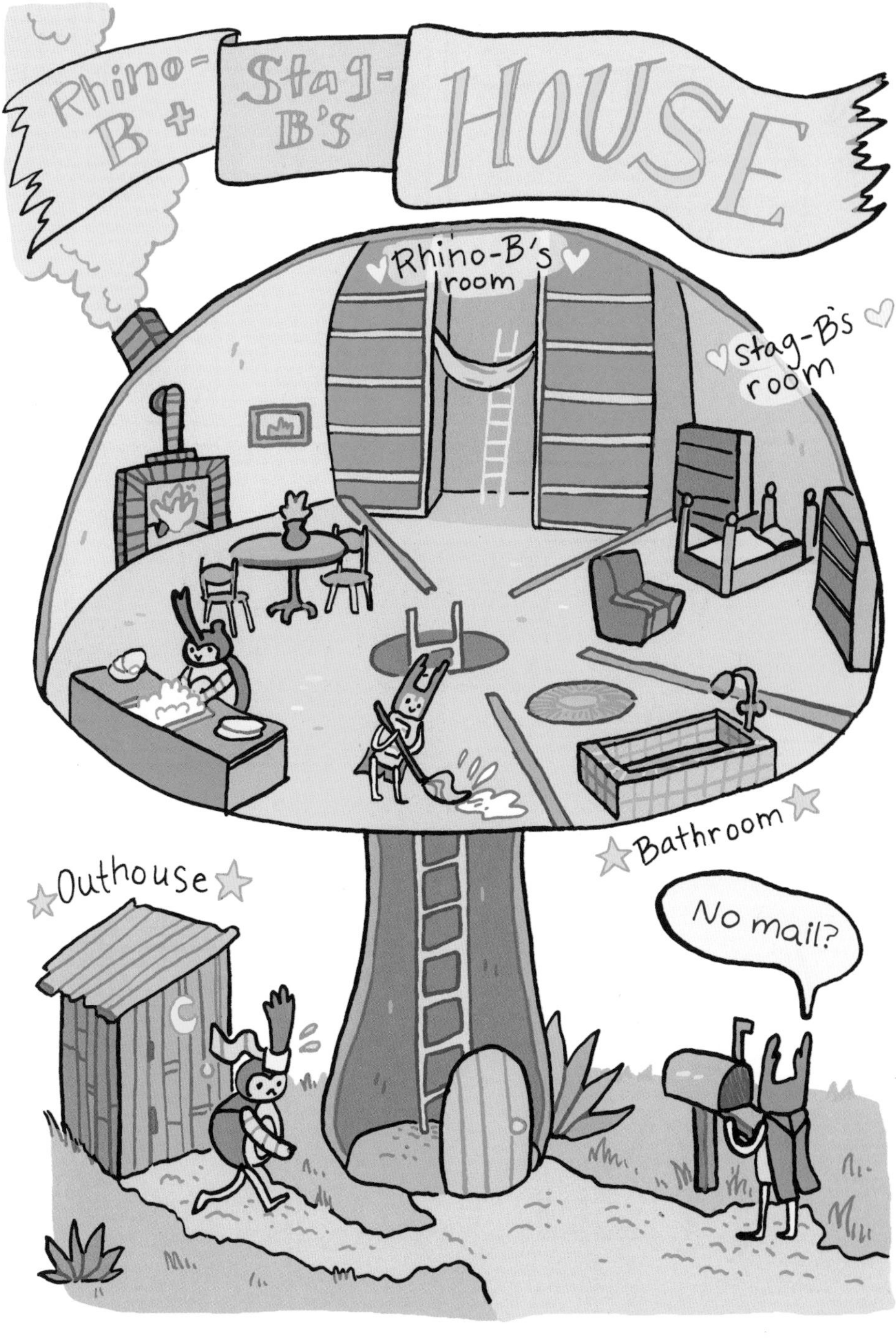
Rhino-B + Stag-B's HOUSE
Rhino-B's room
Stag-B's room
Bathroom
Outhouse
No mail?

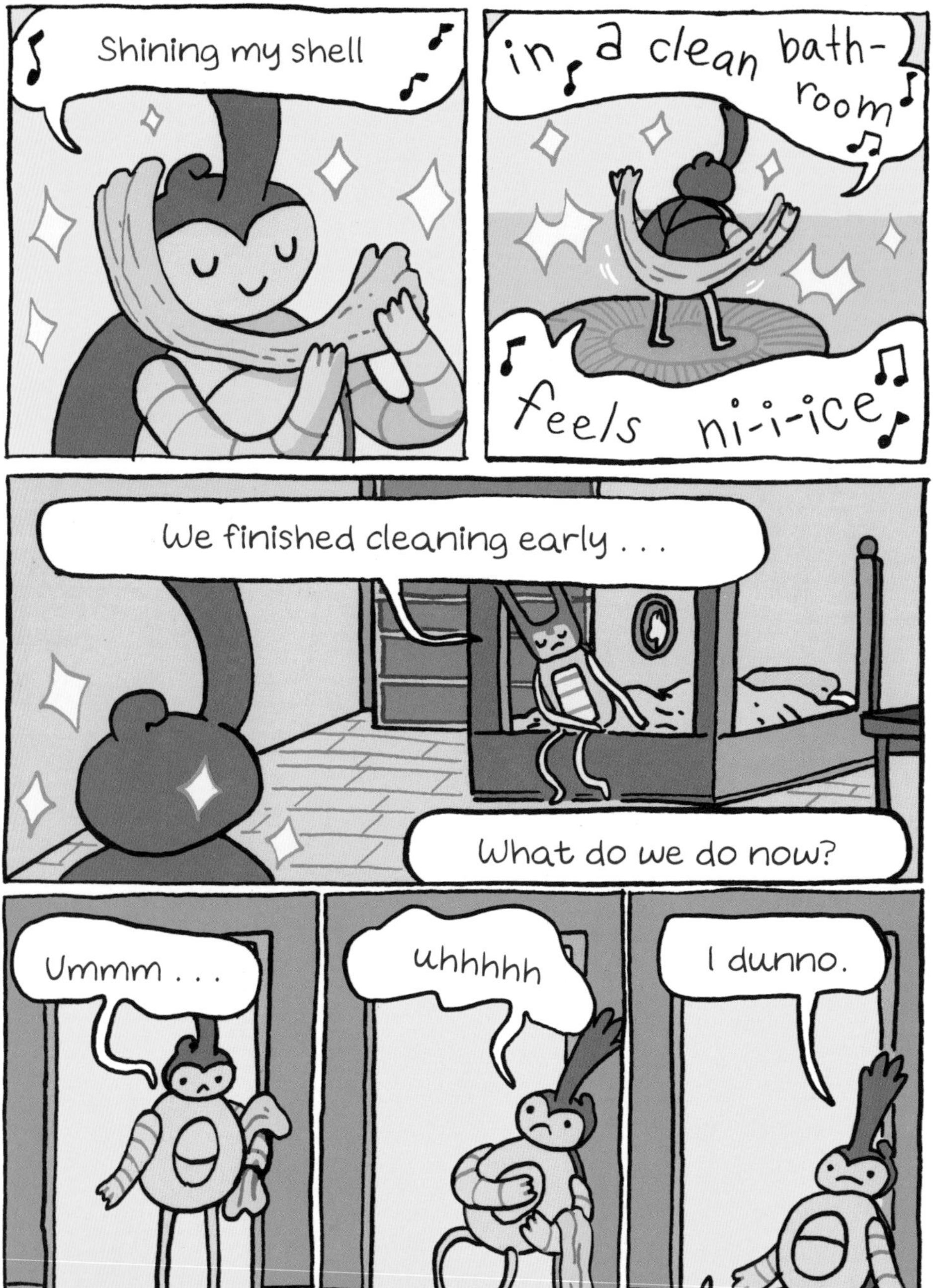
Shining my shell
in a clean bath-room
feels ni-i-ice
We finished cleaning early . . .
What do we do now?
Ummm . . .
uhhhhh
I dunno.

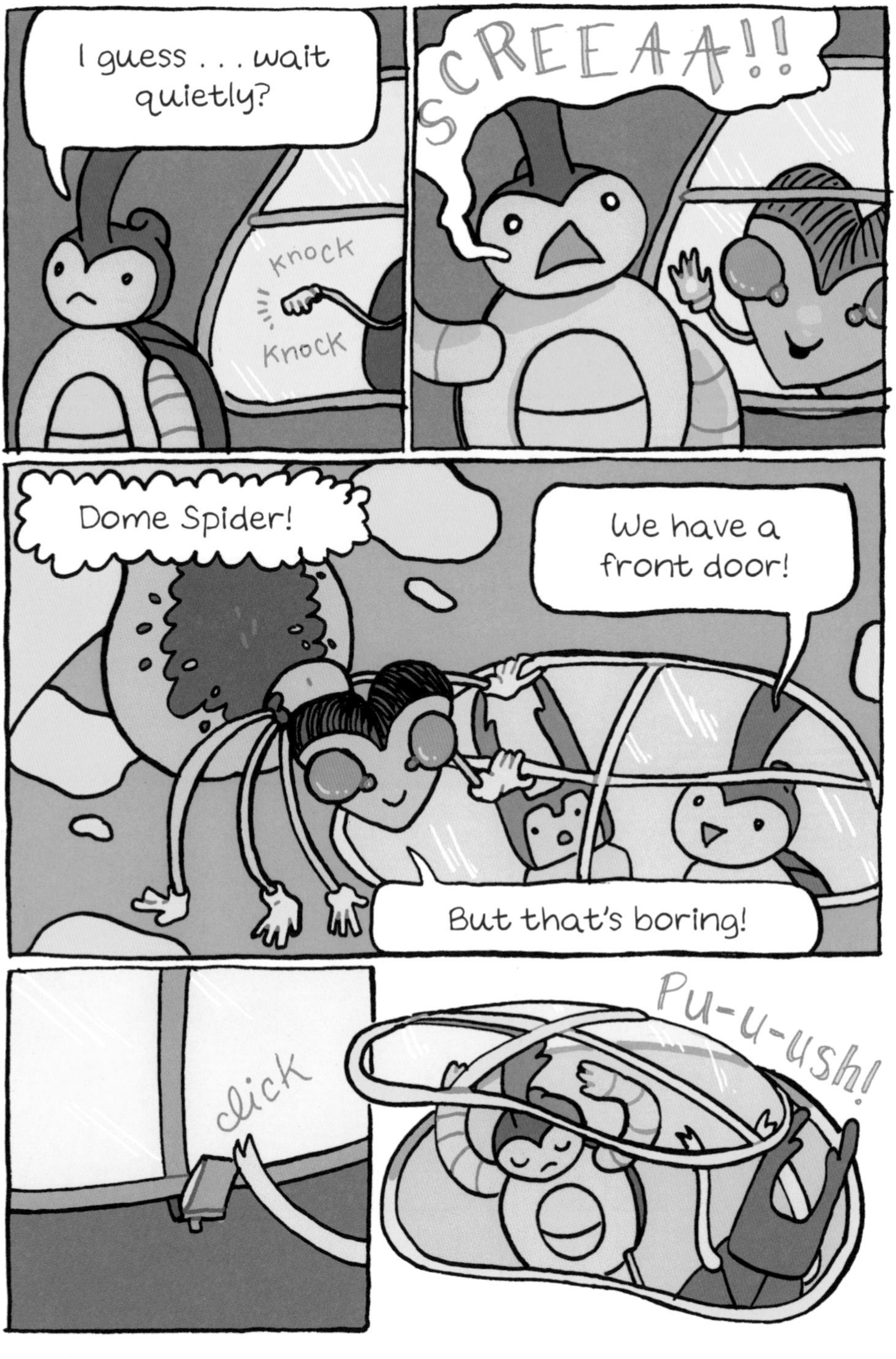
I guess . . . wait quietly?
knock
knock
SCREEAA!!
Dome Spider!
We have a front door!
But that's boring!
click
Pu-u-ush!

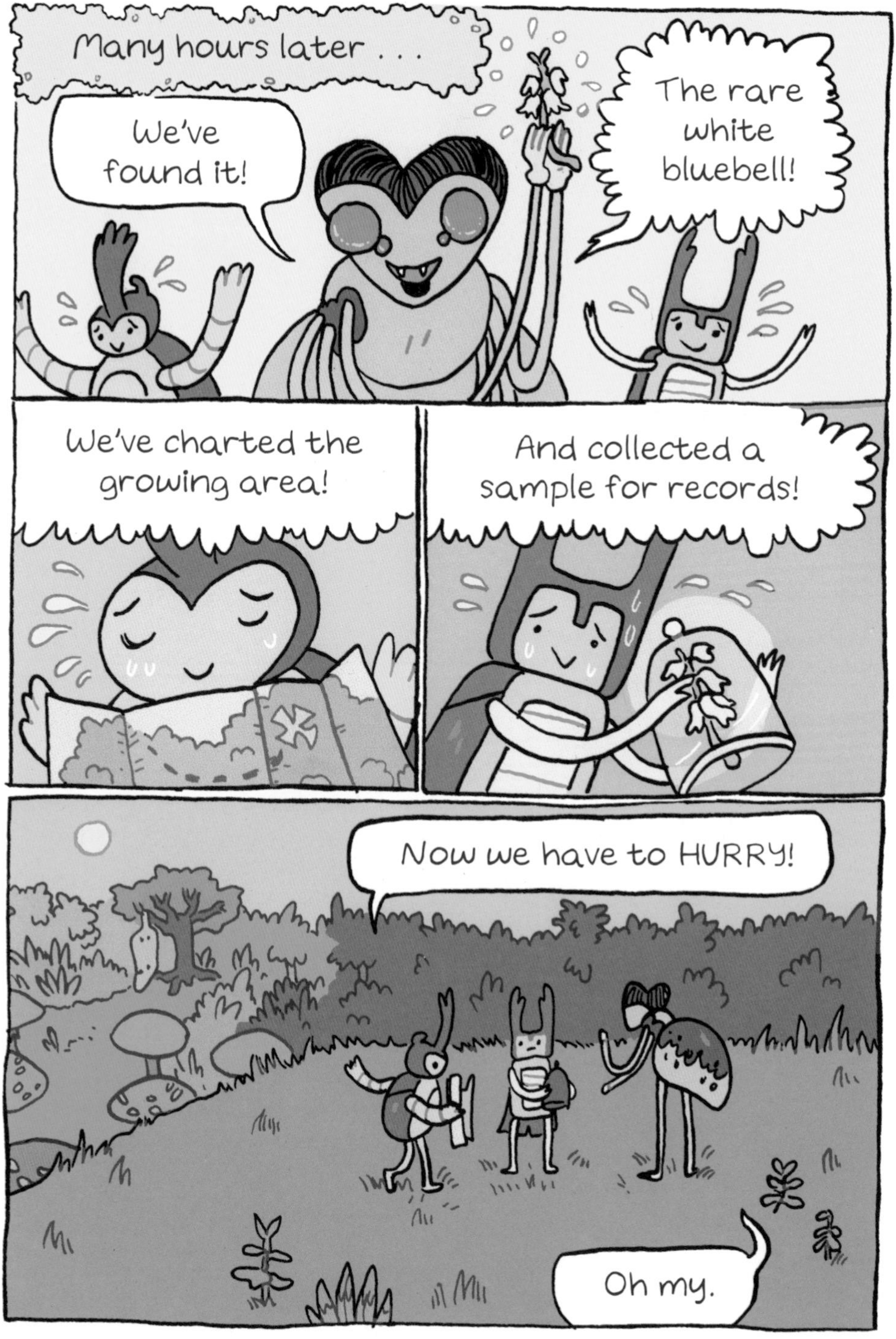
Many hours later . . .
We've found it!
The rare white bluebell!
We've charted the growing area!
And collected a sample for records!
Now we have to HURRY!
Oh my.

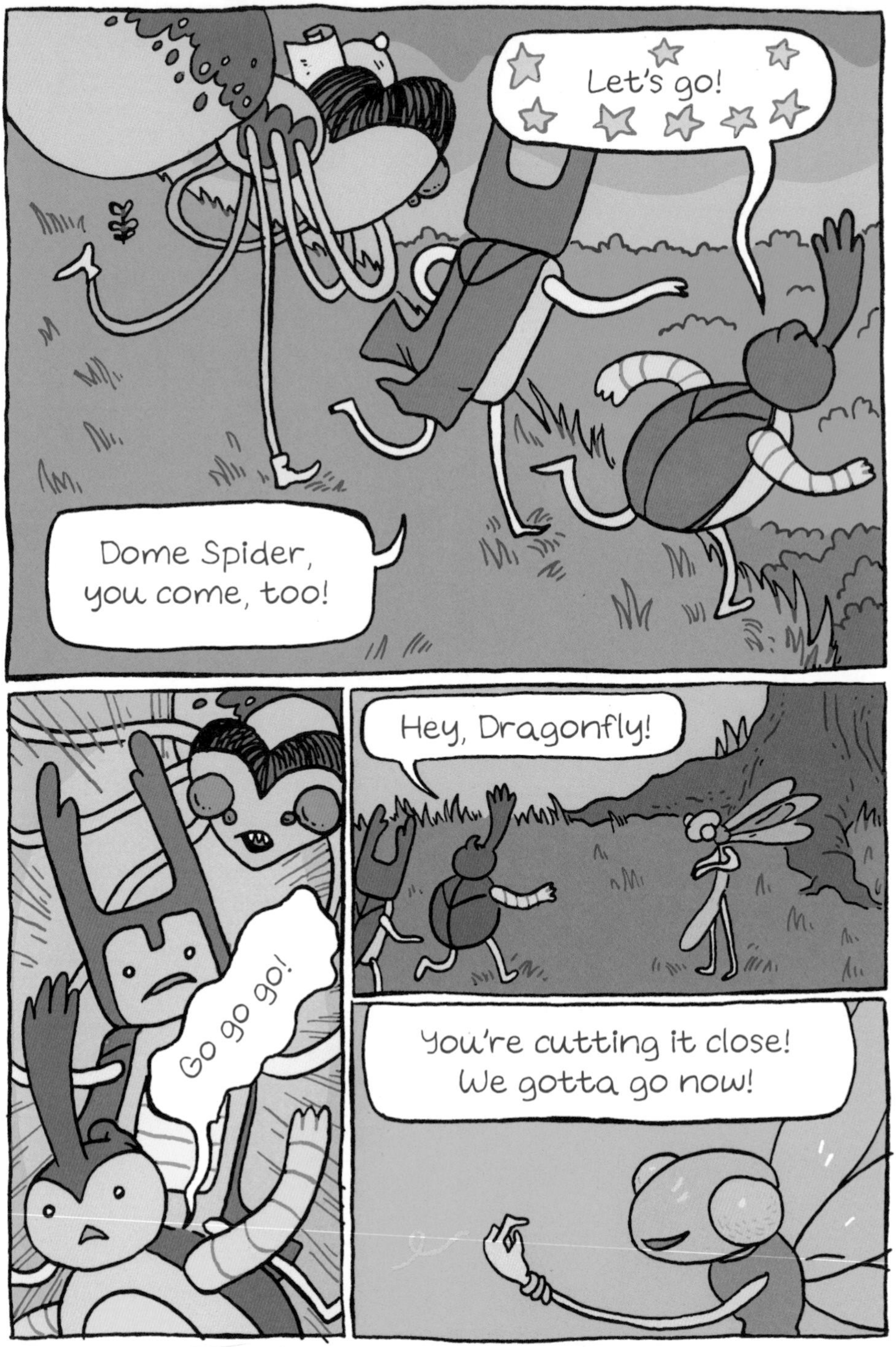
Let's go!
Dome Spider, you come, too!
Go go go!
Hey, Dragonfly!
You're cutting it close! We gotta go now!

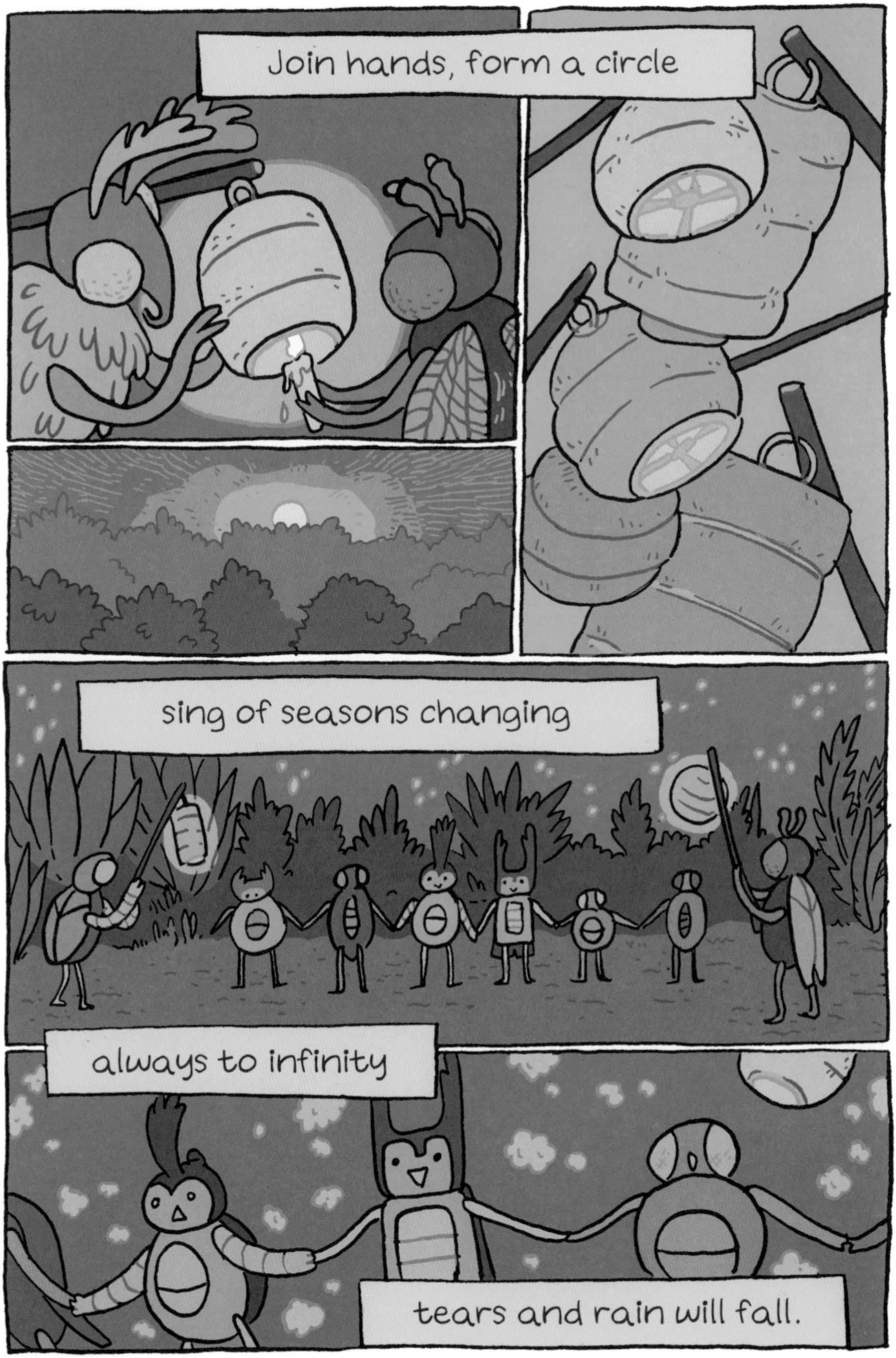
Join hands, form a circle
sing of seasons changing
always to infinity
tears and rain will fall.

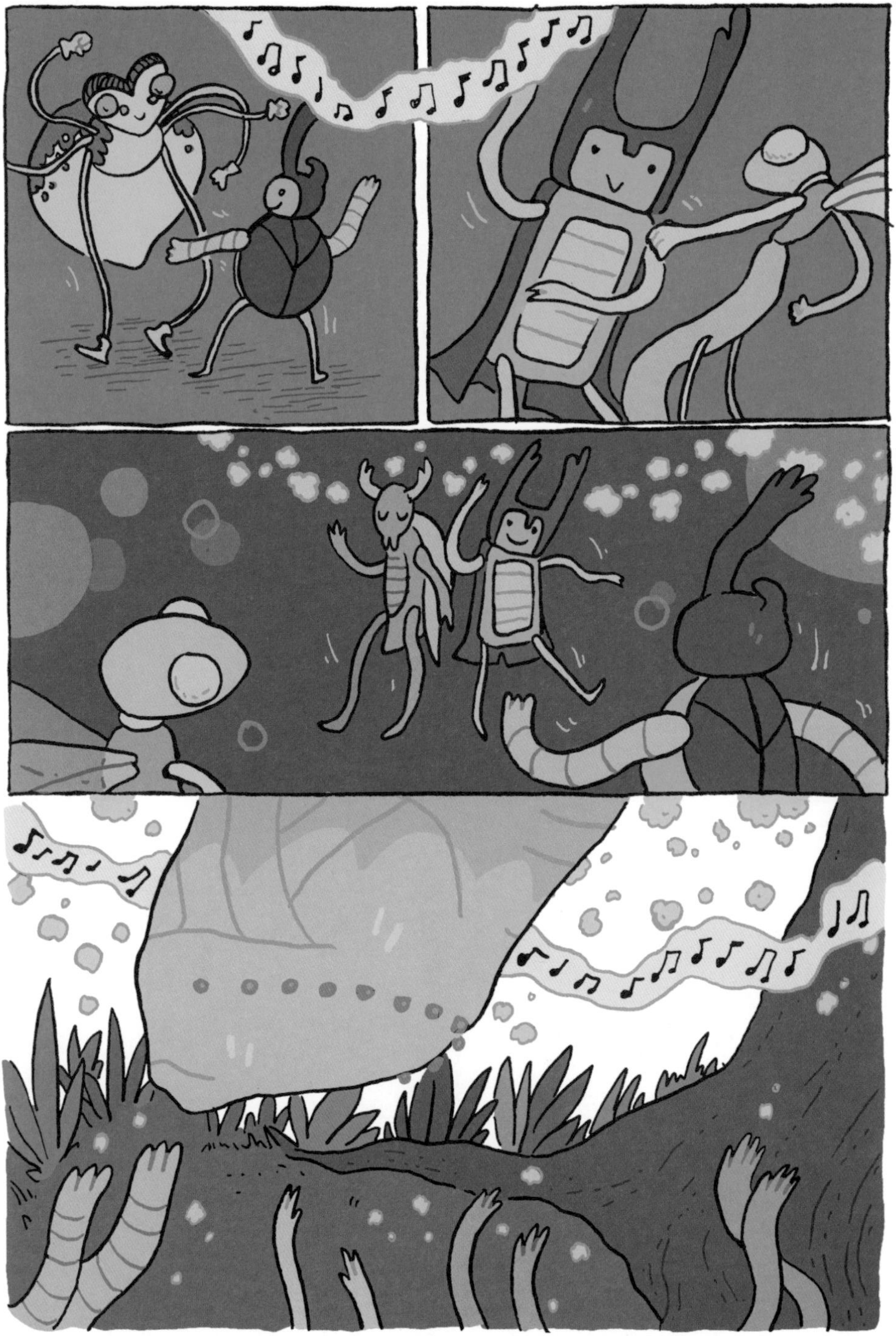

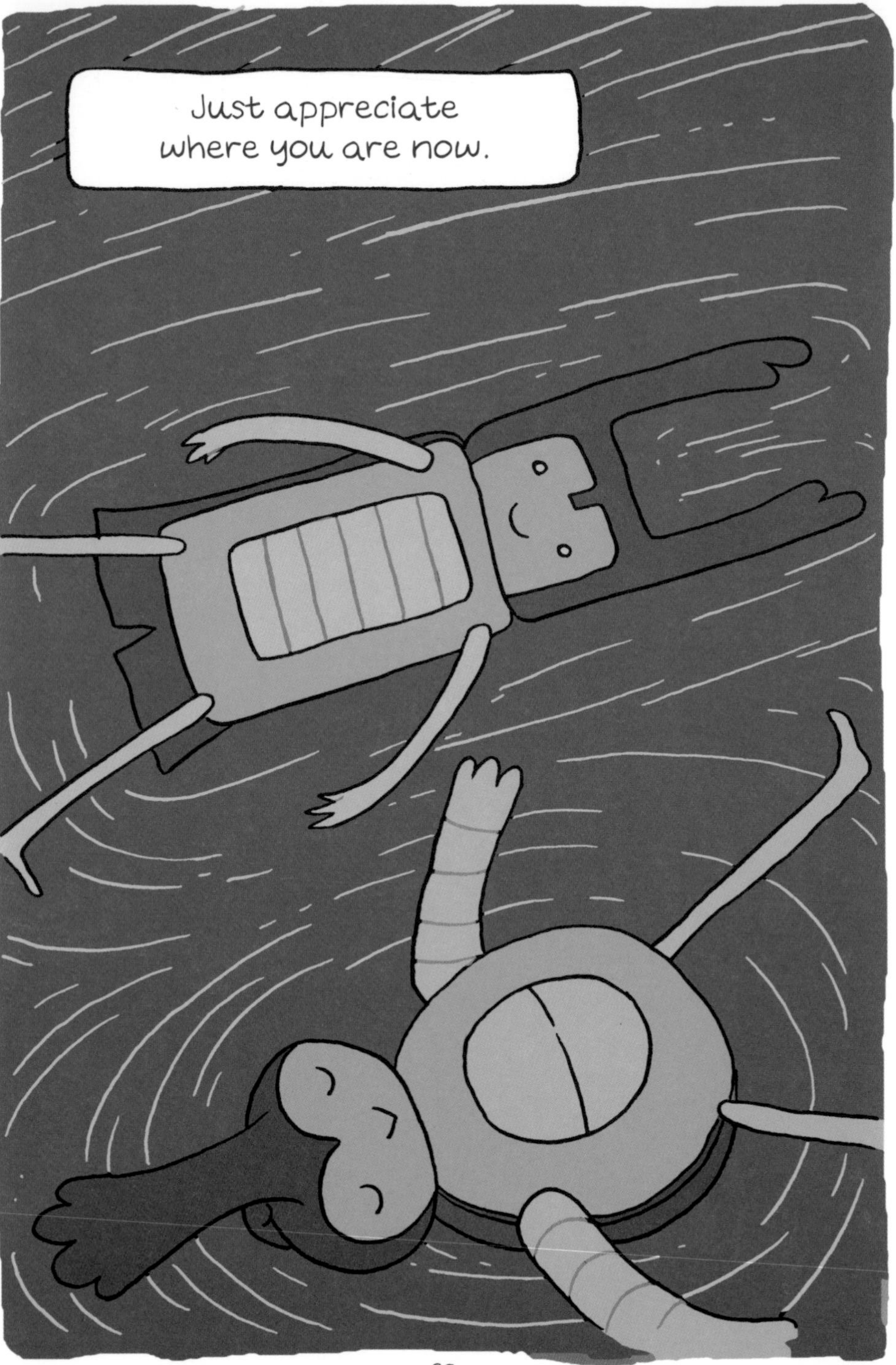
Just appreciate where you are now.

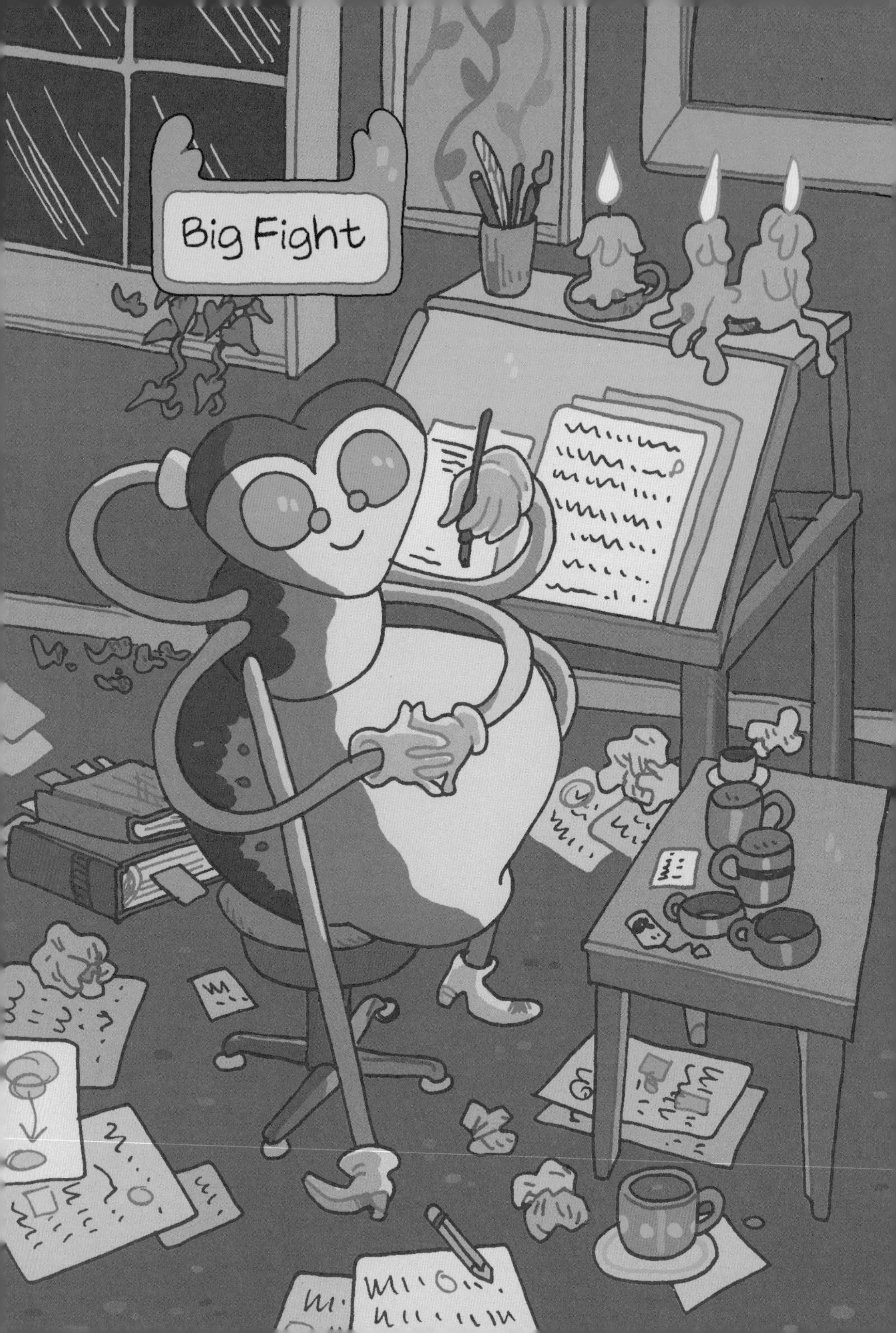
Big Fight

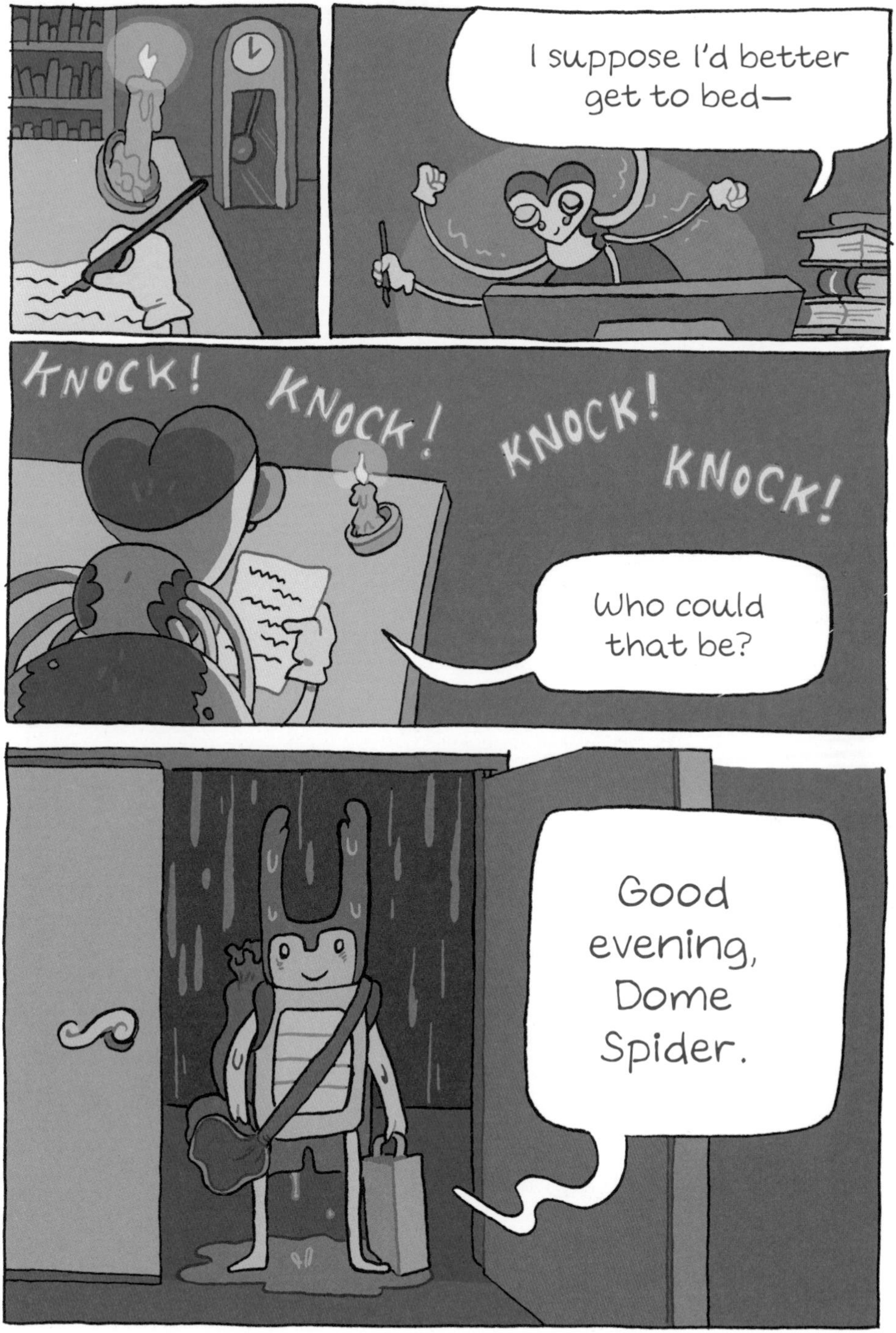
I suppose I'd better get to bed—
KNOCK! KNOCK! KNOCK! KNOCK!
Who could that be?
Good evening, Dome Spider.

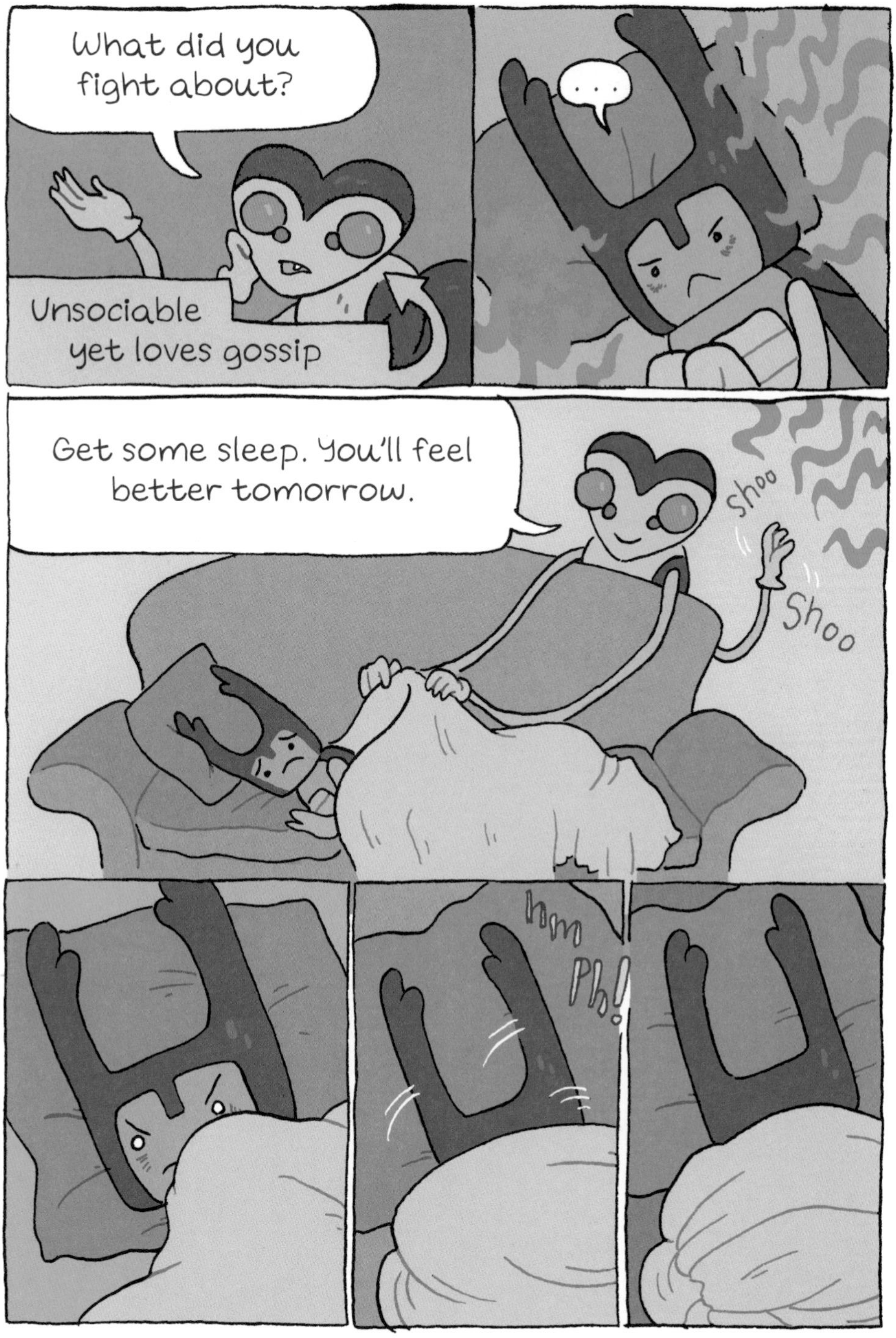
What did you fight about?
Unsociable yet loves gossip
...
Get some sleep. You'll feel better tomorrow.
Shoo
Shoo
hmph!

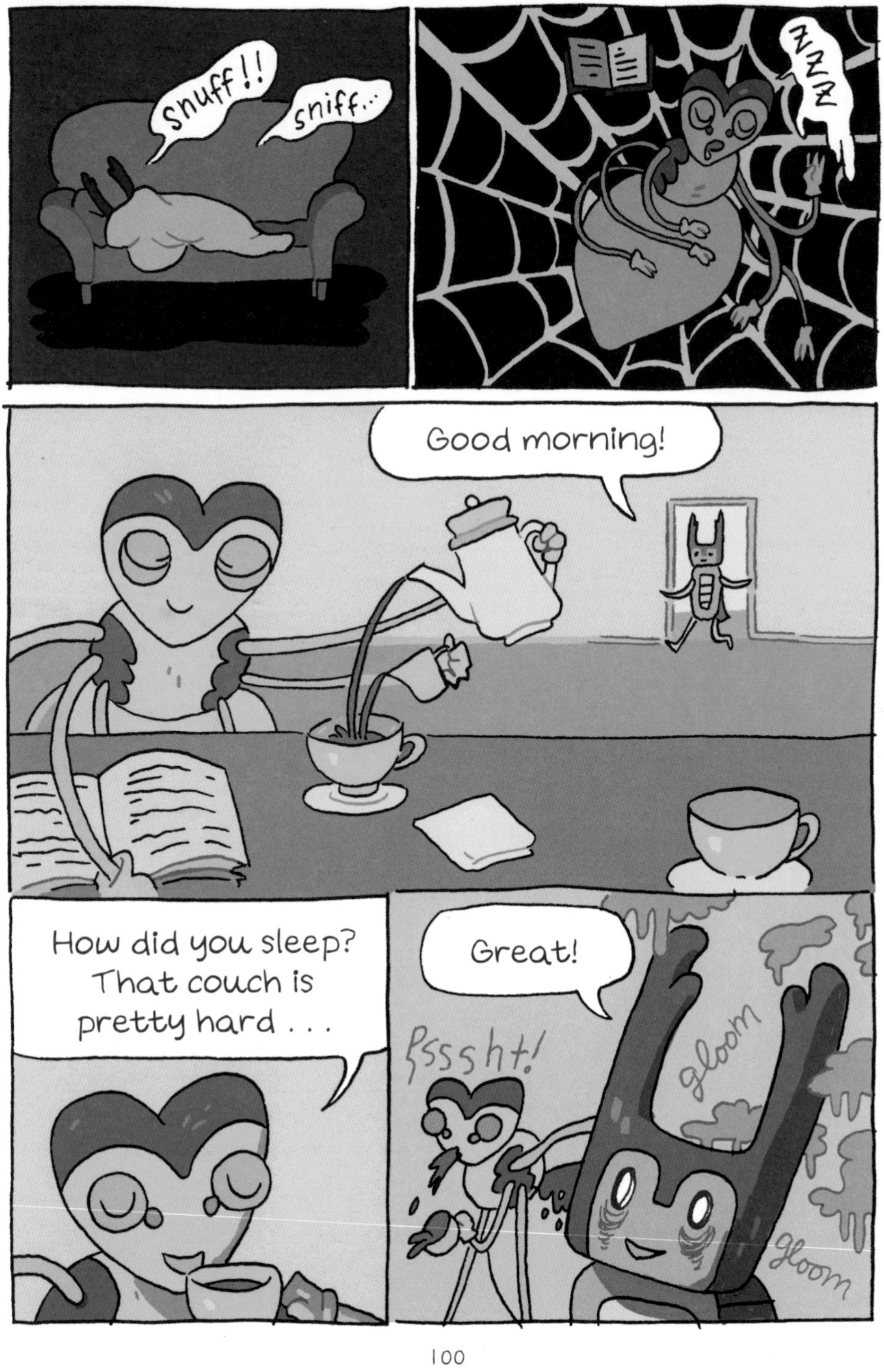
snuff!!
sniff...
ZZZZ
Good morning!
How did you sleep? That couch is pretty hard . . .
Great!
Psssht!
gloom
gloom

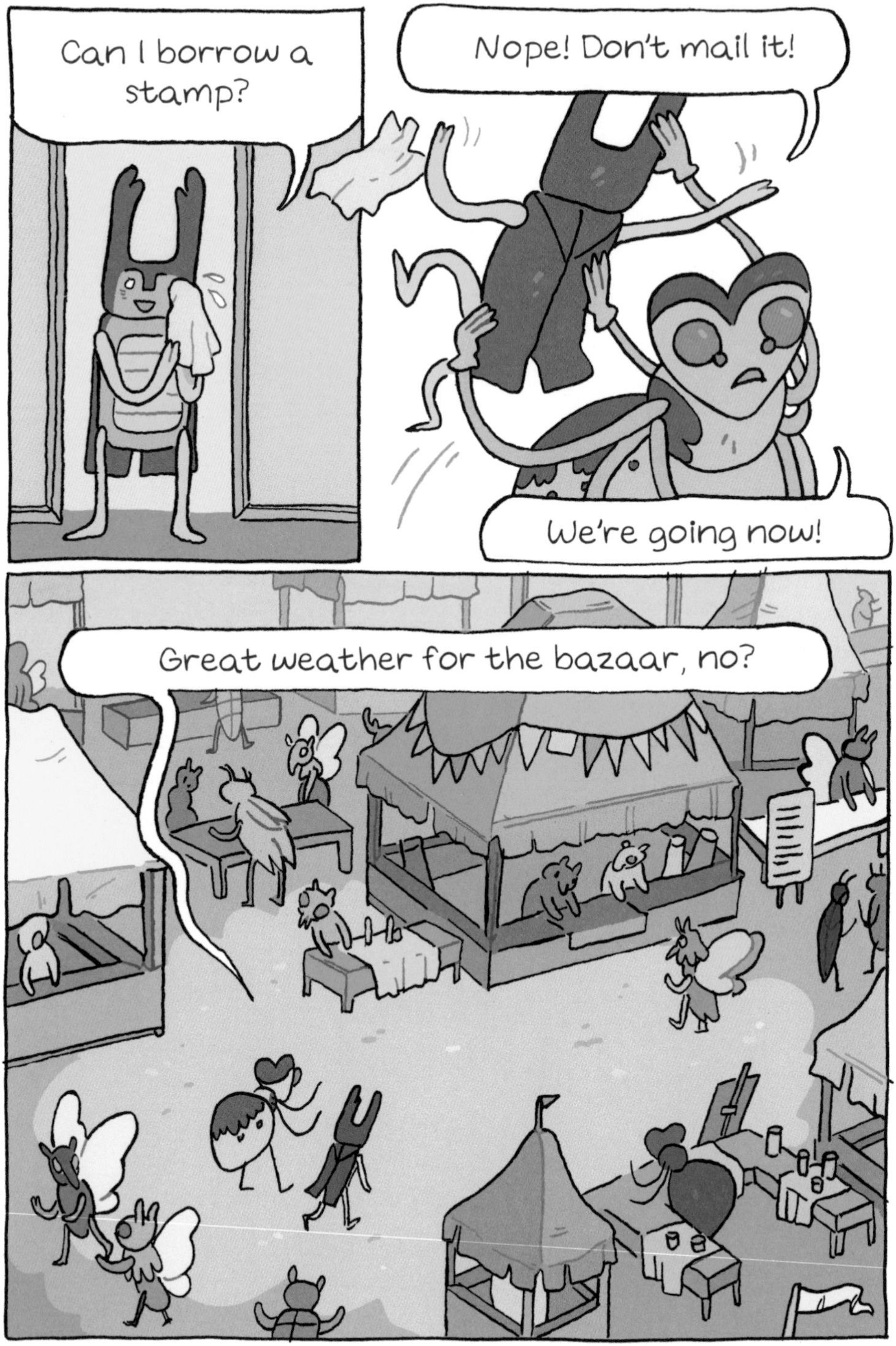
Can I borrow a stamp?
Nope! Don't mail it!
We're going now!
Great weather for the bazaar, no?

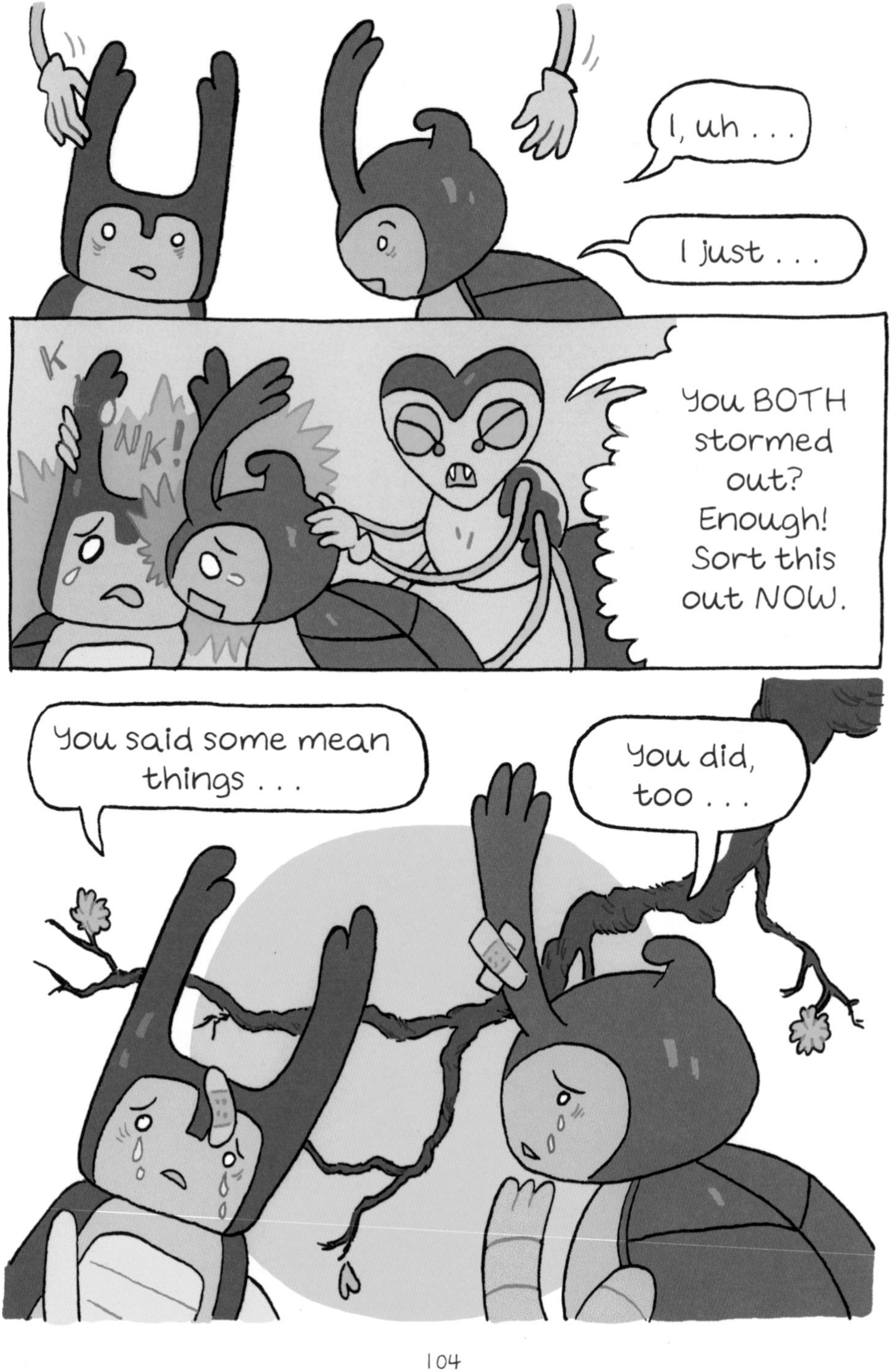
I, uh . . .
I just . . .
KONK!
You BOTH stormed out? Enough! Sort this out NOW.
You said some mean things . . .
You did, too . . .

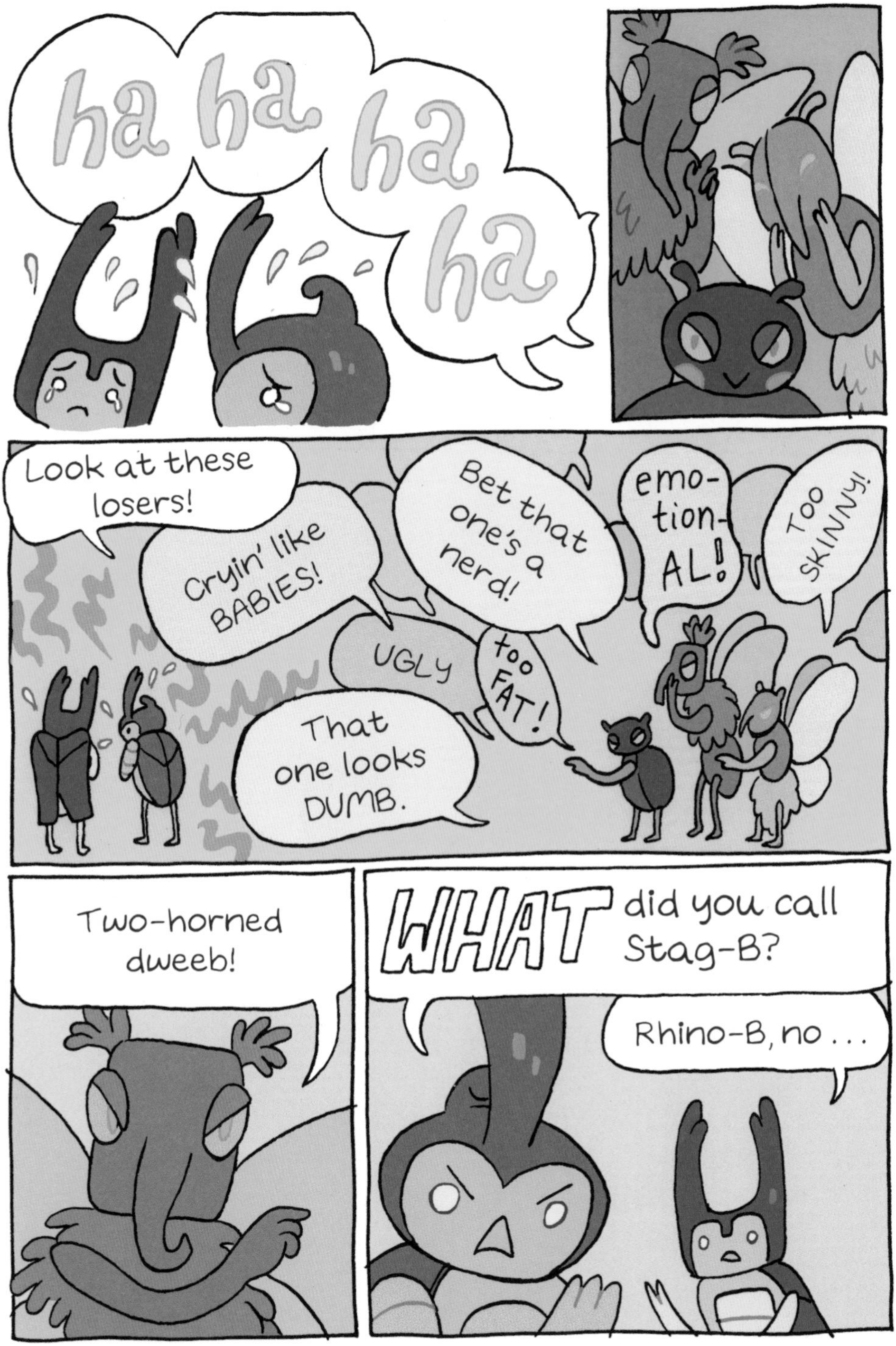
ha ha ha ha
Look at these losers!
Cryin' like BABIES!
Bet that one's a nerd!
emo-tion-AL!
Too SKINNY!
UGLY
too FAT!
That one looks DUMB.
Two-horned dweeb!
WHAT did you call Stag-B?
Rhino-B, no . . .

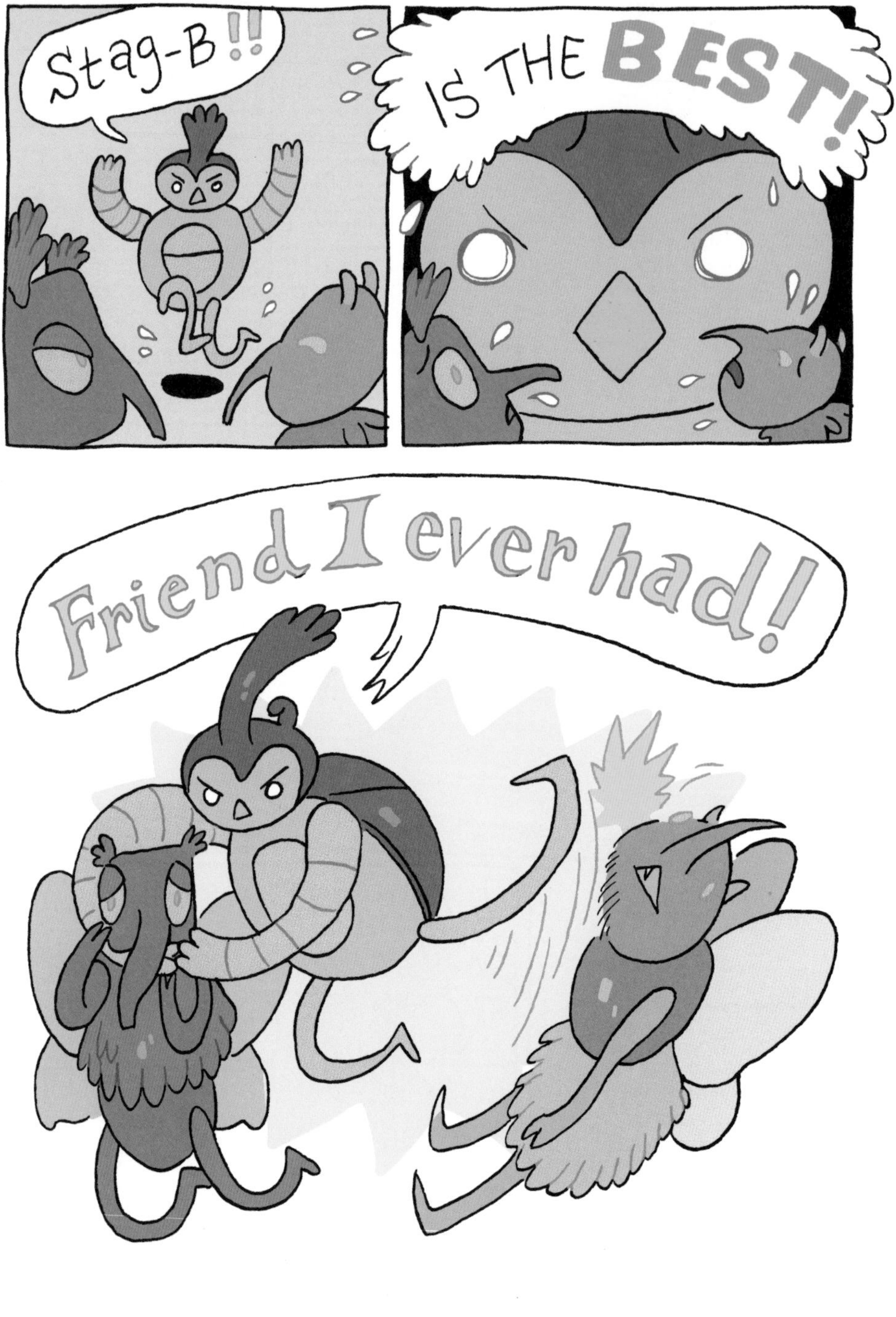
Stag-B!!
IS THE BEST!
Friend I ever had!

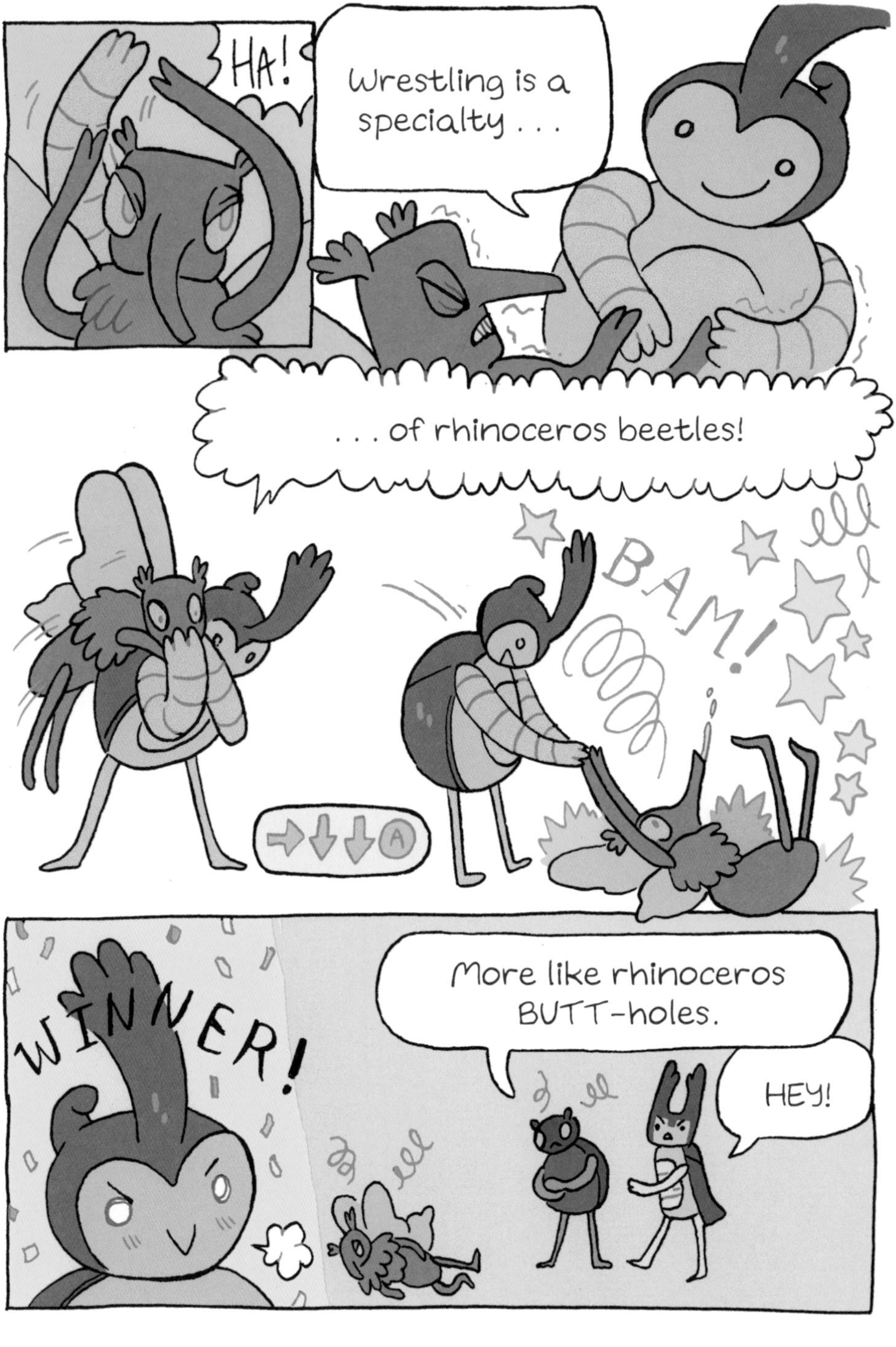
HA!
Wrestling is a specialty . . .
. . . of rhinoceros beetles!
BAM!
A
WINNER!
More like rhinoceros BUTT-holes.
HEY!

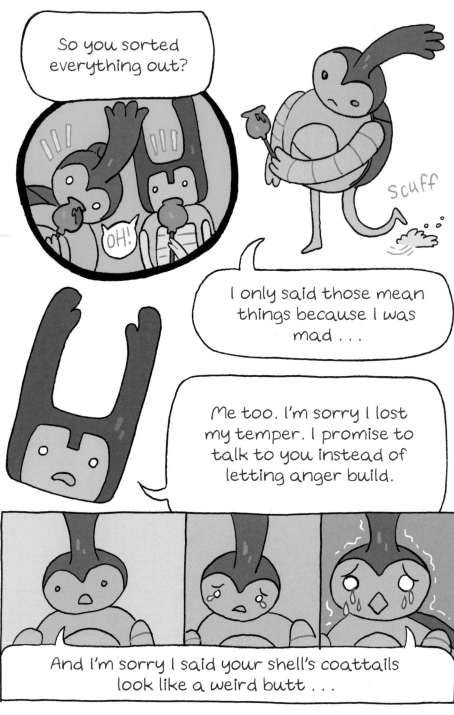

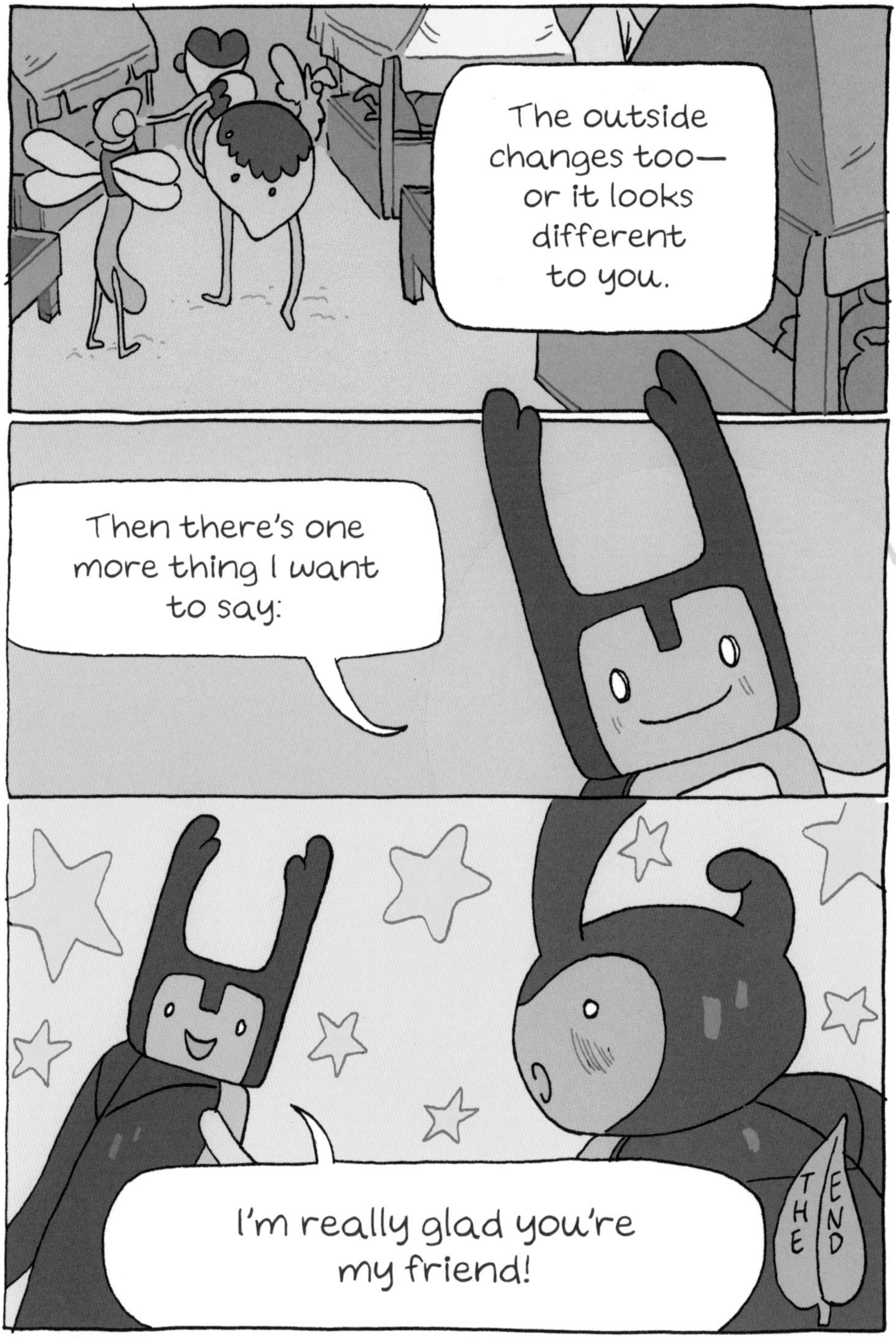
The outside changes too—or it looks different to you.
Then there's one more thing I want to say:
I'm really glad you're my friend!
THE END

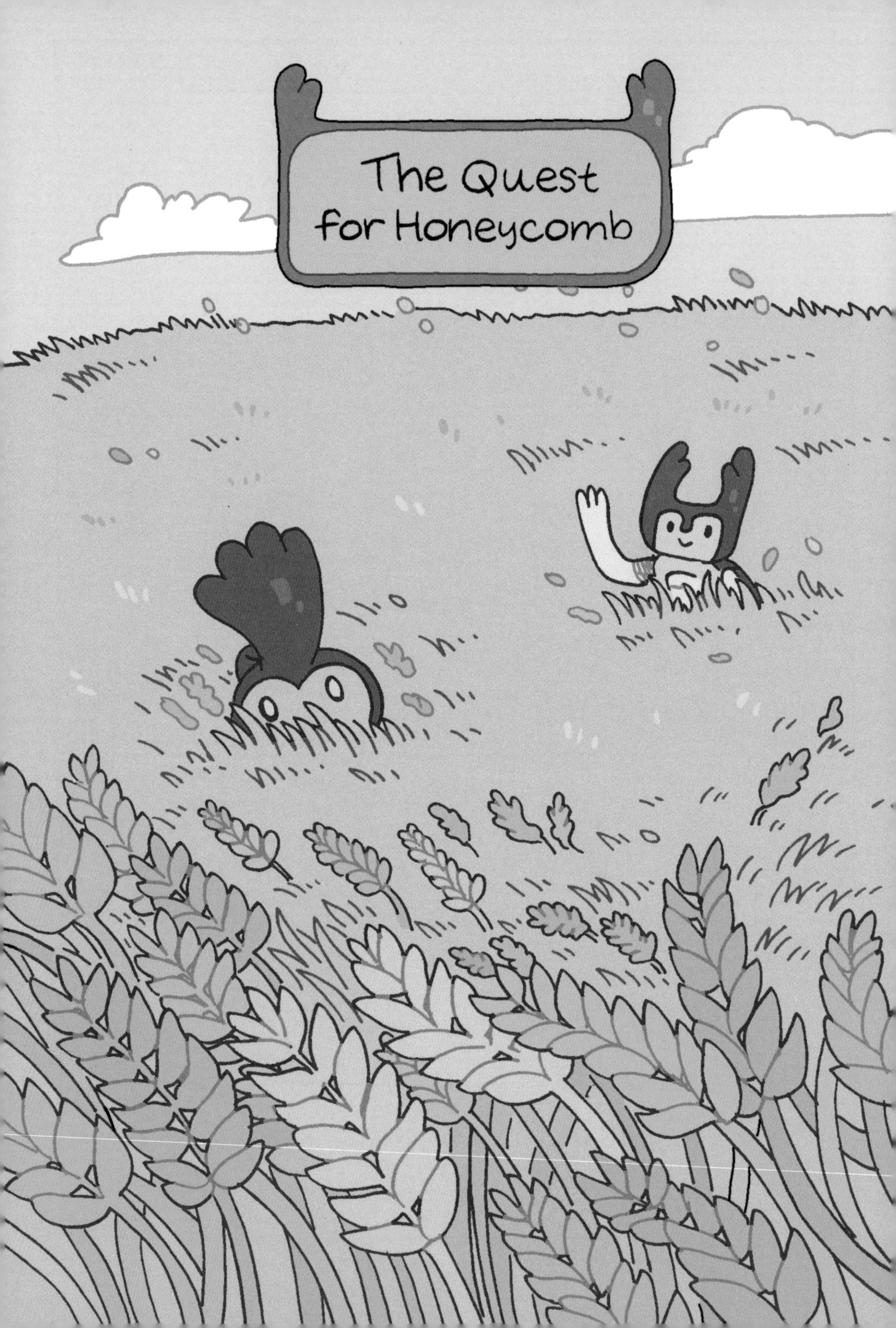
The Quest
for Honeycomb

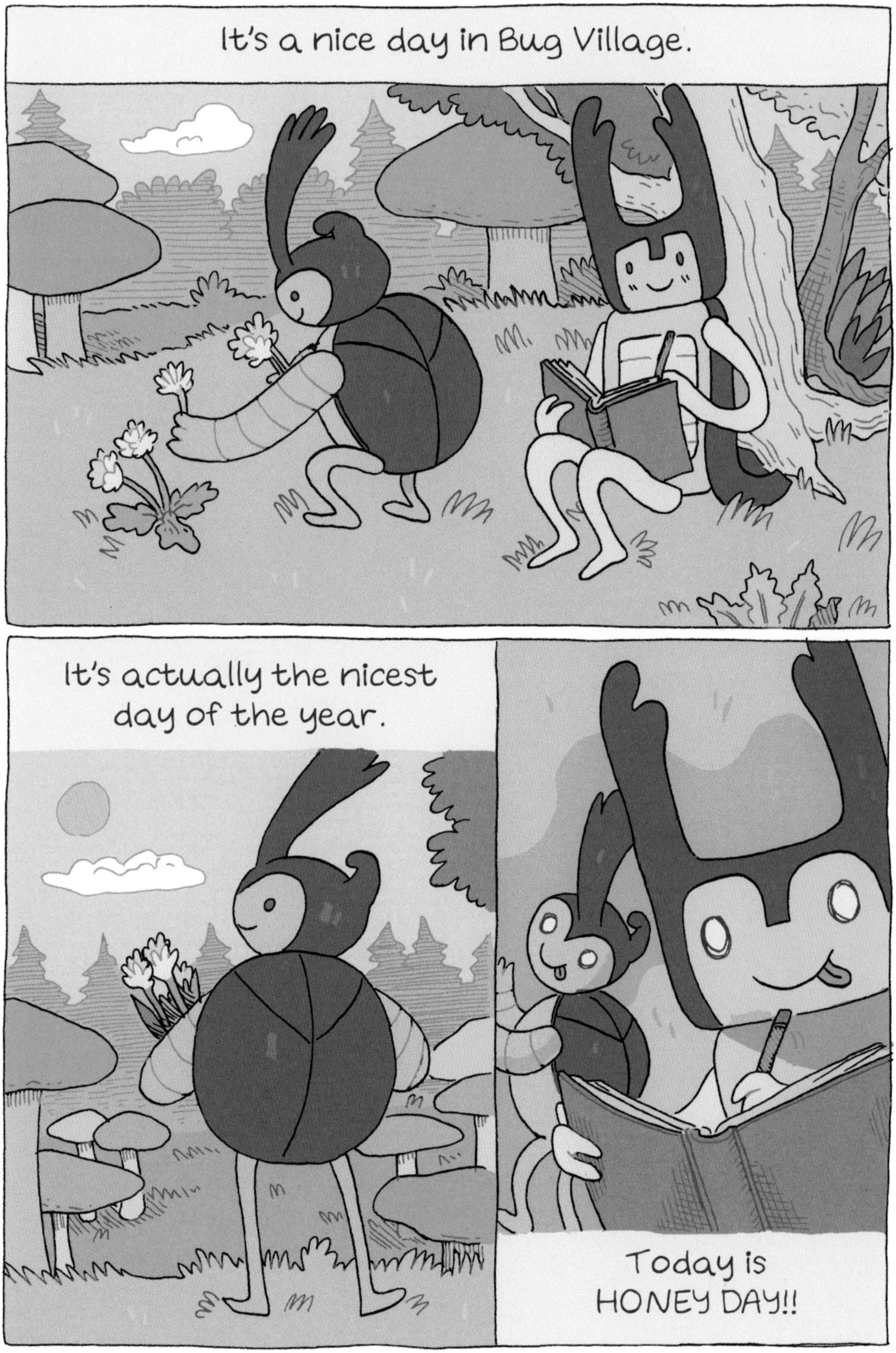
It's a nice day in Bug Village.
It's actually the nicest day of the year.
Today is HONEY DAY!!

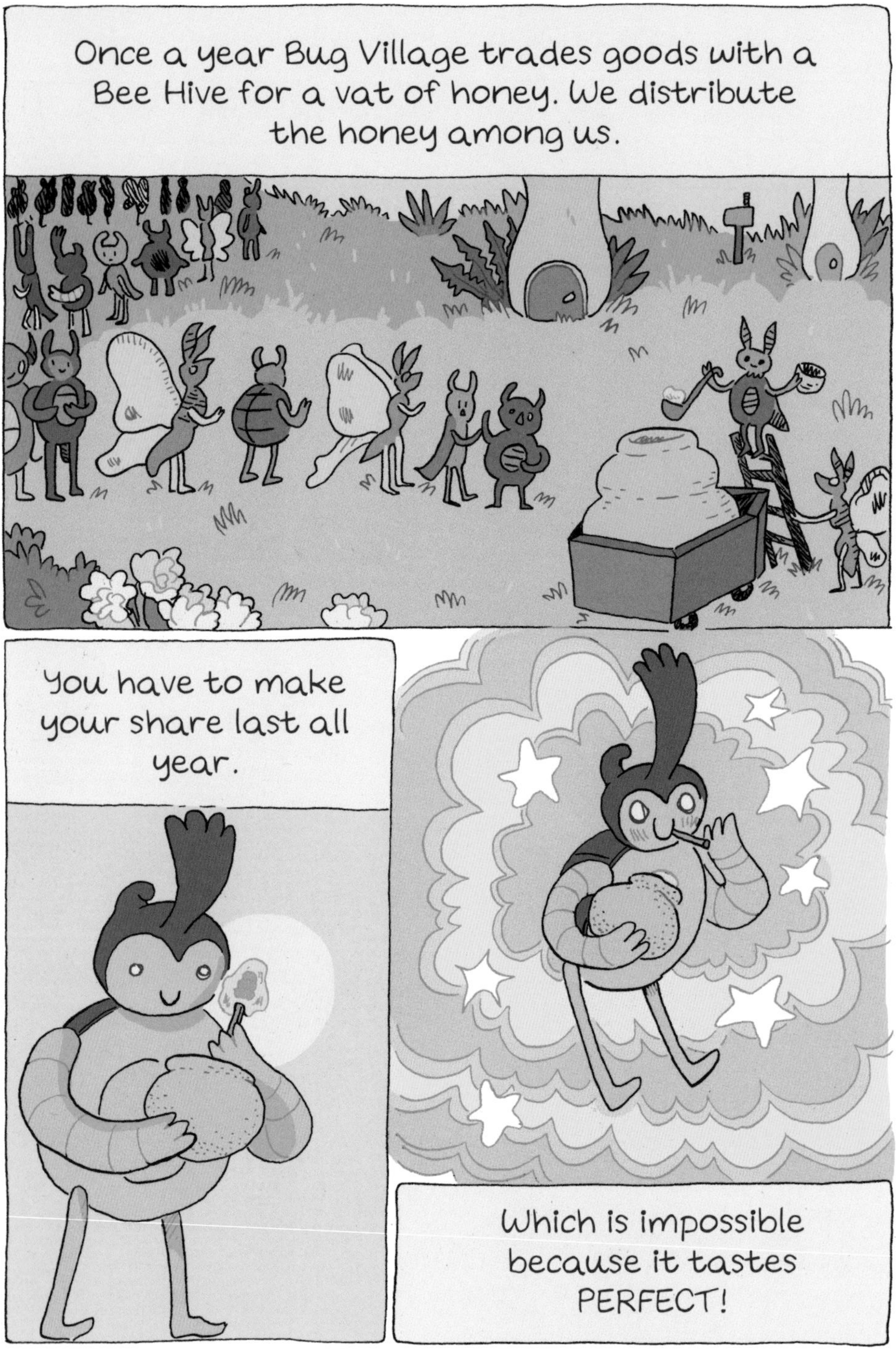
Once a year Bug Village trades goods with a Bee Hive for a vat of honey. We distribute the honey among us.
You have to make your share last all year.
Which is impossible because it tastes PERFECT!

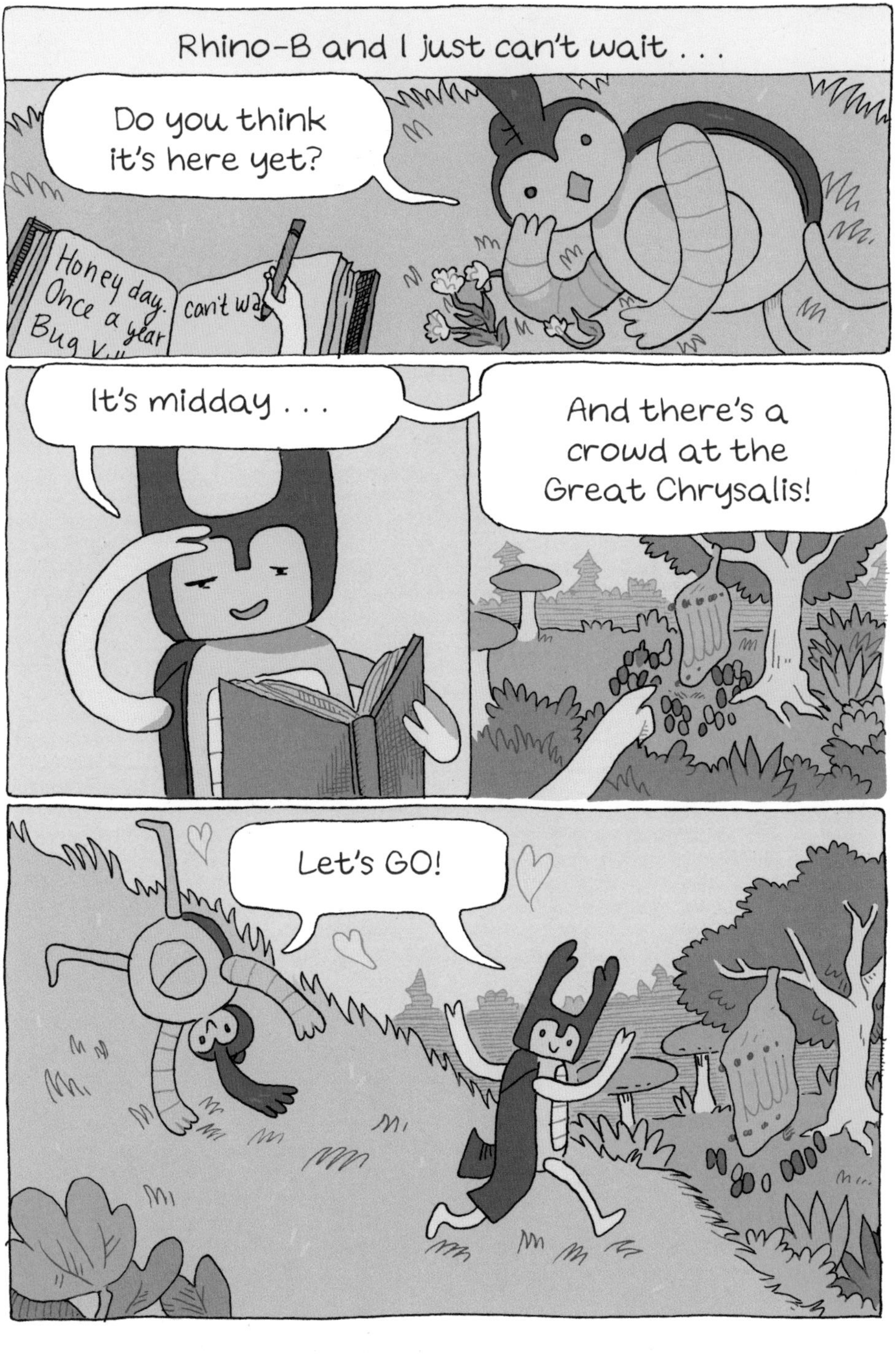
Rhino-B and I just can't wait . . .
Do you think it's here yet?
Honey day. Once a year Bug V...
can't wa
It's midday . . .
And there's a crowd at the Great Chrysalis!
Let's GO!

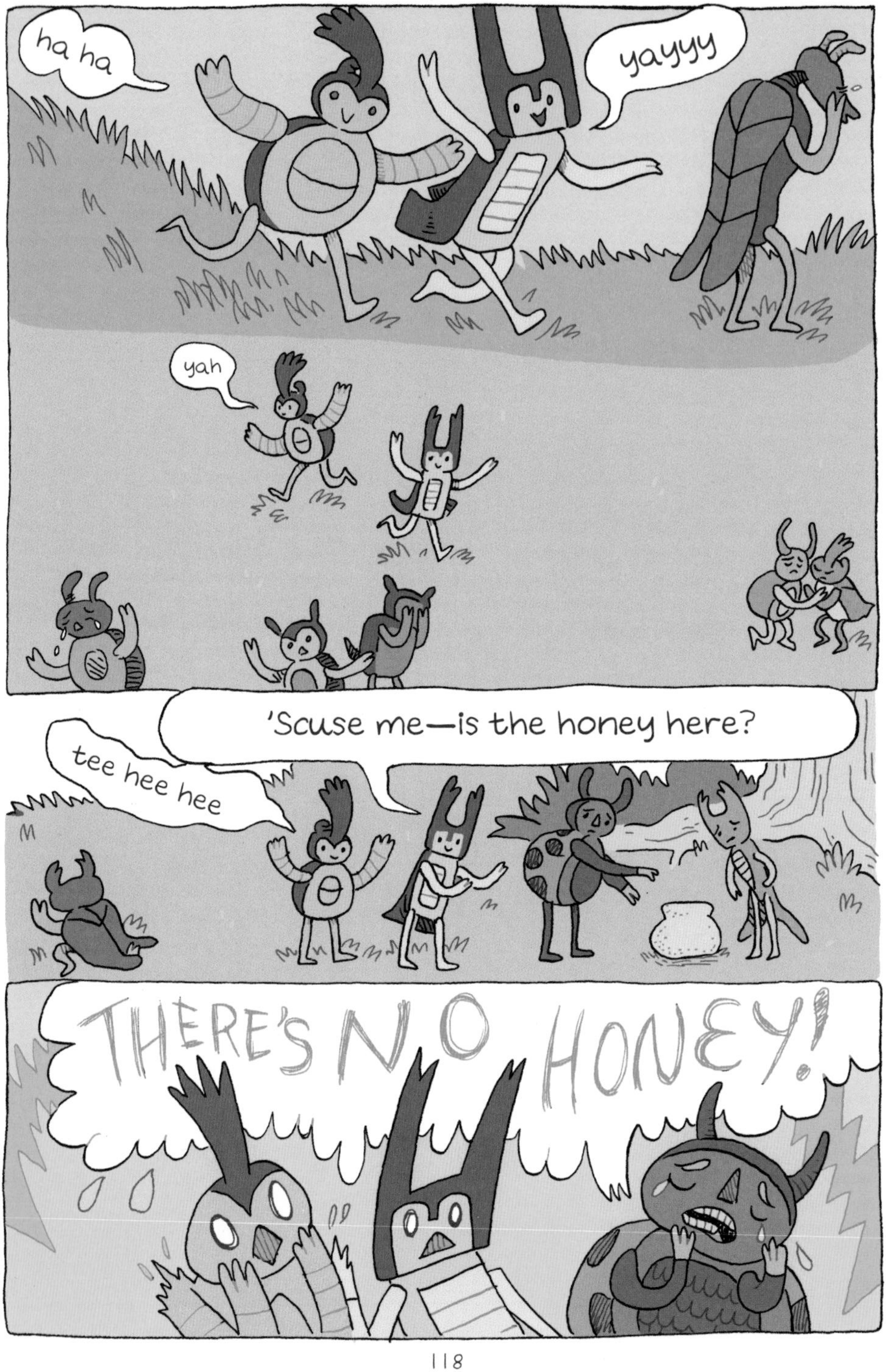
ha ha
yayyy
yah
'Scuse me—is the honey here?
tee hee hee
THERE'S NO HONEY!

119

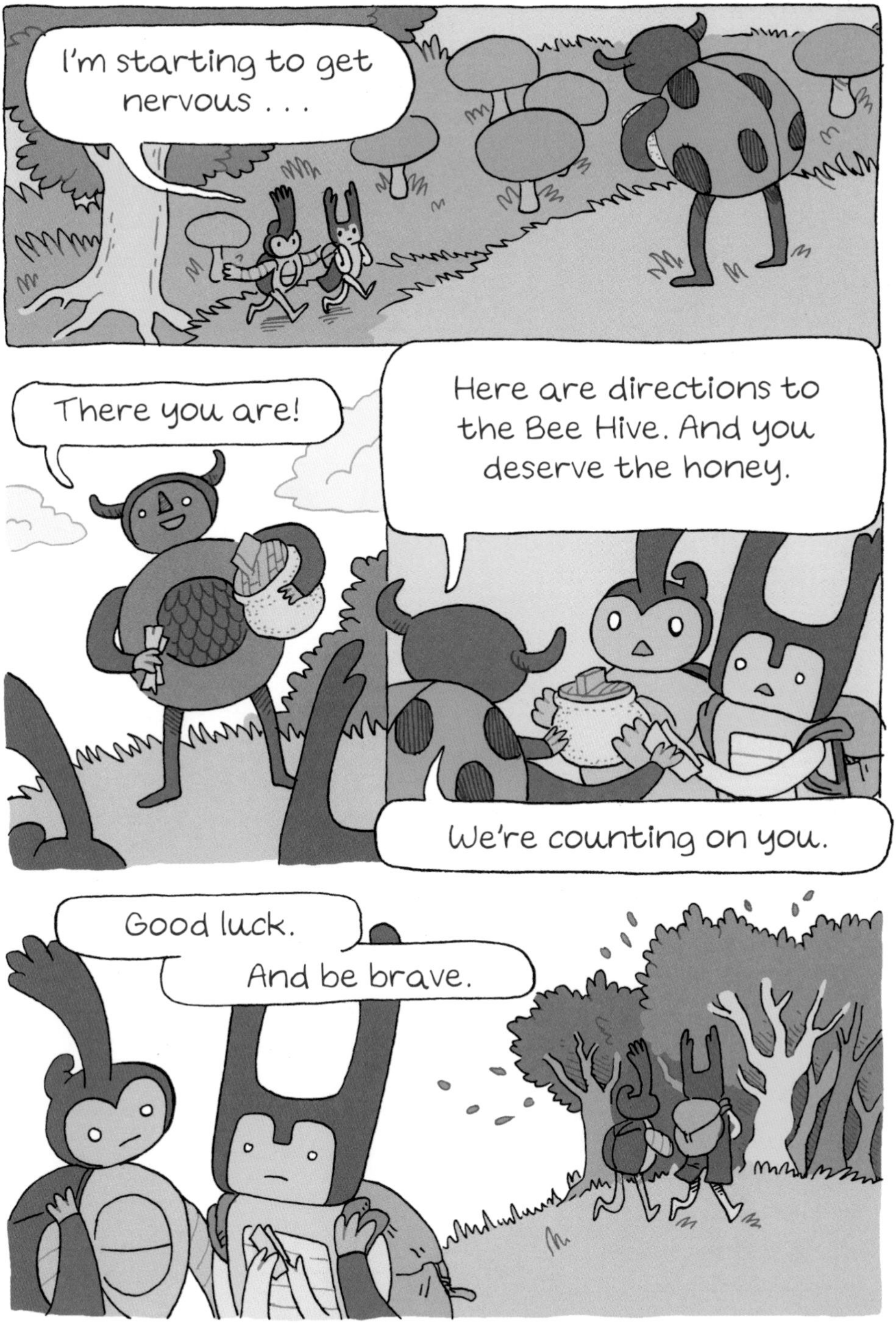
I'm starting to get nervous . . .
There you are!
Here are directions to the Bee Hive. And you deserve the honey.
We're counting on you.
Good luck.
And be brave.

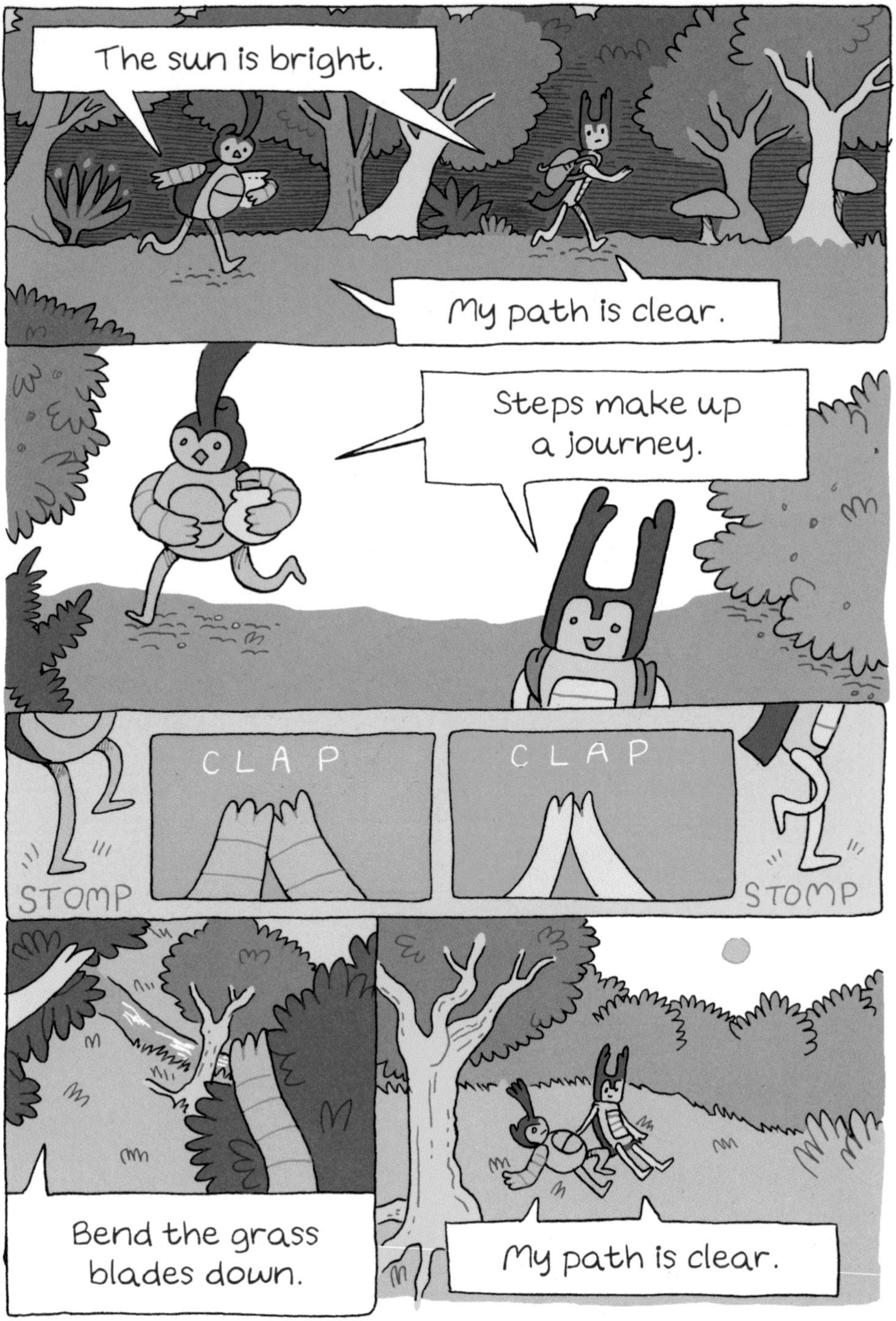
The sun is bright.
My path is clear.
Steps make up a journey.
STOMP
CLAP
CLAP
STOMP
Bend the grass blades down.
My path is clear.

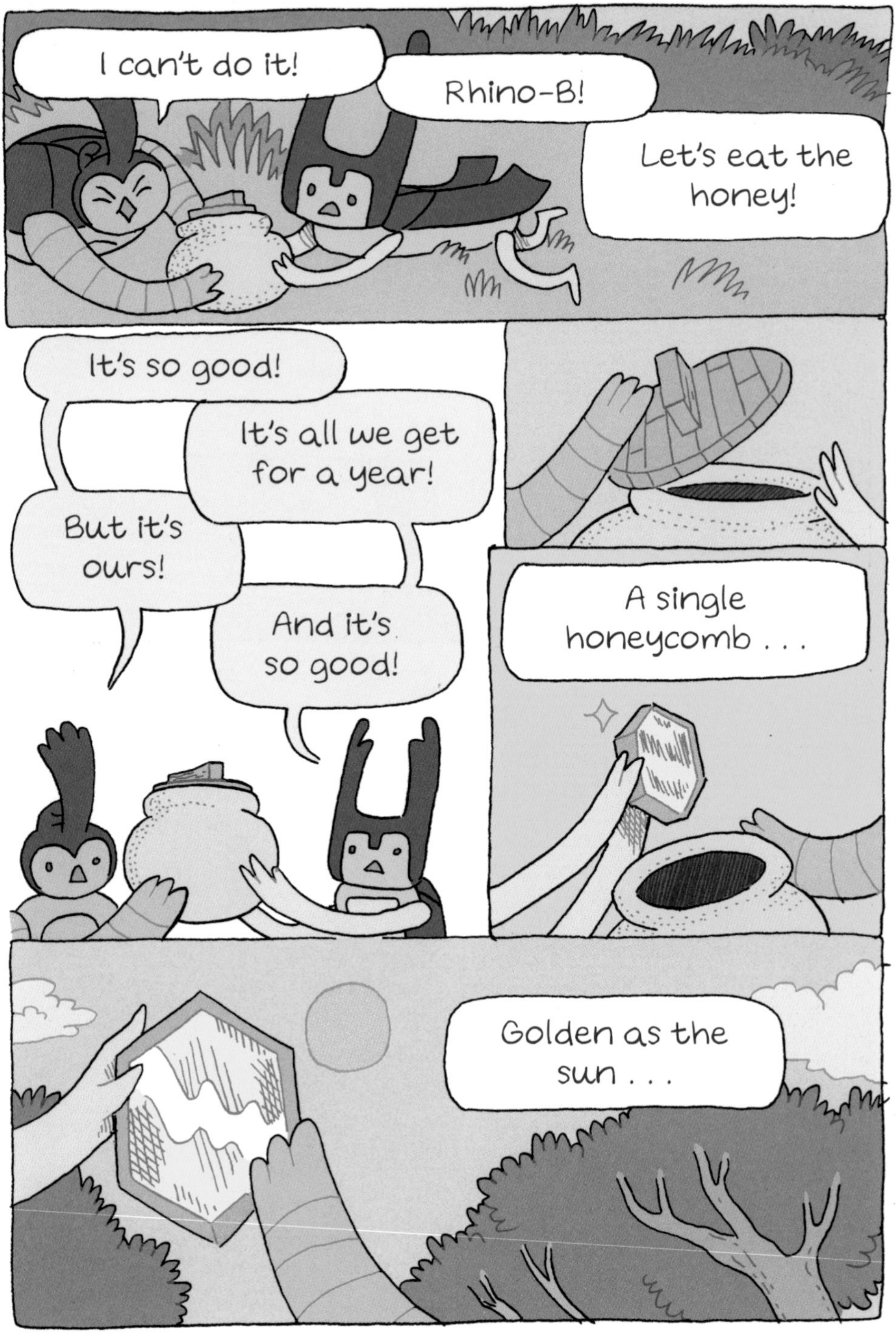
I can't do it!
Rhino-B!
Let's eat the honey!
It's so good!
It's all we get for a year!
But it's ours!
And it's so good!
A single honeycomb . . .
Golden as the sun . . .

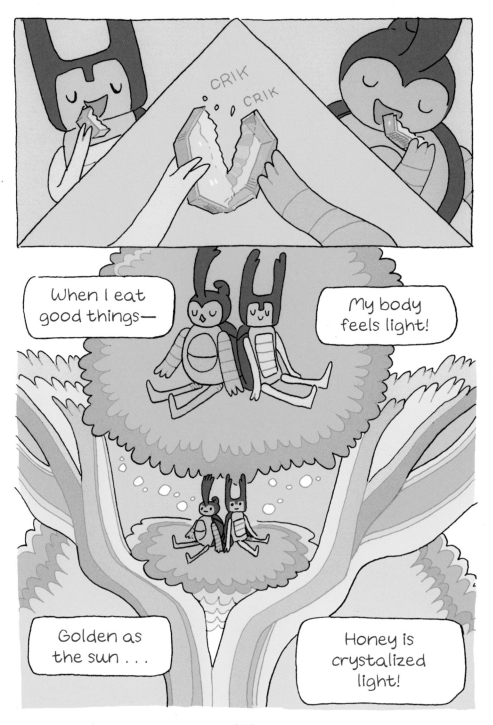

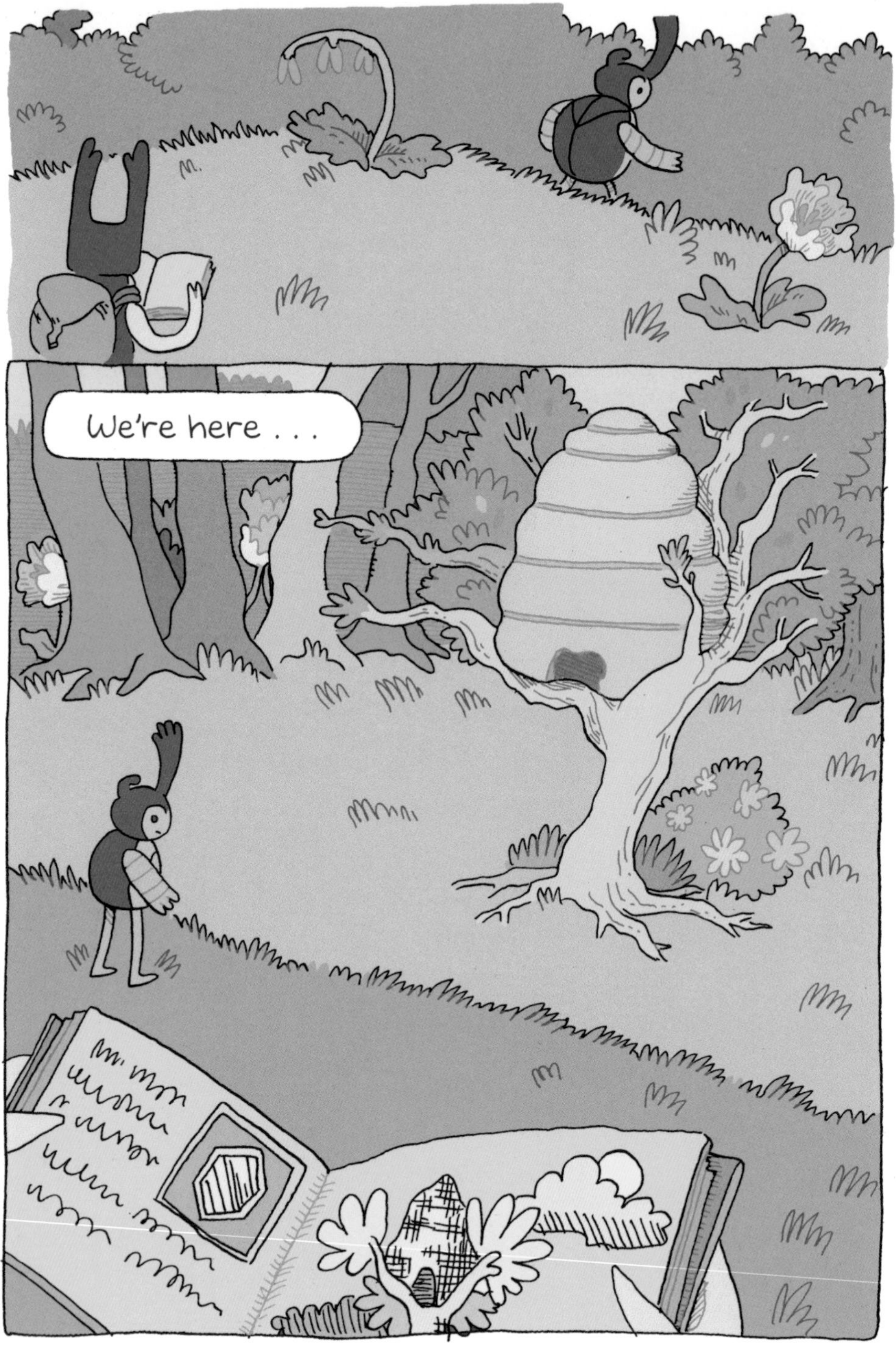
We're here . . .

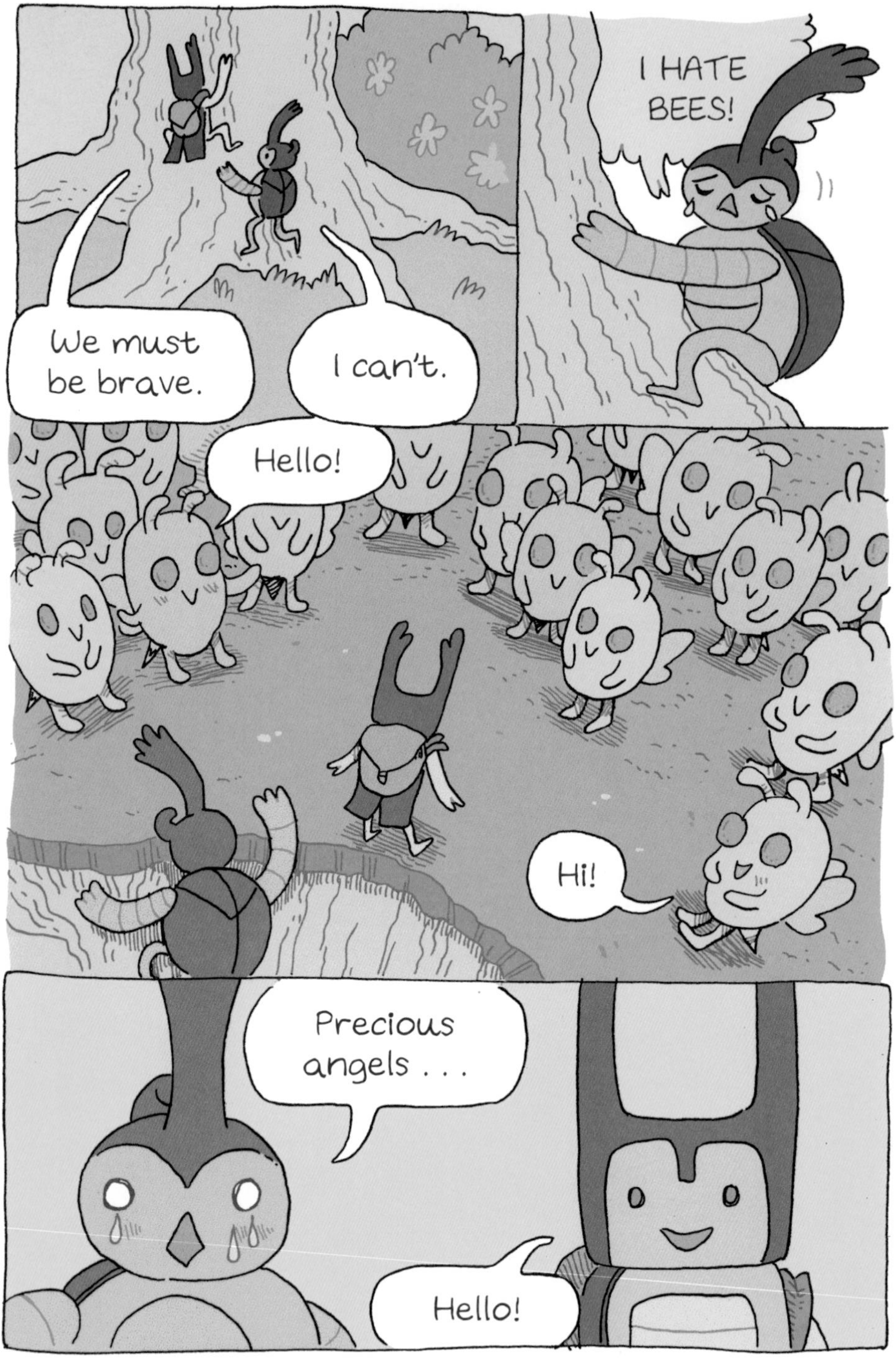
We must be brave.
I can't.
I HATE BEES!
Hello!
Hi!
Precious angels . . .
Hello!

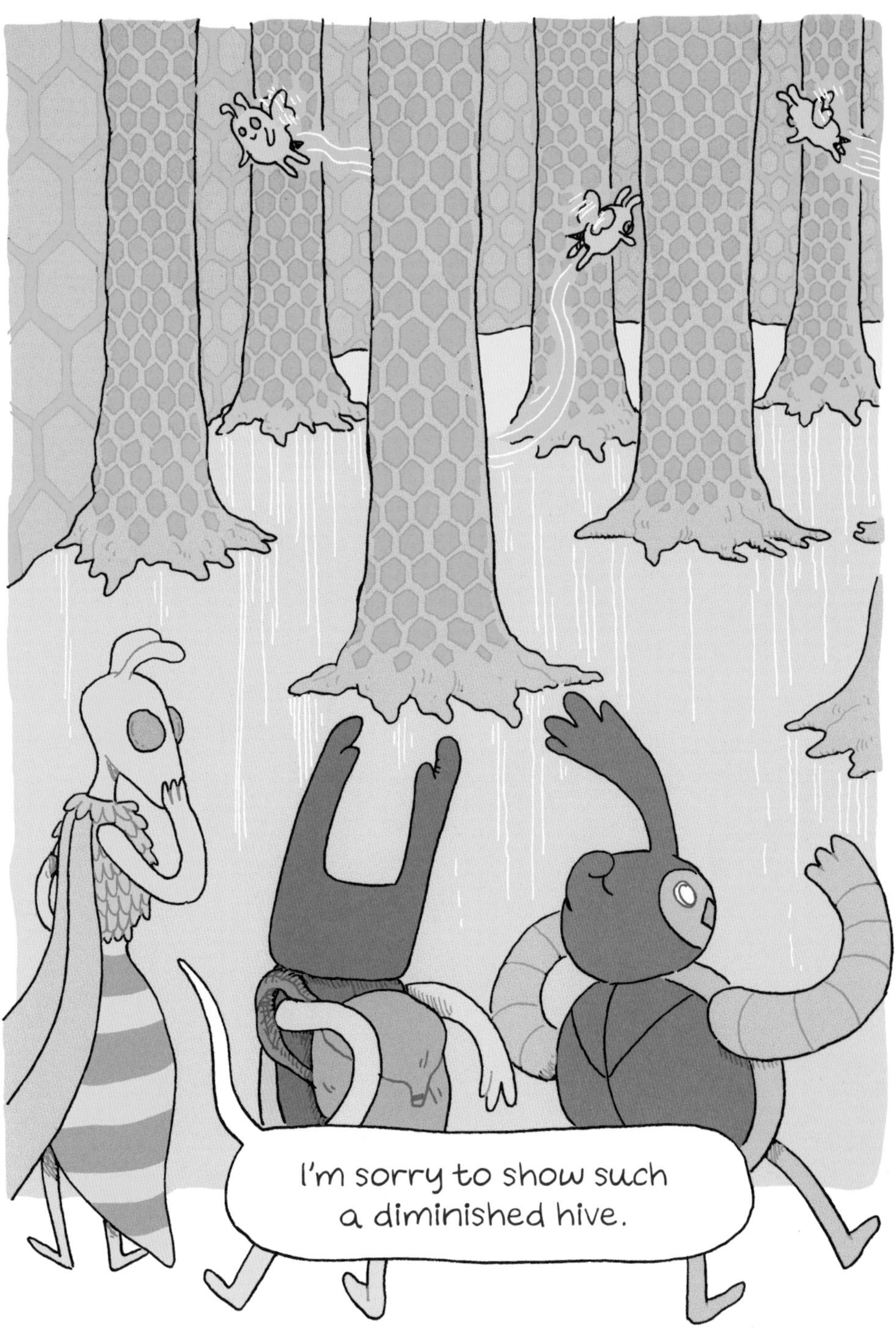
I'm sorry to show such a diminished hive.

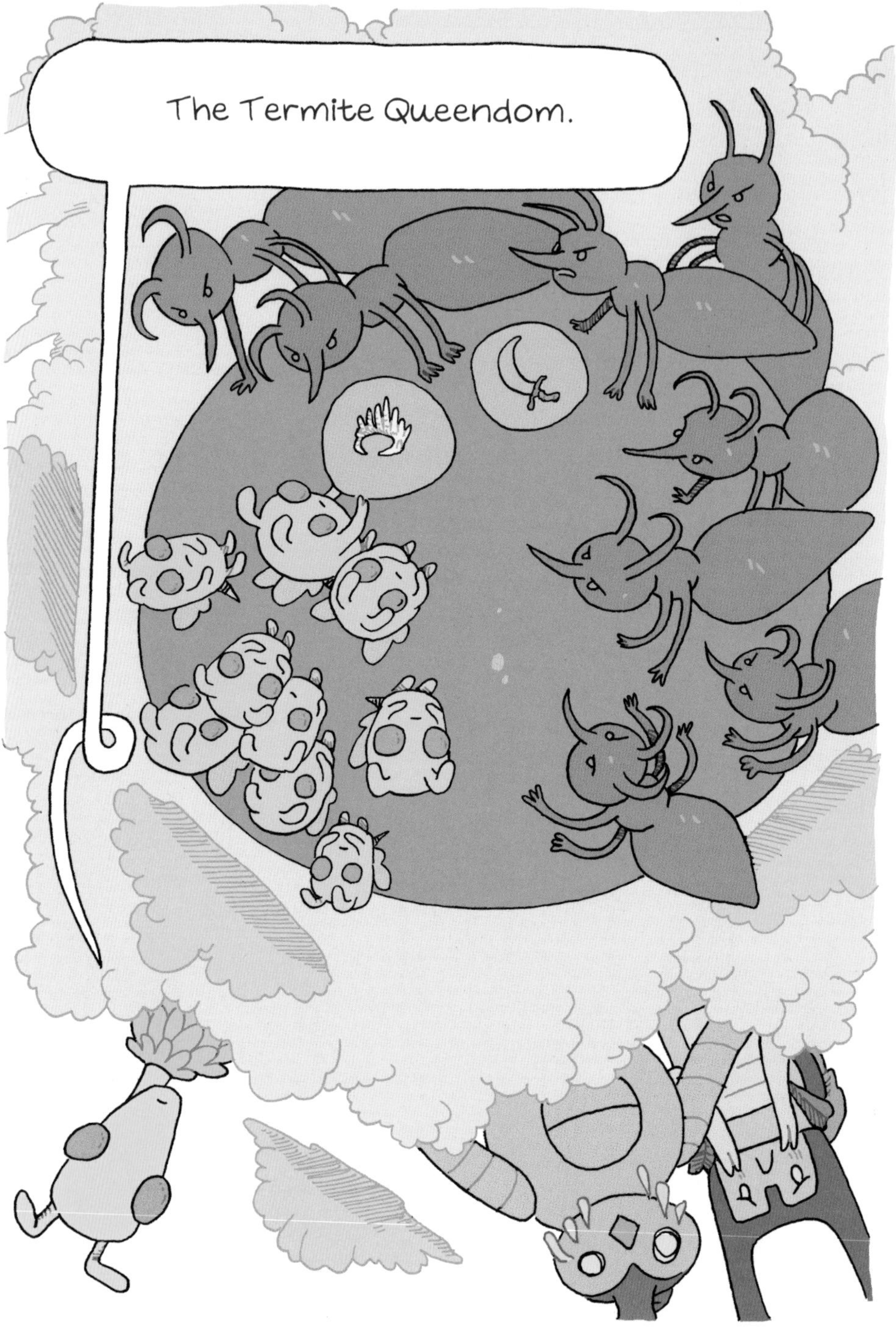
The Termite Queendom.

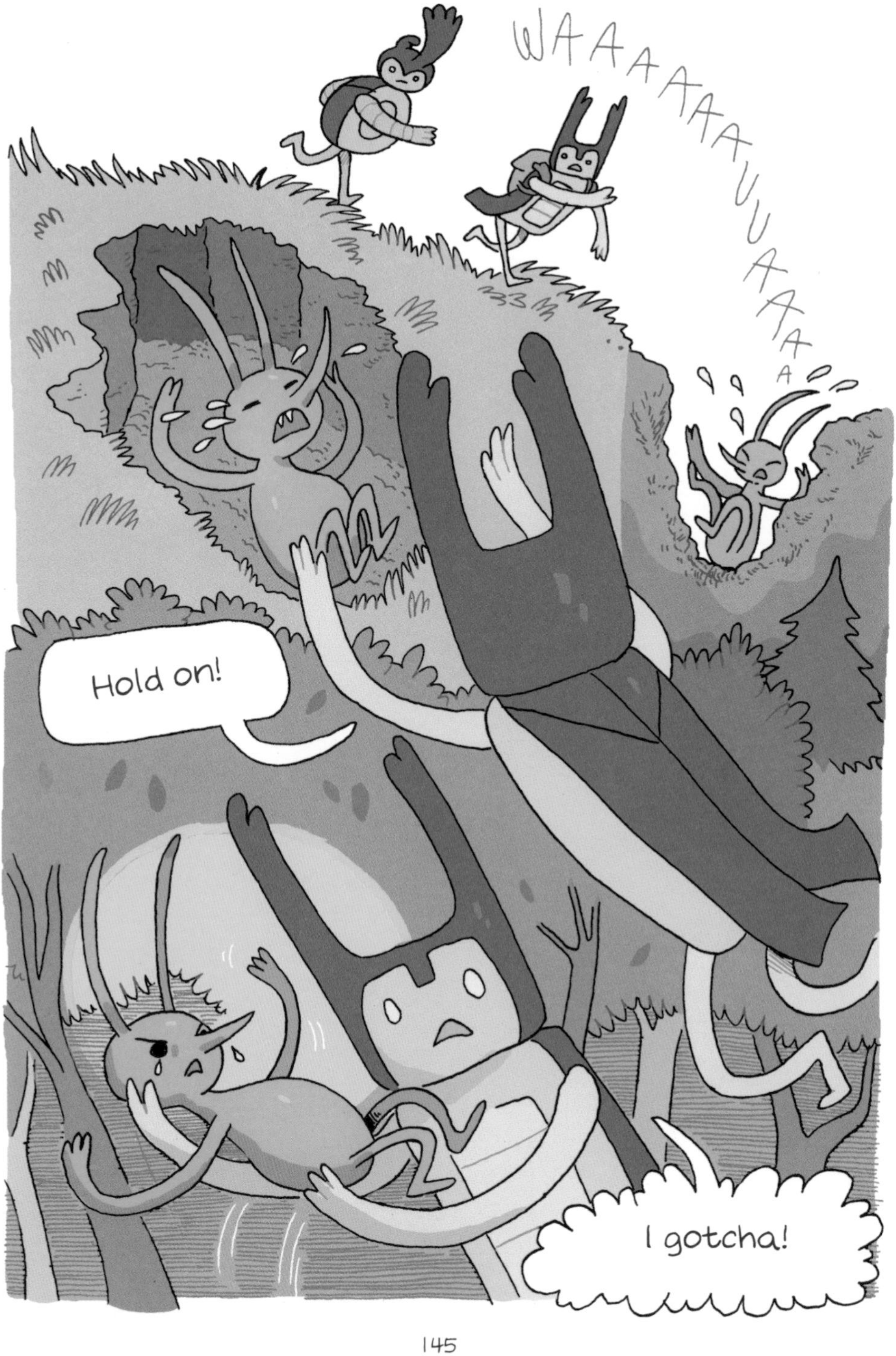
WAAAAAAUUAAAAA
Hold on!
I gotcha!

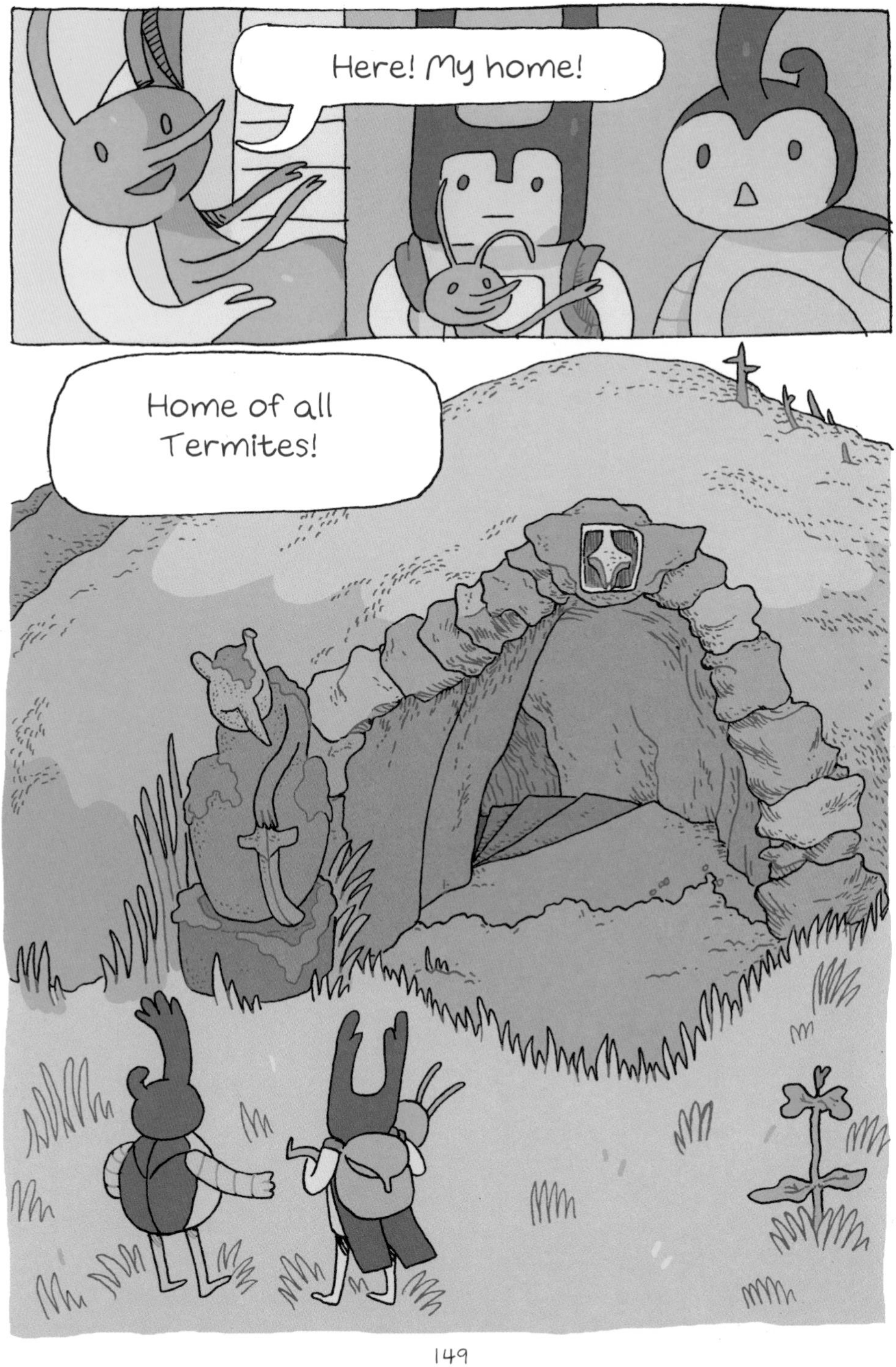
Here! My home!
Home of all Termites!

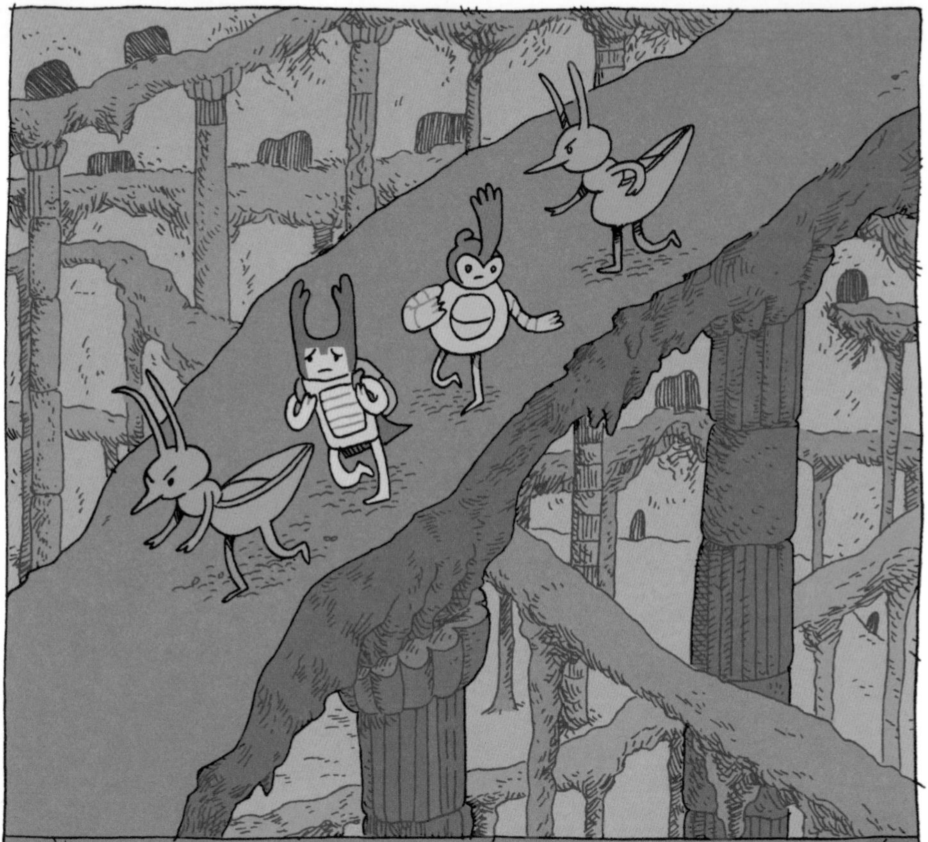

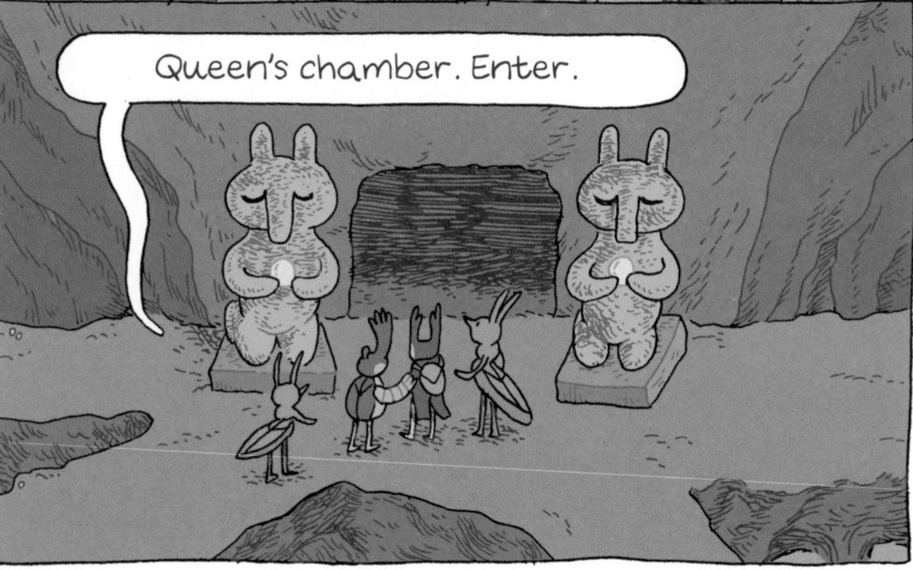
Queen's chamber. Enter.

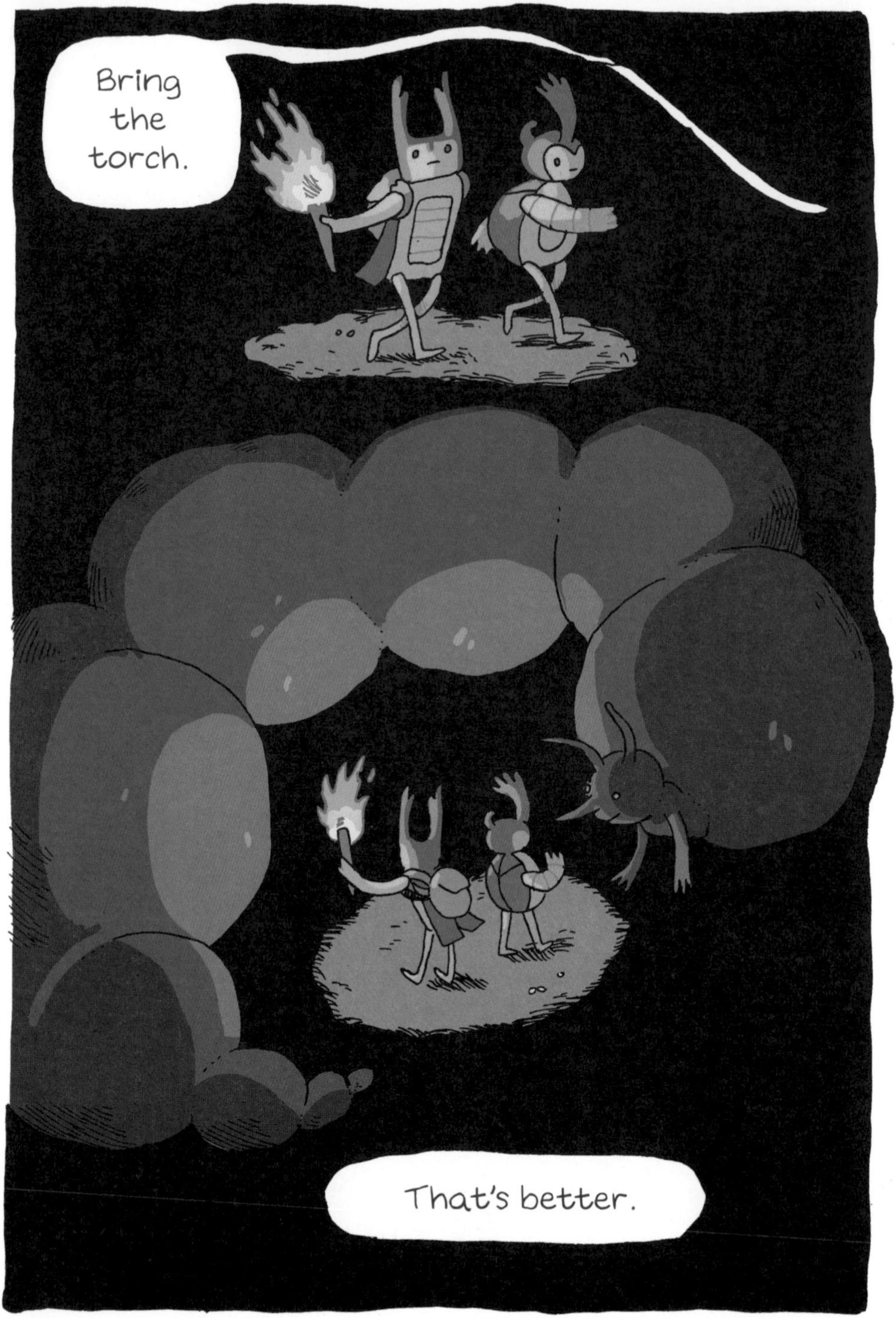
Bring the torch.
That's better.

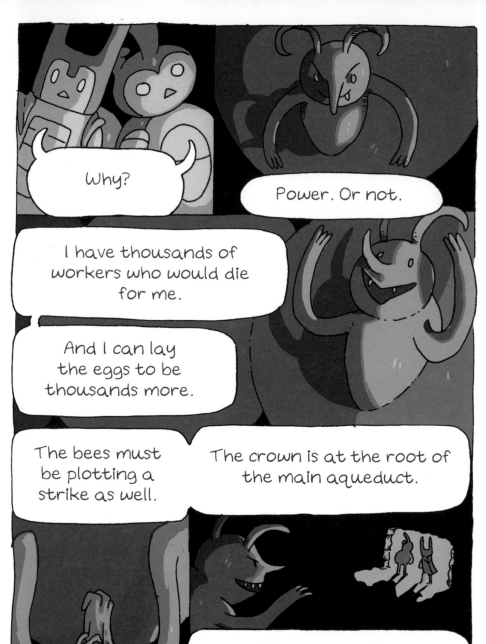

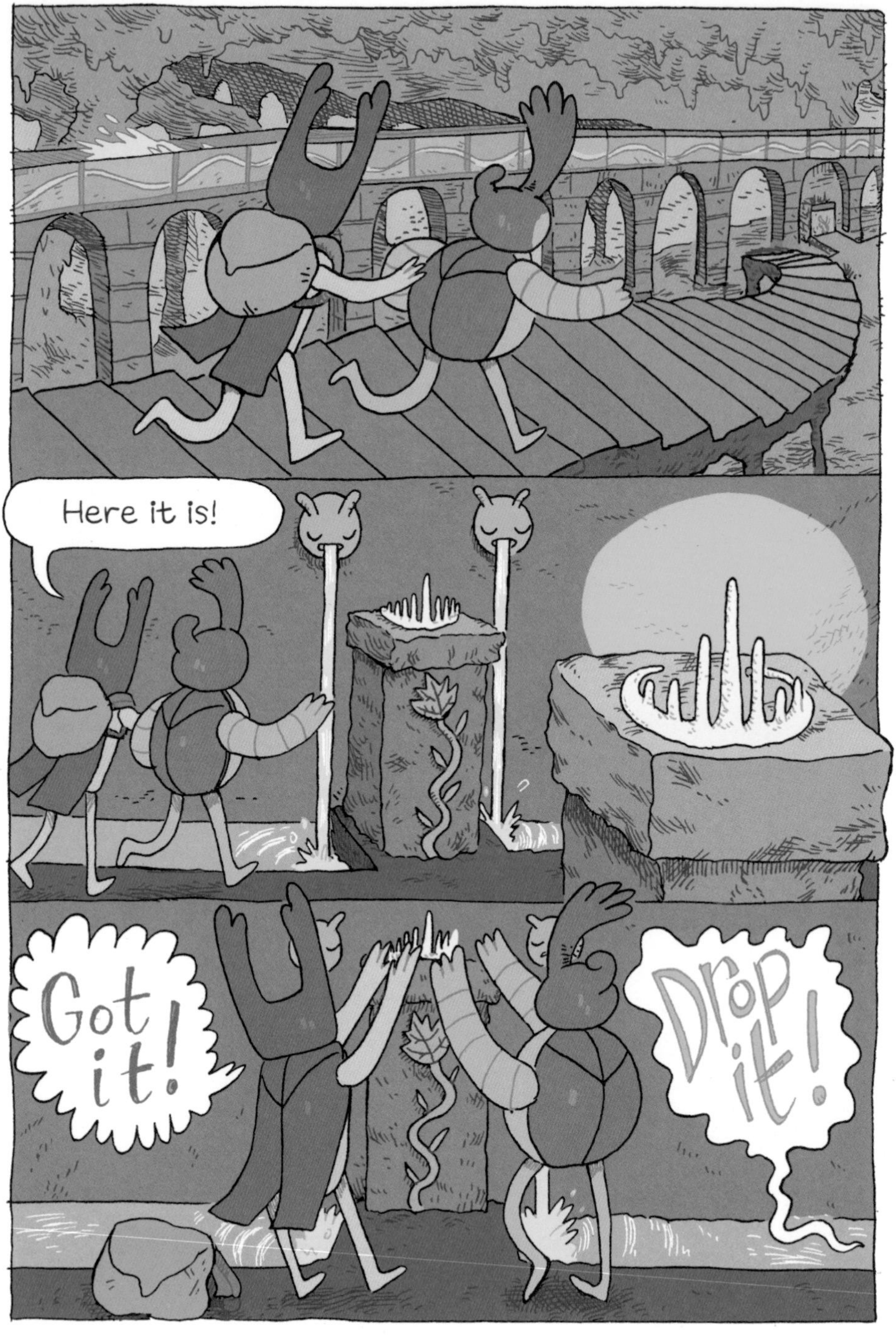

Here it is!
Got it!
Drop it!

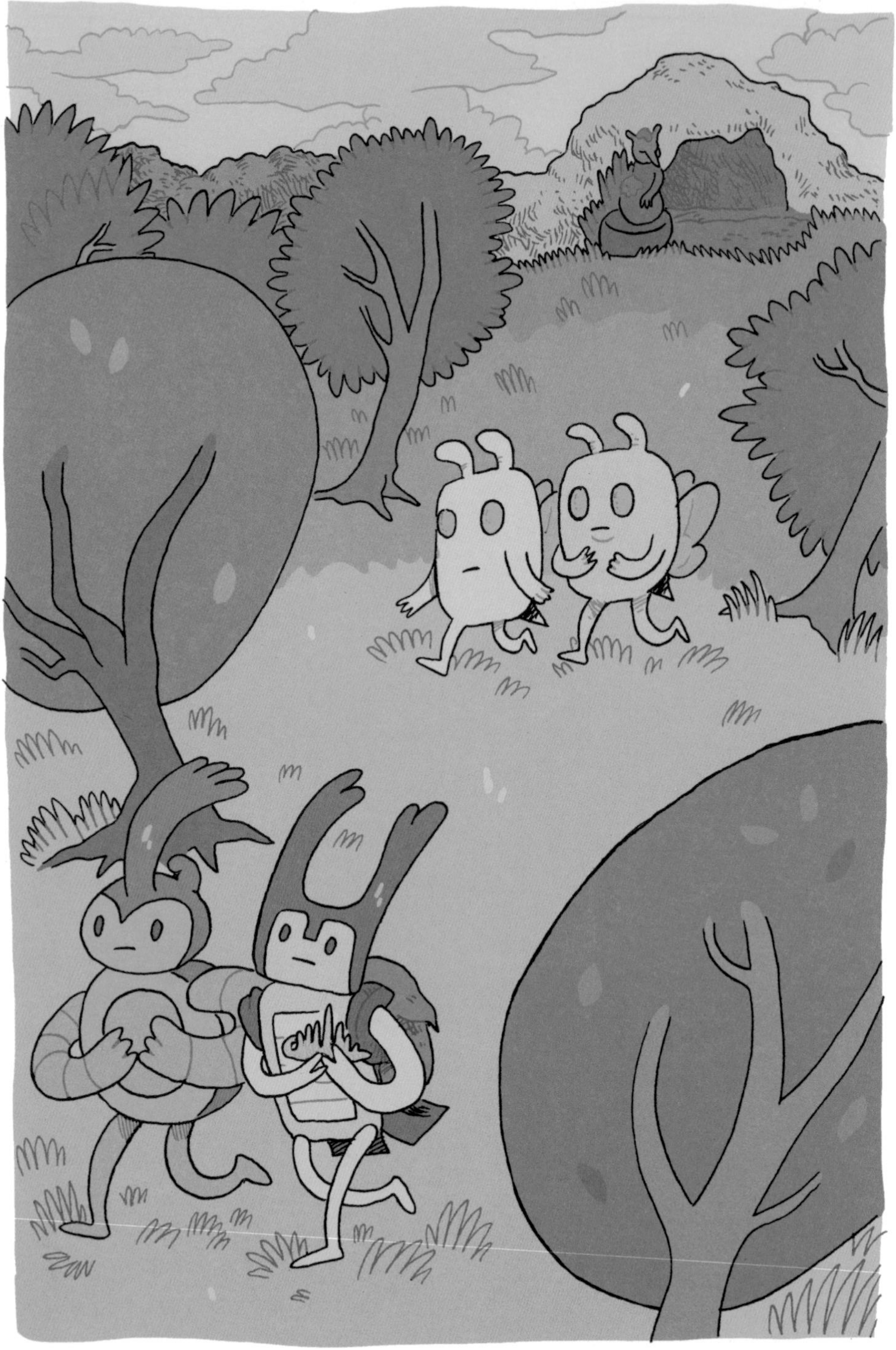

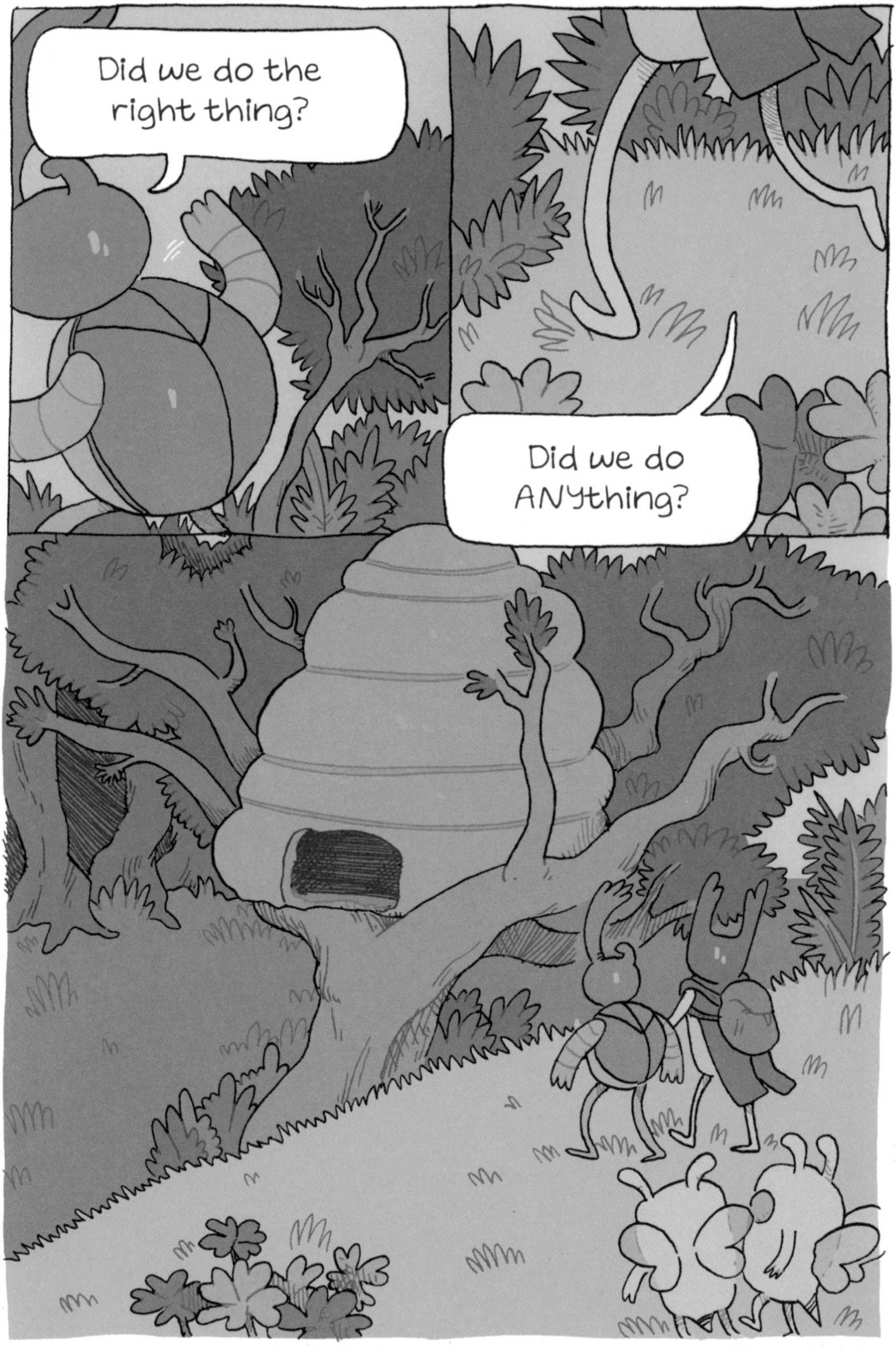
Did we do the right thing?
Did we do ANYthing?

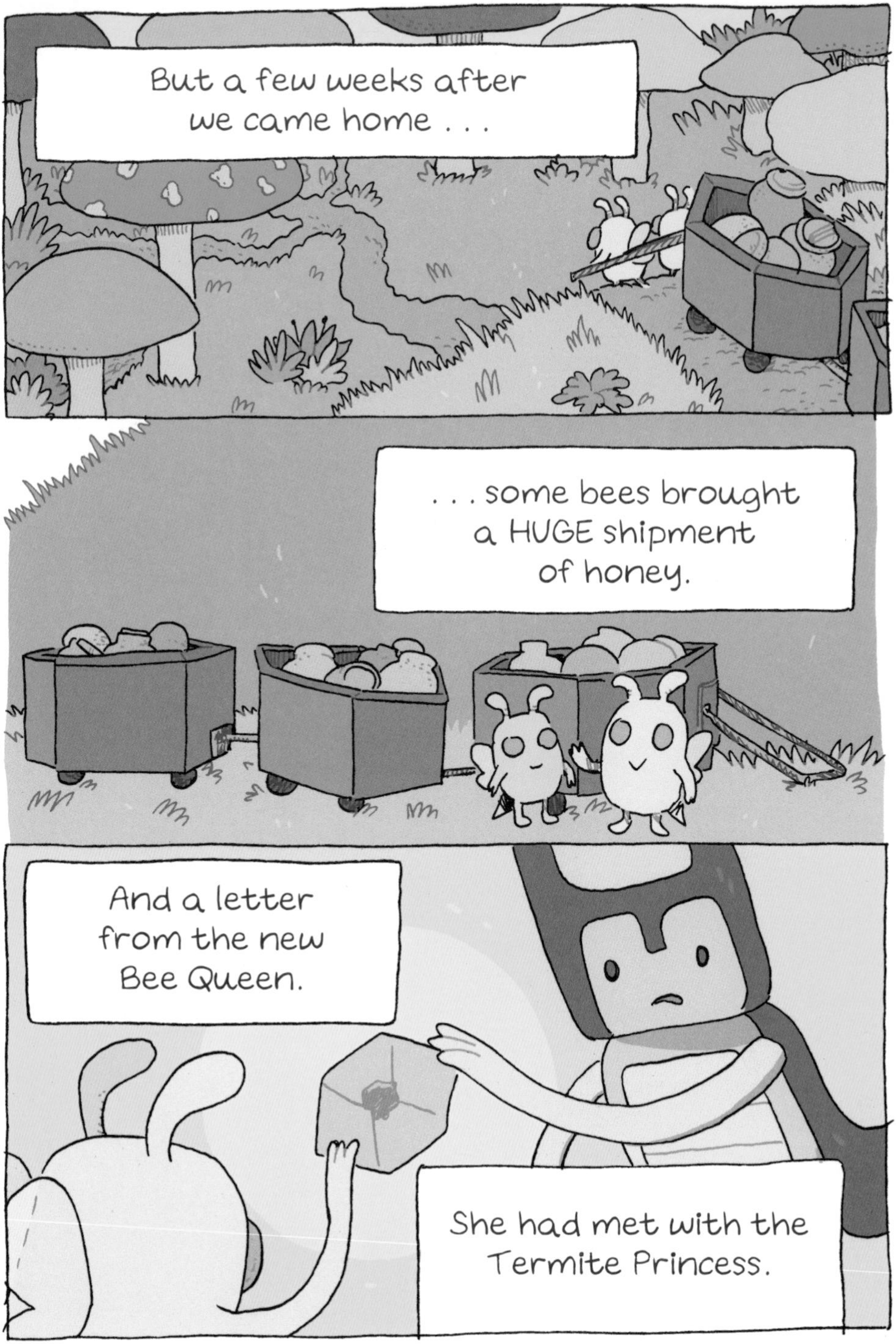
But a few weeks after we came home . . .
. . . some bees brought a HUGE shipment of honey.
And a letter from the new Bee Queen.
She had met with the Termite Princess.

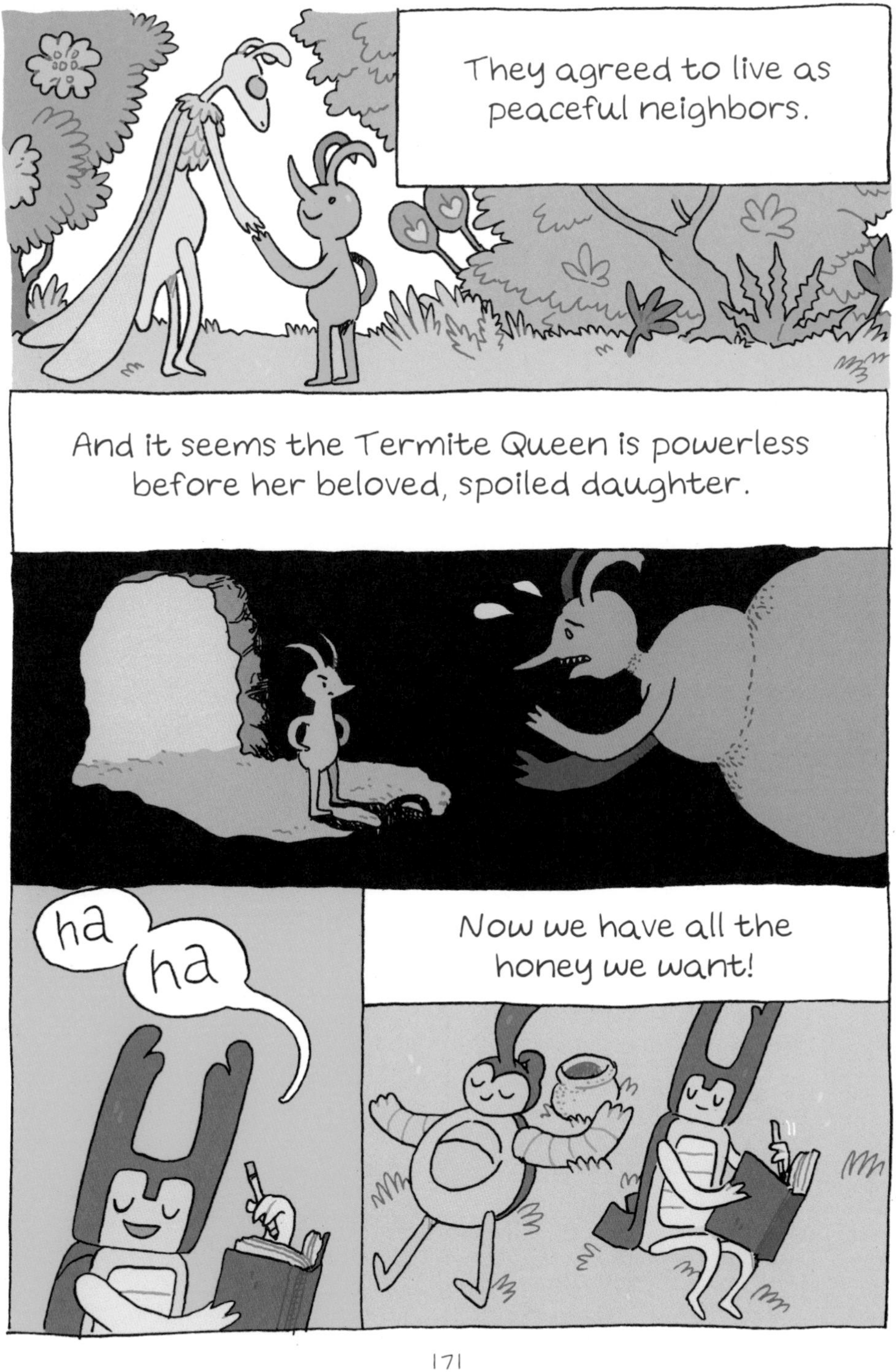
They agreed to live as peaceful neighbors.
And it seems the Termite Queen is powerless before her beloved, spoiled daughter.
ha
ha
Now we have all the honey we want!

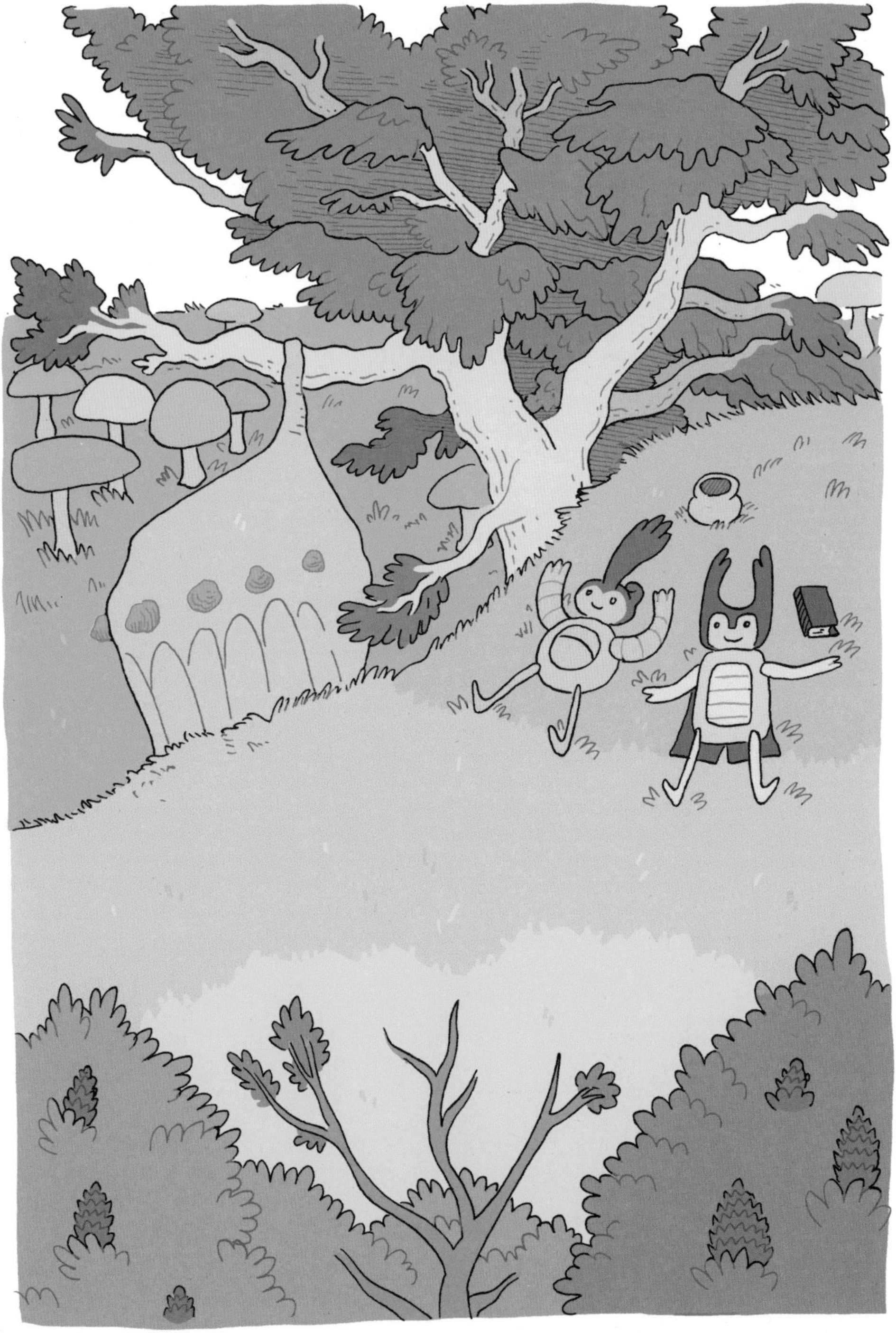

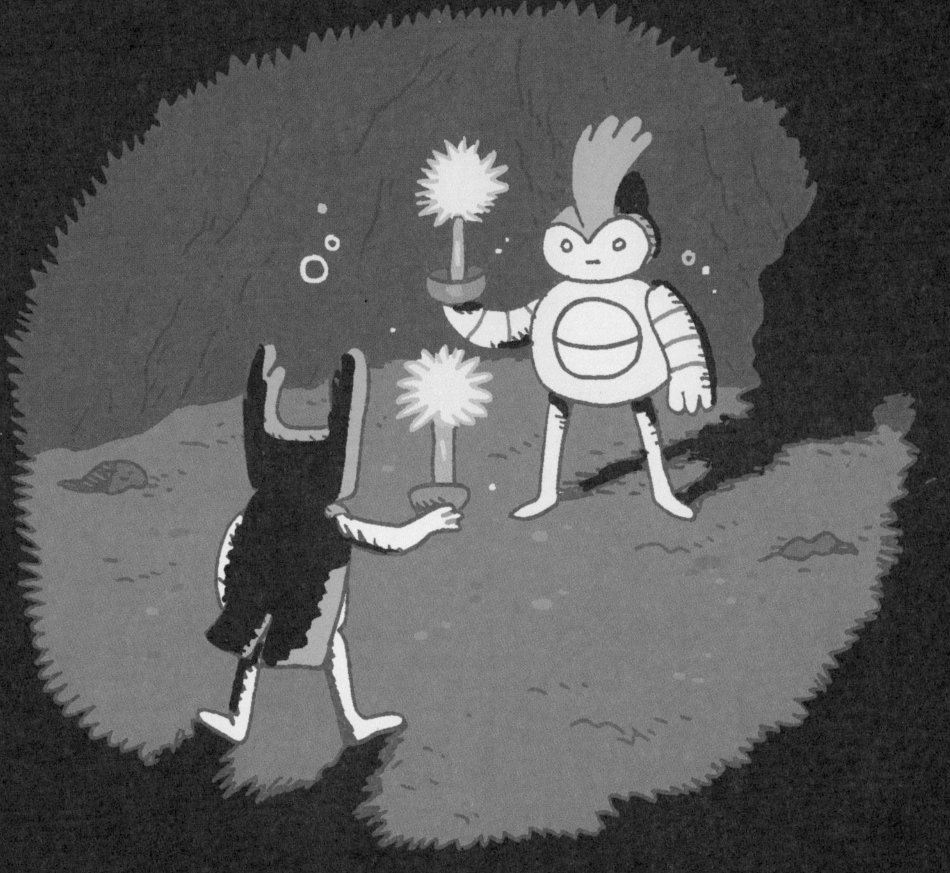

In the Dark

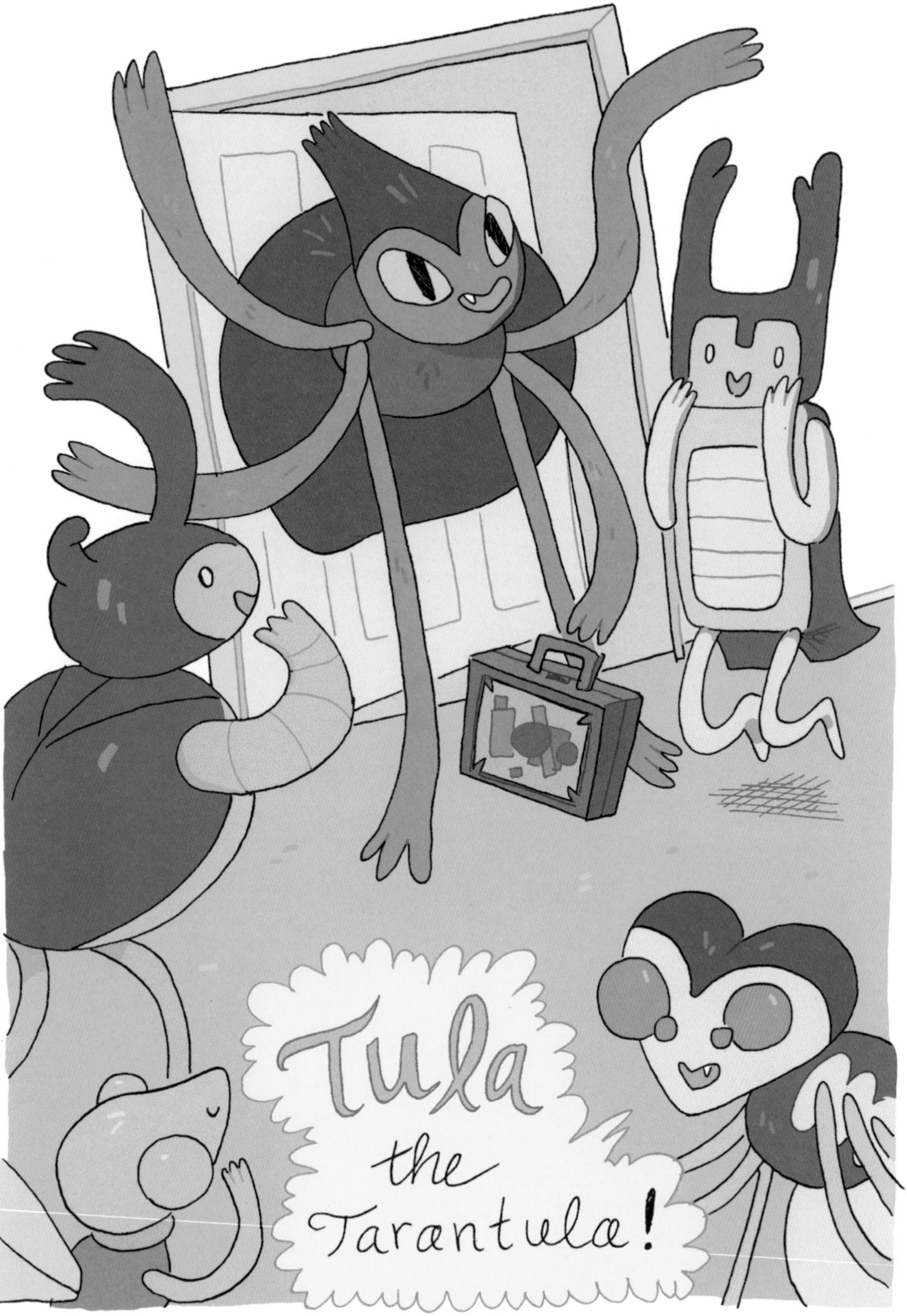
Tula the Tarantula!

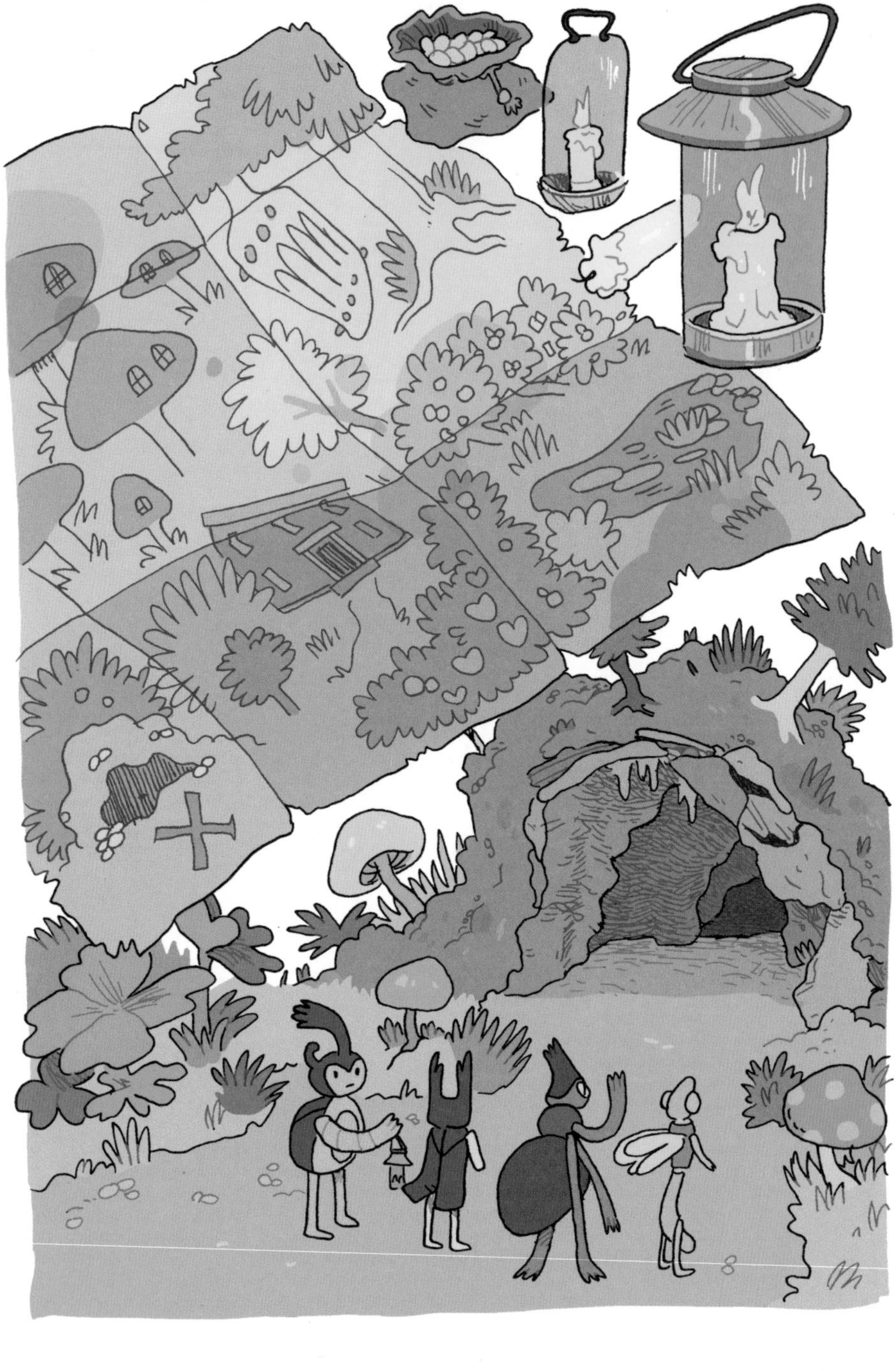

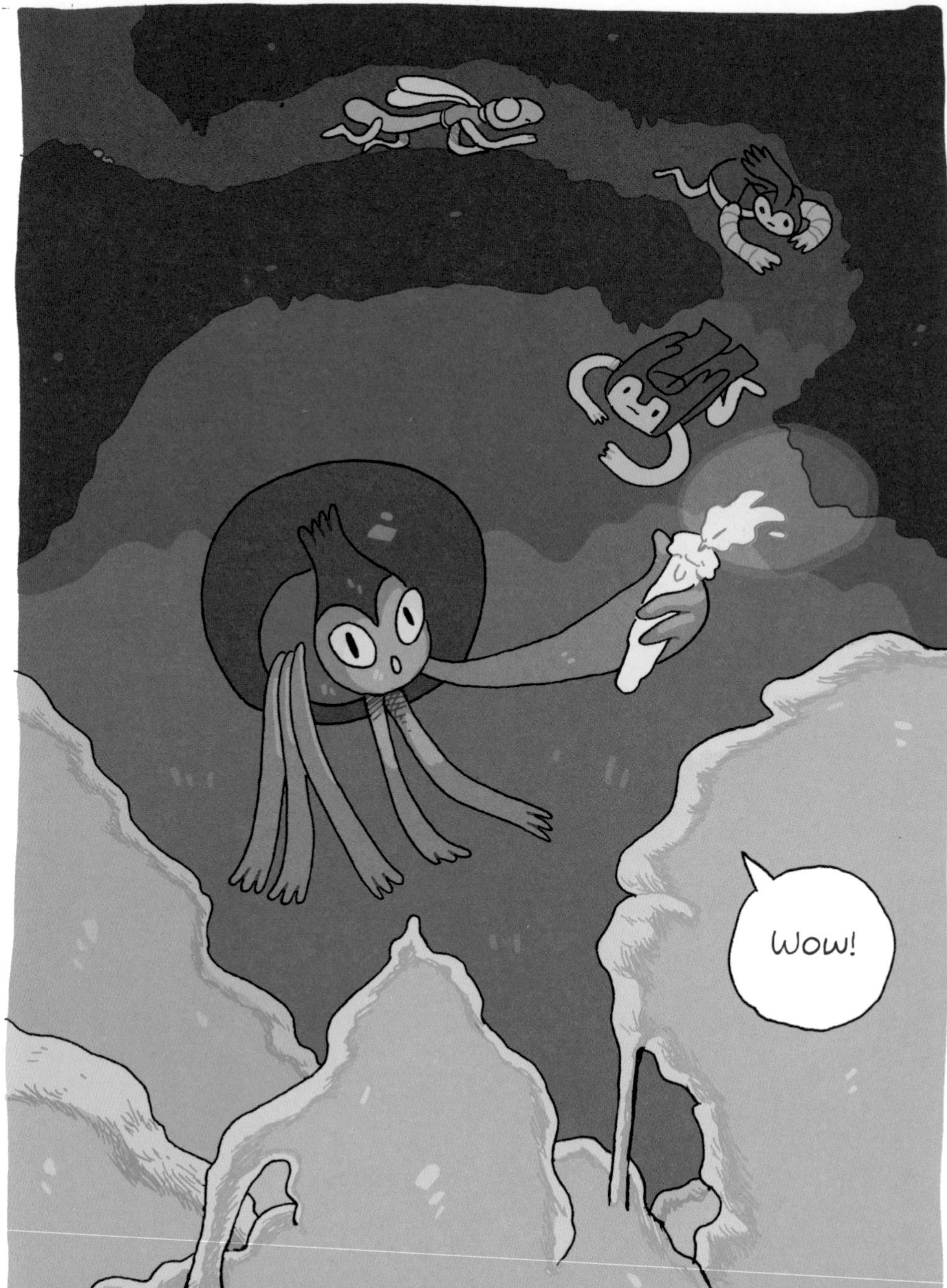
WOW!

190

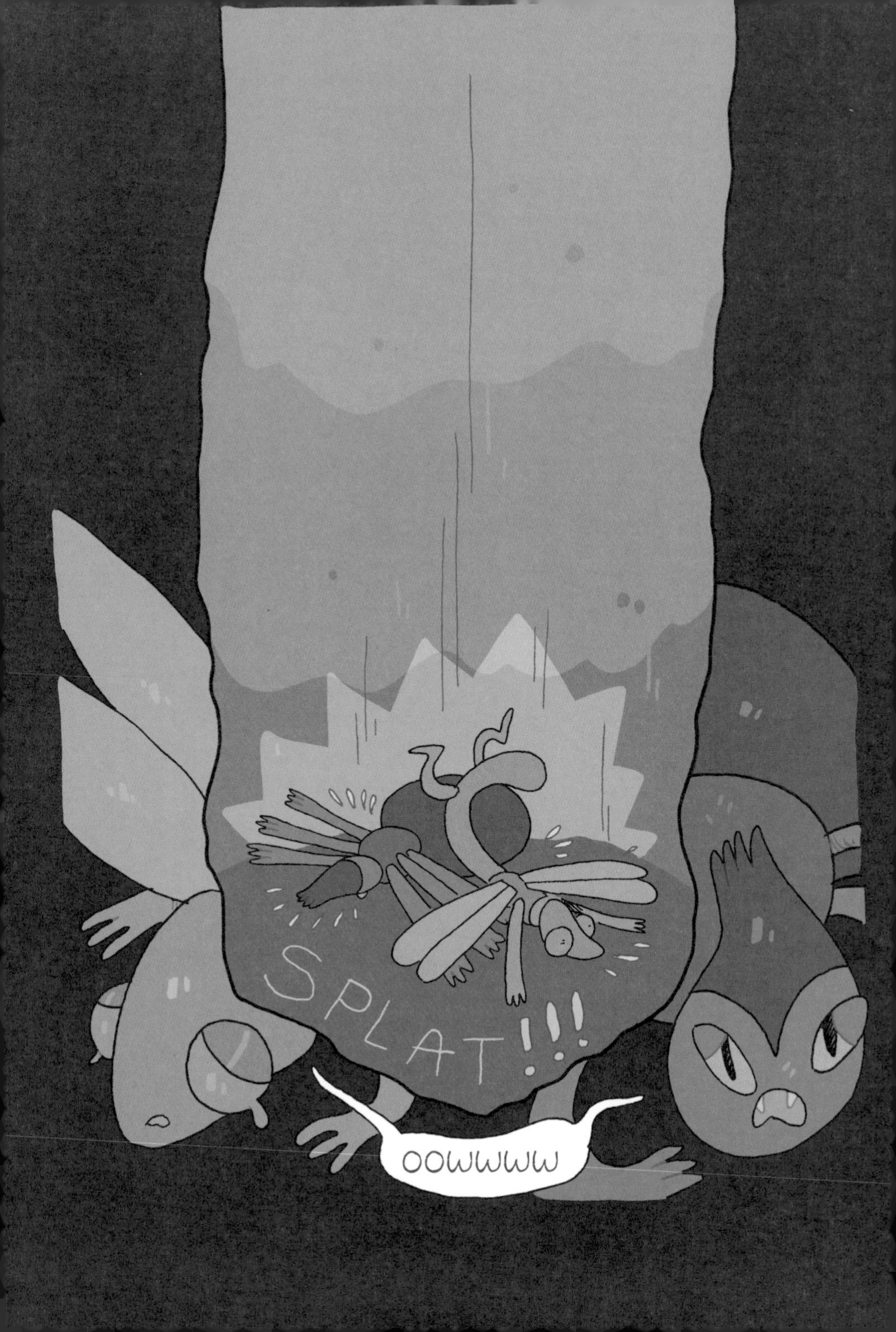
SPLAT!!!
OOWWWW

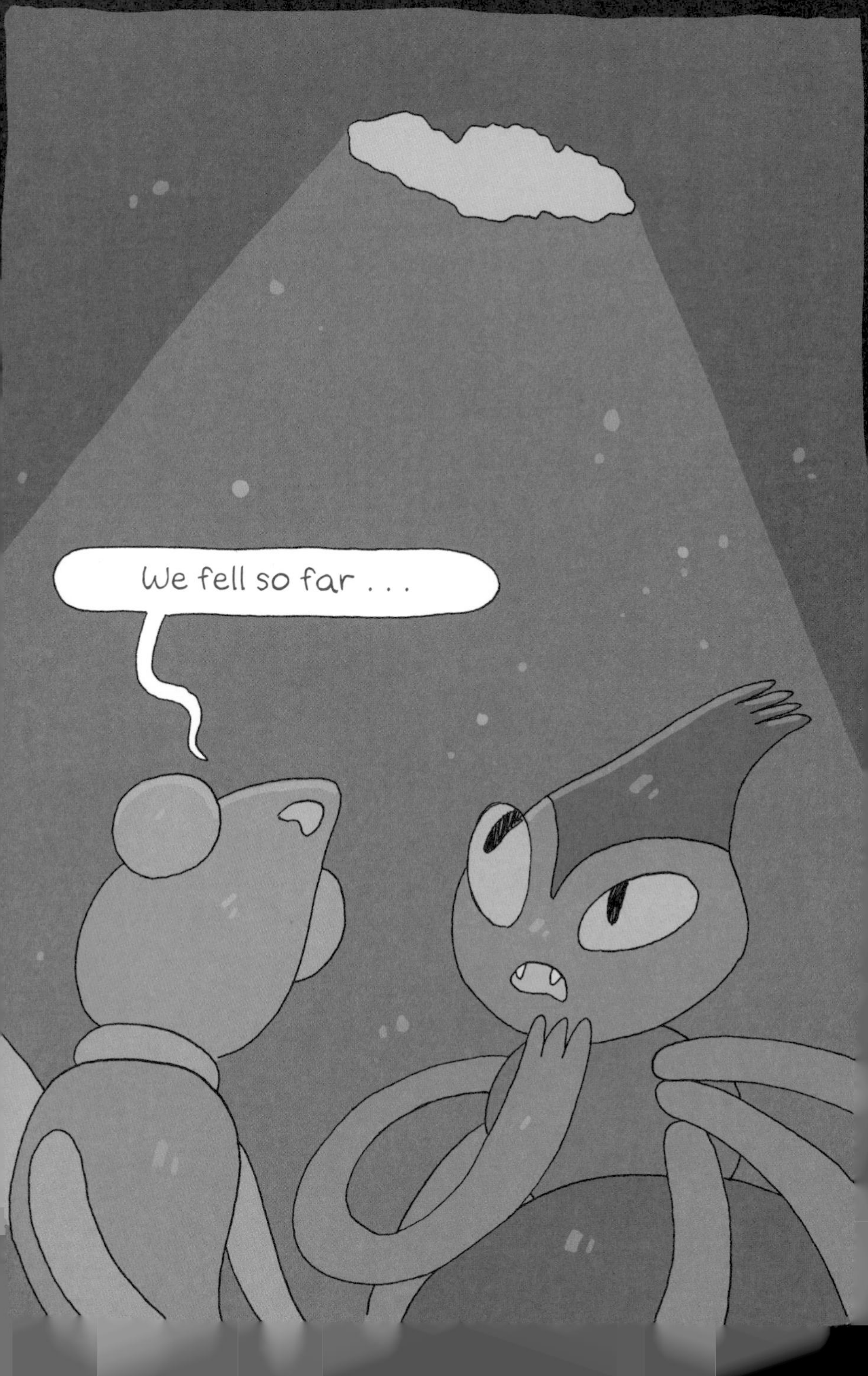
We fell so far . . .

the future is hopeless
I'm powerless
my soul is a rotten berry
everything is ending

the world is warm
my life is bright
I can feel my power
everything is limitless

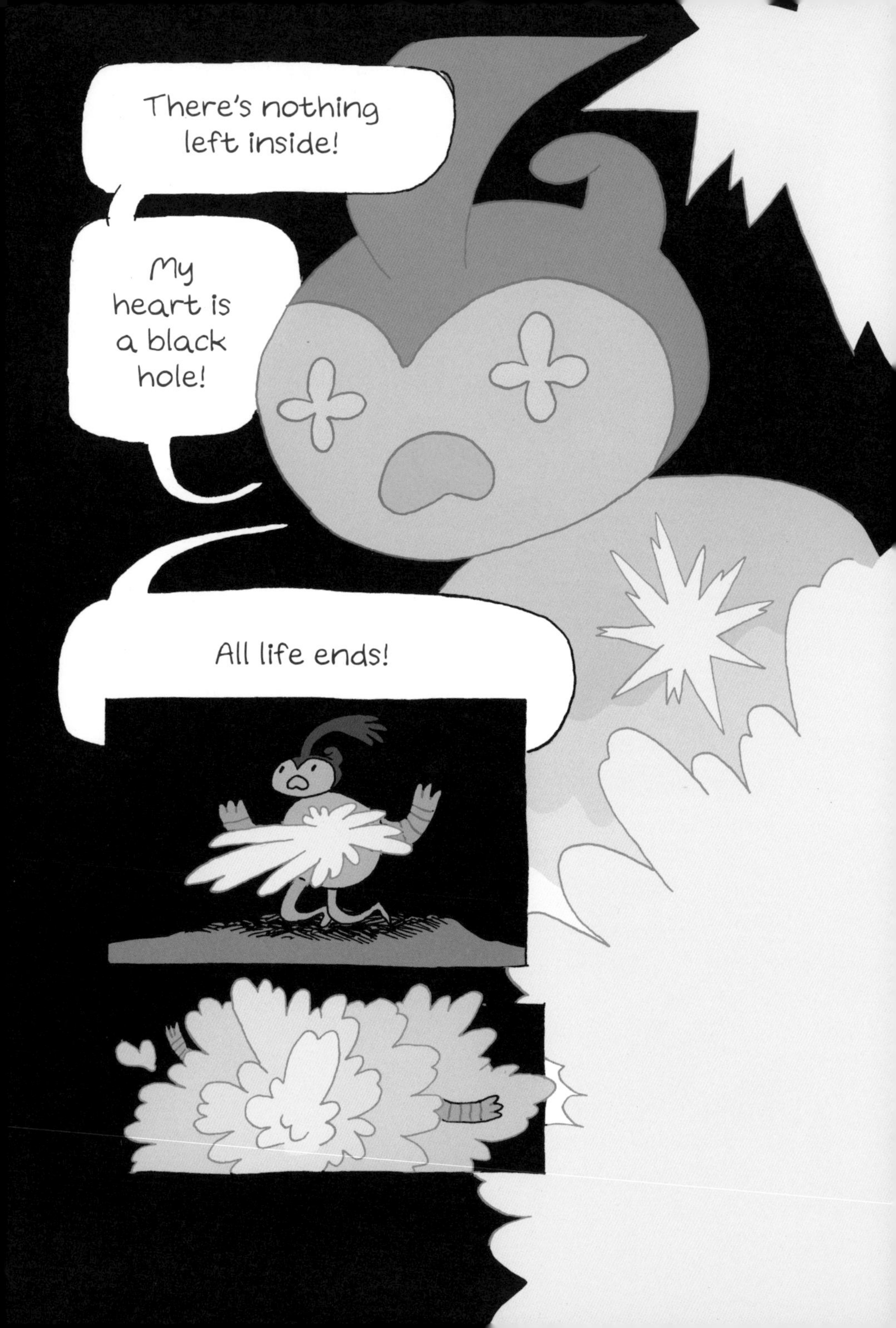
There's nothing left inside!
My heart is a black hole!
All life ends!

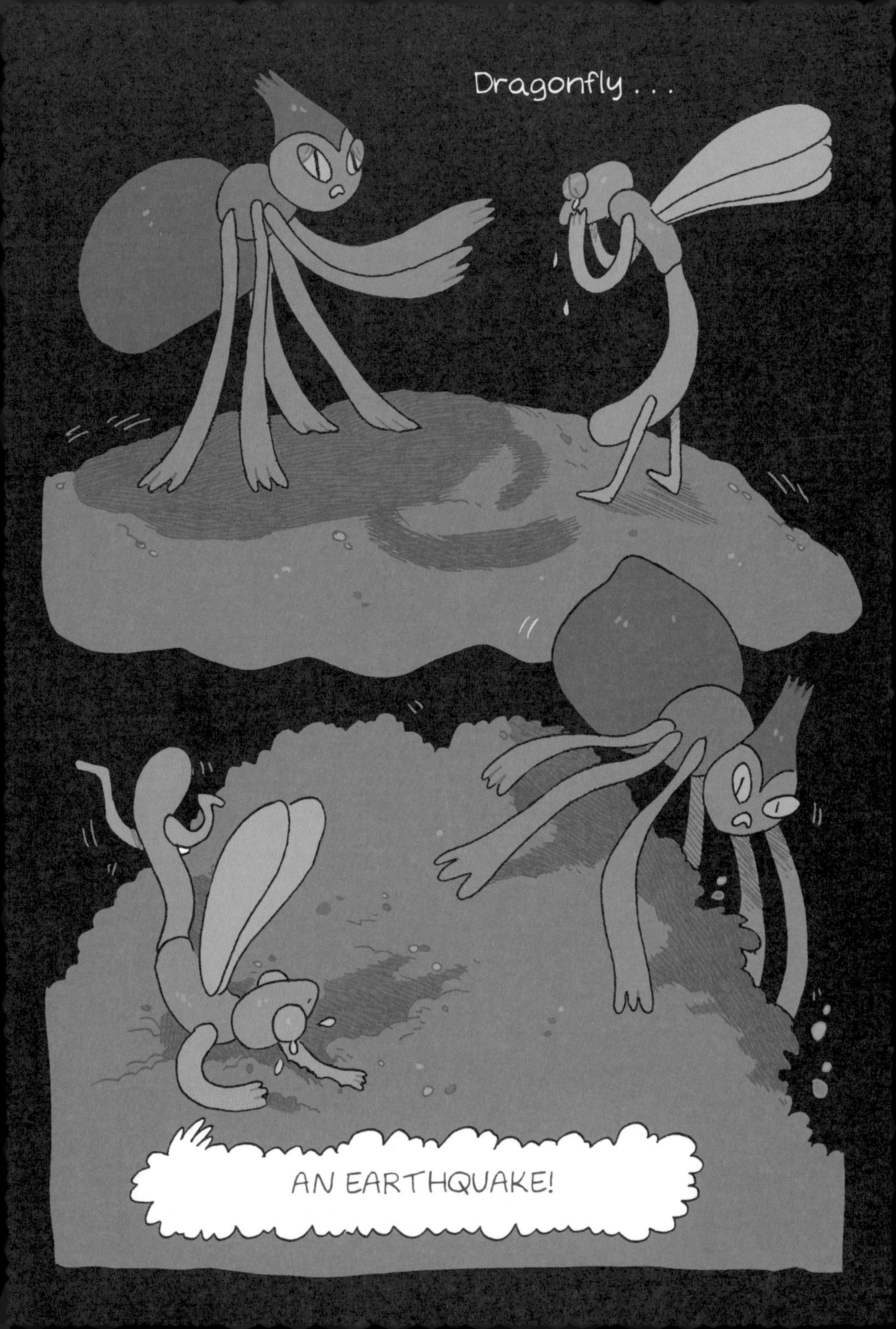
Dragonfly . . .
AN EARTHQUAKE!

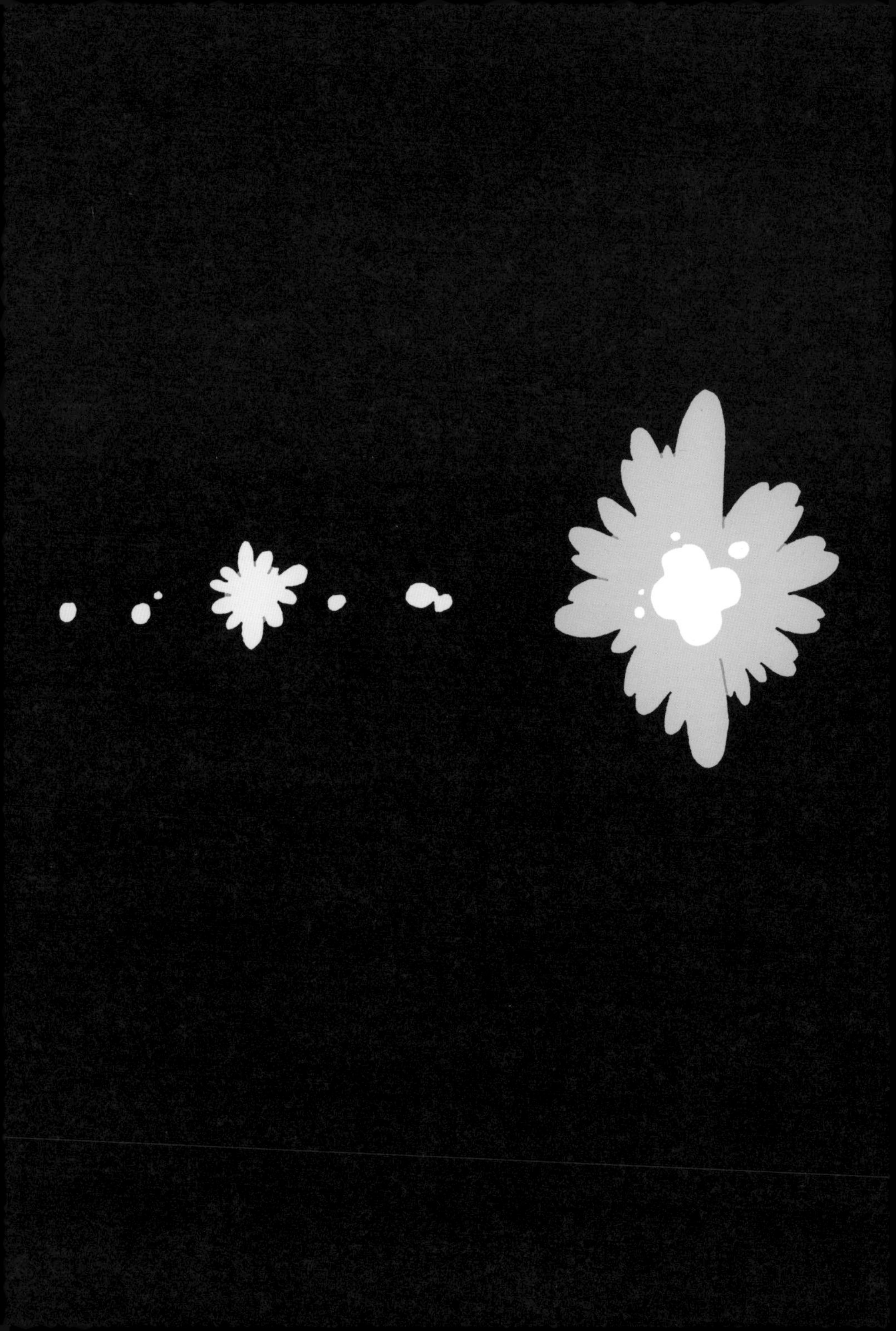

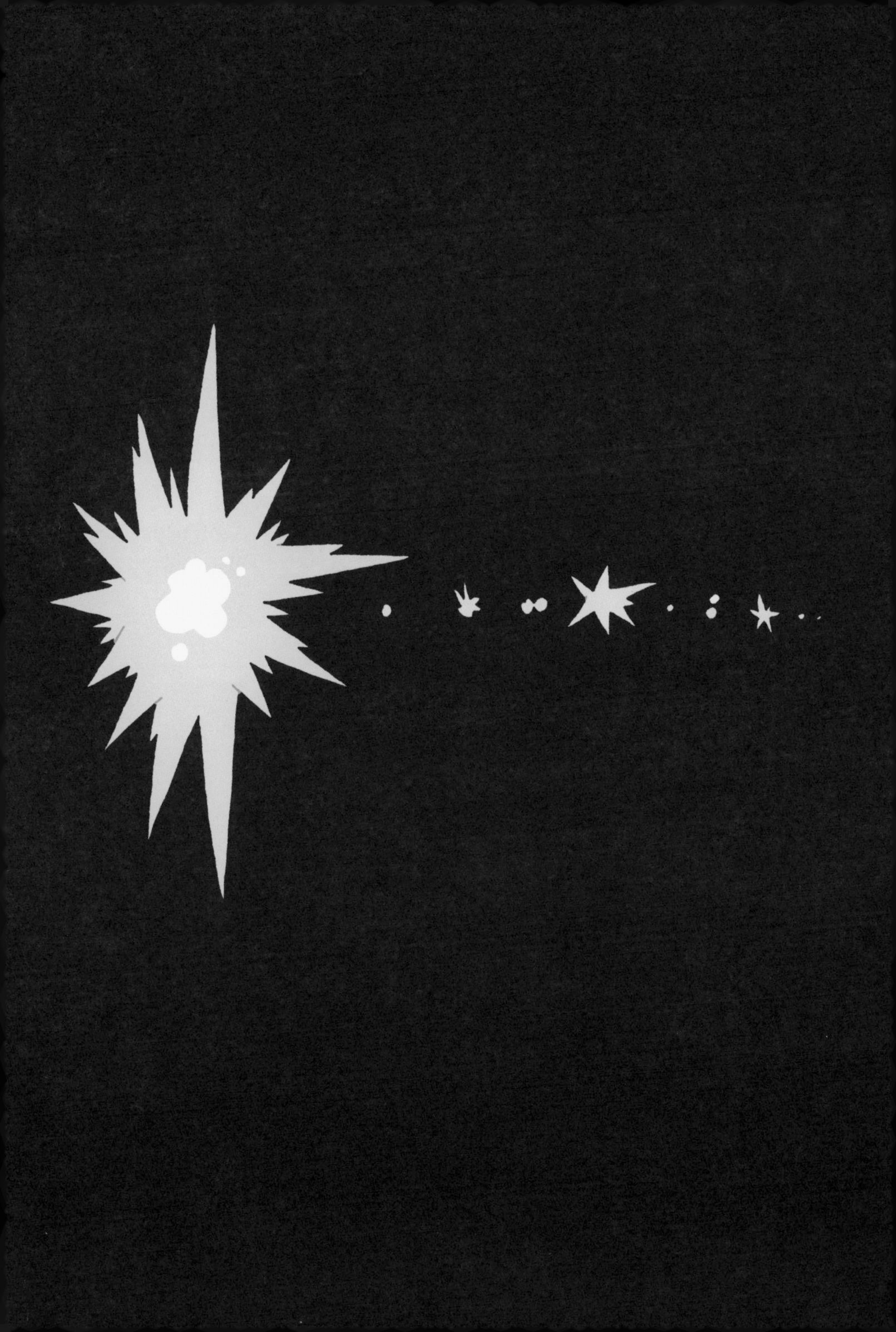

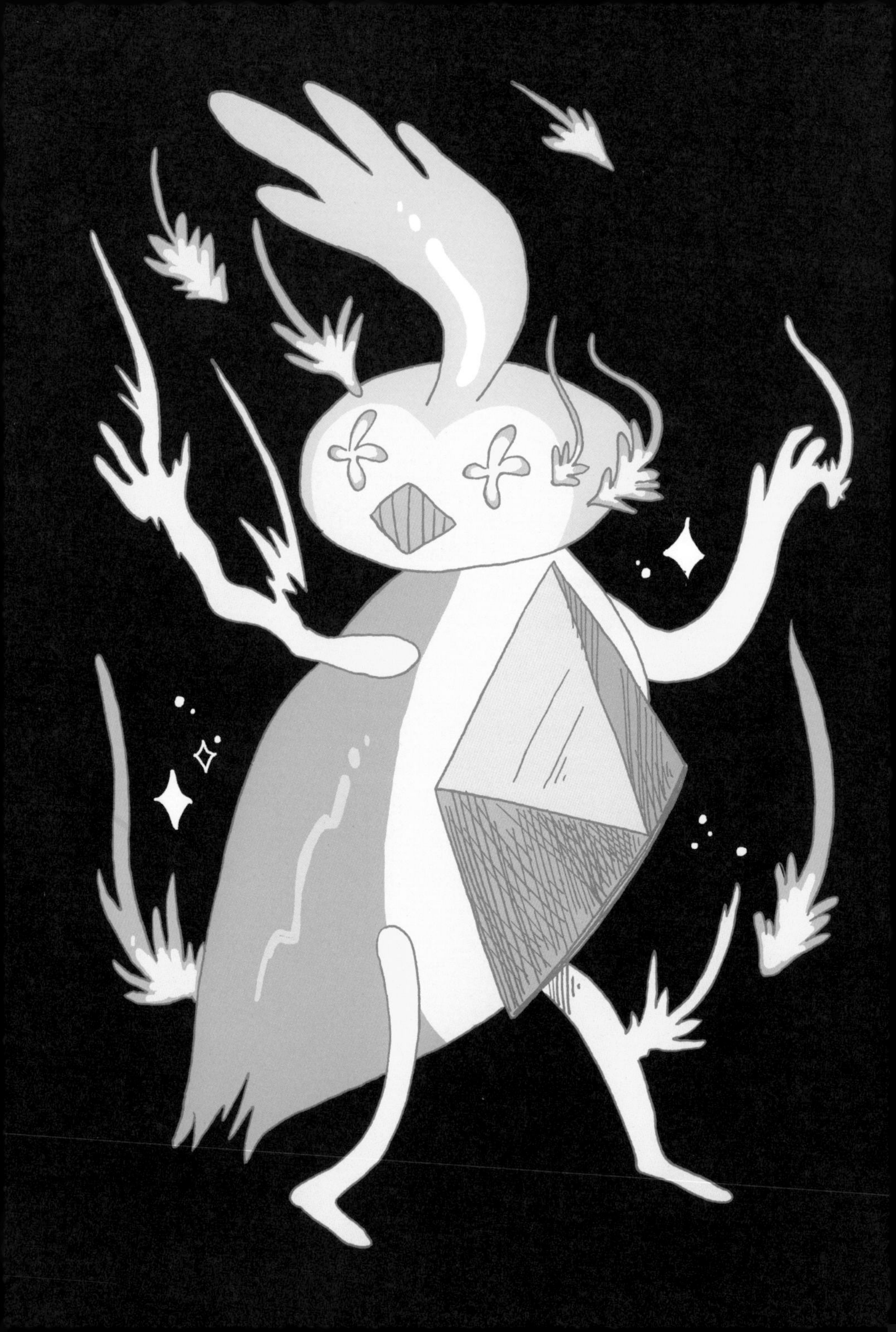

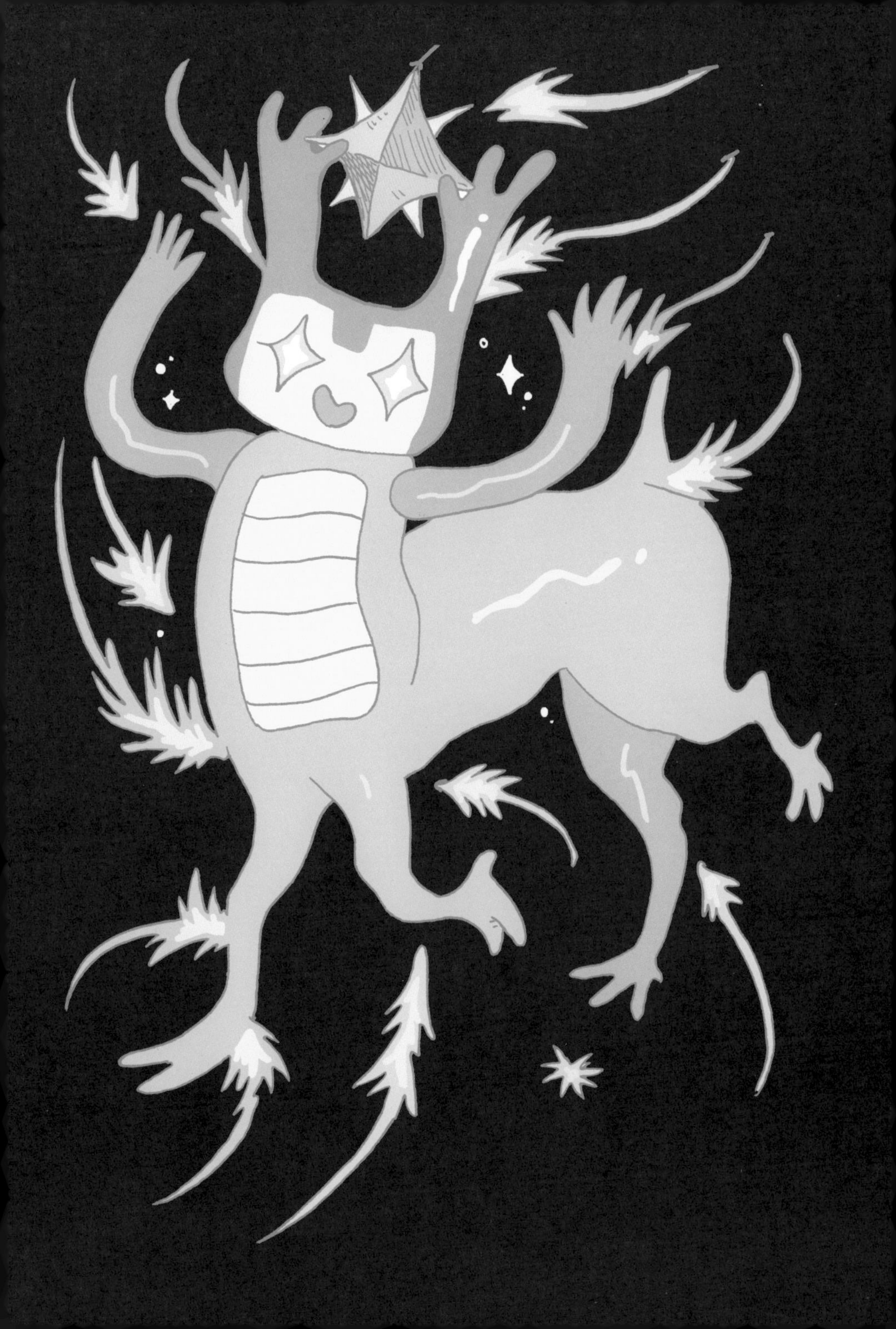

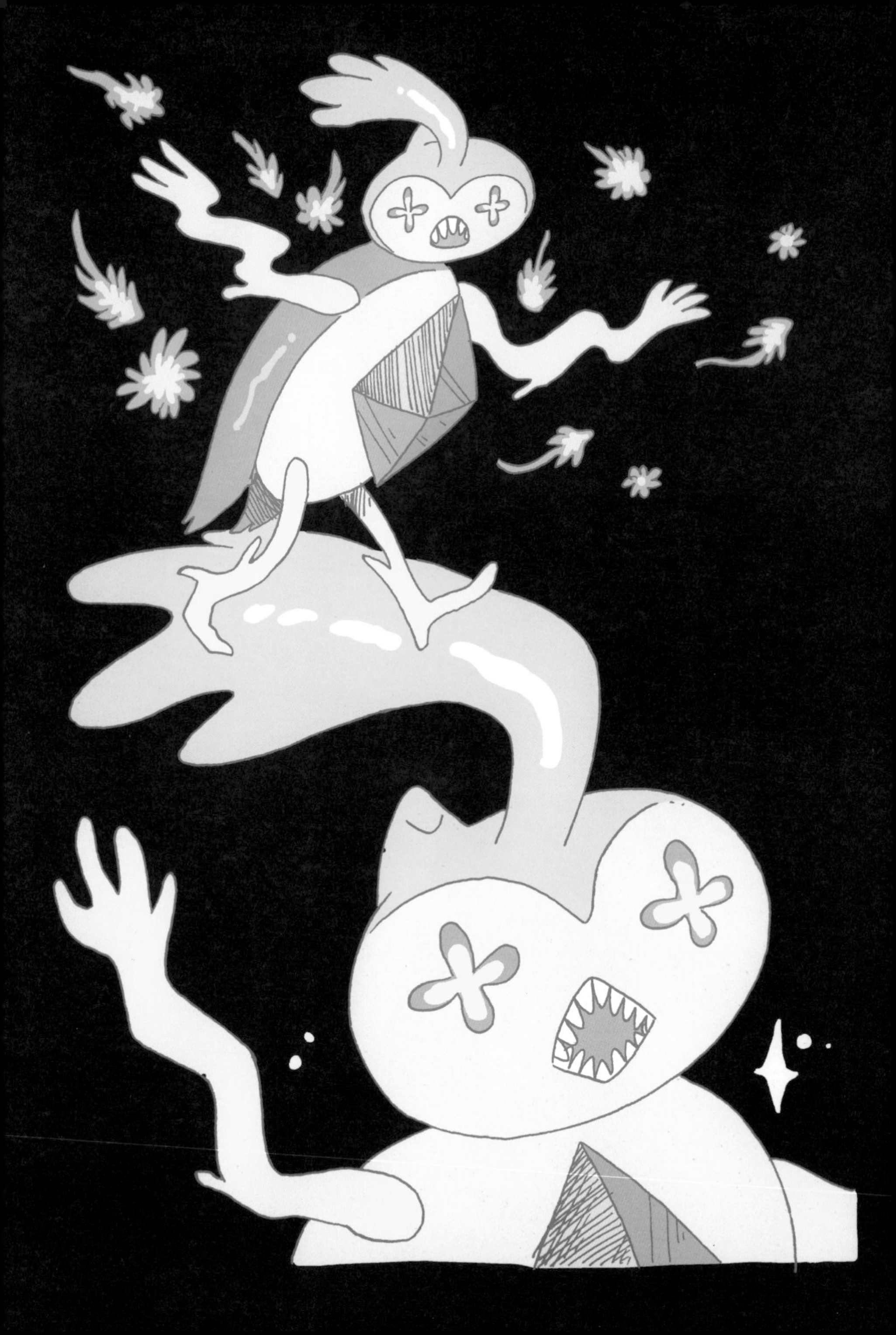

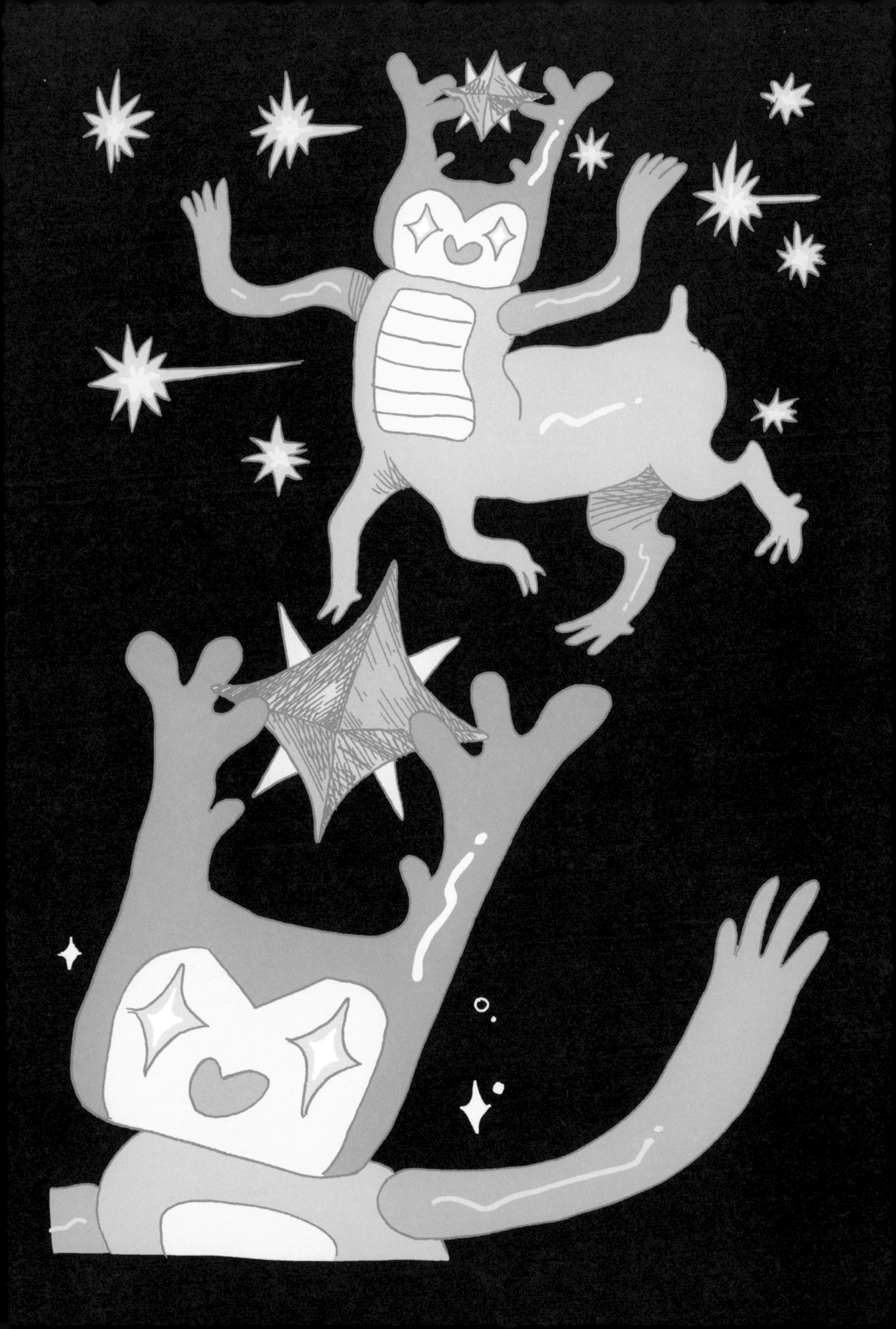

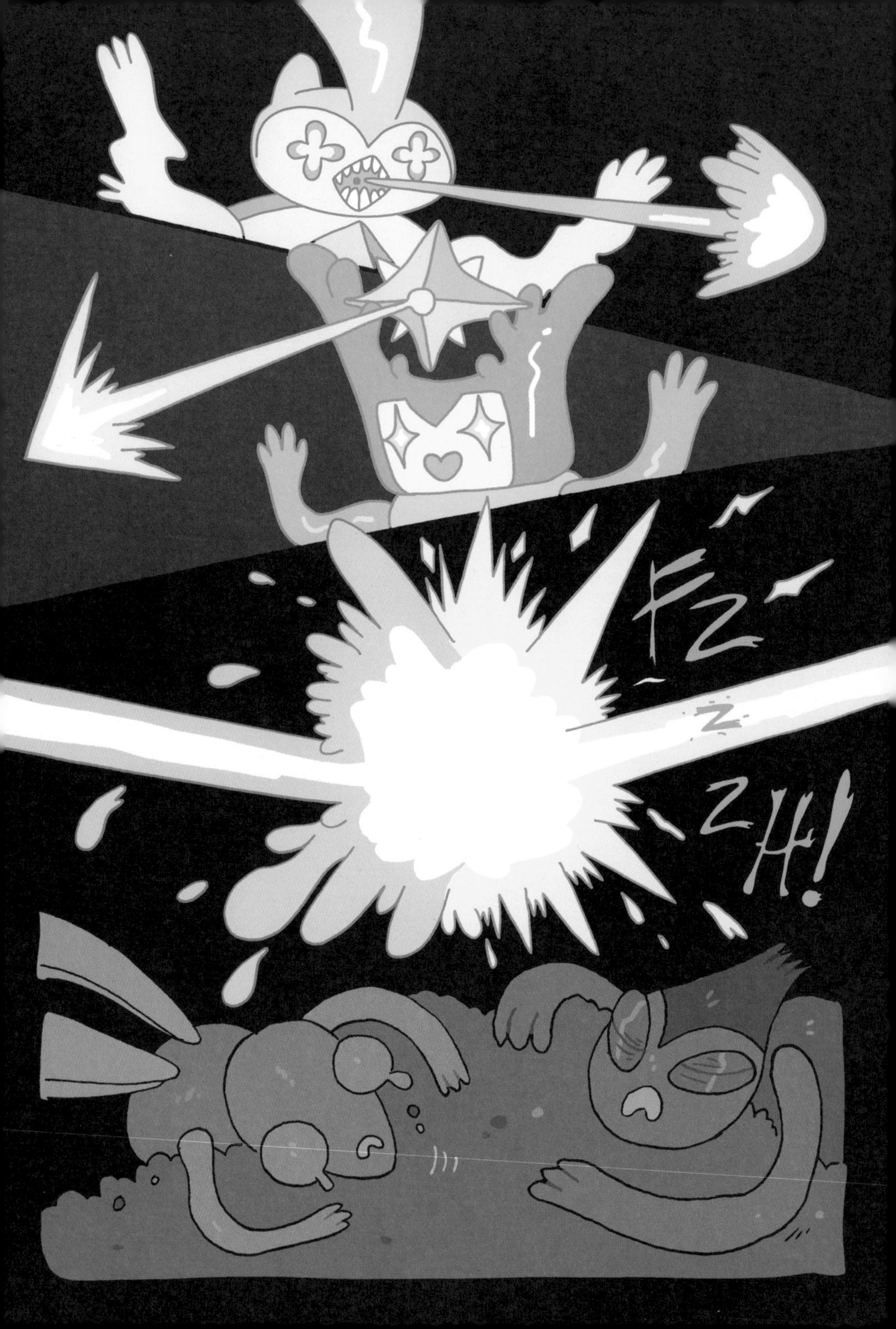
FZZZH!

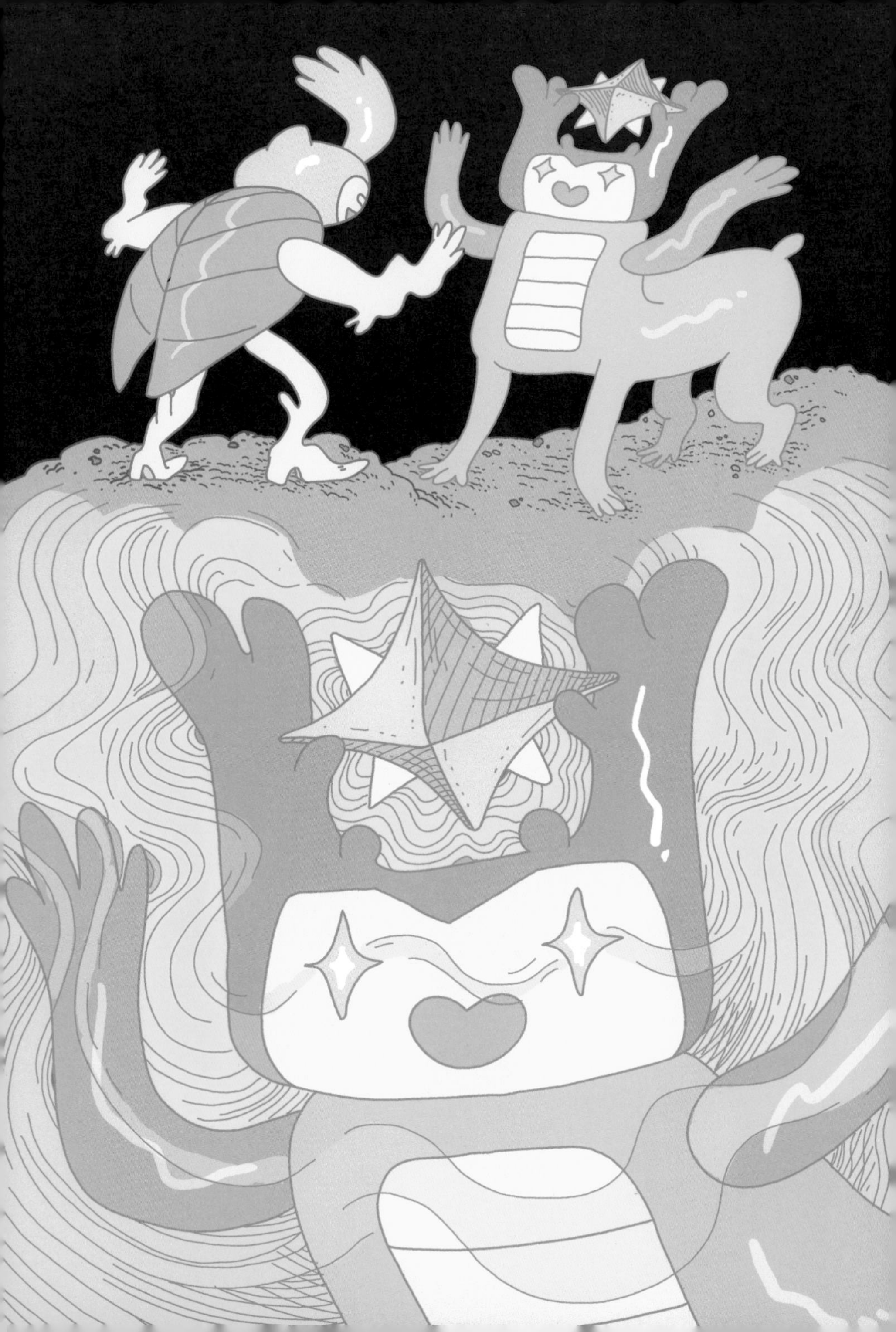

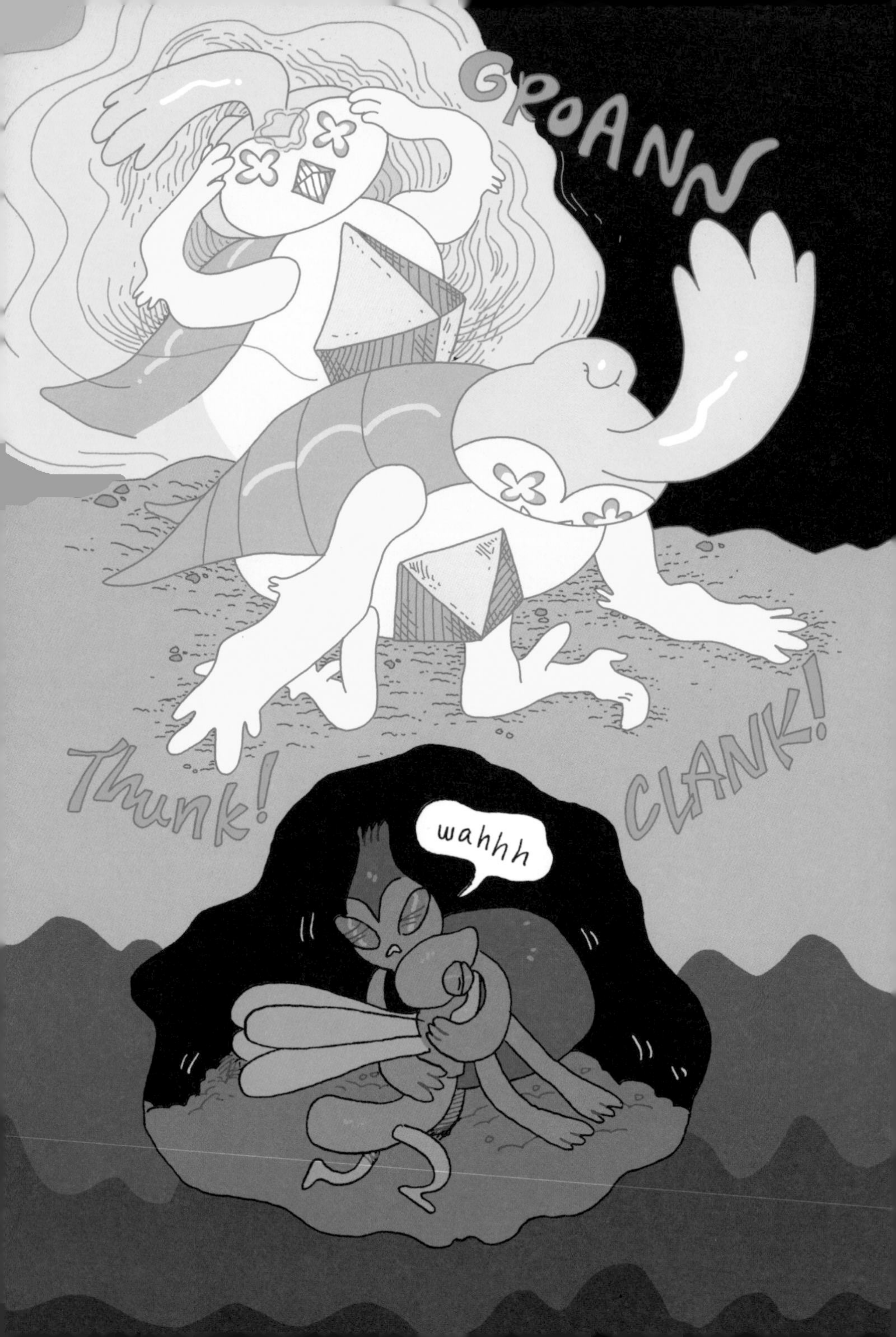
GROANN
Thunk!
CLANK!
wahhh

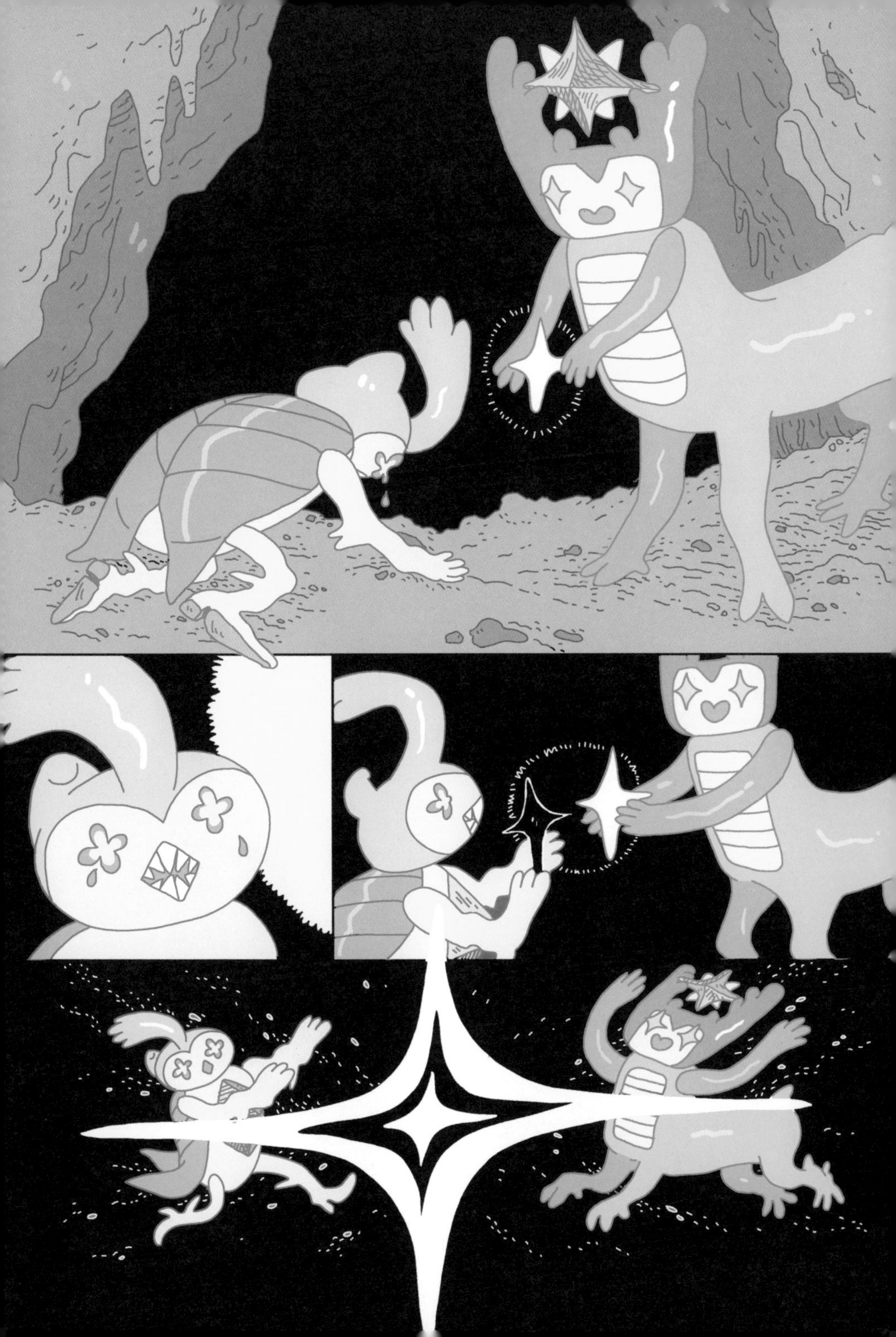

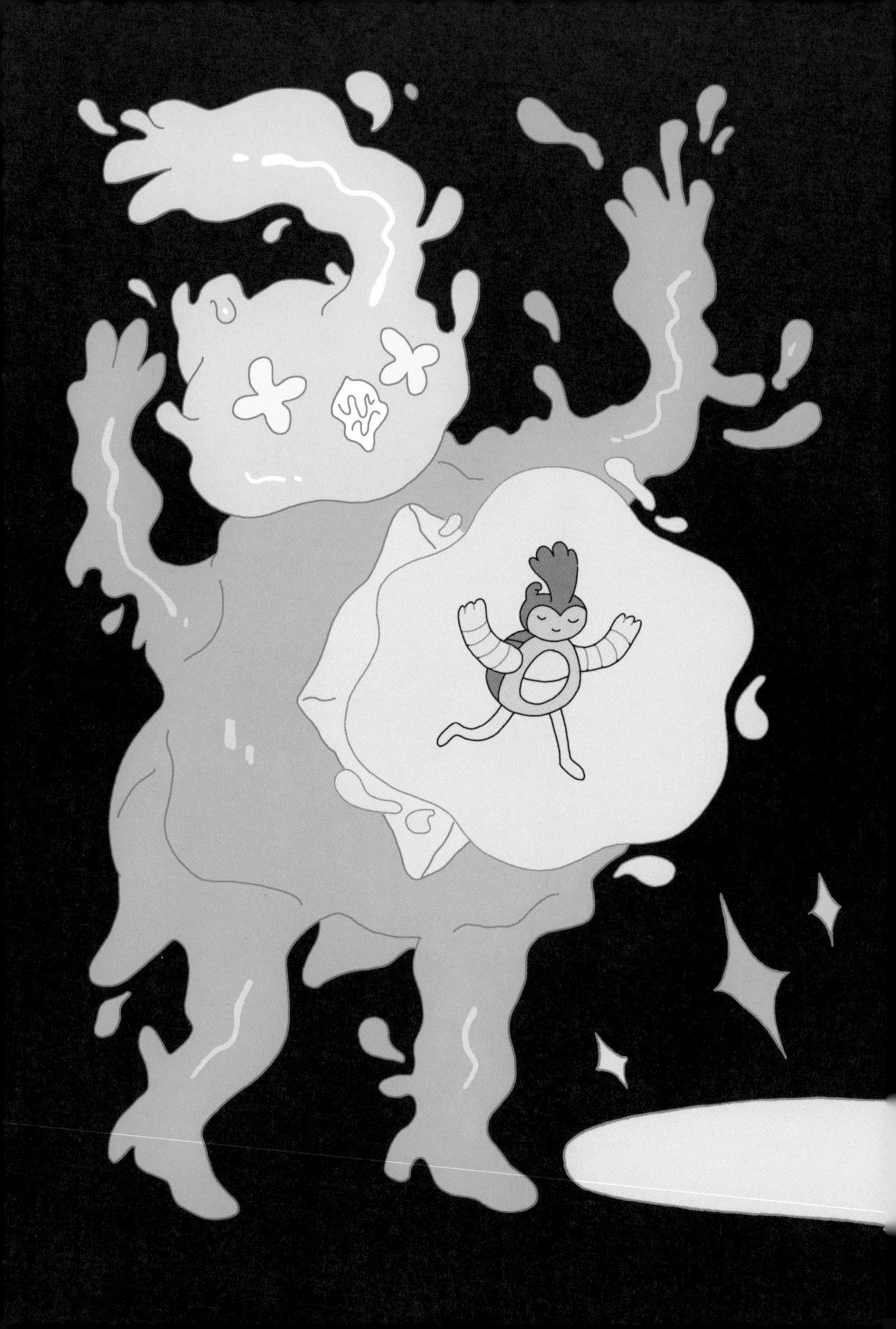

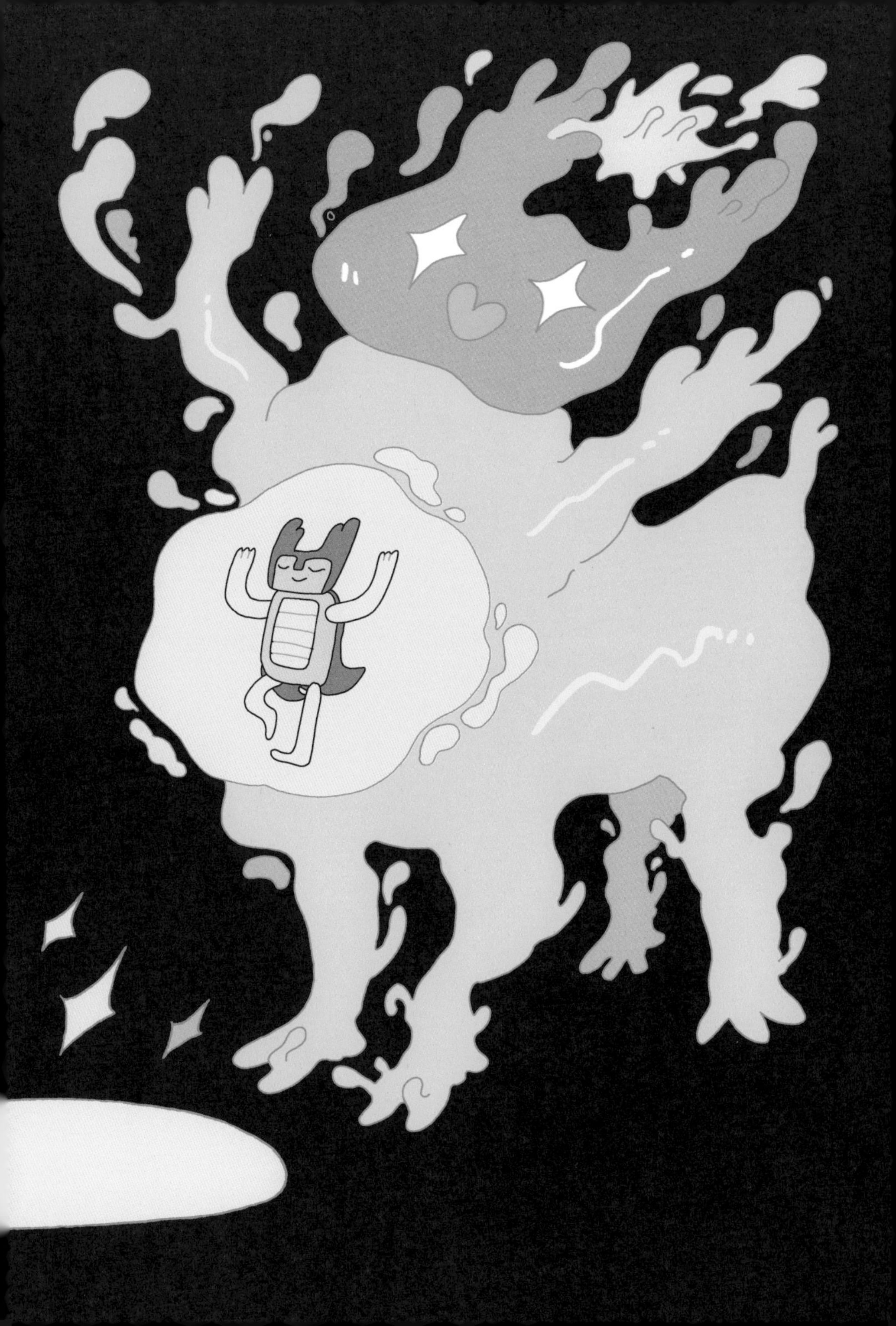

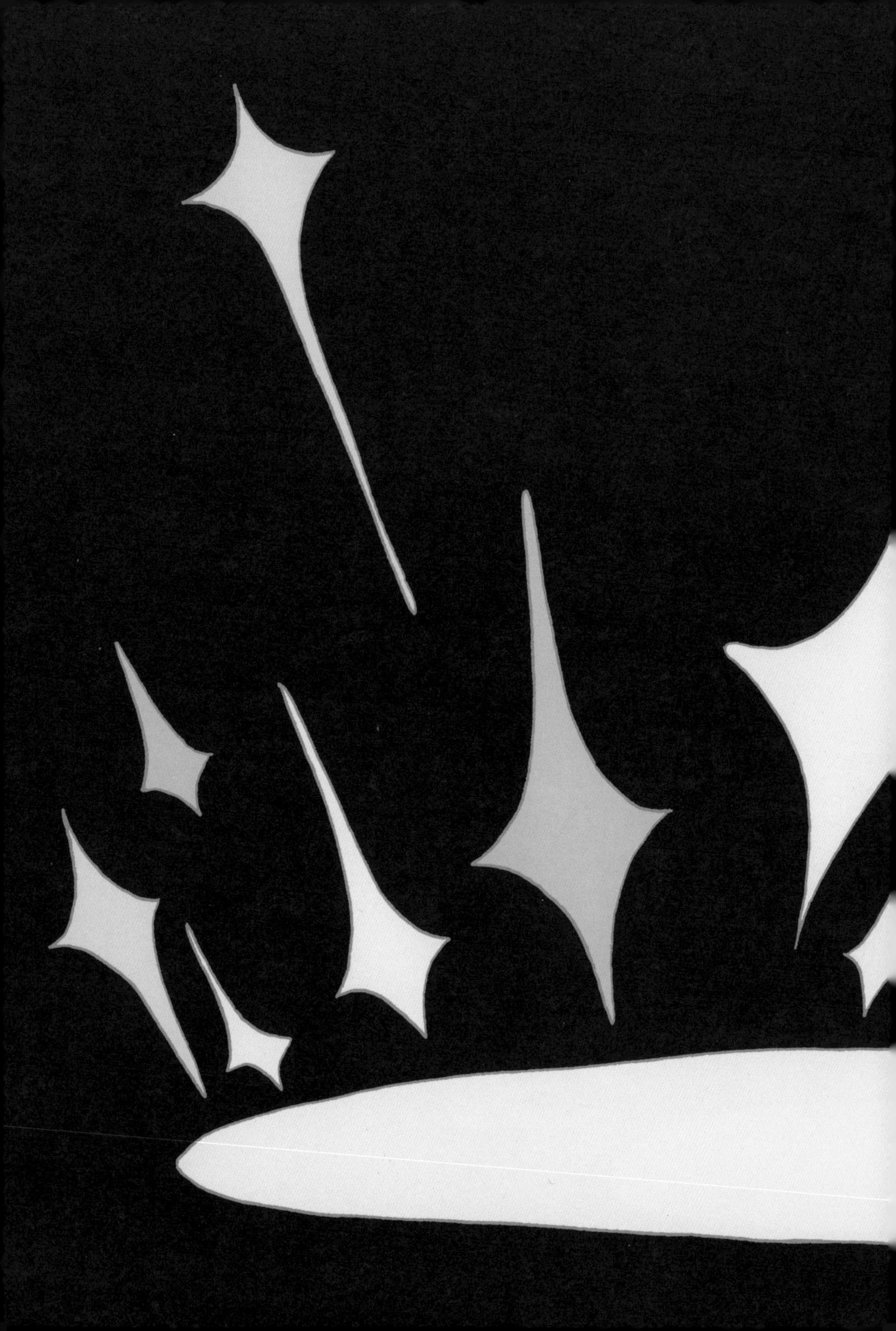

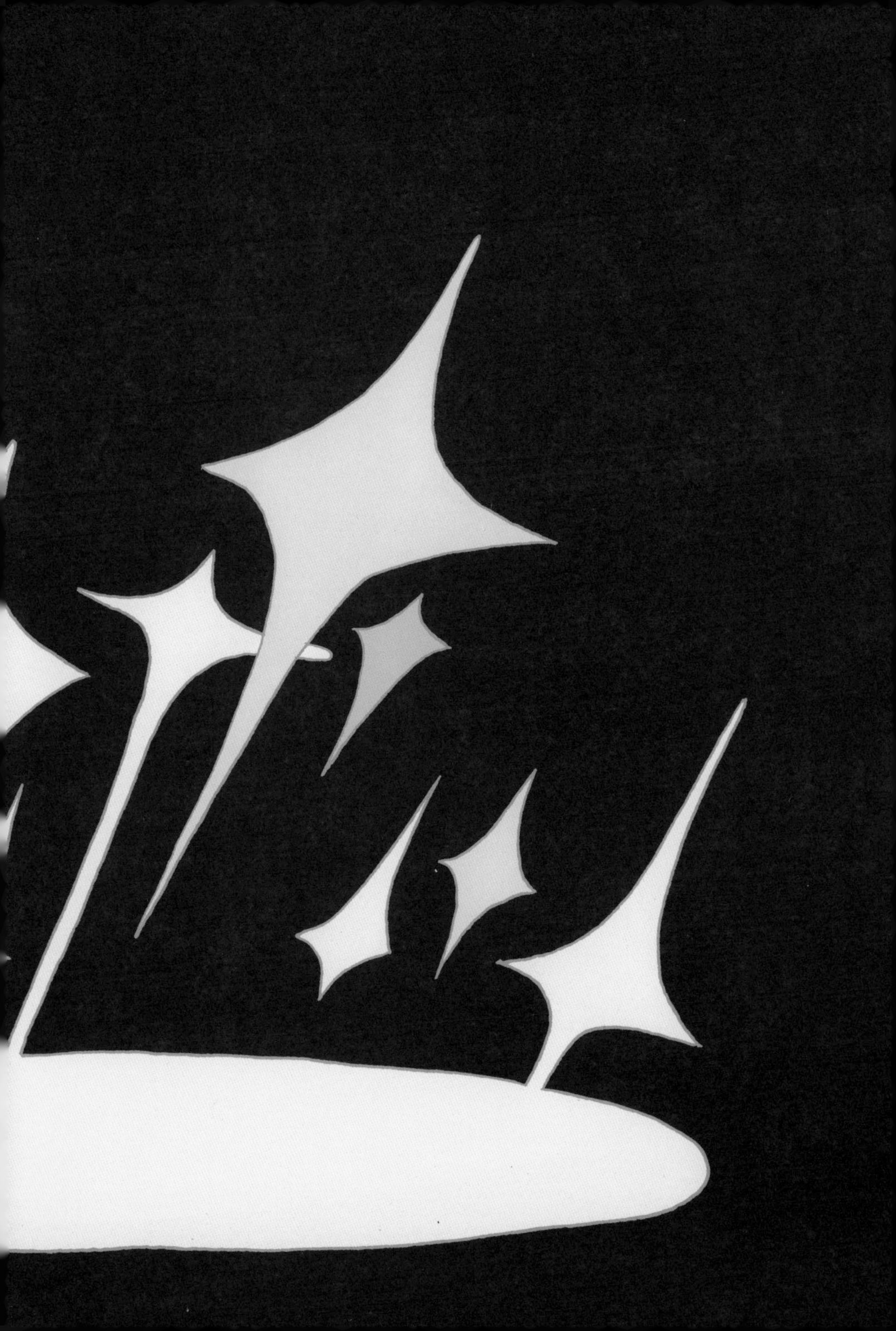

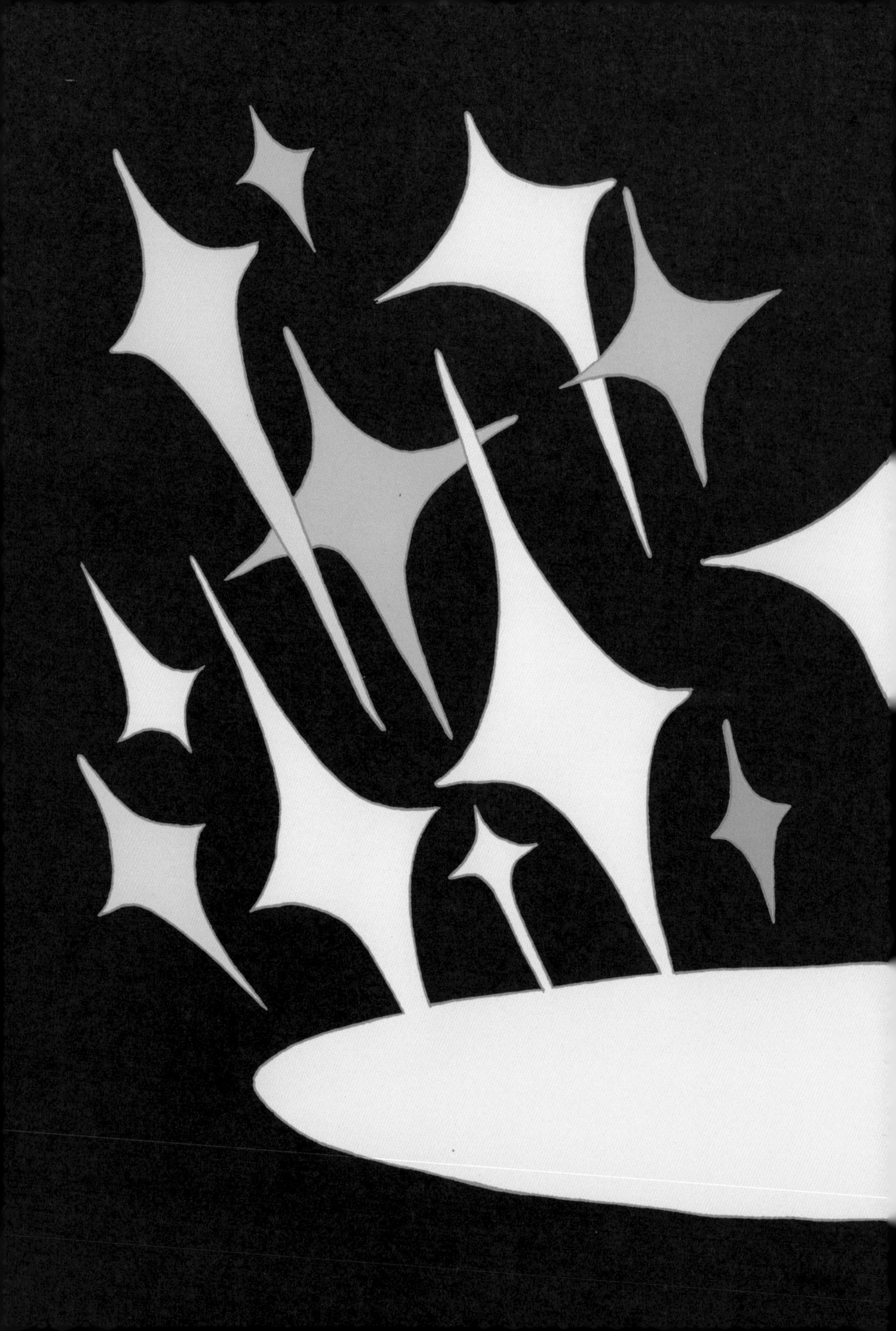

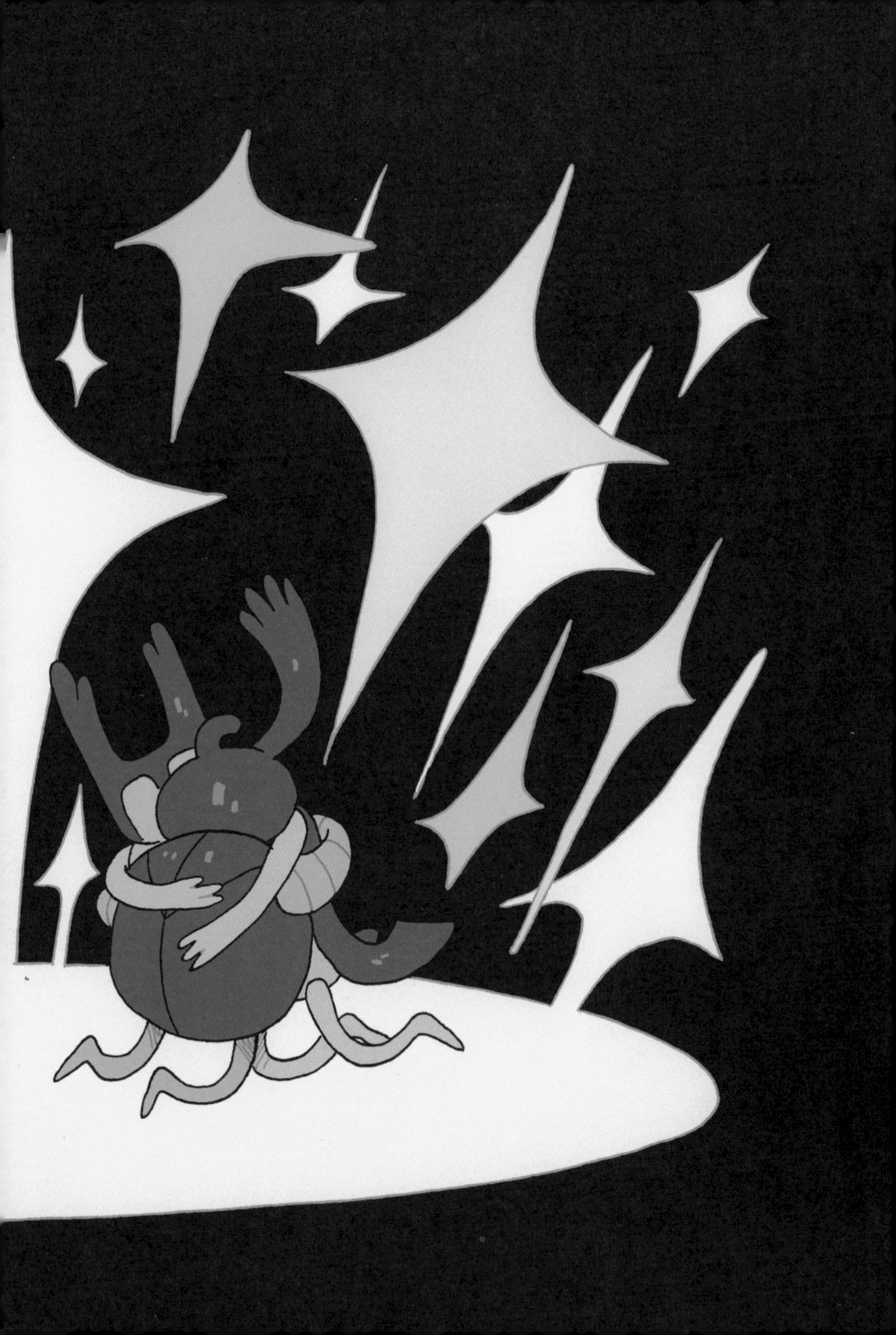

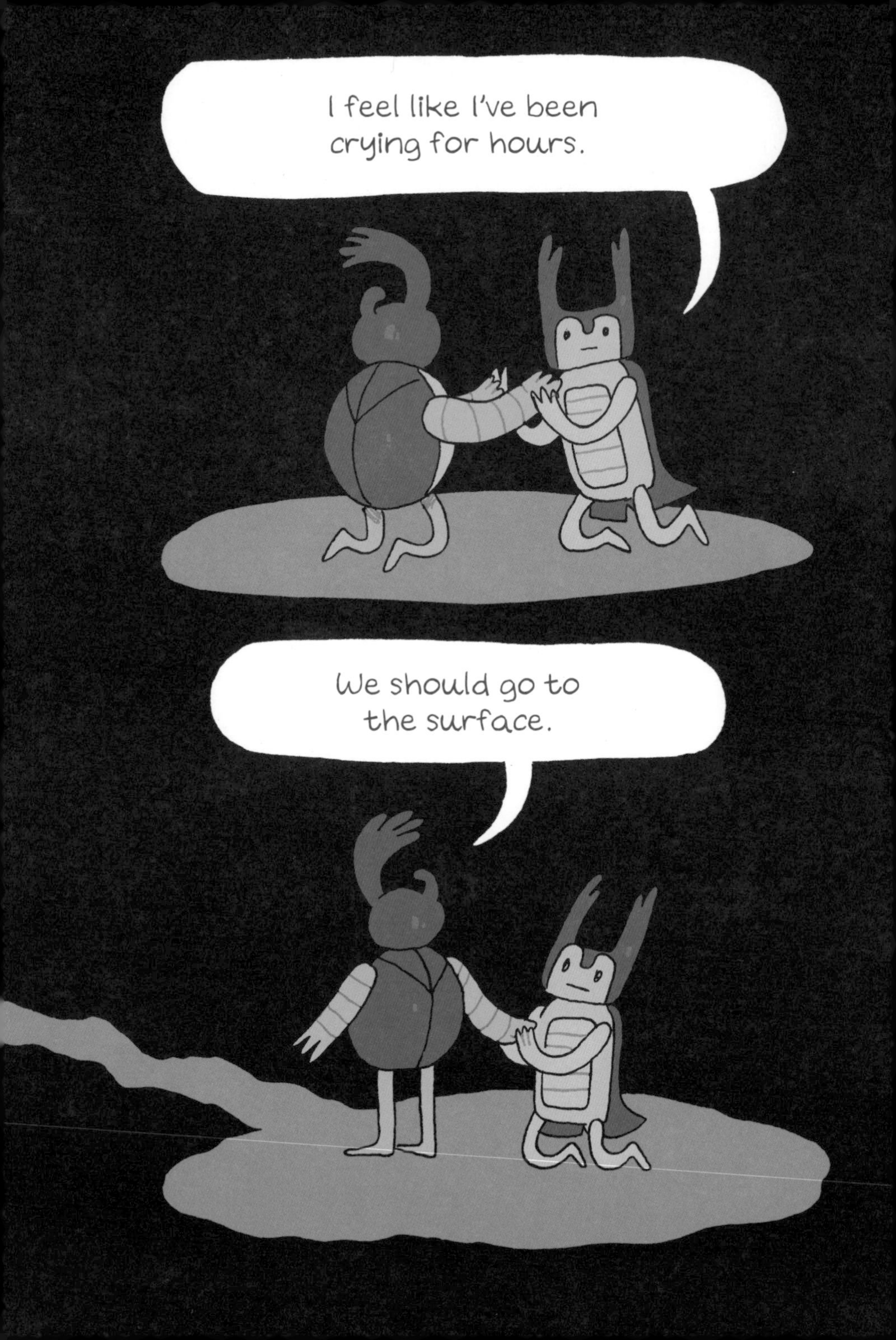
I feel like I've been crying for hours.
We should go to the surface.

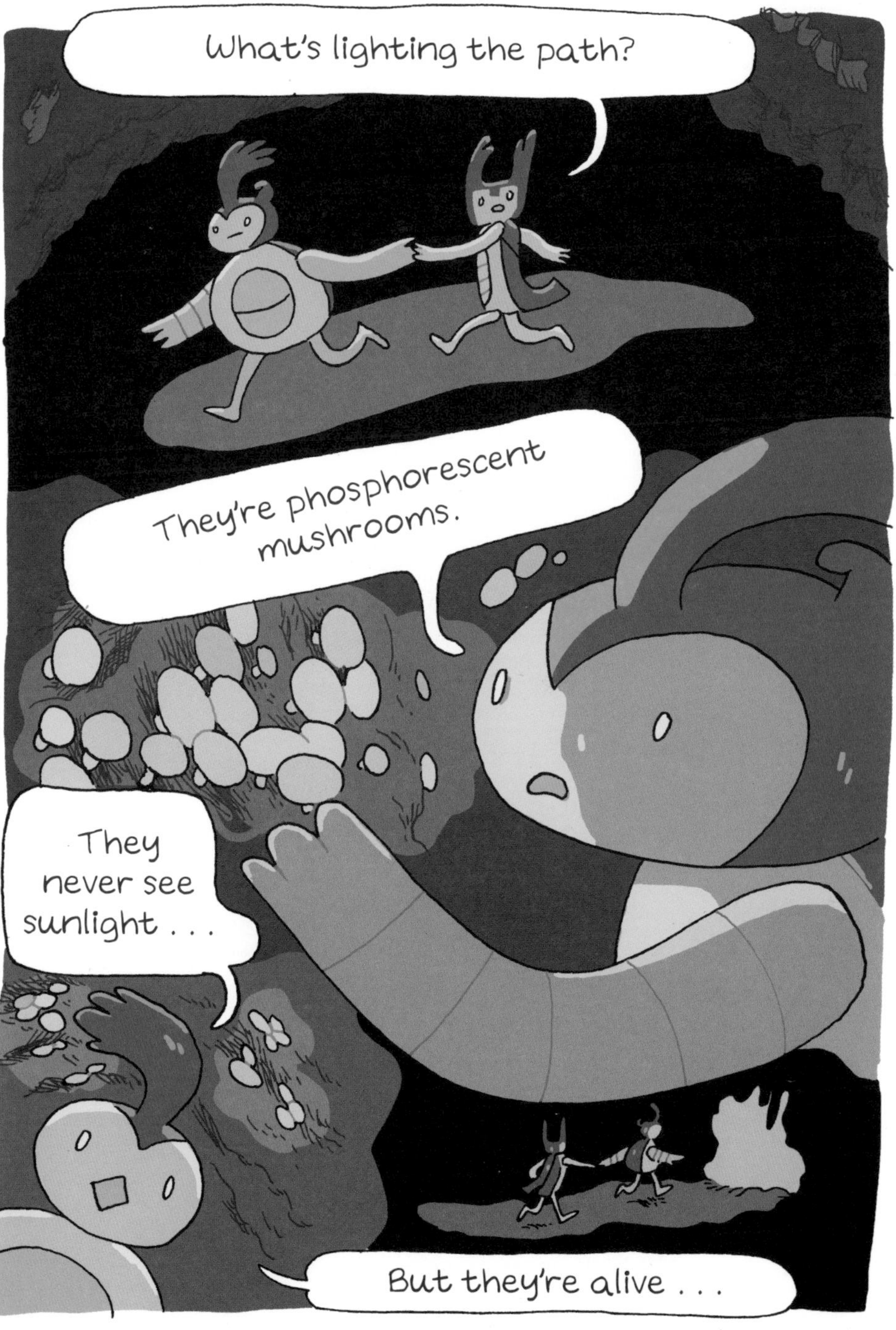
What's lighting the path?
They're phosphorescent mushrooms.
They never see sunlight . . .
But they're alive . . .

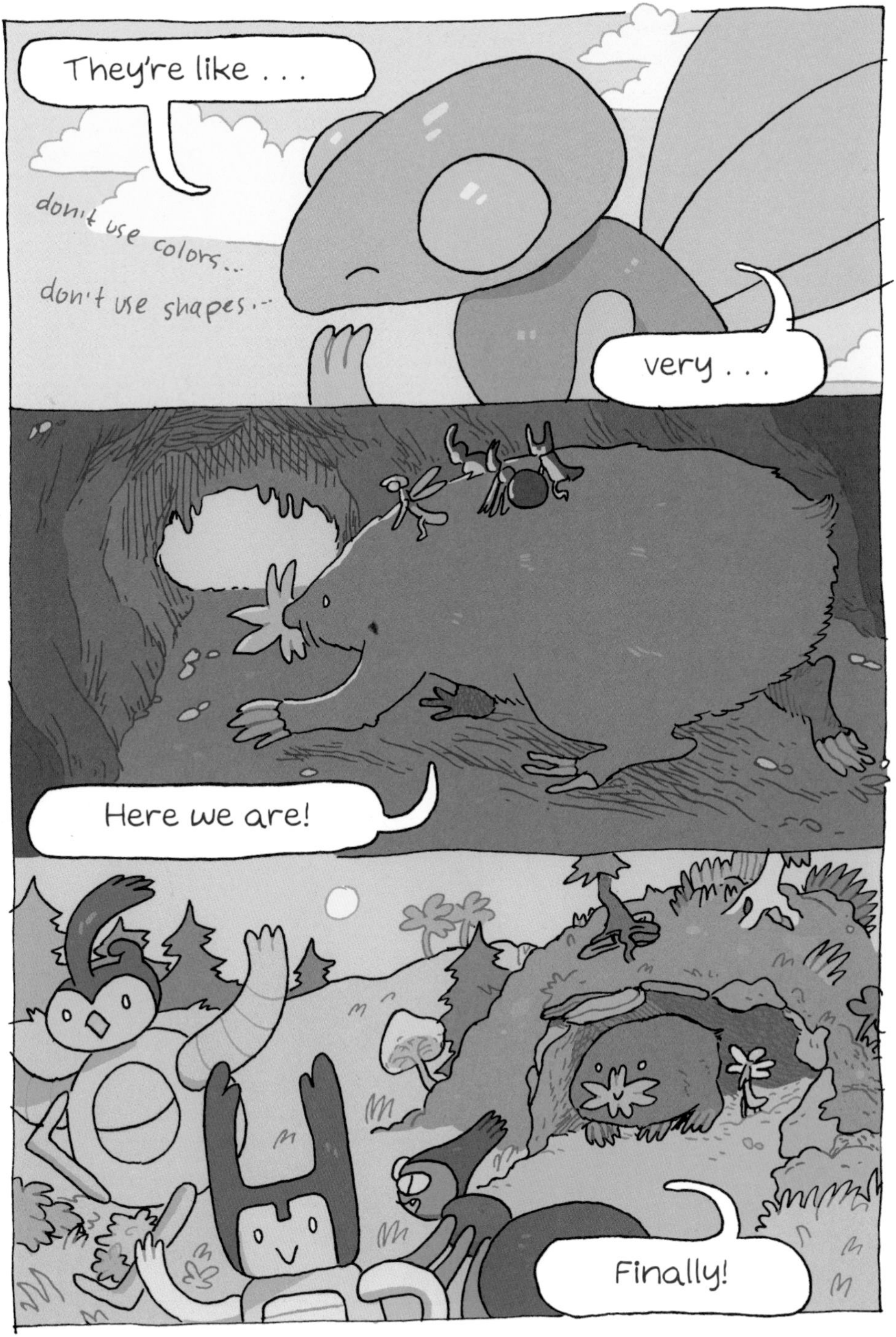
They're like . . .
don't use colors...
don't use shapes...
very . . .
Here we are!
Finally!

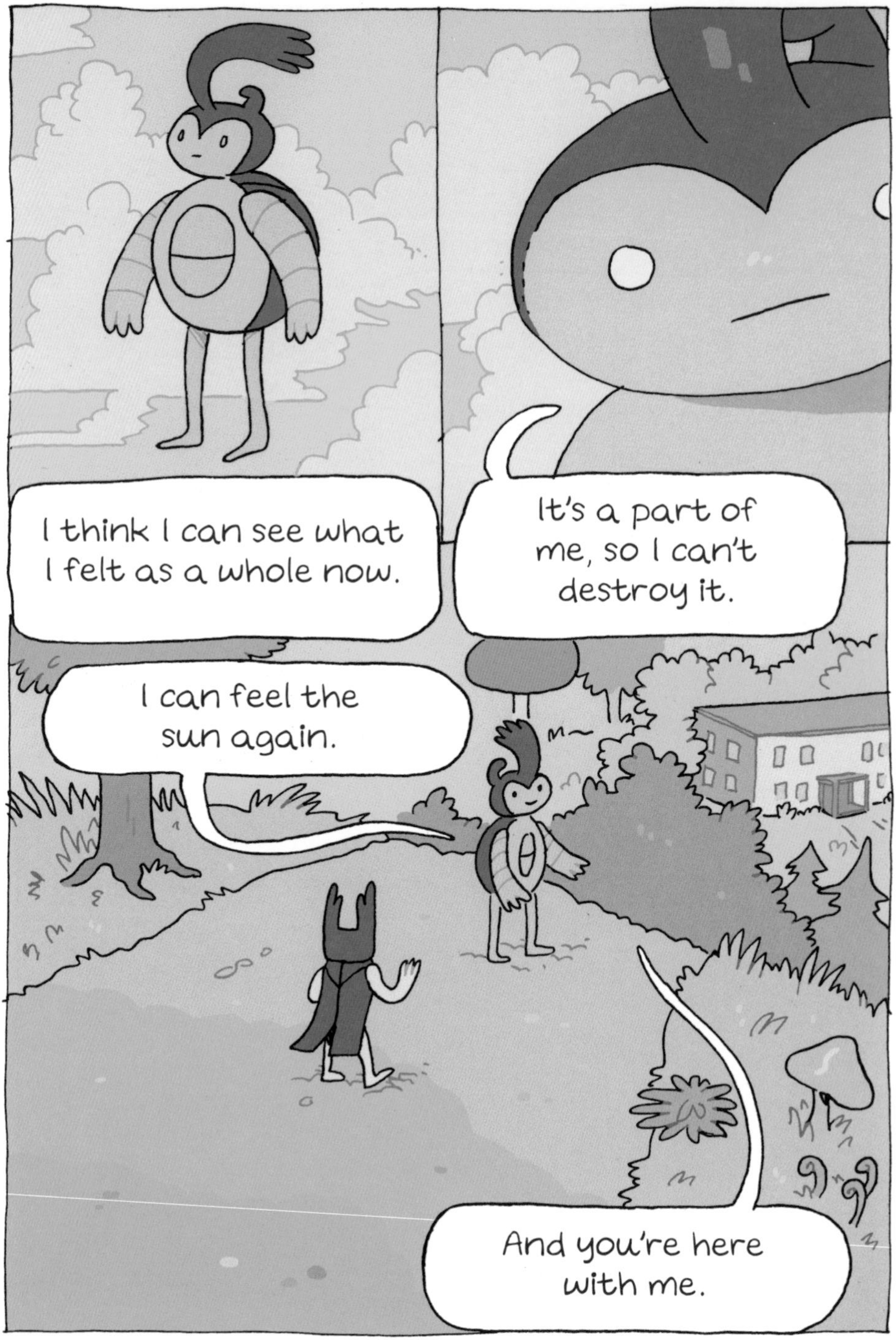
I think I can see what I felt as a whole now.
It's a part of me, so I can't destroy it.
I can feel the sun again.
m~
And you're here with me.

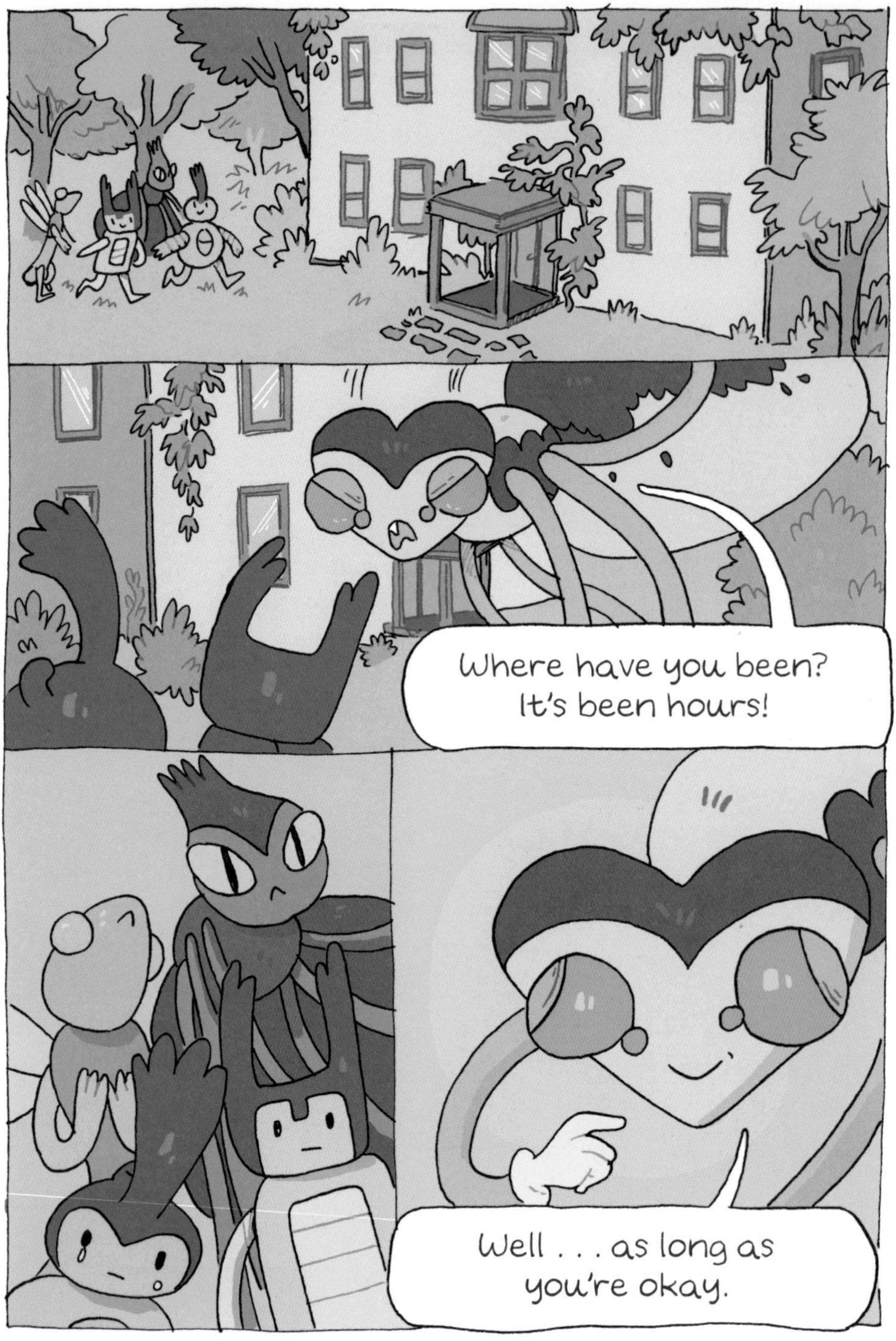
Where have you been? It's been hours!
Well . . . as long as you're okay.

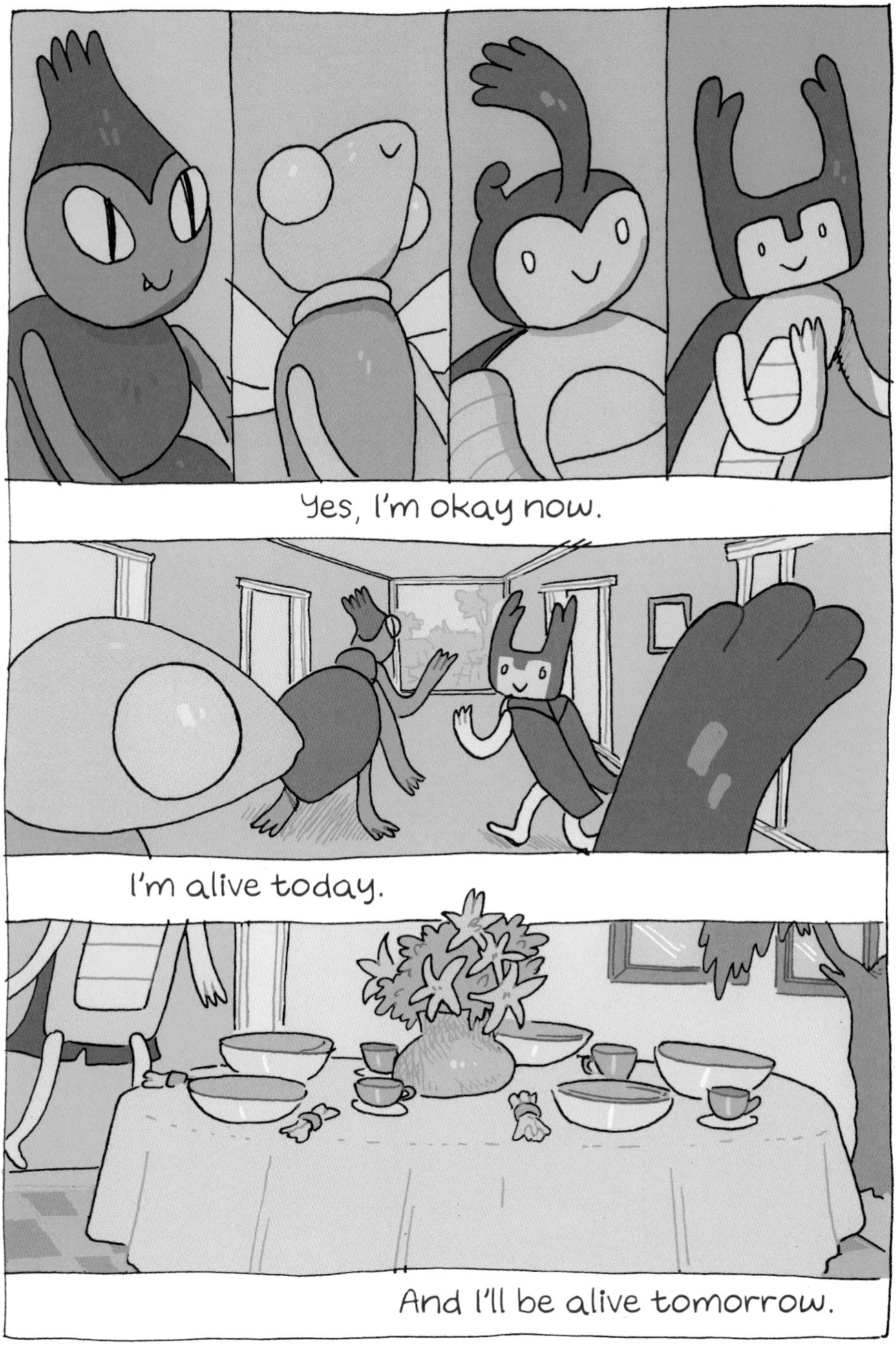
Yes, I'm okay now.
I'm alive today.
And I'll be alive tomorrow.

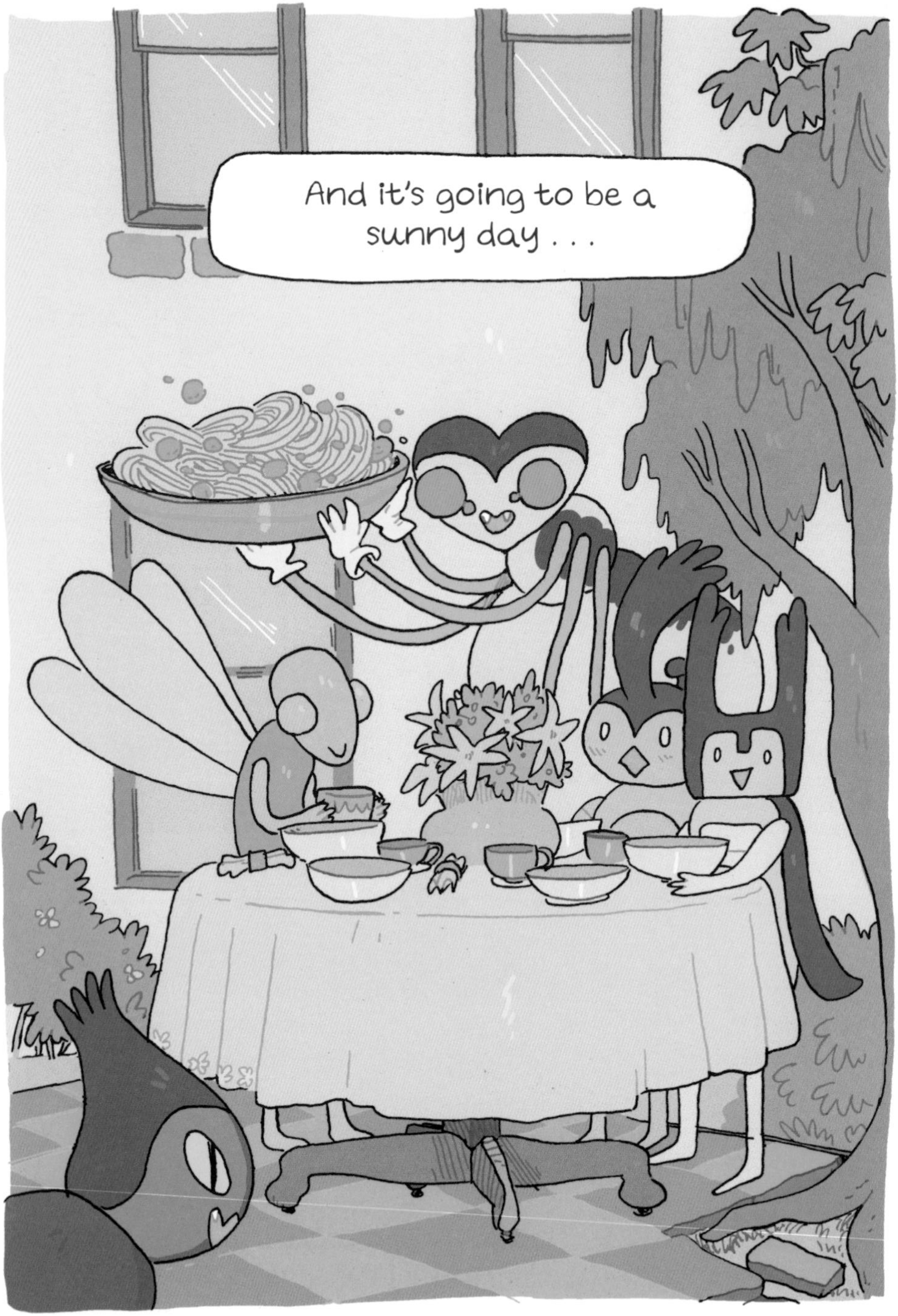
And it's going to be a sunny day . . .

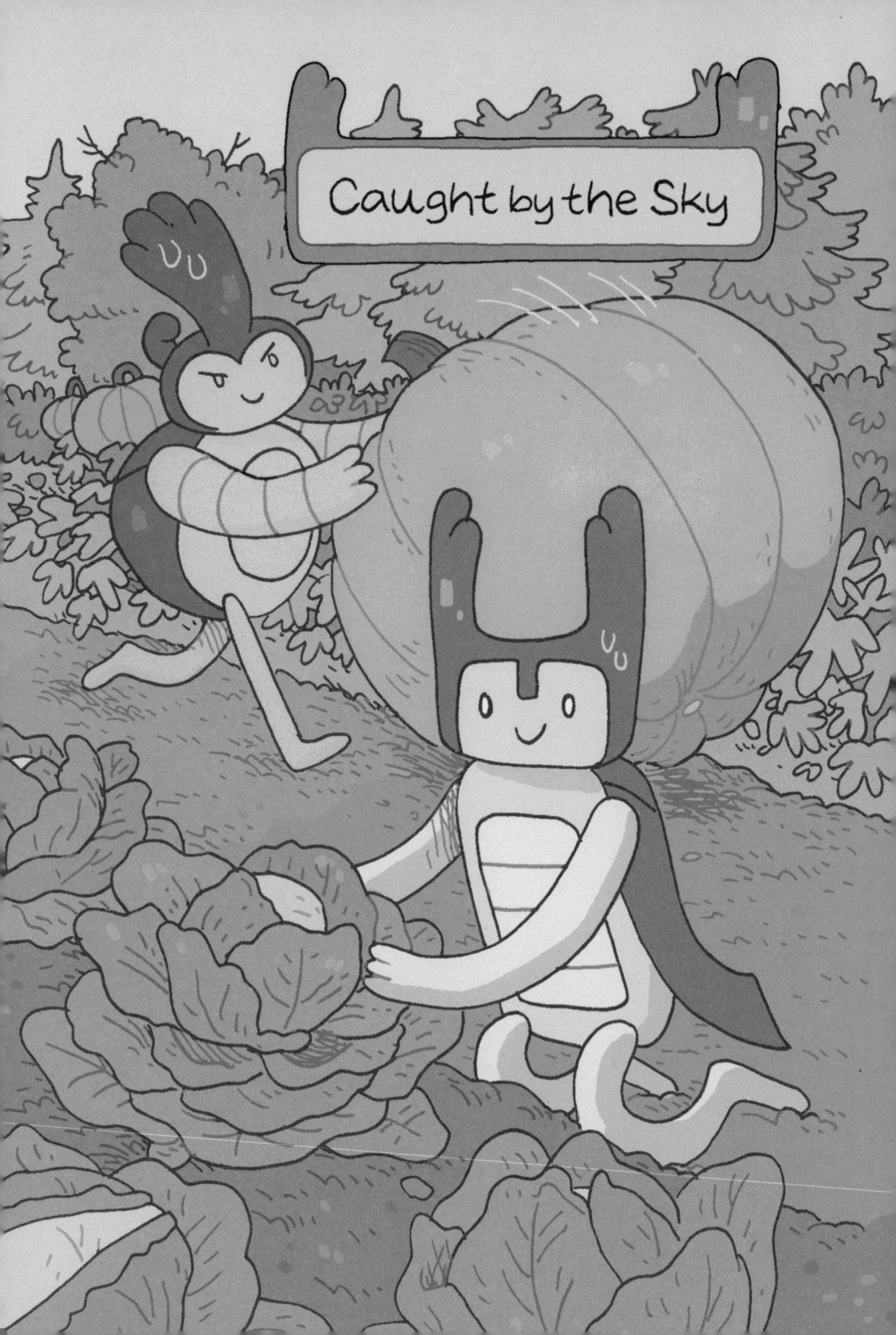
Caught by the Sky

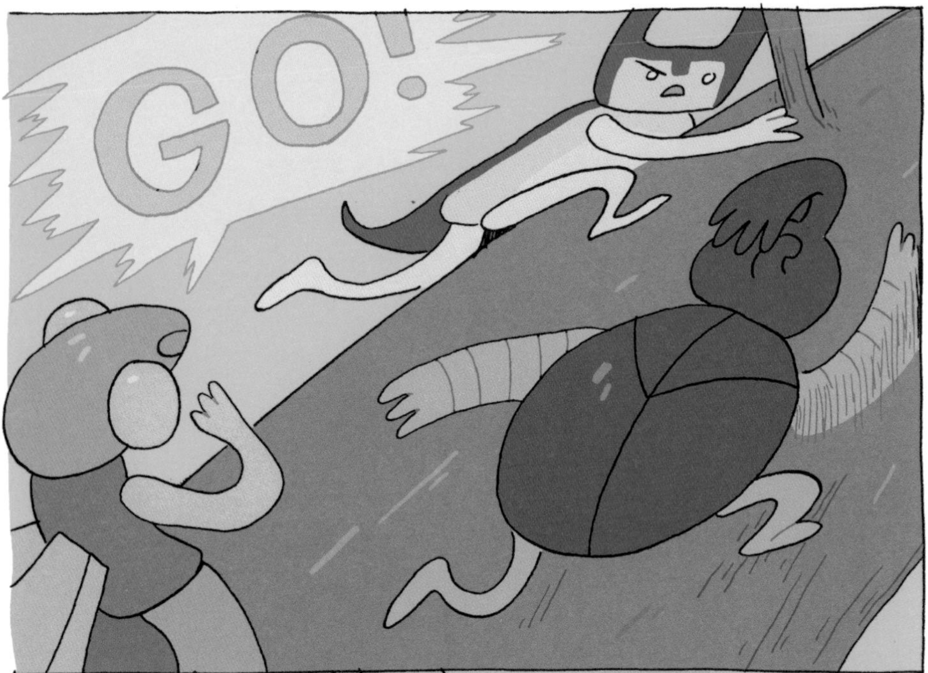
GO!

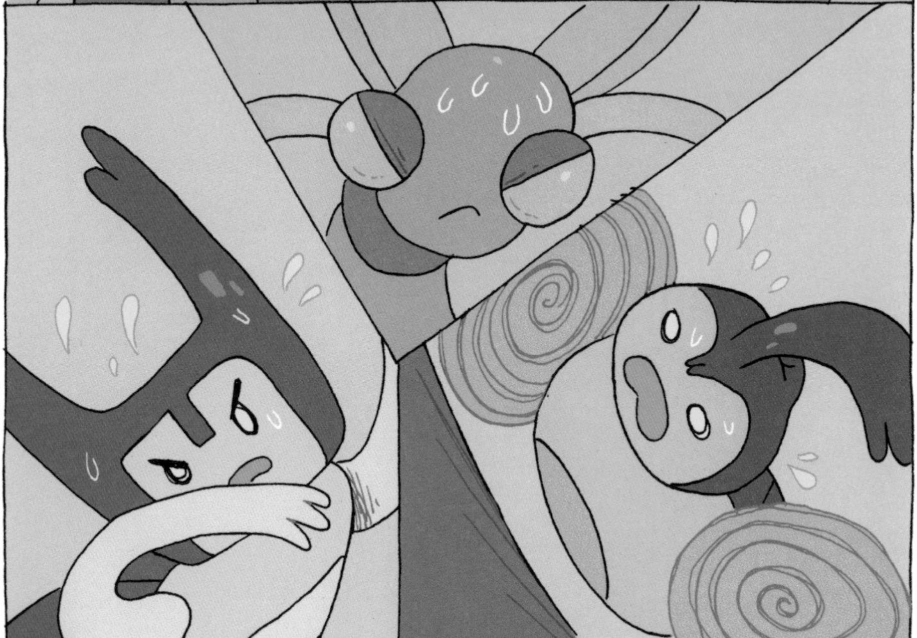

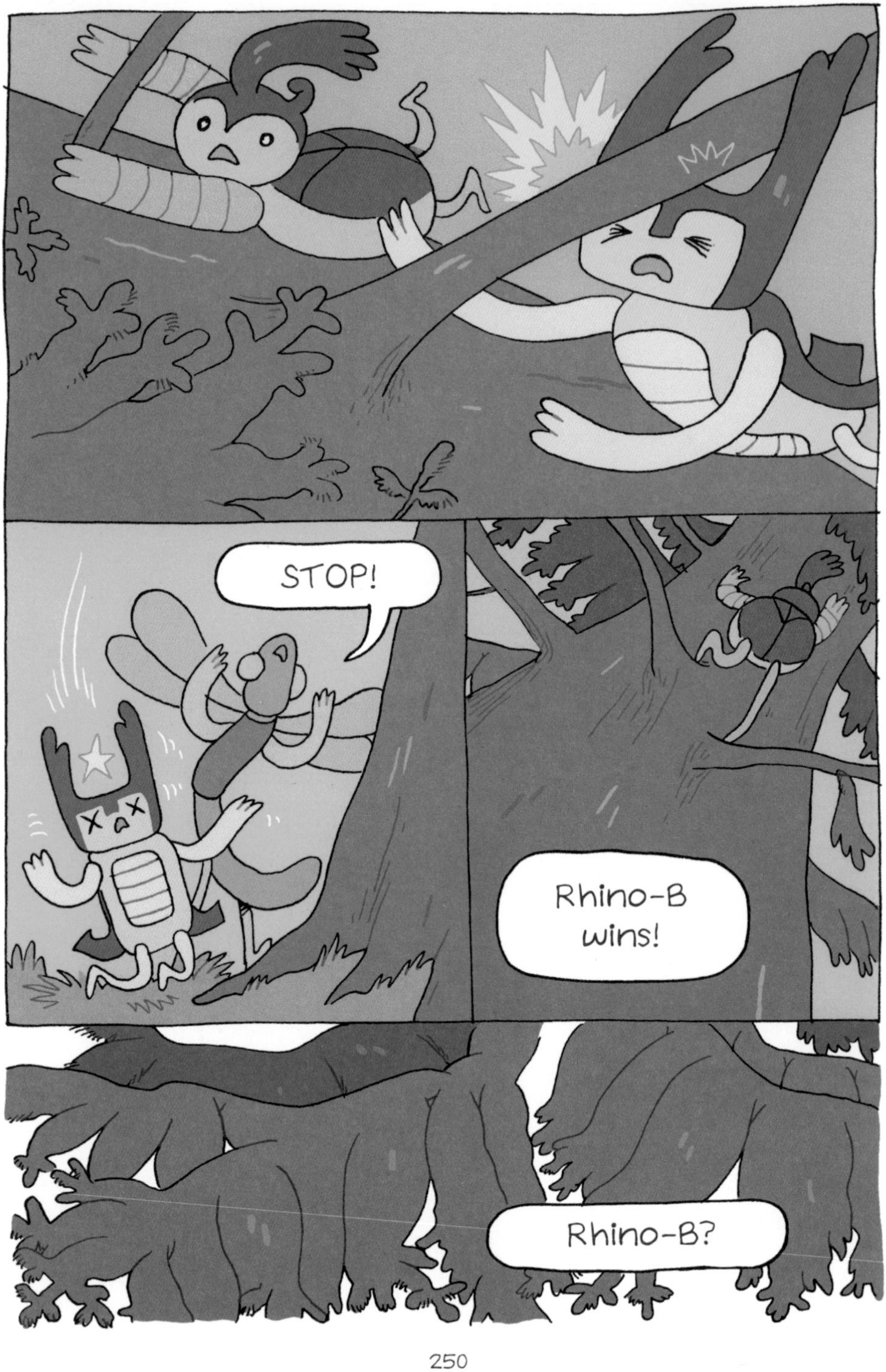
STOP!
Rhino-B wins!
Rhino-B?

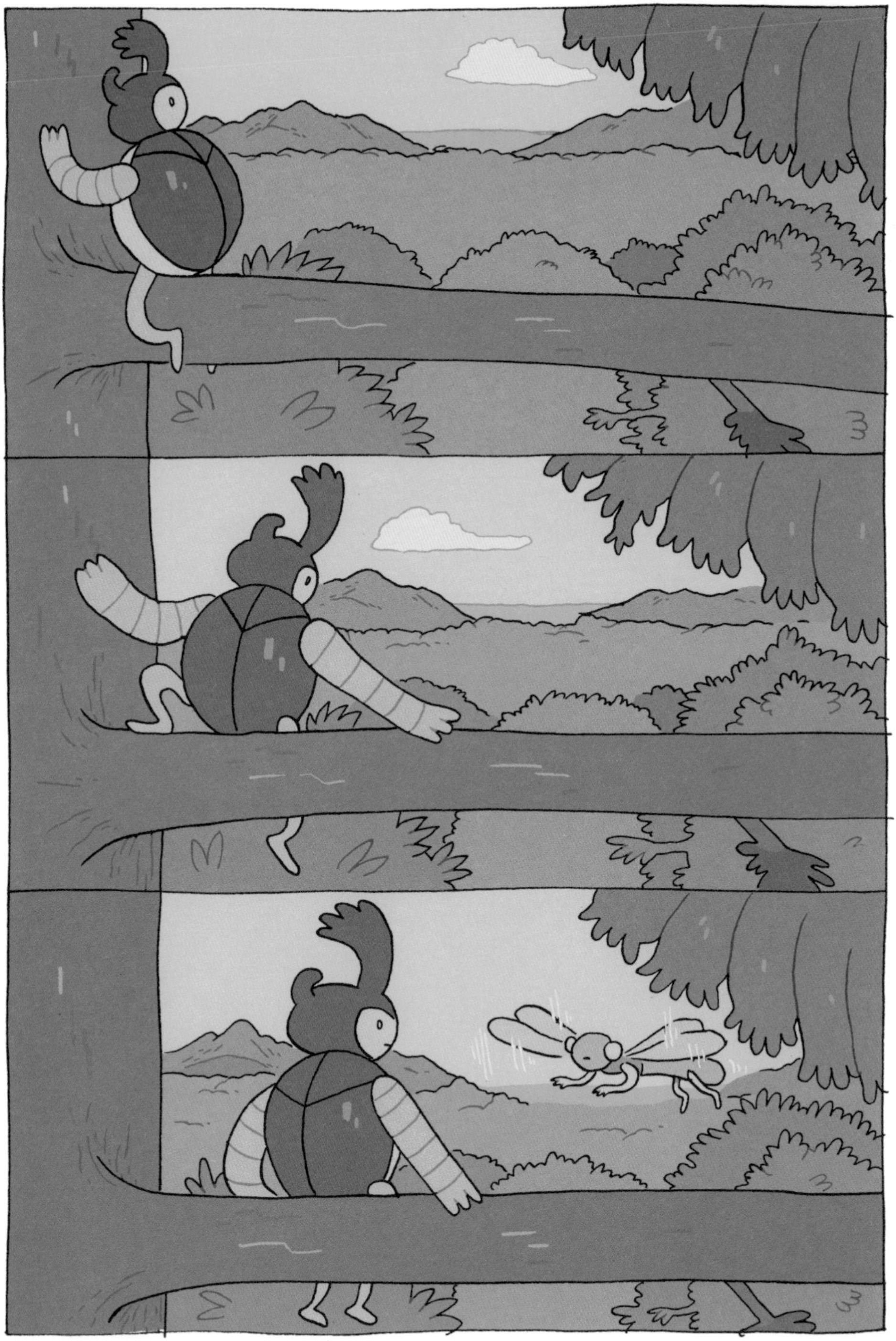

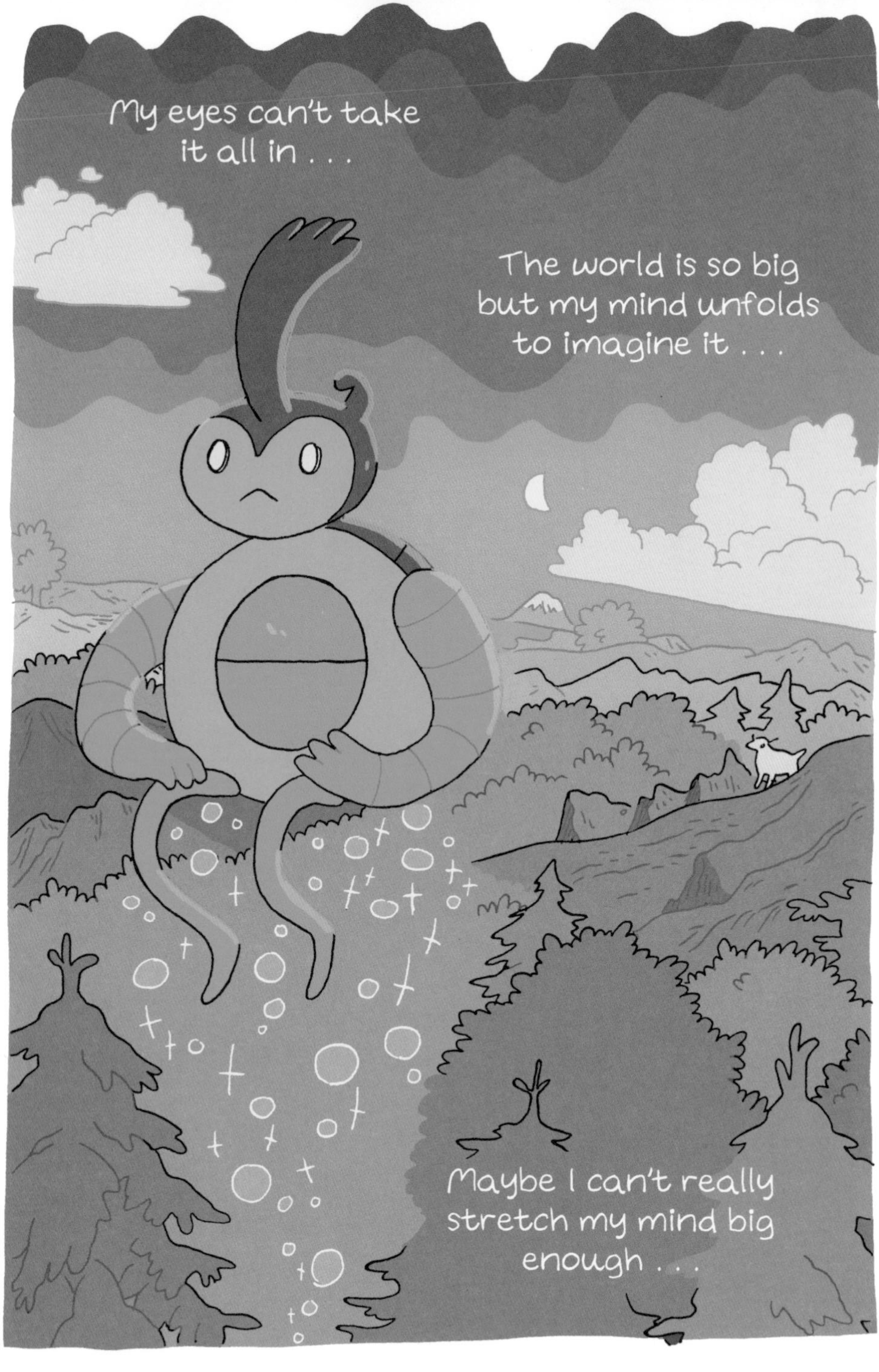
My eyes can't take it all in . . .
The world is so big but my mind unfolds to imagine it . . .
Maybe I can't really stretch my mind big enough . . .

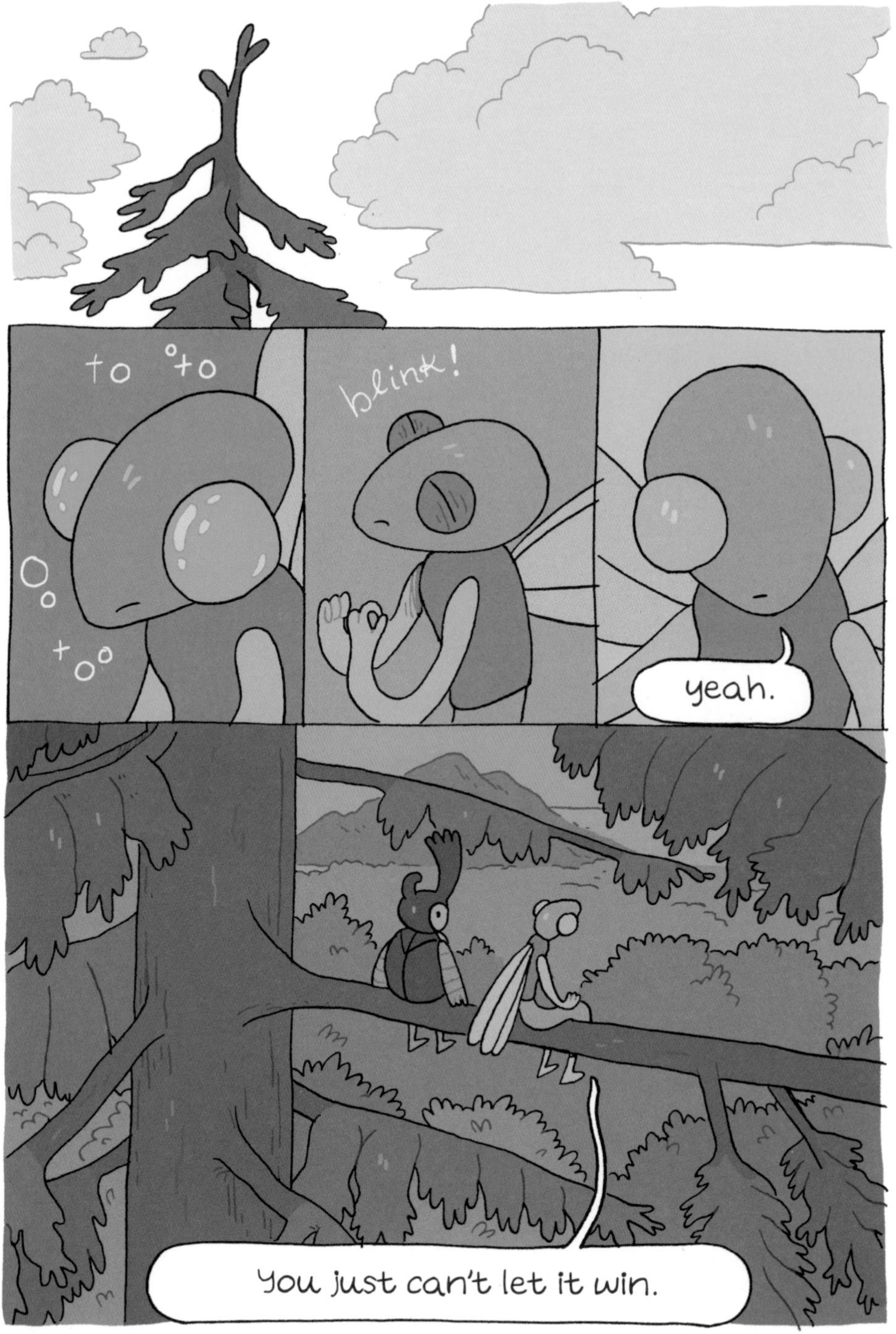
to to
to o
blink!
yeah.
You just can't let it win.

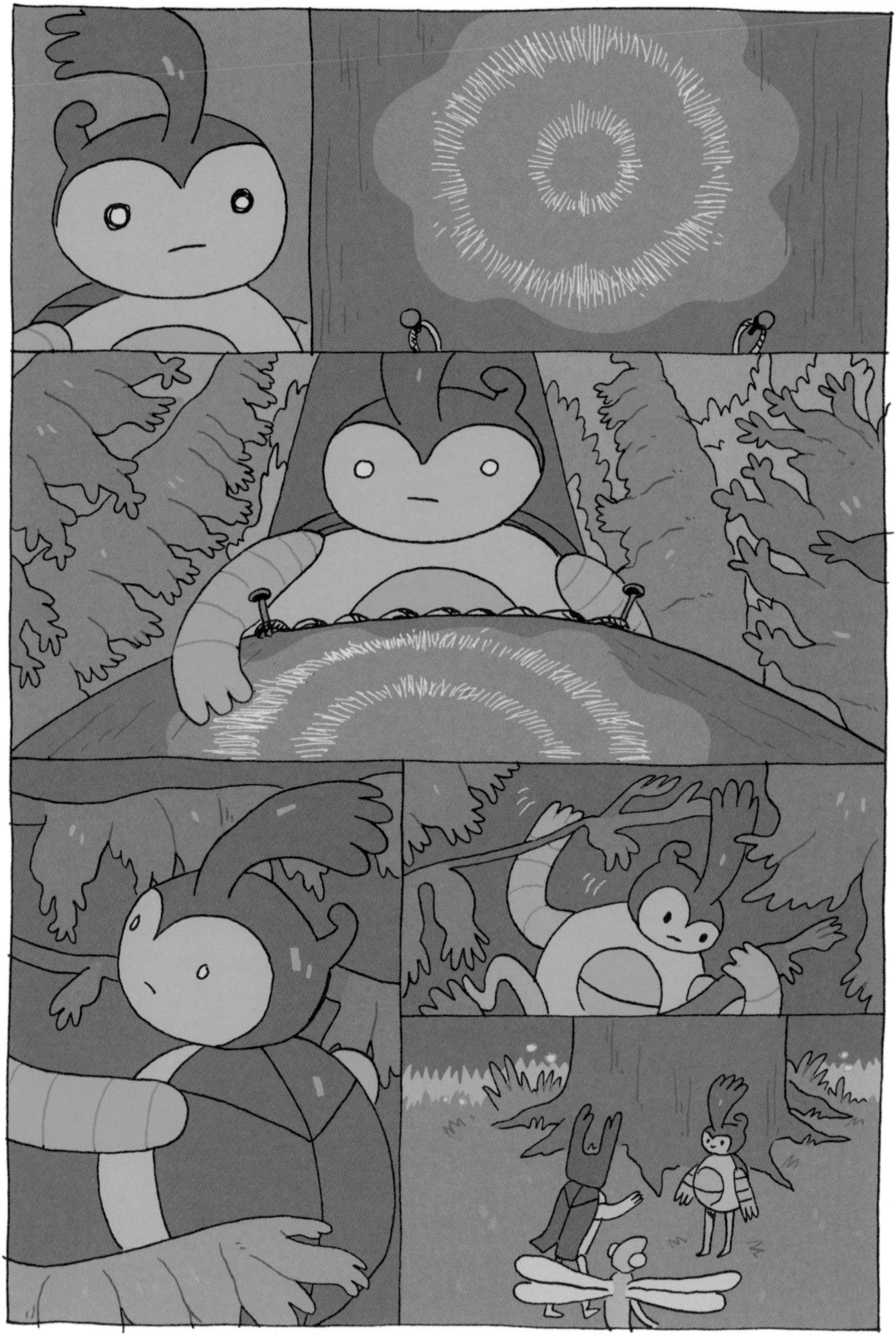

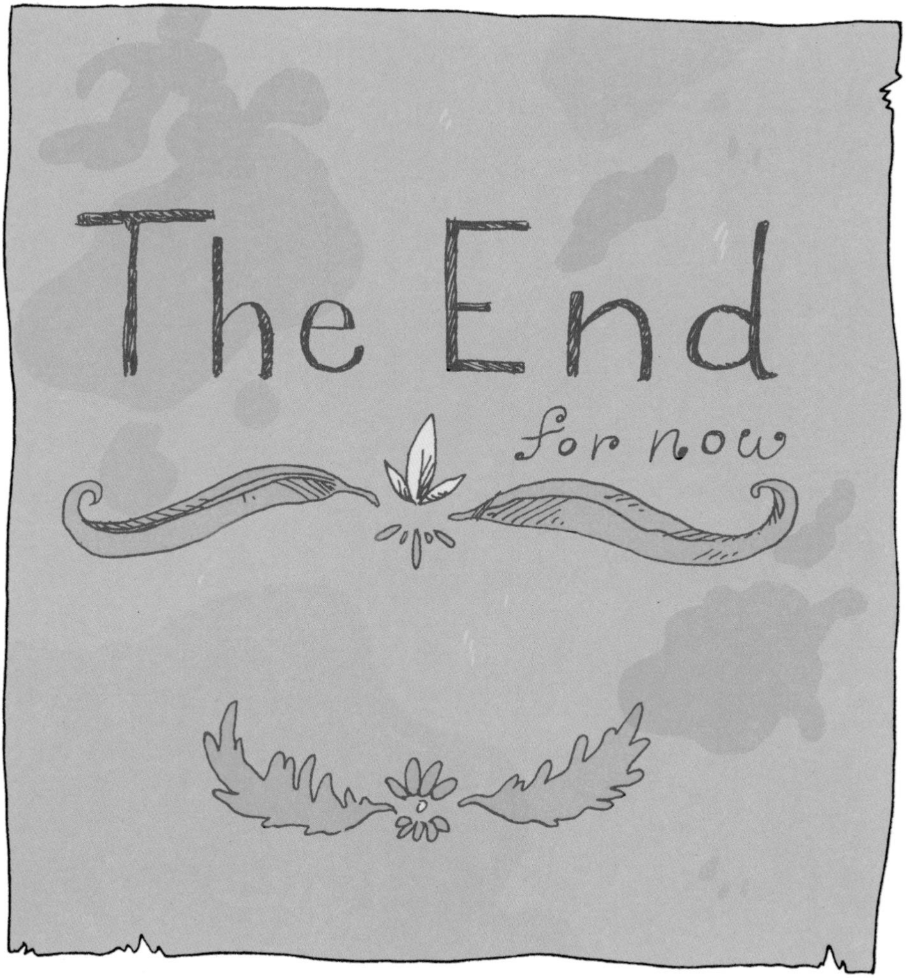
The End
for now

BEETLE FACTS!

There are over
twelve hundred types of stag beetle and over three hundred types of rhinoceros beetle. Stag beetles and rhinoceros beetles use their horns to wrestle one another and dig into the ground. In both types of beetle, males have much larger horns than females. Although a stag beetle's mandibles look like big scary jaws, they cannot bite humans.

The largest beetle is the Hercules beetle, which is a kind of rhinoceros beetle. They can grow up to seven inches long.

A beetle's life cycle resembles that of a butterfly. They are born from eggs as larva, big white grubs that live underground and feed on rotting wood. When it's time for them to become adults, they pupate. Butterflies pupate in chrysalises aboveground, but beetles pupate underground. After their bodies develop, they emerge as adults and live aboveground. Adult beetles eat tree sap and fruit. After they mate, females burrow underground and lay eggs. Lifespans vary depending on species, but some beetles can live for two to three years.

Beetles live all over the world. What kind of beetles live near you?

Laura Knetzger

grew up in Washington State, near Seattle. She wanted to be a cartoonist since she was eleven years old. She went to art college in New York City, and now she lives in Seattle.

She has a pet cat named Chilly. Chilly is a gray tuxedo cat. Cats are definitely Laura's favorite animal.

Laura got the idea to make Bug Boys as she was watching a documentary about bug collecting called Beetle Queen Conquers Tokyo. She drew two cute cartoon bugs as she was watching the movie, then tried to make up stories about them.

Her hobbies are reading, playing video games, and knitting. Laura's favorite food is udon noodles with tempura on top.

Bonus Comic

Rhino-B! We're working on making some Bug-size Giant technology!

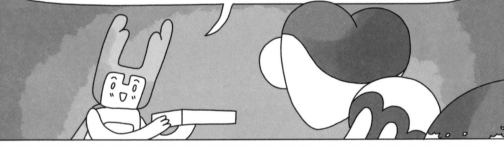

I couldn't figure out how to use this just from studying Giant stuff, so we built one to experiment on.

But I still don't get it. Do you?

Rhino-B?

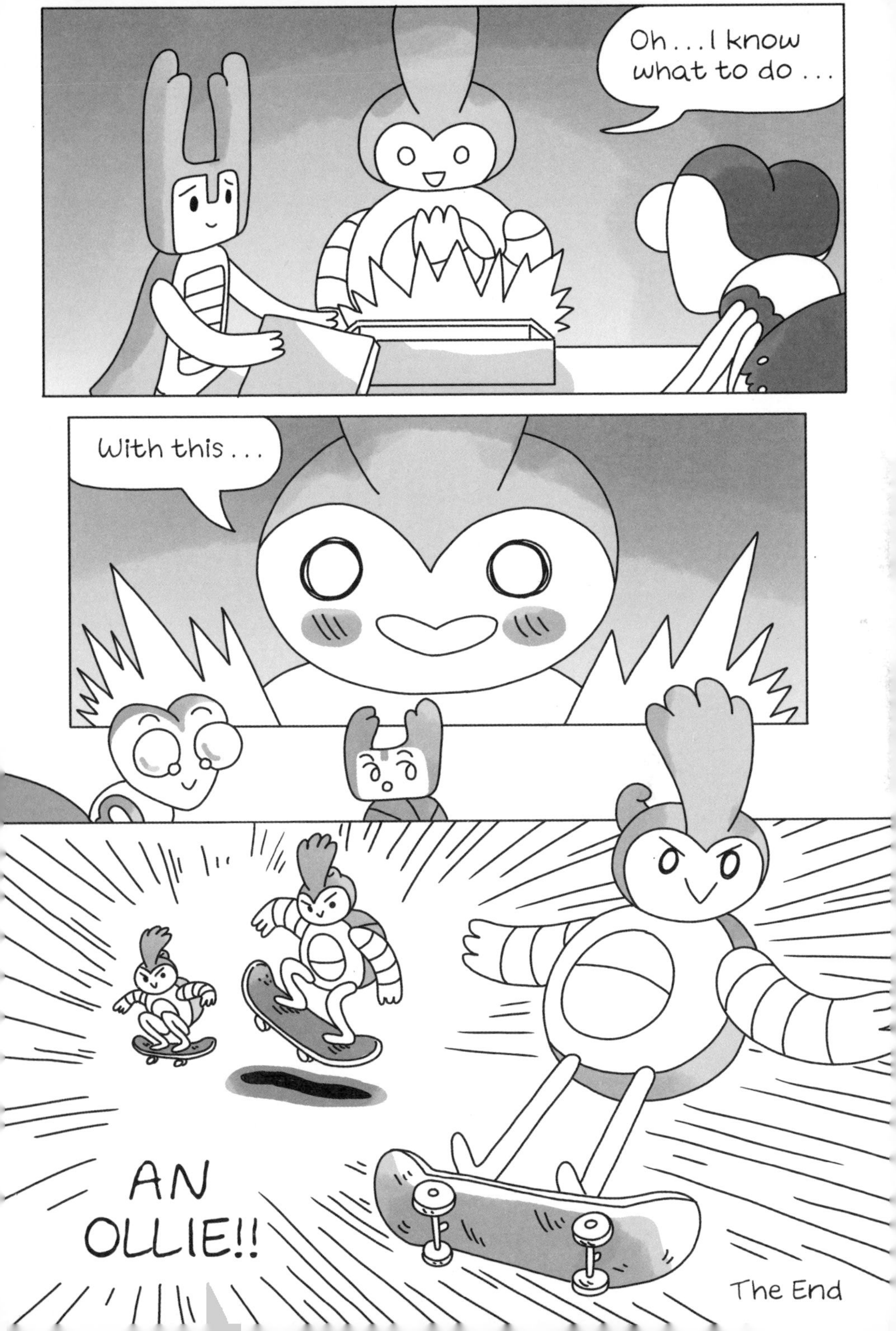

Oh . . . I know what to do . . .
With this . . .
AN OLLIE!!
The End

How to Draw Rhino-B

Step One: Draw
the head.

Step Two: Draw
the body.

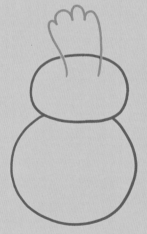

Step Three: Draw
the front horn.

Step Four: Draw
the arms.

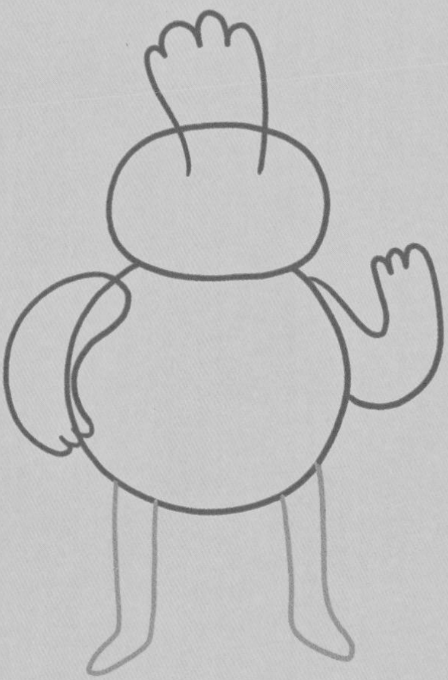

Step Five: Draw some legs.

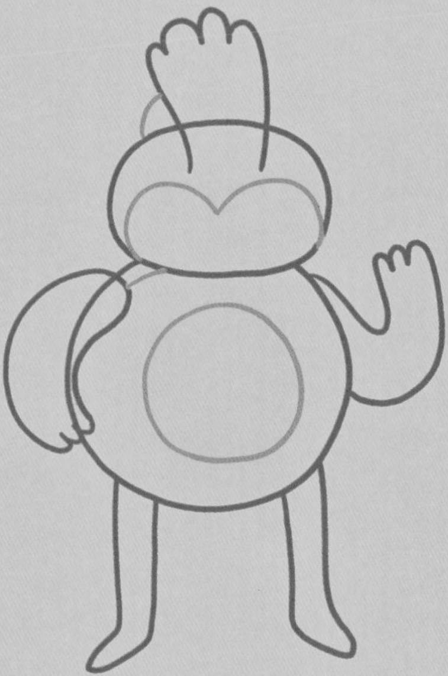

Step Six: Let's add some details.

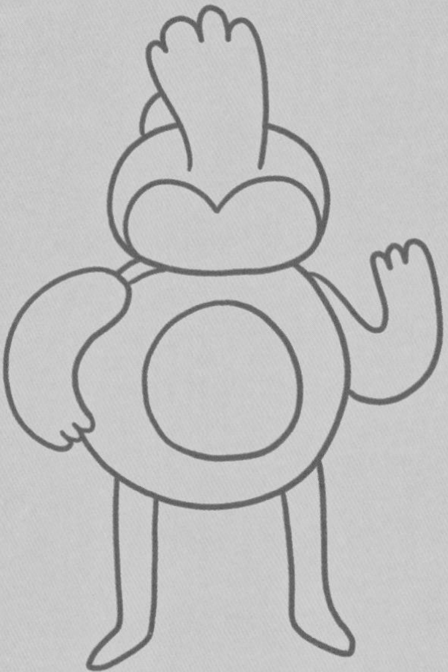

Step Seven: Erase those extra lines.

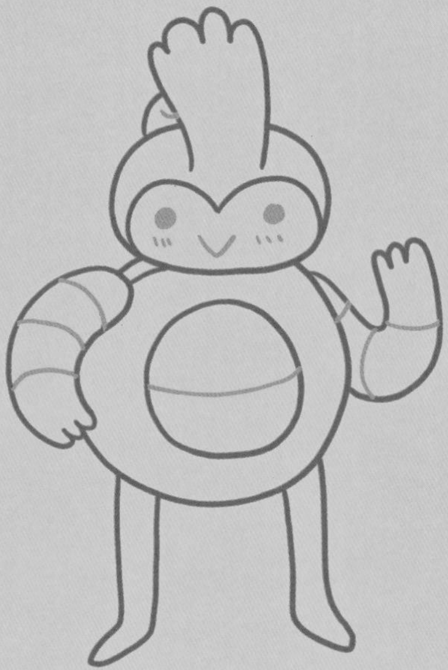

Step Eight: Finish off with a face and more details!

How to Draw Stag-B

Step One: Draw the head.

Step Two: Draw the body.

Step Three: Draw the horns.

Step Four: Draw the arms.

Step Five: Draw
some legs.

Step Six: Let's add
some details.

Step Seven: Erase
those extra lines.

Step Eight: Finish
off with a face and
more details!

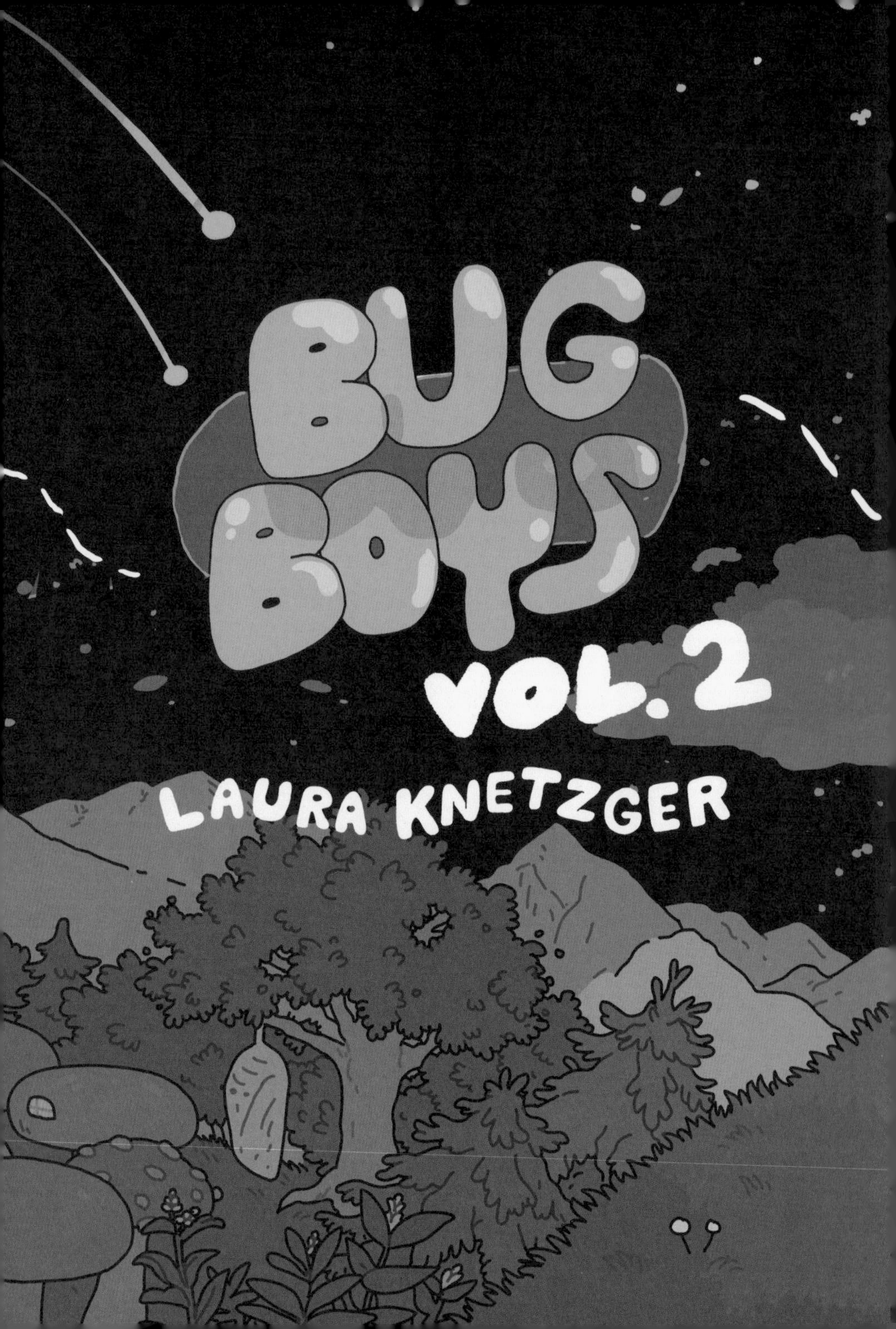
BUG BOYS
VOL. 2
LAURA KNETZGER

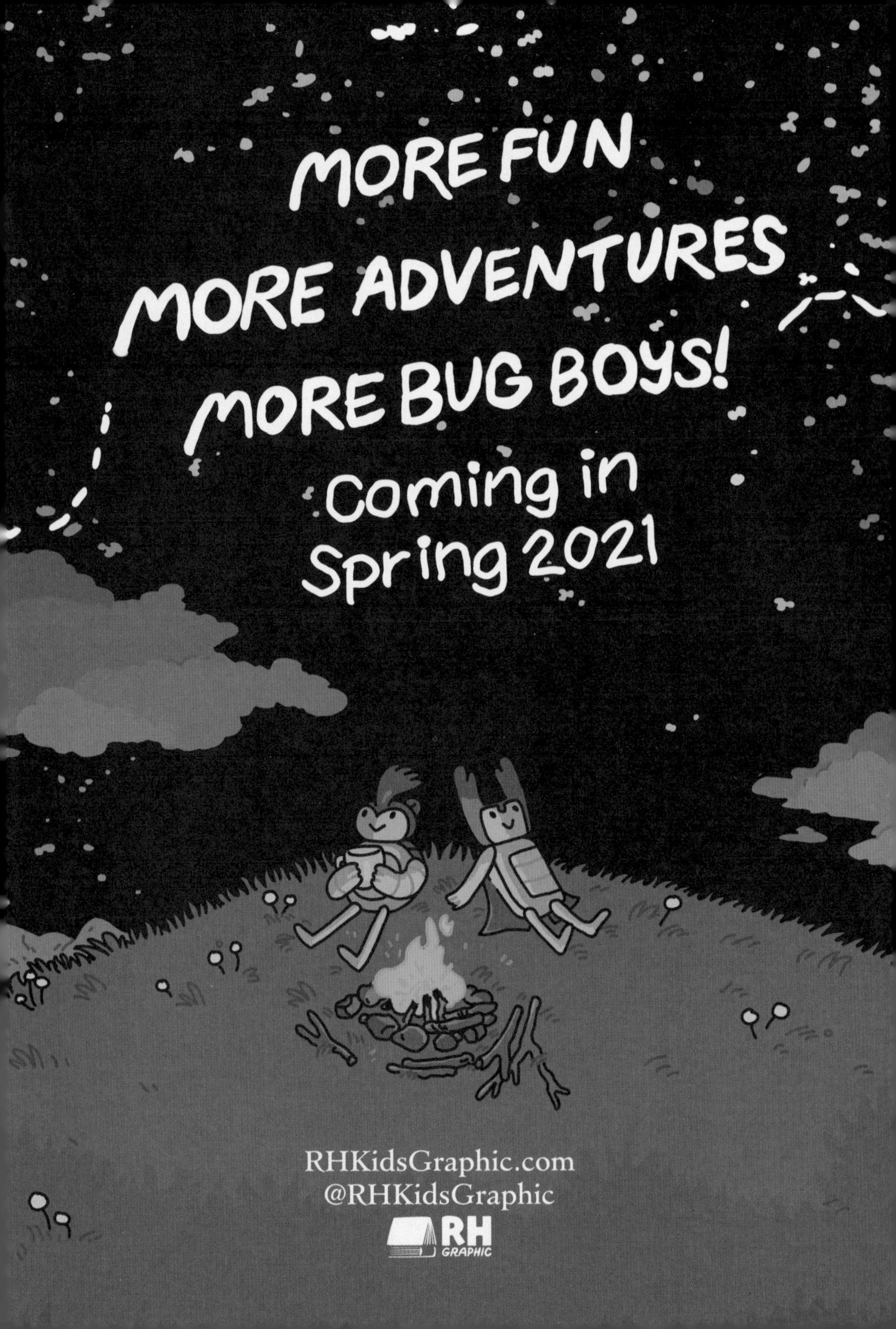
MORE FUN
MORE ADVENTURES
MORE BUG BOYS!
Coming in Spring 2021
RHKidsGraphic.com
@RHKidsGraphic
RH GRAPHIC

RH GRAPHIC
THE DEBUT LIST

BUG BOYS
By Laura Knetzger

BUG BOYS
LAURA KNETZGER

Bugs, friends, the world around us – this book has everything!
Come explore *Bug Boys* for the fun, thoughtful adventure of growing up and being yourself.

Chapter Book

THE RUNAWAY PRINCESS
By Johan Troïanowski

THE RUNAWAY PRINCESS
Johan Troïanowski

The castle is quiet.
And dull.
And boring.
Escape on a quest for excitement with our runaway princess, Robin!

Middle-Grade

ASTER AND THE ACCIDENTAL MAGIC
By Thom Pico & Karensac

Aster and the ACCIDENTAL MAGIC
THOM PICO
KARENSAC

Nothing fun ever happens in the middle of the country . . . except maybe . . . magic?
That's just the beginning of absolutely everything going wrong for Aster.

Middle-Grade

WITCHLIGHT
By Jessi Zabarsky

Witchlight
Jessi Zabarsky

Lelek doesn't have any friends or family in the world. And then she meets Sanja. Swords, magic, falling in love . . . these characters come together in a journey to heal the wounds of the past.

Young Adult

FIND US ONLINE AT @RHKIDSGRAPHIC AND RHKIDSGRAPHIC.COM